Also by Kirk Mitchell

PROCURATOR

NEW BARBARIANS

CRY REPUBLIC

NEVER THE TWAIN

BLACK DRAGON

WITH SIBERIA COMES A CHILL

SHADOW ON THE VALLEY

FREDERICKSBURG

HIGH DESERT MALICE

DEEP VALLEY MALICE

CRY DANCE

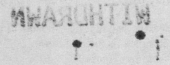

SPIRIT SICKNESS

Kirk Mitchell

BANTAM BOOKS

New York   Toronto   London
Sydney   Auckland

This edition contains the complete text
of the original hardcover edition.
NOT ONE WORD HAS BEEN OMITTED.

SPIRIT SICKNESS
A Bantam Book

PUBLISHING HISTORY
Bantam hardcover edition published July 2000
Bantam mass market edition / April 2001

All rights reserved.
Copyright © 2000 by Kirk Mitchell.
Cover art copyright © 2000 by Jamie S. Warren Youll.
Map by Jeffrey L. Ward

Library of Congress Catalog Card Number: 00-026106.
No part of this book may be reproduced or transmitted in any form
or by any means, electronic or mechanical, including photocopying,
recording, or by any information storage and retrieval system,
without permission in writing from the publisher.
For information address: Bantam Books.

ISBN 0-553-57917-7

Published simultaneously in the United States and Canada

Bantam Books are published by Bantam Books, a division of Random
House, Inc. Its trademark, consisting of the words "Bantam Books"
and the portrayal of a rooster, is Registered in U.S. Patent and
Trademark Office and in other countries. Marca Registrada. Bantam
Books, 1540 Broadway, New York, New York 10036.

PRINTED IN THE UNITED STATES OF AMERICA

OPM   10   9   8   7   6   5   4   3   2   1

SPIRIT
SICKNESS

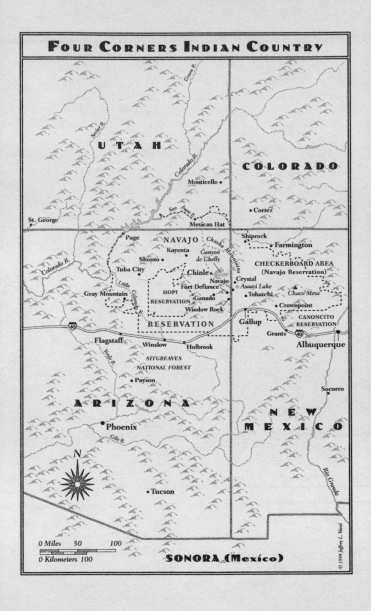

FOUR CORNERS INDIAN COUNTRY

UTAH

COLORADO

Sevier R.

Green R.

Colorado R.

• Monticello

San Juan R.

St. George •

• Cortez

Mexican Hat

Shiprock •

Page •

NAVAJO

Chuska Mountains

• Farmington

Colorado R.

Kayenta •

Canyon de Chelly

Shonto •

CHECKERBOARD AREA
(Navajo Reservation)

Tuba City •

Chinle •

Crystal •

Little Colorado R.

Navajo •

Asaayi Lake

Chaco Mesa

Gray Mountain •

HOPI

Fort Defiance •

• Tohatchi

RESERVATION

• Ganado

• Crownpoint

Window Rock •

Gallup •

CANONCITO RESERVATION

RESERVATION

40

Grants •

Albuquerque •

Flagstaff •

Winslow •

Holbrook •

SITGREAVES NATIONAL FOREST

Verde R.

• Payson

A R I Z O N A

N E W

Socorro •

M E X I C O

• Phoenix

Gila R.

N

Rio Grande

• Tucson

0 Miles   50   100

0 Kilometers 100

SONORA (Mexico)

© 1999 Jeffrey L. Ward

ANNA TURNIPSEED FELT RIDICULOUS—AND A LITTLE frightened that, after so many years, she was doing something this *native*.

Still, she hiked away from her condominium complex and out into the open desert west of Las Vegas. It was almost 4:00 P.M.; the air was cool. The only sounds were her footfalls on the slope and the droning of wild bees among the yucca blossoms. Clasped in her arms was a receiving cradle woven by a grandmother she couldn't remember. Twenty-six years ago, Anna had come home from the Indian Health Service hospital in it. On that day, a beaded deerskin bag had been attached to the frame to receive the stump of her navel when it dropped off. The bag and the remnant of her umbilical cord were long gone, but the cradle survived. A specimen of Modoc basketry this finely crafted would fetch at least $2,000 on the artifacts market. Not that she'd ever sell it.

Anna was going to burn her cradle.

Last week, she'd gone home to her ranchería, or mini-reservation, on the California-Oregon border. Her mother, confined to a nursing home with Alzheimer's, had failed once again to recognize her, so only a granduncle had been there to listen to the horrors of her first year as an FBI agent. Uncle Boston was generally believed by the local Indians to be a practitioner of spirit power, although his detractors thought of him only as the fired gas station attendant who, half-blinded by cataracts, had pumped ten gallons of diesel fuel into the gasoline tank of a brand-new Jaguar. Shamans had always had their supporters and critics. But everybody agreed Boston was a traditionalist. Traditionalists never trimmed their eyebrows, and Boston's had grown into unruly white tufts over his clouded eyes. Right off, he asked Anna if she still had a dried hummingbird or mole in her possession. *No,* she'd replied, coming close to smiling. He went on to ask what things from her childhood she'd kept. When she mentioned the receiving cradle hanging on the wall in her study, he gasped. *"Jesus Christ—are you out of your mind?"*

"Why?"

"You can't keep somethin' like that. It should've been destroyed as soon as you outgrew it."

"Mama never said anything."

"Then she's been crazier longer than I thought."

"Most first cradles are made of tules, aren't they?"

"Yes."

"Mine's willow, which is harder to weave. It's gorgeous. Grandma's best work."

"We're talkin' about mortal danger here, girl—not art. Burn the goddamn thing before you have any more bad luck!"

It seemed bizarre that your well-being could depend on what you kept or threw away. Yet, on the 650-mile drive back to Las Vegas, the idea began to appeal to Anna. Here was something she could do—other than depend on her partner's occasional visits—to make her feel safer. Her emotional and physical torments of the past five months finally made sense. She had violated Modoc ways. Now, the remedy appeared to be equally simple.

So she took her cradle off the wall and carried it out into the desert behind her condo complex.

There were storm clouds to the northeast, but it was sunny where she walked. She wore a light jacket to conceal her service pistol. Since being released from the hospital four months ago, she hadn't stepped out of her condo without her handgun and her cellular phone. It felt suicidal to go anywhere unarmed and cut off from backup. She knew that this feeling bordered on paranoia, but she couldn't shake it. The world was far more dangerous than it had seemed a year ago. Demons walked it. Living, breathing demons who left mutilated corpses in their wake.

She came to a dry wash. A good place to torch something without setting fire to the surrounding brush.

Stooping, she laid the cradle on the sand and studied the diamond pattern one last time. What did the design mean? Were the diamonds an arrangement of stars? What had her grandmother been saying to her infant granddaughter? Had the old woman—a bronze-faced munchkin in the family photographs—foreseen in the night sky the perils of Anna's current occupation?

Maybe it was unlucky to ask things like this.

Anna honestly didn't know. Connecting with her heritage felt like communicating through two lemonade cans separated by a thousand miles of string. Falling back on her culture felt like sifting through the wreckage of a mind-set nearly obliterated by missionaries and the government bureaucracy. *"Shit,"* she whispered, feeling like a fraud. Growing up, she'd paid little attention to Uncle Boston's "chiefy talk." It'd sounded so corny to her. So Hollywood Indian.

She let her frustration pass. This was a holy act, she supposed, and she had to keep a quiet head.

At last, she ignited a butane lighter and touched the flame to the exquisite handiwork. The tinder-dry cradle erupted into a crackling orange fireball. The heat made her scamper back on her heels. The frame unraveled, and the blackened willow withes curled on the ground like angry snakes before crumbling into ash.

Anna was watching the smoke dissipate and wondering if she felt any sense of liberation—when her cell phone rang in her pocket. She took it out. "Hello?"

"What're you doing, lady?" That comforting Oklahoma drawl. Her partner, Emmett Parker.

"Spring housecleaning. Where are you—your office?"

"No, I left Phoenix three hours ago. I'm more than halfway to Gallup."

She'd hoped Emmett might have been headed for Las Vegas. But just hearing his voice made her feel better. Or was this tiny mood swing the first dividend from the cradle's destruction?

Emmett paused.

She was familiar enough with his range of silences to realize that this one was troubled. "What's wrong?"

He let out a long sigh.

"Em . . . ?"

"Something's happened out here. Something awful . . ."

THE MESA AIRLINES COMMUTER descended out of the western sky into Gallup, New Mexico. Emmett Parker waited outside the terminal doors, watching the landing lights get bigger against the clouds.

Already, he was wondering if he'd made a mistake by asking Anna Turnipseed to come here. Too soon for someone in her condition.

Then he saw her, and pleasure overcame his doubts for a moment.

She was first off the plane, a small but shapely young woman with bobbed brown hair. She came slowly down the airstairs and across the tarmac to him. It was breezy, and she used her right elbow to make sure her windbreaker was covering her pistol. Her eyes, once open and frank in her oval face, seemed pinched and wary tonight. She gave him a cool peck on the cheek. "Hi."

"How was your flight?" He took her bag from her.

"Okay."

"Any turbulence?"

"Not much."

They walked in silence toward his car. The bronze-colored Bureau of Indian Affairs Dodge was the reason Emmett himself hadn't flown in—he would've been dependent on the FBI for ground transportation. Which meant working to their drumbeat.

The parking lot lights revealed the small circle of burn on Anna's forehead that had required a skin graft. The scar would be with her the rest of her life, an indelible reminder of the instant last January when an insane bastard had taken the flame of an acetylene torch to her face. Emmett quickly put that memory out of mind. As if his unspoken thoughts might infect hers. Some thoughts were like germs. "Get a chance to grab a bite before leaving Vegas?"

"No," Turnipseed said with a bright tone that sounded forced. "But I'm not hungry."

They got in his sedan.

Sniffling, she shed her jacket, then switched on the dome light to fish a wad of Kleenex out of her purse. There was an iridescent glimmer of feathers among her FBI credentials folder, hairbrush and keys. "What's that?"

She wiped her nose, then showed him. A mummified hummingbird. "For luck," she explained with an embarrassed look. "Uncle Boston insisted I take it."

"He came down to Vegas?"

"No, I drove up for a couple days."

Emmett started his engine. Until now, she'd said nothing about going home to her ranchería for a visit. But that wasn't what bothered him. All of a sudden, Anna Turnipseed—Cal Berkeley graduate in sociology, first in her FBI Academy class in academics—was carrying a Modoc charm. He didn't dismiss the old powers out of hand, but the shift in Turnipseed's belief system was too abrupt for comfort.

Frowning, Emmett set out for Window Rock, the Navajo tribal capital.

She avoided his eyes.

Turnipseed was Modoc, and he was Comanche. As ethnically different from each other as a Swede from a Mongolian. And she was still a rookie, despite a brutal inaugural year in the field, while he was a vet with fourteen years of chasing psychopaths around the West. Gulfs. Each time he looked at the possibility of this relationship dispassionately, he saw the unbridgeable gulfs between Turnipseed and him. "Sure you don't want to get something to eat here in Gallup?"

"I can wait."

"Got your choice in Window Rock," he plunged on. "McDonald's, Church's chicken or Taco Bell Express. And a Dunkin' Donuts in Tse Bonito, just this side of the capital . . ." Emmett whipped around a tanker truck lumbering up the long grade with a load of diesel for one of the tribally owned coal mines. "Don't know when we'll get a chance to eat again."

"I'm really not hungry." But finally she looked at him. "Unless you are."

"Nope." His stomach had been in knots ever since he'd seen her deplane as if descending into the next lower level of hell.

The speedometer needle vibrated around eighty-five. He backed off the pedal a little. But not much. The FBI's Gallup office had a big jump on them to the crime scene. The shoulders of Highway 264 glittered under his headlights: the remains of countless empty bottles tossed from cars returning to the dry Navajo Nation from Gallup's bars and liquor stores. Generations of broken bottles. Like discarded dreams, he thought.

Turnipseed lowered her side window as if she suddenly needed air, but quickly powered it up again. Unusually chilly for the last week of May. A slow-moving front out of the Pacific Northwest had brought wave after wave of light rain to the Colorado Plateau over the past three days. "Want me to put the vent on outside flow?"

"Please," she said. "How'd you get us involved in this?"

"I didn't. The U.S. Attorney in Phoenix did. He phoned me right after lunch. Said the Navajo government had requested me—"

"Specifically you?"

"Yeah, and an FBI agent of my choosing to ramrod the investigation . . ." Emmett had recognized this to be the only chance to get Turnipseed back on the bicycle. There was no right kind of case to ease her return from convalescent leave, so he'd said to the federal prosecutor that he wanted Special Agent Turnipseed of the FBI's Las Vegas field office to form the other leading half of the task force. Emmett's choice of partner had seemed to surprise the man, who knew as well as anybody that the Law Enforcement Division of the Bureau of Indian Affairs—and BIA Criminal Investigator Emmett Parker, especially—had no affection for the FBI. But the U.S. Attorney had readily agreed, knowing that now the Department of Justice and the Department of the Interior would share a high-profile investigation in Indian Country under the direction of a Modoc woman from California and a Comanche man from Oklahoma. It didn't get any more politically correct than that. "So," Emmett went on, "I phoned the FBI agent of my choosing."

Turnipseed noted, "But you didn't do that until four o'clock. And the U.S. Attorney called you right after lunch, right?"

True. He'd driven all the way to Holbrook before he felt up to persuading her to meet him in Gallup. "Sorry," he fudged, "but I wanted to get a jump on the drive. Didn't want to give your Gallup office any more time than necessary to screw up the scene." That wasn't the main reason, although the FBI was eminently capable of fucking up a crime scene. He'd been afraid she would refuse to come. Rookies who had a violent first year often resigned. They had no normal years under their belts to assure them what ordinary law enforcement life was like. It was all blood and terror to them. She was too young to hang up a promising career, even if it was with the Federal Bureau of Interference. First in academics at Quantico: Nobody shone that brilliantly by accident. Yet, on the phone with her, these arguments for sticking it out had deserted Emmett, and he'd wound up merely saying, "Look, I can use your help on the Navajo rez, Anna." Following a seemingly endless silence, she'd abruptly asked him how she was to get there. He'd been tempted to add something foolishly personal at the end of their exchange, something he'd come close to saying a dozen times since January. But, as on all those other occasions, he'd wound up checking the impulse.

Turnipseed and he now crossed from New Mexico into Arizona.

"Window Rock," he announced a few minutes later, sounding more cheerful than he felt. "First time here?"

"Yes." But Turnipseed made no comment about the Navajo tribal capital's strip malls and fast-food restaurants, the streets still stained reddish brown by winter's mud. Window Rock was like the other far-flung towns of northern Arizona and New Mexico, except for the off-white tribal flags flying everywhere in daylight. But these had been struck at sunset.

Emmett sped past the Navajo Nation Inn, a 1950ish Travelodge look-alike at which he'd reserved two rooms. He and Turnipseed had no hope of seeing them before dawn.

The dash clock read 8:07.

The night was depressingly young.

At the traffic signal, he turned up Navajo Route 12 and watched the golden arches of the McDonald's recede in his rearview mirror. Hot coffee would have been a godsend, but he might still get a cup at the police headquarters before continuing north to the settlement of Crystal, where the incident command post had been set up in the chapter house there, a kind of community hall.

A police Ford Expedition four-wheel-drive was waiting for him at the turnoff to the Department of Law Enforcement. "Parker . . . ?" a self-assured voice asked over the Arizona state mutual aid frequency. "That you in the Dodge sedan?"

Emmett reached for his mike. "Affirm. Who's talking at me?"

"Sergeant Yabeny." The Navajo cop pulled out onto the highway, laying down a gust of exhaust smoke as he led the way north. "I'm to take you to the scene."

Emmett followed. "Copy."

He'd never met the sergeant but soon admired his driving. They took the deserted four-lane at nearly ninety and swiftly put the lights of Window Rock behind. A sliver of moon had risen over the Chuska Mountains. It dimly revealed that culture-straddling duality of Navajoland: squat hogans side by side with white-style cabins or mobile homes. Quanah Parker, Emmett's great-great-grandfather and the last chief of the Comanche, had built a spacious ranch house off grazing fees he collected from wealthy Texans and never looked back. While Quanah stubbornly hung on to his native religion, especially peyote use, he'd found the material culture of his people to be dispensable. A romantic fog obscured how adaptable most Indian societies had proved.

He told himself that Turnipseed was adaptable. She'd buck the odds and not quit.

She reached over and turned off the vent flow-through. "Where's the medical examiner coming from?"

Emmett replied, "Gallup. But we can tap your D.C. forensic support, if needed."

"That's okay with you?"

"If needed," he repeated. Less was more when it came to help from the FBI.

Sergeant Yabeny began slowing for the outskirts of Fort Defiance, once the site of a U.S. Army post, now one of several federal housing collection points for those thousands of Navajo who'd abandoned their hogans and, in some cases, their elderly relatives in the boondocks.

"How were the victims found?" she asked. Good—she was finally freely talking.

"Civil Air Patrol out of Farmington. A lucky sweep over Crystal Wash near Canyon de Chelly . . ." The main Navajo reservation, known as the Big Rez to differentiate it from lesser holdings, contained 17.5 million acres, making it roughly the size of West Virginia. But to suggest that it was wilderness, even though parts of it were desolately lonely, would be inaccurate. Nearly 200,000 Navajo—or *Dine,* the

People, as they called themselves—lived in these canyons and on these desert steppes. The largest surviving tribe of full-bloods in North America. If anything, that meant *somebody* had to have seen. "I'm assuming ground units got to the site mid-afternoon," he concluded.

Yabeny's brake lamps blinked on and off three times, warning Emmett to slow for a Navajo Housing Authority tract. Here there were no reminders of the *Dine* past, just boxy frame houses set like game pieces on a Monopoly board. Streetlights faded out the stars. It could have been East Los Angeles, the heavy calm lying over the cookie-cutter dwellings like a lull between shootings. On the sagging wooden fence backing the development were splashes of graffiti. One read: *Viper Killers.* Another: *G.M. Lives!* Not exactly the Navajo country of John Ford westerns.

"He's turning," Anna cautioned.

Yabeny had veered right, keeping on Route 12 and avoiding the heart of the settlement.

Speeding up, Emmett fell in behind the tribal cruiser once more.

Turnipseed yawned. Another good sign, he thought, although it might have just been the need for more oxygen. They were almost at seven thousand feet. "How far to Crystal?"

"Fifteen, sixteen miles," he said.

"And then down the wash?"

"Who knows. Get off the main roads here, and you can throw away your AAA map." They'd crossed back into New Mexico, which reminded him of the jurisdictional mess this vast reservation involved. Felonies were handled by four different FBI posts with the now and then assistance of the BIA, misdemeanors by six tribal police subagencies and nine sheriff's offices in three states. Emmett expected Yabeny to turn off onto Route 134 toward Crystal, but the sergeant kept to Highway 12, dipping them back into Arizona. Where the crime scene lay. The Navajo police used a New Mexico state medical examiner on this side of the reservation, however, even in the Grand Canyon State, due to epic driving distances—it was shorter from New York City to Boston than from one corner of the Big Rez to the other.

A thick band of clouds was creeping out of the northwest. Emmett hated working a crime scene in rain.

Yabeny braked for the muddy apron of a dirt track, inched off the pavement and stopped. He strolled back to Emmett's car, a slim Navajo of average height in a Pendleton jacket and a pair of stone-washed Levi's. There was no urgency in his body language. No outward grief, either. Just a lean economy of movement and a natural indifference to haste. "This is as far as you can go with two-wheel drive," he said, squinting against Emmett's headlights. "We'll have to go on in my unit."

ANNA SAT IN THE front bucket seat beside the sergeant. She'd taken off her windbreaker and now realized that she was twisting the nylon in her hands. She made herself stop.

Marcellus Yabeny wasn't from Patrol, as she'd expected. He was assigned to Window Rock Criminal Investigation Services. He'd muttered something about heading the tribal youth gang task force, although offered no real answer when she asked him if gang involvement was suspected: "We'll see." His flattish face seemed young, but a sprinkling of gray was beginning to show at the back of his head.

Emmett sat in the middle of the bench seat directly behind them, his elbows propped on his knees. Ten minutes of jolting and occasionally ooze-covered road passed under the tires before Parker spoke up and asked Yabeny, "How long had they been missing?"

"Two days," the detective sergeant said.

It was Monday evening. So they'd vanished sometime Saturday.

From the caged prisoner area at the rear of the vehicle wafted a smell Anna had hoped to forget. Stale booze and vomit. They reminded her of times in the cabin in which she'd grown up. It was within sight of the lava beds where in

1873 her ragtag ancestors fended off much of the U.S. Army for half a year. *What made me go back last week? And what the hell am I doing with a dead hummingbird in my purse?* Her father had always said that Uncle Boston was a crackpot, making up what no one in the tribe remembered about the old ways. But that may have been only because her father had a secret that would've outraged traditional Modoc morality even more than the evangelical Christianity on the ranchería.

"Is Lieutenant Tallsalt at the scene?" Emmett asked Yabeny.

"No."

"Where is he, then?"

"Unavailable."

Emmett sat back, possibly in disappointment, Anna thought. Over the phone this afternoon, he'd mentioned that the head of Window Rock CIS was a friend from their days together at the FBI's academy for allied personnel. In the low light of the instrument panel, she studied Emmett's darkly intelligent eyes, the vague wrinkles at the corners of his mouth. He *was* disappointed. Something else occurred to her. He finally looked his age, thirty-nine. In late fall, before the nightmare in California, he hadn't. But his thick-chested body gave off the same old sense of coiled strength.

He caught her examination with a frown, and she faced forward again, feeling the heat rise in her cheeks.

The plain around them was heavily eroded. The gullies were so deep they seemed to have been clawed into the sides of the arroyo by giant talons. The few stunted and twisted junipers to show in the spill of Yabeny's headlights looked like furry trolls waiting motionless for the vehicle to pass before springing back to life.

Emmett let out an impatient breath. It smelled of Maalox.

He'd made no promises over the phone that this would be an easy investigation, a safe one. In that sense, she hadn't felt manipulated. Still, she'd resented his drawing her back to work. The newly assigned special agent in charge of the

Las Vegas office, her boss, had made no such demand. In fact, her SAC called weekly to remind her that the timing of her return was entirely up to her. No pressure. But was that because he considered her to be damaged goods and secretly wished she would take a disability retirement? Emmett genuinely wanted her back on the job, she knew, even though he was presently watching her like a hawk.

The high beams of an oncoming vehicle bounced up the track out of a gully and made Anna shade her eyes with a hand. A tribal cruiser was returning from the scene. The driver pulled alongside Yabeny, lowered his window. The detective sergeant let down his own glass, and the scent of mud, of last year's sheep dung revived by the rains, filled the cabin.

The eyes of the bullnecked patrolman flickered impassively over Anna and Emmett.

Then the two cops talked briefly in their own tongue, falling into the metronomic quality of conversational Navajo. The intonations were so different from English and Modoc, she had no idea how they felt about what they were saying.

Leaning forward, Emmett asked the patrolman, "FBI agent and the medical examiner already up there?"

"Yes," the man said. No hint of an attitude toward these parties.

"How long?"

"I don't know—couple hours or more."

"We got to go," Yabeny said abruptly. He waved farewell to the patrolman and drove on.

Rain speckled the windshield.

Anna asked, "How is it that the two of them were together, Sergeant?"

"Chief's idea," Yabeny said. "Wanted the wives to get some idea of what the guys go through on the job."

"Do you have any female patrol officers?" The chief had wanted *spouses* to get an idea.

"Three," Yabeny replied.

They passed an earth-covered hogan on the rim of the wash. A mud igloo. It, like the others along the increasingly indistinct track, looked uninhabited. At least for the season. None was linked to Crystal by a telephone line.

Emmett had lapsed into a distracted silence. Anna wasn't sure if her problems, Lieutenant Tallsalt's unexplained absence, or the fact that the FBI agent out of Gallup had beaten him to the crime scene by several hours was the cause. She turned to catch him running a slow hand through his close-cropped hair. Then his gaze riveted on something through the windshield. She turned her head to see it: a cold, chromium-blue glow breaking over the ridge directly ahead.

The front of the four-by-four sank downward, and she braced her hands against the dashboard. Yabeny gunned the engine. But instead of climbing the far side of the gully, the vehicle sideslipped. Lumps of mud thudded against the wheel arches. As the sergeant let up on the accelerator, Emmett asked, "You in four-wheel?"

"Yes."

Emmett got out, slamming his door behind him. He went to the rear of the Ford, stepped up onto the bumper and rocked the whole vehicle.

"Hang on a minute," Anna told Yabeny. She joined Emmett outside. The night air felt strangely dank for the high and arid Colorado Plateau. There was something fetid about the mud churned deep by the tires of numerous vehicles. It stuck to her low-heeled shoes. Emmett helped her up onto the bumper, and she clung with her fingertips to the roof trim.

"Go," Emmett told Yabeny.

The tires flailed more mud, but then dug in, and the Ford wallowed up the bank and onto the crest of the ridge. All the lurching made the recently knitted bones of Anna's right elbow and ankle buzz. Her war wounds from the last case.

She could feel Emmett's eyes on her again. The cruiser jounced up onto the crest, and he shouted for Yabeny to stop.

Crystal Wash had finally come into view.

Midway across it, three floodlights triangulated on a dull black vehicle, creating a kind of ash-tinted moonscape through which Navajo uniformed cops and the plainclothesmen of various agencies sifted. It took her a moment to realize that the vehicle they were focused on, which was mired up to its wheel hubs, was a Ford four-by-four like Sergeant Yabeny's. Except that the paint had been scorched off and the plastic lenses of the emergency light bar atop the roof melted into glistening puddles.

"Nobody told me they were burned," Emmett said to her, almost apologetically.

chapter 2

PARKING AT THE CRIME SCENE WAS LIMITED TO THE TOP
of a sandy embankment on the south side of Crystal Wash.
Beyond that Emmett saw only mud. Detective Sergeant
Yabeny nosed his vehicle among those already crowded there.
Three beat-up tribal cruisers, a coroner's pickup with a cab-
high refrigerated camper and a new Chevy Suburban, probably a bucar. FBI parlance for *bureau car*. Yabeny shut off his
engine. The floodlights penetrated the windows. Neither the
sergeant nor Turnipseed budged. Her face was turned just
enough for him to see that she wasn't blinking.

At last, there was a soft rustle of nylon. But it was just
Turnipseed untwisting her windbreaker as if thinking about
putting it on.

Emmett got out alone.

A portable generator was growling among the vehicles.
From it, a cable snaked down the embankment and branched
out across the muddy flats to each of three floodlights. They
trapped the burned-out cruiser in their glare. The abandoned
Ford Expedition had been cordoned off with yellow tape
strung on a circle of aluminum poles. This was to prevent
the trampling of any possible evidence around the sport utility. Nine men stood just outside this perimeter, facing the
ruin of the vehicle. Some wore the tan uniform of the Navajo
police. Some plainclothes. The wet silt beneath them was
heavily trampled, and their trousers were muddied up to the
shins. There were fewer tracks inside the ribbon, which gave

Emmett the hope that, so far, only the first cop to arrive on the scene, the medical examiner, and perhaps the Gallup FBI agent had approached the vehicle.

Evidence didn't stand up well to company, even allegedly expert company.

He glanced back.

Turnipseed was still sitting with Yabeny inside his cruiser. The sergeant's reluctance to get out was less worrisome to Emmett than hers. A traditional *Dine*—if Yabeny were one—saw death more as a spiritual contaminant to the living than a release for the deceased from earthly pressures. But that was Yabeny's problem. Turnipseed's paralysis was a different matter. It had personal implications for Emmett. He was almost certain she was on the brink of resigning. She was sitting there telling herself that chasing sick bastards through Indian Country was no way to make a buck.

Through the mud-spotted glass, her face was as still as a mannequin's.

That's right—if you remain inside the cruiser, the issue is decided. So what'll it be, Anna?

Her door opened.

She stepped down onto the damp sand, her face pale but determined, and put on her badly wrinkled FBI windbreaker.

Yabeny got out too.

Reaching Emmett, Anna wetted her lips with the tip of her tongue. "Where were they headed?"

The victims, she meant.

Good question. The same one now foremost in Emmett's mind.

The jeep trail ended on the embankment, cut off by a flash flood that had burst down the wash long ago. Surely, a tribal patrolman with twenty-six years' experience would have appreciated the perils of venturing up a muddy wash in an especially wet late spring. Even the bladed roads on the reservation could be made impassable by a brief downpour.

Where had Officer Carbert Knoki been bound?

Emmett looked upstream, out to the last dim throw of the

floodlights. The wash tapered down to a car's width between two sandstone monoliths that resembled pillars. There, maybe. Had Knoki been racing for cover under fire? Pursued by one or more vehicles? Or had he even been driving his own cruiser?

"Let's go," he said quietly to Turnipseed.

She fell in beside him without a word. Yabeny followed at a distance.

Emmett had worn hiking boots and now regretted not having warned Turnipseed about Navajoland mud. She stopped him, lightly grasping his arm for balance as she plucked her left shoe out of the slime and put it back on. The drizzle wasn't enough to soak through Emmett's parka anytime soon, but the droplets were a ticklish irritation on his face. They came down in shimmering veils, and each floodlight was now encircled by a halo of rainbow.

All the cruiser's visible windows were sooted over. Water-filled holes showed where frantic attempts had been made to dig out the tires.

They slogged on.

A white man in an FBI sweater broke away from a cluster of patrolmen and trudged up to meet them. Strands of silver-blond hair swept back from a domed brow in an attempt to cover a thinning crown. There was a softness around his mouth that made him look more sensitive than he probably was. Hands stuffed in his pockets, he didn't offer to shake. His aloof, cerebral air put Emmett off at once. "Parker and Turnipseed?"

"Yeah," Emmett said.

"Reed Summerfield, out of Gallup. Been expecting you."

"Anna," she muttered. It seemed obvious the two hadn't met before. Two FBI agents out of eleven thousand. Emmett knew by first name most of the BIA's eighty criminal investigators to have survived the latest budget cut.

In disgust, Summerfield gestured at the muddied front of his sweater. "Grand place for a crime scene. Had to get down on all fours to check the gas tank."

"Was it punctured?" Emmett asked.

"Yeah. That probably explains the accelerant splashed all over the interior and—"

"Where are the victims?" Anna butted in.

Summerfield looked down at her as if he'd never been interrupted in his life. But then smiled humorlessly. "I'll let the examiner show you in a minute."

"Why didn't the windows blow out?" Emmett asked.

"One did," Summerfield replied. "The left rear to the prisoner cage. I'm sure that's when the fire inside got hot enough to make the bodies unrecognizable."

Emmett caught the sudden stiffening of Turnipseed's shoulders. "What about foot tracks around the vehicle?" he asked the Gallup agent.

"Enough of them to indicate an all-out effort to get the cruiser unstuck—before the perps gave up, torched it and hiked out."

"Two of them?"

"That's right," Summerfield said with a yawn. Feigned nonchalance or genuine boredom? He was an odd duck, even for an FBI agent. "We can confirm that much by the two sets of tracks."

"Which direction did they go?"

"Southeast, toward the town of Navajo. Unfortunately, impressions in this soup collapse in on themselves as soon as you take your next step."

"What about any tracks up on the plain?"

"Erased by last night's downpour." Summerfield yawned again. "Listen, you two mind if I take off pretty soon? Haven't slept since the call came out on this early Saturday morning."

"By all means," Emmett said generously.

But Turnipseed wasn't ready to let him go. She dabbed the rain off her upper lip with her jacket sleeve. Or it may have been cold sweat. She asked, "Were tribal police first on the scene, Reed?"

"Yes," Summerfield answered. "Yabeny was closest when the report came in from Civil Air Patrol . . ." The sergeant was standing a few yards away. He, like all the other members of his department present, was watching Summerfield, Anna and Parker with an air Emmett couldn't quite put his finger on. Quiet resignation that, in this case, they were reduced to guides and luggage bearers for the feds? Or did they know something about the late Carbert Knoki that made expressions of grief seem out of place? In Emmett's experience, Indian cops carried on like their white counterparts when one of their own was slain. Angry tears, fists through locker room walls. The whole nine yards. "Were you alone, Marcellus?" Summerfield called to Yabeny.

"Yes." But then the detective sergeant added somewhat defensively, "With another unit just a couple minutes behind me."

Emmett wondered why that mattered to Yabeny.

But then Turnipseed took the conversation in another direction, and Emmett didn't want to override her. "Who checked the interior?"

"I did," Yabeny replied.

"Just you?"

"Yes."

Her tone was a bit strident, but Emmett found that understandable. Even desirable, given her need to be taken seriously by the tribal police. "Before or after the other unit showed?" she demanded.

"After," Yabeny answered tersely.

Summerfield yawned for a third time, then motioned over a middle-aged Hispanic with a myopic stare. He wore a pair of old-style rubber galoshes with metal fasteners, the kind the nuns at the boarding school had made Emmett wear on rainy days. "Dr. Esquivel, this is Agent Turnipseed from my agency and Investigator Parker, BIA. They'll be heading the task force."

"Who's leading?" the medical examiner asked curtly.

Emmett said without hesitation, "Agent Turnipseed." Her eyes snapped toward him, but he ignored her surprised look.

Box her in so there's no graceful way for her to retreat.
"Okay now for us to take a look, Doctor?"

"I think so." But Esquivel turned to Summerfield. "Unless . . . ?"

"It's their show. I was here just to shoo everybody away until they arrived."

"Let's get it over with." Esquivel stooped heavily to pass under the yellow ribbon, his kit in one hand and a small pry bar in the other.

Delaying Turnipseed a moment, Emmett took a tiny ceramic jar from the pocket of his parka. "Tincture of benzoin," he whispered as he used two fingers to gently smear the aromatic balsam under her nostrils. He could feel her rapid breaths pulsing on the back of his hand. Her frantic gaze was imploring him to say the words he couldn't simply because they would be untrue. *It's going to be all right.* The coming minutes promised to be ghastly. He gave himself a daub of benzoin, then dropped the jar into his pocket. "You're an investigator, not family," he coached.

She nodded without comment.

Yabeny tossed Emmett a big cell flashlight, and Parker lifted the ribbon for Turnipseed to duck under.

Esquivel used the pry bar to open the heat-warped rear door to the caged prisoner area of the Ford. A flesh-crawling screak came from the partly fused hinges as they gave. The balsam under Emmett's nose scarcely masked the half-sweet, half-charred stench that wafted out of the tomb of the compartment. He suddenly realized that he'd smelled it ever since arriving at the scene.

The examiner stood aside. Turnipseed pressed her lips together.

Two shrunken and blackened figures, prone, faced each other in the portion of the cruiser normally reserved for inebriates. One was female, judging from her broader hips. The victims appeared to be on the verge of punching each other with their outreached fists. "That's called the pugilistic attitude," Emmett explained under his breath, wanting to believe that if it could be explained it could be endured. "Involuntary muscle contraction from the heat of the fire. Doesn't mean they were alive at the time they were doused with gasoline."

Turnipseed slowed but kept coming on.

Emmett could hear the ooze sucking at his boots and her shoes. He halted, and she leaned slightly against him.

Officer Knoki's melted wool uniform was plastered to him like a wetsuit. His badge was still affixed to the left side of his chest, although the brass had been darkened by the flames. Knoki was resting on his holster, so it was impossible to tell for the time being if he'd managed to keep his service pistol.

Emmett doubted it.

Enough of the woman's face remained intact to give the illusion of a look of horrified astonishment. Again, a trick of the heat. Despite his resolve to memorize everything he observed, Emmett's mind wandered for a moment: *She came out to see what her husband's work was like, and all he showed her was the death she'd imagined a thousand times for him.*

"What was her name?" Turnipseed asked.

"Aurelia," Esquivel replied. "Aurelia Knoki."

Emmett cleared his throat. "Ages?"

"He was forty-nine," Yabeny replied from behind the ribbon. "She was forty-seven."

The couple's hands were unbound. This had been immediately apparent because of the pugilism, but now the significance struck Emmett. The Knokis had been overpowered—and maybe killed—miles before the four-wheel-drive cruiser had sunk into the mud of Crystal Wash. Their murderers had had no need to restrain the couple while transporting them.

Taking them where? Emmett asked himself.

Esquivel took an ear-and-nose speculum from his kit, braced a knee on the frizzed carpeting of the tailgate and crouched between the two corpses. "Confirmation depends on the presence or absence of carbon monoxide in their blood," he intoned. "But let's see if we can get a tentative idea."

Emmett said, "He's trying to determine if—"

"I know," Anna cut him off.

Esquivel inserted the speculum up one of Aurelia Knoki's nostrils. Had she been alive at the time of the fire, smoke stains might be found there. A pinprick of speculum light escaped from the dead woman's nose, spilling over his pulpy, white hands.

Quick and merciful. That's what Emmett hoped it had been.

The examiner was taking too long. A faint sickening feeling was coming over Emmett when Esquivel finally said, "Gross tissue damage. Can't tell from her nostrils." Emmett expected the man to start searching for the cause of Aurelia's death, but instead he promptly turned to her husband's body.

Waiting, Turnipseed gripped Emmett's upper arm.

The second examination made Esquivel scowl. "Same problem. We'll have to wait for the autopsy."

Turnipseed's hand fell away from Emmett's arm.

How much had this cop seen before the blackness? His wife dying? Had Carbert felt the flames curling around him, sucking the air out of his lungs? Emmett, the boarding school inmate, had grown up on a Roman Catholic mythology filled with saints condemned to the pyre. So he had imagined this death many times before. To most tribes, fire was something of incalculable good that had been snatched from the dangerous abodes of malevolent beings by ancient heroes, either human or animal. Or part both.

Turnipseed was breathing shallowly again.

"Anna," Emmett said, "I need to look around. You stay here as Dr. Esquivel's witness."

Her eyes showed panic, then disbelief that she was being deserted at this moment, but finally anger. "Go ahead." She gave him her back.

Emmett glanced at the victims' footwear and the shards of heat-tinted glass peppering their bodies. Then he waded around to the driver's-side door and shone the flashlight down through the window onto the floor mat. It was covered with clumps of fire-dried mud. This crude clay was also baked onto the steering wheel and the gear shift lever where the driver had touched them.

Carbert Knoki's citation book was still in the space between the bucket seats, the browned tickets bulging out of their basketweave leather cover.

Pivoting, Emmett examined the ground within six feet of the door. There were no ejected casings from Knoki's department-issue .40-caliber pistol, so he doubted that the officer had been engaged in a firefight while trying to get the cruiser unstuck. The lack of bullet holes in either the vehicle's glass or body gave further credence to this assumption.

His beam froze on a section of wooden handle.

Kneeling, he pried a round-nosed shovel out of the muck, careful to touch it only by the lower portion of the shaft. "Sergeant Yabeny," he asked, rising, "is this issued gear?"

"No. We just carry little trenching tools in the units."

Emmett gave the spade over to the Navajo evidence technician, then passed under the ribbon to the detective sergeant. "You canvass the neighbors?"

"What neighbors?" Yabeny asked, frowning up into the drizzle.

"We passed four hogans on the way in."

"Five. That's what our computerized housin' map shows. Five residential ID numbers on Crystal Wash Road. Three are unoccupied. One's just a summer place. And we talked to the Tsinnajinnies. Those are the only folks who live in this drainage year-round. Saw nothin', heard nothin'."

"Not even vehicle lights?"

Yabeny hesitated, then said, "Right."

"How far is their place off the road?"

"Quarter-mile."

Emmett wiped the benzoin off his lip with his handkerchief.

Pavlov, the Russian behaviorist, had been right. Instead of covering the stench of death, the balsam now always evoked it for Emmett. He'd put some on only to make certain Turnipseed did. "Take a stroll with me, Sergeant?"

Yabeny dipped his head once. Without enthusiasm.

They kept to the north fringe of the wash. Rocks provided stepping-stones there. Emmett wanted to know two things. The first was the destination the murderers had in mind. The second was what kind of man Carbert Knoki had been, and this was why Emmett had drawn the sergeant away from the other Navajo. Tomorrow, he'd ask John Tallsalt, Yabeny's boss at CIS. But it was useful to see a victim from more than one point of view. "How long had you known Knoki?"

Yabeny paused, perhaps having suspected that this was coming. "Ever since I came on the department."

"When was that?"

"Eleven years."

"You two friends?"

That required another pause. "Not really."

"Clan connection?"

"Nope."

"Where'd he and his wife live?"

"Mobile home in Navajo," Yabeny replied. A small community north of Fort Defiance distinguished only by its silent tribal lumber mill. Closed by debt and controversy within the tribe over harvesting trees off sacred mountain ranges. Emmett and Turnipseed had passed through Navajo on their way out of Window Rock.

He called a brief halt and, turning eastward, studied the floodlit Ford. The scene had an air of crafted unreality, like a movie set. Only Turnipseed seemed divorced from it, although she was still standing motionless at the rear door to the prisoner compartment. "What kind of guy was Knoki?"

"Okay." Yabeny shrugged. "Took care of his relatives." That was a hint that the dead man had been more traditional than modern, although Emmett would wait to pin that down with Tallsalt. Modern-behaving Navajos were known for putting self over family interests. Like the rest of America, which had Social Security to salve its conscience.

Emmett knelt and ran the flashlight beam along the rippled bed of silt that lay between him and the narrows. Not a single shoe impression. "What kind of cop was Knoki?"

"Old school," Yabeny said without having to think.

Coming to his feet again, Emmett asked, "In what way?"

"Bert loved goin' after those bootleggers. Drug dealers too. But mostly the rumrunners. Said they were bringin' down the whole Navajo Nation."

Emmett considered this. Reason enough to kill a meddlesome patrolman. Tallsalt had once told him that an ambitious liquor smuggler could clear $5,000 a month. More during the summer months, when young people partied out-of-doors. A fortune on this reservation, where the median income was $1,500 a year.

"Did Knoki report to the station before going on patrol Saturday?" Emmett started walking again. The mud slopped over the tops of his boots.

"No. Just radioed in as he left his trailer in Navajo." Yabeny chuckled under his breath. "Said he had a ten-fifteen/code one-oh-one along with him."

The code for a female prisoner. Emmett smiled, but then asked, "Was there any bitching about the spouse-ride-along program?"

"Some. Lot of the guys were afraid somethin' like this would eventually happen. But the chief ordered it, so we shut up."

They had reached the sandstone pillars. Again, Emmett scanned for prints. None. "What time did Knoki log on?"

"Sixteen hundred." Four o'clock, Saturday afternoon.

"Any distress calls?"

"Nope."

"Any transmissions from him at all?"

"One. At twenty-eleven hours he made a traffic stop on Route 134 near the Asaayi Lake turnoff."

"Did he call in the license plate?"

"Uh, no. At least the dispatcher didn't log it. We're lookin' into that."

"Disposition of the stop?"

"Bert said he scratched the driver for excessive speed."

All at once the charred citation book had evidentiary importance. The lab might be able to make out the writing on Knoki's copy of the ticket.

Fifty yards west of the pillars, the flash flood had undercut the steep gravel embankment, gouging out a cavity large enough to entomb the Ford with minimal effort by shearing off the overhang with the shovel.

This, no doubt, is where the killers had been taking the Knokis. The absence of tracks, human or vehicular, suggested that they had known this place without having had to visit it recently. They just hadn't counted on the deep mud. Or maybe figured that they, as locals, could deal with it. Their first mistake. Emmett hoped that many more were to follow.

"Finished?" Yabeny asked. As if this accident of terrain meant nothing to him.

"Yeah," Emmett replied. He turned back toward the floodlights.

chapter **3**

ANNA FUMBLED FOR HER SEAT BELT RELEASE AS YABENY
pulled alongside Emmett's sedan where they'd left it on the
highway six hours ago.

A heavy, wet stillness lay over the plateau as she and
Parker got out. The Navajo sergeant mumbled a goodbye
and sped away.

Emmett unlocked the passenger-side door for her, and she
got inside. The digital clock in the instrument panel read 3:09.
Condensation coated the windows, and the interior of the car
was clammy. While Emmett warmed up his engine to run the
defroster, images of the scene in lower Crystal Wash flashed
inside her head, gruesome beyond imagination. Imagination
was a candle flame compared to the searchlight of reality.
She'd witnessed an autopsy last winter in Las Vegas, but
never before had she been caught up in the dizzying, cyclonic
blur of a homicide scene. The smells. The overpowering presence of the wronged dead.

A salty taste of blood touched her tongue.

She'd been absently gnawing on the inside of her cheek.
She stopped.

Until now, working on her notes had helped her fend off
these jarring mental pictures. She'd pored over the pad even
while being bounced around inside Yabeny's cruiser, clamping a flashlight under her arm while she deciphered and corrected her atypically oversized scrawl. On many of the pages,
her hand had been trembling too badly to leave legible

words. But she'd been frenetically busy ever since Emmett returned from his hike down the wash with Yabeny and thrust a steno pad into her hands. "You've got the initial report," he said. She had resented the task until she realized that it would distract her from the horror.

And so most of the night had trickled away in a welter of chores. Angle selection and documentation of photographs. Close-ups on the bodies. On the vehicle. The tracks marking the suspects' escape route up onto the plain. She made a sketch of the entire scene—without Summerfield's assistance, as the Gallup agent had left for home within an hour of Emmett's and her arrival. Under her direction, the remaining cops formed a search line inside the ribbon and inched along like the minute hand of a watch, flashlight beams bobbing over the boot-honeycombed surface of the mud. Evidence from inside the cruiser was carefully labeled and packaged. Endless detail to cram her mind, leaving room for little else.

And now, abruptly, her notes were finished.

There was nothing to do but sit. And remember.

Emmett's headlights swept over the rain-jeweled sagebrush as he turned south onto the highway. She inhaled. The stench of charred flesh was still locked inside her head. She'd asked Emmett about it, and he muttered something about the burnt molecules getting attached to nasal hairs. Only time would rid her of it, despite the application of benzoin before and repeated washings after.

She let down her side window.

The fragrance of wet sage temporarily rescued her from the stink. It reminded her of home, the sagelands of northeastern California. The same raucous stars were overhead, now that the clouds and their drizzle had drifted eastward into the heart of New Mexico. But there were limits to her nostalgia. It alone couldn't entice her all the way back to that tar-paper shanty in Modoc County, which held its own horrors for her even though the shack had been long abandoned to the ranchería's gangbanger wannabes, who—according to

Uncle Boston—sniffed glue, paint and gasoline there, or made love to their girls on a filthy sheepskin. On her trip home last week, she'd avoided her parents' wrecked house.

She put up the window. Her clothes were damp, and the air chilled her.

Emmett cleared his throat. "Little town of Navajo's along the way. Yabeny gave me directions to the Knokis' trailer. Mind if we swing by?"

"No." She didn't. The busier the better, despite the lateness of the hour. She wasn't looking forward to sleep.

Neither was Emmett, apparently. Otherwise, the detour by the victims' mobile home could wait until tomorrow. He was still trying to grasp something just beyond his reach. In his restless wandering at the crime scene, she'd glimpsed an investigative approach different from her own. She liked to connect the dots; Emmett seemed to be in constant search of an overview. Not that he lacked respect for detail; his uncanny memory attested to that. But his preference was to rise above the confusion of the scene. As if each new case was a vision quest, the spiritual journey undertaken by a Plains Indian to help him separate intention from accident. Fit the pieces of the universe together in a comprehensible whole.

Did Emmett himself see it that way? And was Uncle Boston setting her on that kind of path? If not, the hummingbird in her purse was simply grotesque.

Emmett took a side road and drove slowly past a lumber mill. A silent and darkened relic of the time when all the reservations had welcomed industry. Its towering incinerator chimney pointed like a cannon at the stars. In the yard, piles of rain-soaked wood chips gave off a vinegary smell. At the end of the pavement was a seedy cluster of a dozen mobile homes.

They located the Knokis' double-wide by number. Like cops everywhere, Carbert Knoki hadn't hung out a name plaque, even though everybody in town probably knew where he lived.

Pulling into the driveway, Emmett cut his engine, switched

off the headlamps and sat back. An older-model Mazda coupé was parked on the cracked cement pad near the rear of the trailer. The dogs in the area were barking. Emmett scrutinized the exterior of the mobile home by the sulfurous glow of its entry door light, his expression weary. Anna looked at the trailer—and was struck by the sense that no one lived here anymore. She quickly shifted her attention to details. Distraction in details. Carbert Knoki had been frugal with the skirting: the Astroturf-covered wooden stoop beneath the door had been pulled out a few inches, revealing a six-foot-wide gap.

The porch light.

It occurred to her that the Knokis had left it on Saturday afternoon with every expectation that they'd be returning home in Sunday morning's darkness. Now, they were en route to the University of Arizona Medical Center in Tucson to be autopsied.

At least there were no children.

She'd heard Emmett ask Yabeny about that, and then had felt self-absorbed for not having thought to inquire. It should've been her first concern: any offspring left by a cop killed in the line of duty. The sergeant explained that the Knokis had had a baby boy, but he'd developed medical problems as a toddler and died at the pediatric hospital in Salt Lake City. Twenty years ago.

Two investigative dots defied connection. "Em . . . ?"

"Yeah."

"A couple of things at the scene didn't make sense to me . . ."

"Go on," he said.

"Carbert had his boots switched on his feet. Same with Aurelia's shoes."

"What's the second thing?" he asked.

"That side window in the prisoner cage didn't explode out, like Summerfield said."

"Why not?"

"The glass was sprayed all over the Knokis. And it'd

been cooked by the flames. So I'd say the window was bashed in at some point *before* the vehicle was set on fire."

He reached over and gave her shoulder a squeeze. "Good for you, Anna." He let go of her and grabbed his door latch.

She'd liked his touch. But then she realized that he hadn't answered her. "What's this all mean?"

"In the morning," he said. "I'll let Tallsalt explain . . ." His friend, the tribal Criminal Investigation Services lieutenant who'd absented himself from tonight's crime scene. "I left a message with Yabeny for John to meet us for brunch at the inn. Come on."

She felt a menstrual-like pinch in her gut. "Are we going *inside*?"

"Yeah. Yabeny told me where to find the key."

The driveway paralleled a chest-high redwood fence that separated the Knokis' narrow lot from those of their neighbors on the west and east. A large black dog on the opposite side followed their progress, barking. Suddenly, it leaped up, fangs glinting, and startled Anna with a deep, ferocious growl. The animal's eyes seemed terrified. A planter ran the length of the fence. No plants in it. Just fist-sized rocks. The west slope of the Chuska Mountains, like her own Modoc high desert, was too harsh an environment for anything but native species, which grew too glacially slow for landscaping purposes. Besides, she didn't believe that the Navajo were into manicuring their terrain. It was intrinsically white to believe that nature could be improved upon.

Emmett took special interest in one particular rock. Picking it up, he shook it, producing a muted rattle. The hollow rock was artificial. Inside was a house key.

They were turning for the Knokis' entry door when a neighbor's porch light flared on, adding to the sickly yellow atmosphere. The black dog fell silent. A Navajo in his mid-thirties peered tentatively from his doorway, then seemed relieved to see Anna and Emmett. "Who're you?" he asked as the dog slunk between his legs and into the safety of the room behind him.

"Police," Emmett replied.

"Dine?"

"No, federal."

The man came down his steps to the fence. He had a cleft lip. "You found 'em." It wasn't a question.

"Yes," Emmett said after a moment. "Dead."

The neighbor nodded fatalistically. "Thought so."

"Why?" Anna demanded.

"Well," the man said grudgingly, "all the dogs in the park been goin' *loco*." A faint Hispanic accent, unlike that of the other *Dine* Anna had met tonight.

"So?"

He jerked his lips—the Navajo way of politely pointing—at the Knokis' trailer. "Guess they been tryin' to make it home."

A shiver went up Anna's backbone. By *they* the man wasn't referring to the dogs. But, for the moment at least, her curiosity was sharper than her unease. "How long have the dogs been acting this way?"

"Couple months, on and off. But real bad the last two nights."

She asked, "And you are . . . ?"

He must have thought that Emmett or she might be at least part Navajo, for he gave the traditional introduction, starting with his mother's and father's clans. ". . . And my name's Hank Whitesheep."

"Investigator Parker from the BIA, and I'm Special Agent Turnipseed, FBI." They shook over the fence. Whitesheep had a laborer's weathered face but a tender hand. No calluses. Nor was there any conviction in his languid grip. "Were you related?" Anna decided not to mention the Knokis by name to a man who apparently believed the spirits of the murdered couple were already haunting their former home.

"Not really, ma'am."

Emmett felt the need to clarify. "What about clan relation?"

"Well, sir, the woman and me were sort of related that way," Whitesheep answered. "No big thing to either of us."

In Anna's brief experience, people who called cops *ma'am* or *sir* were either recently out of the military or had served extended time in jail or prison. Whitesheep had a civilian slouch. "When did you last see them, Hank?" she asked.

"Oh, Saturday afternoon. One o'clock, two o'clock. Before I went to Bashas' Market in Window Rock."

"How'd they seem to you?"

"Okay, I guess. Aurelia said Bert was goin' to make a cop of her." Whitesheep's grin faltered as he appeared to realize that he'd used the Knokis' names.

"Were they having trouble with anyone? Maybe somebody here in the park?"

"No, ma'am."

"If you happen to recall anything along that line, do you mind leaving a message for us with the Navajo police?" She handed him one of her cards, and Whitesheep gave a shrug that said he wasn't going to make any special effort. Then he ambled back inside his trailer.

Emmett had already started to unlock the Knokis' entry door.

GILA MONSTER AWAKENED at the sound of an automobile engine.

It vibrated the thin aluminum skirting that surrounded all of the mobile home—except behind the porch steps. They could be scooted open and closed like a secret entrance to the dark, dusty lair in the crawl space beneath the trailer. There he had scratched out a burrow. A nest from which to spring the Blood Atonement. The merciless final reckoning.

His eyes opened a crack.

There was a car in the driveway.

He stirred from his cold-blooded sleep, lifted his heavy head off his pillow of the rear axle and listened.

They have no purpose, the Voice intruded, *other than to lure you to your destruction and damnation on that heathen nation, for they know you must one day kill them to free yourself from their evil!*

The engine died.

He thought he could hear muffled human voices in the silence that followed. He was so used to the barking of the dogs, the noise now passed for silence.

Along every six feet of skirting was a narrow panel perforated with ventilation holes. He must go to one of those panels to be able to hear anything.

Laboriously, he rolled over onto his belly and reached out with his right forefoot. As always during cool weather, his paw trembled slightly as he groped for the lip of the burrow. The crawl space was almost lightless, but he could visualize the rippling of his powerful, scaly forelegs as he inched upward and then across the ground. His skin was beautifully beaded: bands of pink, orange, yellow and white. His face was completely black, so anyone peering into his burrow would see nothing—until it was too late.

His forked tongue flitted out between his front teeth and tested the air. He was picking up the taste of things warm and blooded.

This was confirmed when he reached one of the panels, pressed his goggle-eye up to it and peered out. His heart leaped with excitement: A slender native woman stood at the fence, talking to the dimwitted neighbor. Their words were a muted jumble, barely making a dent in the questions fluttering around inside his racing heart—*Was she Moth Woman? And has Moth Man accompanied her at last?* It was absolutely critical they come together.

His only memory of her was now fourteen years old, yet it might be she.

He imagined seizing her, pinning her throat in his massive jaws and unleashing his poison—sweet to his own tongue—flowing along the grooves in his upper and lower teeth, spilling into her with the hot intensity of semen. And then impaling both Moth Man and Moth Woman with his javelin.

That is what the Voice told him to do.

But there was another voice within him, his own perhaps, that painted a recurring picture—almost a memory—of her stirring a pot of mutton stew over an open fire, a marvelous stew he had never savored but missed just the same. A perfect stew that satisfied every kind of hunger and emptiness. She made the haunting *lol-lol-lol* sound of the Moth People as she worked the ladle in graceful figure-eights.

Gila Monster scuttled back a few feet.

From the entry door nearby came the soft crunch of a key being inserted into the lock. The woman was still at the fence, so she had not come alone. But she had finally turned, and her face was revealed. It was not she. Too young.

Make it impossible for them to follow you, the Voice cautioned, *and punish all who try!*

"I will," Gila Monster whispered.

EMMETT WAITED FOR ANNA before going through the door. The light switch just inside activated an overhead fixture that illuminated the common living room and kitchen area. The furniture was neither new nor threadbare. The kitchen seemed compulsively clean, although the odor of tobacco smoke hung in the double-wide. One or both of the Knokis had smoked. That could potentially affect the autopsy findings in regards to carbon monoxide. Another mental note.

Anna stepped around him, her mud-caked shoes creaking over the linoleum floor.

He saw that his own boots were a mess.

"What are we looking for?" she asked, as if she were in a mausoleum.

"The reason Yabeny was so damn reluctant to tell me where the hide-a-key was." Emmett went to the end table beside the sofa. *Field & Stream. Indian Country Today.* Last Thursday's issue of *Navajo Times*. About what he'd expected. He sensed that there was nothing blatantly unusual about the Knokis that might have marked them for death. But he'd been wrong before. Every human being alive had a point of vulnerability secreted away in their past. A warm, sticky spot of hidden decay.

Anna gestured at the empty counter space, the dishrag hung over the faucet spout to dry. "My God."

"What?"

"The poor woman left this kitchen as if she knew she was going away forever."

Emmett decided not to add anything to that. He went to the mail caddy beside the telephone and answering machine on the breakfast counter. She joined him there, watched as he sorted through the envelopes, opening only those that had been opened already. Bills and credit card statements. No charges so exorbitant as to cast doubt on Bert Knoki's ability to cover his expenses with his department paycheck. One number ten envelope had been slit open but looked personal enough for Emmett to pause. Handwritten, possibly a woman's script, addressing Bert as *Hosteen* C. Knoki, a title of perfunctory respect probably from another Navajo. The return address was P.O. Box 444, University Park, Arizona. A down-at-the-heels Phoenix neighborhood. The postmark was almost three months old.

He set the letter down on the counter. There were limits to how far he would invade the privacy of the dead. At this point. He returned all the mail to its caddy and checked the answering machine. No messages.

Turning, he strode for the back. The lightly reinforced floor shook under his boots.

There was a small utility room off the kitchen. A door gave access to the east side of the yard.

Flicking on the nightstand lamp, Emmett surveyed the bedroom. A lumpy-looking bed with a George Washington coverlet and six pillows. People with difficulty breathing at night piled up their pillows.

Outside, the dogs were going crazy again.

Atop the bureau was a framed copy of a nineteenth-century lithograph: angels carrying a baby up into heaven from its cradle and bereaved parents. Anna gravitated toward it while he opened the top drawer of the nightstand. Inside were less recent issues of *Field & Stream* and a snub-nosed .38 Special revolver with a lock inserted inside the trigger-guard to prevent firing. Did the now childless Knokis have children over often enough to warrant this? Probably. Navajo extended families were enormous; Bert and Aurelia were bound to have had numerous nieces and nephews. If not, Knoki had been extraordinarily cautious—until Saturday night. Had he feared his own gun being used against him for some reason? Also inside the drawer was a small hide bag filled with corn pollen. To ward off evil. The Navajo equivalent of Anna's hummingbird, which still bothered Emmett. Was she hanging on by a thread that slender?

Leaning against the door jamb, he watched Anna going through the medicine cabinet. "Bert had high cholesterol," she announced, rattling the pills in a plastic vial as proof.

"Navajo diet," Emmett said. "Not many vegetables, except corn in season. Lots of mutton. Greasy fry bread." He paused, then asked, trying not to sound too worried, "How're you doing, lady?"

"Fine," she answered without looking at him. "One of the Knokis was pulling out all the stops to try to quit smoking. Patches *and* gum."

"You did well tonight," he went on.

She seemed to be on the verge of responding to that when the lights in both the bathroom and the bedroom bumped off and on, then went out for good.

Emmett rushed back into the kitchen. All the lights in the entire place were off, and the refrigerator moaned down to silence. Yet through the window over the kitchen sink he could see Whitesheep's porch light shining.

He flipped on the switch to the garbage disposal. It didn't fire up. The barking outside grew frenzied.

Spreading his parka, he drew his .357 Magnum revolver. He saw by Anna's silhouette that she had taken out her 9mm pistol.

The hysterical yapping of the dogs was drifting east through the backs of the tiny lots. "Get my flashlight from the glove box . . ." He kept a small black metal one in his jacket pocket, but it was useless for distances. "Then meet me around back." As soon as he caught her nod, he pushed through the utility room door and sprinted to the rear fence.

He stopped, gripping his revolver in both hands before him.

The dogs had fallen silent. He strained to catch the sound of footfalls fading up the first ridge of the Chuskas, which rose just beyond some sort of flat expanse that reflected no starlight.

Nothing.

Anna appeared at his side. Taking the big flashlight from her, he wheeled and knelt, then ran the beam along the bed of gravel Bert Knoki had laid down instead of turf in this side yard. The surface was too rough to register any kind of foot impression. He raised the beam to the circuit breaker box attached to the wall of the mobile home. Its cover was ajar.

But before checking it, he shone his light over the fence.

The few acres there below the slope had been used once by the lumber mill, for they were carpeted with wood chips. Another poor medium for tracks.

"Hear anyone?" Anna asked breathlessly.

"No." Holstering, he approached the box. The main breaker had been thrown.

"Prank?"

"Maybe." But then as he started for the evidence kit in the trunk of his car, he said, "Maybe not. Don't touch it." He couldn't believe that someone had been here to ransack the home of a murdered cop. There'd been no sign of that. But someone had been here.

Balls, Emmett thought. *This joker has balls.*

Returning to Anna, he dusted the switch with black powder. She held the light for him. Clear latent fingerprints depend on sweat or body oils being deposited by the toucher. The tape Emmett applied to the powdered surface came away with virtually nothing to suggest the friction ridges—the distinctive loops and whorls—of a human finger. Instead, he could faintly discern a peculiar beaded pattern. Almost like snake scales.

"Gloves?" she asked, the beam wavering in her increasingly unsteady grasp. She had to sleep soon. So did he.

"If so, I've never seen a pair like it."

Emmett locked up and returned the key to its artificial rock.

He drove three hundred yards up the dirt road to Asaayi Lake at a crawl, holding his door open and flashlighting the surface for tracks, then doubled back into the abandoned timber yard behind the trailer park. Neither Anna nor he found anything of note among the rotting wood chips.

An hour later, as he pulled into the lot of the Navajo Nation Inn and parked facing the rising sun, Anna brought something to his attention. Dawn revealed two hand-sized prints on the passenger side of the windshield. The resemblance to anything human ended with their size and the number of digits. Five. Beyond that, they were undeniably reptilian. Emmett could even see where the claws had left scratches in the water spots on the glass—as if the thing had braced itself against the windshield to leer inside the sedan.

chapter 4

ANNA SUSPECTED SHE WASN'T ALONE IN THE QUEEN-
sized bed.

But opening her heavy-lidded eyes seemed impossible, so
she drifted off again, letting a wave of protective oblivion
swell over her. Then the certainty that she was flanked by a
pair of charred corpses jolted her. She kicked off her covers
but quickly made herself lie perfectly still, listening for the
faint sighs and hisses of putrefaction she'd heard from the
back of the torched cruiser in Crystal Wash. Only the hammer-
ing of her own pulse filled her ears, but she could smell burnt
flesh. She was convinced of it. The stench was overpowering.
Her trembling fingertips brushed lizard skin, cool and scaly. Or
was it the alligator pattern left on human skin by searing
flames?

Bolting upright, she gasped.

You're dreaming, you're dreaming. She cradled her stuffy,
aching head in her hands. The Knokis wouldn't let go of her.
They were smothering her with their incoherent pain. This is
what death felt like. A crushing weight. Utter hopelessness.

They're here with me.

A whirring noise suddenly came from the nightstand. She
pressed her hands over the clock radio, hoping to muffle it.
But the sound persisted. Her purse. It was coming from her
purse. She hesitated, then unzipped it. She jerked her hands
back in fright as something tiny and black burst from the
purse and flitted around the room. It hovered briefly at the

window, then swept back to the bed and whirred close to her eyes. Little wings gusted wind into her face. This wind stank of death.

She pounded the wall with her fists.

The floor in the next room creaked as feet landed heavily on it.

She crawled down the center of the bed, holding her arms rigidly against her sides, terrified that now, with her mind slowly clearing, she'd still find the Knokis beside her. It was irrational, all of it.

And horribly real.

She reached the door the same instant Emmett jiggled the locked knob from the outside. *"Anna?"* As soon as she opened the latch, daylight flooded the room, temporarily blinding her. "What is it?" he asked frantically, bursting inside. A tall shadow moving through the dazzle.

"Nothing," she replied.

He barged past her with revolver in hand, searched the bathroom and then shoved her clothes aside in the closet partition to make certain no one was hiding there. He came back to her, his face screwed tight and his chest heaving, seemingly oblivious to the fact that he was trooping around the Navajo Nation Inn in just a pair of jockey shorts. "Did somebody try to break in?"

"No." She sank onto a corner of the bed, seeing that the Quantico T-shirt she used for a nightie was clinging to her sweat. There was no sign of Uncle Boston's hummingbird around the room, and she saw that her purse was still zipped shut on the nightstand.

He shut the door and clicked on the bedside lamp. Only then did she realize that the fresh, cool air had felt heavenly on her skin. He sat in one of the chairs at the table, was still gripping his revolver—although loosely now. "Dream?"

She nodded.

Absently, he began rubbing one of his pectoral scars. From the Gaze at the Sun Suspended finale of the Sun Dance, she knew. A decade ago, while on an undercover assignment for the FBI in South Dakota, he'd submitted to the torturous ritual. Hanging off a pole on rawhide tethers attached to his flesh with skewers. He'd never really explained why to her. There were still distances between them she didn't feel comfortable closing. On his left hand was a more recent scar. A stab wound suffered during their last case together.

"The dreams will keep coming back for a while," he told her, dropping his hand from his chest.

"Thanks," she said dejectedly. Then his worried look drew a humiliated laugh from her. "I'm sorry, Em."

"Don't be," he said. Sternly.

She switched off the bedside lamp to avoid his stare, and the darkness behind the blackout curtains came as a comfort now. There was a quiet metallic rattle as he laid his weapon on the table. She believed that she could catch his scent through the unshakable odor of char. It was pleasant. Like honey and leather. Quanah, his middle name and that of his feared war chief ancestor, meant *fragrant*. She'd learned this from a Comanche dictionary. Certainly not from him.

"This is silly," she muttered, irritated at herself. "What's the time?"

"Almost nine."

Three hours of tossing and turning since she'd left him and gone to bed. The slit in the curtains let in a narrow strip of light, and by it she watched Emmett's silhouette sit back.

"It just felt like the Knokis were *here*," she said defensively.

He kept silent.

"You probably sleep like a baby."

"Not in a long time," he admitted.

"Is that what I have to look forward to?"

"You'll manage."

"Are the dreams worse when cops are the victims?"

Emmett didn't reply. A moment later, he came to his feet. "Let's try to grab a couple more hours of shut-eye before we meet with John Tallsalt." The Criminal Investigation Services lieutenant had left a message that he'd meet them at eleven in the inn's coffee shop. *"Now,"* he grumbled, "let's see if I can tippy-toe back to my goddang room without being arrested for indecent exposure."

"Don't go." Having said it, she wished she could take it back. He was riveted to the floor in apparent confusion. "I just don't want to be alone," she amended.

But it was too late.

He sat beside her on the bed. There was just enough light to make out the glint of his pupils hard on hers, hungrily on hers. He was in her hands, and that frightened her. His face was moving slowly toward hers when she did the unforgivable. She shrank from him. Ever so slightly. Not from revulsion—all her impulses at the moment ran counter to that in ways she found unexpectedly thrilling. But he instantly froze, stung, then got up and snatched his revolver off the table.

"I can't stay here and not touch you," he said.

Then he went out.

EMMETT FEIGNED INTEREST in the menu while he awaited John Tallsalt. He hadn't slept after he'd returned to his room from Anna's. Finally, forty-five minutes ago, he'd given up on bed and showered. On the way to the coffee shop, he'd rapped twice on her door without breaking stride.

Tallsalt was already thirty minutes late.

Nothing on the lunch menu appealed to Emmett. And mutton stew and fry bread were the traditional Navajo breakfast. He grimaced. His tastes for the first meal of the day were strictly midwestern: eggs, pork, gravy and biscuits.

But his mind wouldn't stay fixed on food.

Anna.

What had happened was acceptable as long as he understood the nature of his own emotional defenses. His libido had settled on a frigid love object as the means of sparing him a fourth failed marriage. Even had he lapsed with Anna in her overheated room, his own tabu against intimacy with a co-worker would have soon kicked in, and his relationship with her would've quickly been brought back within sensible bounds. In short, he'd turned himself into a lightning bug whirling pointlessly around a night-light.

Still, he was surprised by how disappointed he felt. Crushed.

Stupid. If only because there were advantages in having an Indian partner. Not once had Anna asked him what human-sized reptilian paw marks were doing on his windshield, even though she'd helped him lift the impressions to pass them and the partial print off the Knokis' main circuit breaker on to the Gallup FBI office, which would rush this potential evidence and Bert Knoki's burnt citation book on to that shrine to Western Rationality in Washington: the FBI laboratory.

Anna's face had revealed nothing.

Ishi, the last surviving member of the Yahi who in 1911 staggered half-starved out of the manzanita thickets of California's northern Sierra into a white world with which he'd had no previous contact, had been shown an aeroplane in flight by anthropologists from Berkeley. The scientists waited with barely contained glee for the ignorant savage to be dumbfounded by the sight of a human being riding the air. Ishi's kindly face revealed nothing. Flight had been completely within his understanding. Half-mythic, half-animal tricksters, like Coyote, could conjure up the incredible. The Indian point of view was not narrowly superstitious. It allowed for *anything*.

Anna Turnipseed wouldn't be knocked off balance by the apparently incredible. Maybe the dead hummingbird in her purse only meant she was now open to letting the incredible back into her tightly wrapped twenty-first-century life.

And as far as her nightmare, it had amounted to the other shoe dropping for Emmett. He'd been expecting, almost hoping for a crack in her facade ever since he'd watched her deplane from Gallup yesterday evening.

Emmett gave up on the menu, tossed it to one side.

The surrounding tables were jammed elbow-to-elbow with late breakfasters and early lunchers, mostly tribal bureaucrats being wooed by corporate types. The low buzz of chatter sounded technical. Coal, timber, uranium and a huge tract of land that held the headwaters of several of the Southwest's most vital rivers were being discussed. The *Dine* were amply endowed with resources. And with the BIA beginning to give up its old regency over all the tribes, real power was being exercised in Window Rock. It was also being contested. Indian progressives against Indian traditionalists. Entrepreneurs against environmentalists. All the battle lines familiar to the wider world, but with an overlay of Navajo culture.

Had Officer Bert Knoki somehow figured in one of these conflicts?

He was pondering this when a muscular figure strolled up to the please-wait-to-be-seated sign. The man wore the uniform of a tribal police lieutenant. Campaign hat tilted rakishly forward. Sharp creases in his green-striped trousers. Slowly, he ran his eyes over the tables. Emmett let him go on searching a minute, taking the opportunity to scrutinize his only close friend among the Navajo. Except for a bit of gray in his mustache, John Tallsalt hadn't changed much in the eight years since their academy stint together at Quantico. The same penetrating and un-Navajo gaze that women accused of undressing them: The man's eyes looked to the quick of everything, even though his own people found staring impolite.

At last, Tallsalt turned to the hostess. Whatever he said was suggestive enough to make her blush, but she quickly recovered and pointed at Emmett, seated across the room.

Smiling wryly, Tallsalt strode toward him.

He was large for a Navajo, even for those with some blood of the stocky Pueblo. Emmett suspected the genes of a Castilian goat trader somewhere in his lineage. The lieutenant doffed his hat and took the chair opposite Emmett's—without shaking hands.

Tallsalt righted his coffee cup. "Know what you get when you cross a Comanche and a *bilagaana*?" A white man.

"Pray tell."

"A smart cattle thief."

Emmett kept a straight face. "I find that culturally insensitive."

"Well, we *Dine* would still like to find the cattle you bastards stole from us at Bosque Redondo . . ." When the army interned the Navajo on the parched plains of eastern New Mexico in the 1860s, attempts to turn them into white-style ranchers were thwarted by continuous raids by the Comanche on the government-issued livestock. Finally, Tallsalt offered his hand. "Your face is puffy. You getting laid regularly?"

"Nope."

"Tell me about it." Tallsalt raised his cup to be filled by the waitress. "You didn't hear that," he said, winking at her.

She giggled as she withdrew.

Emmett noticed that the lieutenant's eyes were bloodshot, and the unmistakable odor of gin was on his breath. They'd drunk mint juleps that fall in Virginia, then separately joined AA a year later. "Missed you last night, Johnny."

"Did you?" Tallsalt smiled. "You'll have to forgive me, but I've sworn off felony investigations."

"Why's that?"

"Each time I go, the feds make me feel like I've barged into the wrong pew. So I stick to my misdemeanors and tribal offenses like a good little Injun."

"But you knew I was in on this one."

"*Teamed* with the FBI," Tallsalt pointed out. "What's your partner like?"

"See for yourself," Emmett replied as Anna slid into the chair between them. She was wearing perfume, no doubt in the vain hope of covering the smell of burnt flesh.

"Good morning." Her bright and vacant smile pierced Emmett like an icicle. So this was how she would carry on—blithely, as if nothing of any importance whatsoever had passed between them two hours ago. Tallsalt's appreciation of her sleek looks and the way she filled her jeans was immediately evident. He'd always preferred Indian women, although no woman, native or white, had kept him for long. He was one of those inveterate bachelors who kept his reasons to himself behind a front of jocular banter about not having found *The One*.

"Why the uniform, Lieutenant?" Anna motioned for the waitress to come her way with the coffeepot.

"Pardon?"

"The uniform. I thought CIS wore plainclothes." She looked entirely self-possessed. As if all that had transpired between them in her room had been Emmett's own dream, not the outcome of hers.

Screw her.

". . . Monkeysuit's for the media," Tallsalt was explaining. "They'll be pouring in from Albuquerque and Phoenix this afternoon to find out how this time we managed to lose one of our men *and* his wife."

"Spouse-ride-along is a pretty common program with other departments, isn't it?" Anna asked, holding out her cup to the waitress. Her hand was trembling slightly, Emmett noted.

"Yes," Tallsalt answered, "but the chief had the devil of a time selling it to the men. They already tell their wives everything that goes down at work. Women are always in the know here. Old matrilineal habits die hard, and the guys figure the job's one place they can get away from them." He sighed. "At least the old man'll be spared this afternoon's grilling by the press."

"Why's that?" Emmett asked.

"Checked himself into University Hospital in Albuquerque this morning. Chest pains."

The waitress asked if they wanted to order. No one did. Coffee would do. The breakfast-meeting crowd had finally thinned out, leaving a privacy several tables deep around them. That made it easier for Emmett to ask, "You're acting chief?"

"For no more than a week, I hope," Tallsalt replied. "Lousiest job in the world."

Anna asked, "Why do you say that?"

"I haven't had my second cup of coffee yet." The lieutenant turned to her with a charming smile. That annoyed Emmett. Tallsalt was doing nothing to tone down his attraction, and now Turnipseed seemed to be enjoying his attention. "First time in Window Rock, Anna?"

She nodded. "Beautiful sandstone formations."

"If you have the time, I'll show you the tribal government complex. Best place to view the window in the rock."

Emmett frowned. "What can you tell us about Bert Knoki?"

Tallsalt's smile went out. "A stand-up guy. One of the few in the department I would've trusted with my life. I'll miss him."

"Any relation to you?"

Tallsalt was hesitating before answering when Anna, to Emmett's displeasure, butted in. "Sergeant Yabeny says Knoki was a thorn in the sides of local bootleggers and drug dealers."

"Yes. But if that's your read on this, you're barking up the wrong tree."

"Oh?" she said. "Then what's the right tree?"

"Mexican drug traffickers," Tallsalt answered unequivocally.

Anna said it for Emmett. "What makes you think that, Lieutenant?"

"John, please. Marcellus Yabeny get a chance to tell you two about the aircraft tracks?" Emmett shrugged, and Anna shook her head. Tallsalt continued, "We found landing and takeoff impressions on a small dry lake bed about three miles northwest of Crystal Wash. Wide landing gear, so it was a big enough plane to bring a serious load out of Mexico. That's how the Colombians do it these days, cut a deal with Mexicans to bring the coke the last leg of the trip to the U.S. We've been working these guys for a while. Ruthless bastards."

Emmett asked, "Who are they?"

"Smugglers out of Sonora. Almost sure they have a connection here on the Big Rez, local boys who run the stuff into Santa Fe and Albuquerque."

Emmett didn't care for the lieutenant's effortless slide over a contradiction: He'd just told Anna locals weren't involved. But he decided to let it pass for the time being. "Have you called in the DEA?"

"No," Tallsalt said testily, "because we're tired of them kissing off everything we hand them. When what I have is ironclad, even if it was developed by some poor blanket-ass cops, I'll give the DEA a jingle."

"BIA has a pretty good drug enforcement detail," Emmett pointed out. "Most of us happen to be blanket-asses too."

Tallsalt stared a moment at him. He'd turned uncommonly wary, even for a Navajo, and that more than anything concerned Emmett about the direction the conversation had taken. The lieutenant was the last person on the reservation he'd expected to hold back on him. "I'll keep your BIA unit in mind," Tallsalt said apathetically.

Anna interrupted the eye-lock between the two men. "What you're saying is that Knoki was patrolling Crystal Wash when he stumbled onto a dope drop? And the traffickers felt they had no choice but to kill him and his wife?"

"Something like that."

Anna tossed a prodding glance at Emmett, who finally asked, "How's that account for a couple of Navajo idiosyncrasies at the scene, John?"

"Idiosyncrasies?"

"The Knokis had their boots and shoes reversed on their feet. And somebody made a *chindi* hole by knocking out one of the cruiser's windows."

After a blank-faced second, Tallsalt chuckled.

"What?" Anna demanded as if she were being excluded from an inside joke.

"Thought I'd never accuse Emmett Parker of reading too many Tony Hillerman novels." The lieutenant swiveled in his chair toward her. "You see, Anna, life imitates art. Every federal cop who comes here on a case now takes the cultural approach. Most are real disappointed to learn that the motivations for crime in Navajoland are essentially the same as those in Pittsburgh and San Francisco."

"What's a *chindi*?" she pressed.

Tallsalt straightened the gold-acorn-tipped braids on the brim of his hat. "The spiritual garbage within each of us, even the best of us. It's loosed by death and wanders the night. Eternally. Highly infectious to the living."

"A ghost?"

"Except a ghost might retain some of the good qualities of the deceased. A *chindi* is nothing but pure evil."

"And the switched shoes?"

"So the spirit trips up if it tries to pursue the living."

Her blouse was sleeveless, and she rubbed the backs of her arms. Catching her determined look, Emmett decided that he'd leave it up to her to tell Tallsalt about their predawn experience in the Knokis' mobile home. "What about the smashed-in window?" she asked.

"Maybe the traffickers read Hillerman too. It seems to me the kind of mistake an outsider would make based on limited knowledge. A *chindi* hole is sometimes made in the wall of a hogan to let the beast escape. In the unlikely event somebody was allowed to die inside. But I see no reason for this to be done to a vehicle."

Emmett asked, "Can you take us out to the dry lake where the plane impressions are?"

"Be happy to. Except I'm tied up in the near term. As you can imagine. Special Agent Summerfield went with Yabeny and me that day. I'm sure he still remembers the route."

chapter 5

"I'VE GOT A FEW THINGS TO GO OVER WITH THE TRIBAL president before the press briefing," John Tallsalt explained as he unlocked his office in the Criminal Investigation Services' modest outbuilding behind Navajo police headquarters. Standing aside with an impatient smile, he motioned Anna and Emmett inside, but stayed at the threshold. "Help yourselves to the phone," he went on. "And Emmett—the file you asked about is right there on my desk. Just secure my door when you two leave for the Sonsela Buttes. That's where the dry lake is." He checked his wristwatch before saying to Anna, "I'm sure Reed Summerfield can guide you there with no problem. Surprising the out-of-the-way spots he knows around here." His undercurrent of sarcasm was unmistakable. "Now I've absolutely got to run."

"Go," Emmett said. Grumpily, Anna thought.

Then she and he were alone for the first time since the encounter in her room that morning.

She could hear the wall clock marking off the seconds.

Emmett scooped up the file and sank into the chrome and Naugahyde sofa facing Tallsalt's desk. He cracked the folder and began reading by the light of the high window. She flicked a switch, and the fluorescent fixture stuttered on. He glowered up at it, the crow's-feet deepening around his eyes. Looking thoroughly disgusted. She tried not to sound irked with him as she said, "I'd like to go through that with you." Bert Knoki's personnel file.

Emmett snapped the file shut and tossed it on the sofa beside him. "You going to phone Summerfield or not?"

She frowned at him, but he was studying the opposite wall. It was covered with the lieutenant's commendations and mementos, photos of him with everybody from the senior U.S. senator from Arizona to the manager of the Diamondbacks. The kind of gallery that smacks of political ambitions, which Tallsalt had claimed not to have. There were no family portraits anywhere in the room. She dialed the number for the Gallup FBI office from Tallsalt's Rolodex. The female agent who shared office space with Summerfield had to summon him out of the coffee room. He sounded nonplussed at having his plans for the afternoon changed—he'd just gotten in to work. But he promised to be in Window Rock within forty-five minutes.

Anna hung up and reported this to Emmett, who merely grunted.

Showering that morning, she'd rehearsed a speech, a circumspect one that revealed as much as she dared at this point in her life. That included a confession of how much she cared for him, that during these past months of recovery, Emmett Parker—partner—had proved the only person in the world she could count on. Unconditionally. Was she now willing to jeopardize that by letting Emmett Parker—man—start making conditions of the most intimate sort? "Em . . . ?"

"Yeah."

"About this morning . . ."

His face shifted toward hers, became still with expectation. She knew what he wanted her to say. But finally he asked, "Who's witnessing the autopsies?"

His eyes had turned cold: He had no intention of discussing that morning. A gulf was opening between them. So rapidly—after the glacial development of their friendship—it scared her. When in Las Vegas this spring for the trial arising out of their last case, he'd camped out on her living room couch. It was only on those nights that she'd felt safe enough to sleep soundly. Now, the thought of losing his presence at the bottom of her stairs almost panicked her. Waking to the sound of him humming off-key in her kitchen. Phoning her when he was back home in Phoenix to make sure that she was all right. She said, "One of our Tucson agents is covering the postmortems. I forget his name. Hispanic. You probably know him better than I." She was sure she'd discussed this with Emmett at the crime scene last night. Summerfield, as the agent on the ground most familiar with the federal assets available to the Navajo Nation, had suggested to her how the initial off-reservation tasks might be divvied up, and she'd consulted with Emmett before giving their approval. She was positive this conversation had occurred. For a man who perfectly recalled everything he heard, this contrived amnesia came as a slap.

"Mind if I join you?" she asked tartly.

He picked up the folder without replying, and she sat where it had lain on the small, greasy-feeling sofa. He began passing her pages one at a time. In silence. Above and beyond the growing tension between them, she sensed his distaste for this chore. It was unavoidable in a cop killing: the suspicion that some abuse of power had led to the homicide. Perhaps even justified it. And thus the victim became a kind of suspect. Anna knew of only one other crime that by its very nature so automatically inverted the innocent and the guilty. Rape.

If I die here in Navajoland, will the bureau comb my life for dirt?

By the twentieth page, she felt she was beginning to get a feel for Bert Knoki's career. Even though the material was sprinkled with *Dine* words. Apparently, he'd been one of those academy-to-gold-watch patrolmen valued by some departments as the backbone of the agency while deprecated by others with the bias that a worthwhile cop never passed up the opportunity to advance in the ranks. "No officer-of-the-year awards," she commented out loud. "No commendations from tribal government, other than those marking his terms of service."

"It's not Navajo to stand out," Emmett said churlishly.

Anna pointed at Tallsalt's panoply of plaques, framed certificates and VIP photos.

Emmett wordlessly handed her another page. Careful not to touch her.

One disciplinary action in 1986 had been glaring enough not to be culled from Knoki's file: involvement in a public altercation in Mexican Hat, Utah. Along the northern border of the reservation. Knoki had almost been arrested by San Juan County deputies, who alleged Knoki to have been in the company of a Ute *alzil* . . . "What's an *alzil*?" she asked, looking up.

"Prostitute."

"Oh."

He gave her a sidelong glance. "Oh what?"

"Nothing."

"So he was human. You have a problem with that?"

"Not at all. Hooray for humans." She went on reading. Knoki had contested none of the charges when confronted by Internal Affairs. He took his punishment without uttering a single word in his own defense: two weeks' suspension without pay. Mostly for having been armed during an off-duty incident he refused to explain.

Knoki's pistol.

Last night, with a sickening crackling sound, Esquivel, the medical examiner and Emmett had rolled the patrolman's corpse on his back to see if the man had held on to his weapon. Knoki's holster had been flattened by the weight of his body. The gun was gone. Now that absence translated into a cheerless hope the killers had kept Bert's pistol, unwittingly tying themselves to the crime.

Anna accepted the next page from Emmett.

THE DIRT ROAD TO Sonsela Buttes branched in three different directions, each rutted track identical. Stymied, Reed Summerfield braked, studying the horizon for a hint of anything remotely familiar. The Gallup agent was obviously lost, and Emmett, sprawling impatiently in the back, exhaled. Loudly enough for Anna to half-turn in the front passenger seat and shoot him a look.

Perched on the dashboard was a translation of Zolbrod's *Dine bahane,* the Navajo origin story. In German. The vibration from the engine finally slid the book off the dash and dumped it onto the floor. A Polaroid fell out of the pages. Anna stuffed the book in the glove compartment but didn't notice the photograph on the mat between her feet. Emmett was in no mood to be helpful.

Summerfield's promised forty-five-minute arrival time at the CIS building had doubled to ninety. Then, while puffing an endless stream of brown-papered cigarettes on the drive north, he regaled Emmett and Anna with stories of his recent days at Washington Metropolitan, FCI. He was a former Foreign Counterintelligence agent. There were two basic types of FBI special agents. And criminal agents, of whom Anna was one, were the blue-collar grunts, held in fairly low regard by the more cerebral counterintelligence Brahmins. Unfortunately, for the FCI elite, the end of the Cold War had dropped the bottom out of their glamorous world. Hundreds had been transferred from the centers of foreign espionage—D.C., New York and Boston—and reassigned to a violent crime task force or a health care fraud unit. Somehow Summerfield had missed one of these face-saving postings. He'd wound up in Gallup, a railroad and powwow town surrounded by several dry reservations. He'd been here seven months, three weeks and two days. He kept track of his sentence to this remote posting that precisely.

Thankfully, Summerfield stopped in the shade of the only juniper on the slope. It was hot, now that the low pressure system had moved on. Emmett lowered his window. A breeze whispered through the berry-studded foliage. Another hour of this heat and there'd be no trace of the night's rain on the land. Already, the muddy places along the road were cracking into parquets.

"I just don't remember which way to the dry lake."

Summerfield's ineptitude was turning him surly. For the first time, there was a flash of temper in his rearview-mirror-reflected eyes, a glimpse into a temperament not as affably nervous as it seemed on the surface. The man hated this country and everything in it, Emmett thought.

"Maybe you'll do better," Emmett said, "if you don't have to drive too."

"I can handle it," Summerfield said brusquely.

But he didn't drive on.

Emmett got out and stretched. After a minute, Summerfield and Anna joined him.

"Must be quite a change for you, Reed," Anna observed. "Compared to the hustle and bustle of Washington."

Summerfield scanned the buttes in silence for a moment. "Not at all. It's a challenge to bend the legislative intent of the Racketeer Influenced and Corrupt Organizations Act into an attempt to outwit bootleggers trying to smuggle hooch onto the Big Rez on a Thursday night. And then every few months, almost as regular as clockwork, a tribal cop gets whacked. Before the Knokis, it was a sergeant named Sidney Manygoats. Slashed in the throat with a machete while responding to a public intoxication call. That one took all of ten minutes to solve. His cousin did it. Stinking drunk, of course, and shocked the next morning to discover what he'd done under the influence of the dark water."

"So you find crime in Indian Country pretty senseless?" Emmett asked Summerfield. With an edge.

"Isn't it?"

"Try Oklahoma City, where I worked in the eighties. Though I missed the most senseless blow of all. McVeigh and his buds didn't even need the dark water to pull off the biggest mass murder in this country's history." Starting up the middle branch of the road on foot, he said over his shoulder, "Wait here." He soon left the track and climbed due west in the hope of finding a panoramic view.

*   *   *

ANNA WAS GETTING BACK inside the Suburban when she saw the Polaroid on the floor mat. A fit-looking middle-aged man with a thick mustache smiled warmly across a table at the lens, the arms of his sweater looped around his shoulders and his left hand grasping a cigarette in an ivory holder. The photo had been shot in an outdoor café in Santa Fe, for down the street behind the man was the familiar facade of the Cathedral of St. Francis of Assisi. And taken in the fall. The cottonwood in the middle ground was turning gold.

Anna handed the photograph to Summerfield, who'd sat behind the wheel again. "Surveillance subject?"

The agent's expression turned melancholy. "No," he said after a moment, "nothing like that."

THE RISING GROUND didn't suggest to Emmett the kind of terrain in which he might find a dry lake bed. Usually, these formed on the bottoms of undrained desert basins. But he continued up the rain-softened hillside of volcanic ash, which stuck to his soles like damp talcum powder. The Sonsela Buttes lay between Crystal Wash and Whiskey Creek, both of which eventually wound down into Canyon de Chelly. The advantage to a pilot approaching a makeshift airstrip here, presumably without either landing or runway lights, would be that these rounded plugs of eroded-away volcanoes were higher than anything else in the vicinity. Colliding with a mountain would be unlikely as long as a pilot didn't stray too far east toward the Chuskas. The disadvantage was there was no hard-packed alkali bed on which to land.

Nearing the crest, Emmett caught some sounds that made him slow down. Bleating and the tinkling of bells. Then the protective bark of a dog. He topped the rise, and the perfume of a sagebrush fire sifted over him. Smoke rose from near the base of the only other visible juniper, now that the one shading Summerfield's Suburban was no longer in sight.

Milling around this solitary tree, half-concealed by the waist-high scrub, was a small flock of sheep. A tethered burro stood in the shade. Emmett sang out with what he believed to be a credible *yah-at-eeh*. An elderly Navajo eased up out of the brush, munching on something. He quit chewing as his suspicion mounted. Emmett was Indian but not *Dine*, and that alone could mark him on the remoter parts of this reservation as a skinwalker. A male witch. Approaching, he was careful not to appear overly friendly. That too could be misinterpreted.

Fortunately, the collie mix quickly lost interest in him. Dogs were reputed to be able to sniff out skinwalkers.

"Yah-at-eeh." The old man returned the greeting. He wore a Brigham Young Athletics Department sweatshirt, despite the sultry heat, and a minimum of jewelry. Just a turquoise ring and a silver belt buckle. His wrinkled face continued to register distrust, but he was chewing again. Meat was cooling in a small skillet he'd taken from the fire and set on a flat rock.

"Where you headed with these fine sheep?" Emmett asked.

The old man twitched his lips at the Chuskas. Patches of light green revealed the meadows among the darker shades of the firs and spruces.

"And where are you coming from?"

Another twitch, this one to indicate the plunging depths of Canyon de Chelly to the west behind the man. His spring lambs were just old enough to make the trek to summer pastures, and one of them—probably an orphan—was snuggling around the muddy legs of his army surplus pants.

Emmett showed his credentials. "I'm a policeman with the Bureau of Indian Affairs."

No reaction. Either that or a fastidiously guarded one. Still, the old man turned civil and declared his mother's and father's clans preparatory to introducing himself. "My name is Alva Tsinnajinnie . . ." That set off a ping in Emmett's memory: Last night, Sergeant Yabeny had mentioned this as being the only family that kept a full-time residence along

Crystal Wash. But the area was probably crawling with Tsinnajinnies. "Are you Apache, policeman?"

"No, *Hosteen* Tsinnajinnie—Comanche."

"*Naalani.*" The old man whispered the Navajo word for Comanche. Almost a curse. While the Ute were the traditional enemies of the Navajo, the Comanche had earned a special place as the tribe's bogeymen. Especially to Tsinnajinnie's generation, who were old enough to recall the stories of their grandparents about the *Dine*'s four-year internment by the U.S. Army in eastern New Mexico. Desolate range the free and unconquered Comanche considered their own. So they'd treated the half-starved reservation Indians huddling in holes dug in the ground there as contemptible squatters. But quickly, the old man put aside any inherited prejudice and shook in the Navajo way, slowly and earnestly, pressing his thumb against the back of Emmett's hand. "Do you know your clans?"

"Just one, really. The *Quahadi.*"

"What does it mean?"

"Antelope Eaters." Navajo and Comanche concepts of clan were worlds apart. Navajo clans, of which there were now over sixty, had been diluted beyond recognizable bloodlines to a kind of religious and social fraternity encompassing tribal members scattered throughout Navajoland, with no identifiable common ancestors. Most often, fellow clan members were unaware of their kinship until they rattled off their clan pedigrees as part of introducing themselves. The *Quahadi* were actually a tribal division of the Comanche, not a true clan, but Emmett had better things to do than split hairs with the old man.

"You want something to eat, policeman?"

"I do, *Hosteen* Tsinnajinnie. But there are others with me in a car below."

"There's enough for them too."

Emmett nodded. "Before I get them, I'd like to ask a question . . ." He paused in case there was an objection.

There was none. "Have you ever seen an airplane land among these buttes?"

"No, but there are tracks like this—" Tsinnajinnie held three fingers of his left hand flush to each other. "—over on the lake left sometime by the male rains. No water there now, though."

"And where is this?" Emmett eagerly asked.

Another jink of his expressive lips. Northward. The Navajo divided all natural qualities into male and female. The male rains were the hard cloudbursts of summer.

"How do you think those tracks got there?"

Tsinnajinnie shrugged that he had no answer.

"Do you winter in Canyon de Chelly?"

"I just keep my sheep there with my sister's husband."

"Where do you live?"

"Down the Crystal Wash road." Then he was one of the family Yabeny had mentioned.

"Were you there last Saturday evening?"

"No, I was already goin' for my sheep."

A pinkish glint of sunlight drew Emmett's eye to Summerfield's balding pate. He and Anna had left the Suburban and were hiking over the crest toward them. She looked slight at a distance, but that impression evaporated at close quarters, somehow. Maybe it was her obstinance that made her seem larger than she was.

Emmett turned to the old man again. "Recently, have you seen anybody come into the wash?"

"Nobody but family."

Emmett smiled. "And how many are they?"

"Eleven. My wife and me. Two daughters and seven grandkids."

"Ever see any lights during darkness down in the wash?"

"Not there."

"But you see other lights sometimes?"

Tsinnajinnie picked up the lamb, began stroking its neck. "Fires up in the Chuskas."

"Forest fires?"

"No, smaller'n that." Then the old man lamented, "Everythin's goin' crazy these days, everythin's out of *hozho* . . ." *Harmony* to the *Dine,* roughly translated as *walking in beauty. Hozho* could be undone in an instant by the breaking of tabus, not living in the Navajo way. "I think maybe the fires I seen could be burnin' hogans." A blazing dwelling was an omen of death to these people, so none of this might be literal. Yet, Sergeant Yabeny had hesitated before flatly declaring that the Tsinnajinnies he'd interviewed had seen no lights—had he had the fires in mind? No use asking the old man if there'd been one in the Chuskas Saturday night. He'd been out of the area.

The dog growled, then charged Summerfield. It was within a fang of taking hold of the agent's leg when the old man whistled shrilly, and the collie careened off to the side.

"Thought you got lost," Anna said to Emmett with just the right inflection to indicate that she'd tired of Summerfield's company. Emmett felt a glimmer of vindication. He introduced them to Tsinnajinnie, who put down his lamb to shake. The old man was obviously prepared to clasp hands again with feeling, but Summerfield swiftly disengaged himself, then wiped his palm on his trouser leg. Rather than take offense, Tsinnajinnie shifted his interest to Anna.

"Are you Comanche too?"

"No, grandfather," she replied. "Modoc."

"Modoc," the old man repeated, as if he'd never said the word before. "Where are your people from?"

"Northern California and southern Oregon."

"Lots of trees?"

"Some. But mostly lava beds and grass."

Tsinnajinnie didn't ask Summerfield where he was from. Picking up the skillet by its handle with a dirty bandanna, he offered the fare around, beginning with Anna. Thankfully, Summerfield didn't inspect the limp, lard-white strings. Following Anna's example, he moistened his fingertips before plucking out a hot sample. He held it between his front teeth for a few seconds to cool, then looked pleasantly surprised as he chewed. "Where in the name of God do you get calamari around here?"

"You don't," Anna said. "It's sheep's aorta." And then she seemed to take some perverse delight when Summerfield's color dropped.

"*Hosteen* Tsinnajinnie," Emmett asked, "how far is this male rain lake bed?"

"A short walk." The old man offered him more sheep's aorta, and Emmett accepted. He was suddenly starving, as was Anna, apparently, for she too took another handful.

Summerfield declined a second taste.

Emmett tilted his head toward the north. "Any of this beginning to look familiar, Reed?"

"I don't know," the agent answered. "Maybe if we drove on. What do you think—the road that branches right?"

"I think we should walk from here." Emmett thanked the old man and set out through the flock, checking his watch again. Almost 4:30. The first days of a homicide investigation always went by in a blur. Hard to remember your bodily needs, and if it weren't for the constipation that inevitably ensued you'd probably drop twenty pounds. He sneaked a look behind. Anna and Summerfield were catching up, she with the easy stride of someone used to traversing brushy country and he with the crooked praying mantis hands and minced steps of an urbanite deathly afraid of encountering snakes.

Emmett overheard Anna ask Summerfield if he was married. "God no," he replied. "What kind of sadist would bring a wife out here?"

Emmett shook his head, then bounded up some natural steps formed by a basaltic dike. From the breezy summit, he could finally see the lake bed. It was long and narrow. And irregular in shape. But there was enough distance along its east–west axis for a small plane with sturdy landing gear to touch down and take off again. The lake bed had been created when lava spurted from a small cone and meandered around the north fringe of the much older buttes all the way down to what these days was called Whiskey Creek, leaving a long barricade behind which volcanic ash had been trapped and compacted over time. Or, as the Navajo believed of the lava flows near Mount Taylor in northwest New Mexico, one of the four sacred peaks enclosing Navajoland, it'd been formed when the Hero Twins slew a monster, and the beast's blood dried and blackened into these sinuous masses.

Dotting the surface were two rows of specks.

Anna and Summerfield came up, Summerfield huffing for breath.

"What are those?" Emmett pointed at the specks.

"Signal pots," Summerfield gasped. "Made from coffee cans. The drug traffickers fill them with gasoline, torch them off as the plane circles. *Voilà*—runway lights."

"Did you or Tallsalt's people collect any?" Emmett asked.

"No," Summerfield admitted. "I suppose we can do that today."

"I suppose," Emmett echoed sourly. "I sure as hell can't see the tracks from here."

"Well, they're dreadfully faint."

"Why's that, Reed?" Anna interjected. From this Emmett realized that he'd again grown too caustic for her comfort. "Wouldn't the plane have been heavily laden?"

"I'd say it had more to do with erosion."

"Erosion," she reiterated. Good. She too was repeating the man's idiocies.

"I'd say the impressions were already a few months old when Tallsalt and Yabeny asked me out here."

"And when was that?" Emmett asked.

"Oh, six weeks ago. Perhaps a bit longer."

Tallsalt, you lying sack of shit! Emmett paced around the top of the butte in anger.

"Reed," Anna asked, "did you have any dealings with Bert Knoki?"

"I must have these past months. But nothing specific comes to mind. You know, an incident for which I was case agent . . ." The agent in charge, he meant. "But I hear he had a rather fanciful imagination."

"In what way fanciful?"

"Oh, nothing specific comes to mind, Anna," Summerfield repeated.

So Summerfield hadn't gotten along famously with Knoki, Emmett mused. Not that friction between an FBI agent and a tribal cop was unheard of in Indian Country. But Summerfield was being so coy about this, Emmett made another mental note: *Check with Tallsalt.*

His temper finally under control again, Emmett gestured at the distant Suburban, the road that branched right from the vehicle and eventually switchbacked up to the playa. "Mind driving your unit to the lake bed while Turnipseed and I go on ahead by foot?"

"Not at all." Summerfield's eyes were angry, embarrassed even. He was no fool. Just grossly out of his element.

"Got an evidence kit in the Suburban?"

"This and that."

"Black powder, a camel hair brush and some tape?"

Summerfield nodded.

"Good," Emmett said. "I'd like to try to get some latent prints off those cans. If that doesn't work, we can send the more promising ones back to the lab for fuming." Faint fingerprints could be developed back to visibility by a special process involving fumigation with gases. But Emmett had no intention of messing with prints. What he wanted was a word alone with Anna.

It was downhill to the Suburban, so Summerfield took off at his fastest pace of the day. A stiff jog that resembled power-walking.

Emmett turned for the lake bed, and Anna hurried at his

side as they trotted down the north slope. He noticed, approvingly, that she had indeed brought a pair of hiking boots. And he was gratified that she was enough in tune with his mood not to talk for the moment. A wasted afternoon. It would have been better spent sleeping. That way, when the postmortem findings came in, he and she would have been fresh for any leads that developed out of them.

They slowed for rockier ground.

Then, apparently, Anna couldn't help herself. "You don't give a damn about getting prints of these coffee cans, do you?"

"Nope."

They covered another hundred yards, weaving through the rock sage and sticky-flowered rabbitbrush, before she said, "And Tallsalt told me this morning at the coffee shop I was barking up the wrong tree by looking for local suspects."

"Didn't he, though."

"So if these aircraft tire tracks are more than two months old, what can they possibly have to do with the Knokis getting waylaid by drug-runners last Saturday night?"

"I can hardly wait for John to explain."

"Me too," Anna said.

"But we're not going to ask him right now."

"Why not?" she demanded.

"Because the son of a bitch went through a lot of trouble to salt the task force with his old buddy, E.Q. Parker, from BIA."

"Doesn't that piss you off?"

Emmett glared until she glanced away, then said, "I want Tallsalt to be none the wiser till we find out what he, Yabeny and the rest of this department don't want the world to know about Bert Knoki. Then we'll all have a long sit-down together. And I'll get as pissed off as I fucking well please, Turnipseed."

The sound of the Suburban's horn came blaring across the sage. Summerfield was running the alternating blinker on his headlights as he barreled up the dirt road toward the lake bed. He finally spotted Emmett and Anna, braked and bailed out. He had to shout his message twice before Emmett could understand him.

Summerfield had just heard on the tribal frequency: A patrol unit was responding from Window Rock to the Knokis' mobile home in Navajo—the neighbor-informant believed somebody was under the trailer.

chapter 6

SUMMERFIELD LET EMMETT DO THE DRIVING.

Anna took the backseat. She estimated there was a good chance they'd beat the patrol unit out of Window Rock to the Knokis' mobile home. Reason told her the killers would have no reason to haunt their victims' residence. They'd stay miles clear of it. Yet, someone had been there early that morning when she and Emmett had gone through the place. The rooms had been empty of any apparent physical presence, but someone or something had been there. The dogs in the park had known. That was her one link between reason and intuition.

If the murderers returned to the Knokis', it would be an enormous windfall. But did it also mean they weren't finished killing cops?

Emmett sped over the washboarded stretch of dirt road, never overcorrecting even when the Suburban began to sideslip, keeping a light touch on the steering wheel as he headed toward the distant highway. Summerfield worked the radio. "Window Rock, Frank Two," he transmitted, his voice shuddering from the pounding the shock absorbers were taking.

"Go ahead, Two."

"Be advised myself, Frank Thirty-three and BIA Unit Seventeen are responding from Sonsela Buttes."

"Copy," the dispatcher acknowledged.

Emmett veered onto the highway, and the Suburban

swayed. Anna clung to her armrest. Emmett straightened the front wheels and jammed the accelerator to the firewall. The vehicle no sooner stopped fishtailing than he told Summerfield, "Find out who the RP is."

"Window Rock," the agent transmitted, "who's the reporting party?"

No immediate response. Was the dispatcher asking the communications sergeant if she was allowed to divulge this info to the feds?

"Come on," Emmett grumbled. The sun was almost down to the horizon, and its flat rays were streaming in from the west-facing windows, accentuating his pronounced Comanche bone structure. And bringing out the worry lines.

"Frank Two," the dispatcher's voice finally broke the annoying interference of far-off radio traffic on the reservation, "informant is a Hank Whitesheep, neighbor at space ten. Whitesheep doesn't believe intruder knows he's been discovered."

"Copy, Window Rock." Summerfield hung up the microphone, leaving a sheen of sweat from his palm on the plastic. He then murmured as if touching a feather to his memory, "Whitesheep . . . *Whitesheep* . . ."

"When's the last time you checked your scattergun?" Emmett asked him.

"Let me think—"

Emmett cut him off. *"Turnipseed."*

She reached up and removed the Remington 870 from its roof rack. The safety button was in the off position. She powered down her window. The hundred-mile-an-hour wind howled in, stirring a blizzard of dust off the floor mats. Stinging her eyes and making Summerfield cough. There was a live cartridge dangerously under the firing pin. Four in the magazine. Training the muzzle through the open window, she pried out the shell with a fingernail and pulled the trigger on the now empty chamber. The snick was barely audible over the slipstream.

Pretending, perhaps, to ignore his safety violation, Summerfield raised his voice over the wind. "Mantrap!"

Anna quickly put up the window and rested the Remington across her lap.

"What're you talking about?" Emmett asked the Gallup agent.

"Investigated a Henry Whitesheep at that mobile home park when I first got here. For setting a mantrap at an archaeological site. On supervised release at the time." Parole.

The smokeless incinerator chimney at the shut-down lumber mill on the outskirts of Navajo came into view. Emmett pumped his brakes. "What'd he serve time for?"

"Cranking off two rounds at a tribal archaeology officer while fleeing a stakeout," Summerfield replied. "Back in the early nineties."

"Pot raiding?" Anna asked. Anasazi pottery was still worth a fortune on the black—and gray, or overtly legal—market. The tribe had a special law enforcement branch to protect the relics on its lands.

"Yes," Summerfield said. "Then last year, somebody dug a covered pit at the same site and lined it with punji stakes. Archaeology cop who regularly checks the place nearly stumbled into it." Summerfield reached for the mike again, missing it on his first swipe. "I never could link Whitesheep—"

"Save it," Emmett butted in. They'd left the highway and were tearing up the side road toward the mobile home park. Parker went on, "You and Anna cover the windows while I grab the hide-a-key."

"Right." Then the agent radioed Window Rock that the feds were at the scene.

The dispatcher tried to get an estimated time of arrival from her patrol officer, but Emmett talked over his reply. "Ready, Anna?" She could tell by the tightened cords in his neck that he was resisting the urge to turn his head and examine her eyes.

"I'm fine," she insisted.

Emmett cut the engine and coasted noiselessly the last

hundred feet into the Knokis' driveway. He left the Suburban parked at an angle so Anna would have the solid protection of the engine block between her and the mobile home. Leaping out, she sprawled over the hood on her bare elbows. But the sheet metal was hot, and she jerked up from it and sank to her knees instead. Her recently healed right elbow began throbbing; she'd banged it too hard on the hood. She shifted her shotgun sights back and forth between the front windows and the utility room door. Holding her breath, she watched for any hint of movement. But all the window glass shone black in the failing light.

Summerfield knelt behind the passenger door.

He'd left it half-open as a shield for himself. His 9mm pistol was aimed on the mobile home's west-side windows. One of the scraggly strands of hair he used to try to cover his growing baldness reared up like a coxcomb. And his ungainly crouch made her realize that he had a wide ass for a man.

Despite the tension, she smiled.

Emmett started up the driveway. She tracked his quiet, catlike progress with her peripheral vision. He tested the entry door knob with his free hand—locked—before continuing past the Knokis' Mazda and along the stone-filled planter. Even while opening the hide-a-key rock, he kept his eyes and revolver trained on the trailer. There was no glint off the brass key in his grasp, and Anna realized that the entire park was now in evening shadow. It gave a chilly blue quality to the air even though the temperature still had to be in the eighties. Nobody was stirring. Strange. It was the hour at which somebody had to be returning from work—even on a reservation with a 50 percent unemployment rate. And no dogs were barking this time.

She inhaled, but her lungs already felt full.

Emmett peered all around, his nostrils flared. As if trying to sniff out an ambush. Then he motioned for Summerfield to join him at the entry door. Simultaneously, there came the sound of a weatherstrip seal cracking. Emmett whipped his revolver toward the noise. Whitesheep's door opened slightly, and the ex-con squeezed his grinning face into the aperture. Four feet lower, his dog's muzzle appeared, yapping. But nothing like the hysterical barking in this morning's darkness. Summerfield began to tell Whitesheep something, probably to stay in his trailer. But his mouth must have been too dry, for he wound up just waving for the man to back off.

The door slid shut.

Parker inserted the key in the Knokis' lock.

THE INTERIOR OF THE PLACE was stuffy. Something registered as Emmett swept past the breakfast counter, but he put it out of mind for the moment. In the utility room, he searched for a hatch giving access to the crawl space. None in this model. He checked the inside of the dryer. Amazing, the tight spots a human being could wedge into when desperate not to be found. Empty. Except for a sweatshirt with a snowflake pattern Aurelia might have intended to take with her on the night of her murder, and forgotten at the last minute.

Emmett froze.

The bedroom door was shut. He was certain Anna and he had left all the interior ones open.

Throwing the door back, he waited before entering.

Summerfield treaded heavily on the linoleum behind him. Without turning, Emmett signaled for him to stand still. In case somebody was listening just around the corner inside the bedroom. Or lying prone down below, preparing to punch a flurry of bullets through the thin flooring. Obviously, searches and apprehensions by the Washington Metropolitan Office had been executed by the SWAT team, not the counterintelligence agents.

Emmett burst around the corner, pivoting his weapon from side to side and then from floor to ceiling. He jabbed an urgent finger for Summerfield to cover the foot-high slot beneath the bed, plus the closet door, which was closed.

Then he himself charged into the bathroom, ripped the drawn shower curtain off its rings and flung it aside.

Nothing in the tub.

He backtracked into the bedroom in time to watch Summerfield—despite a pallid face—show some initiative and clear the closet. A wig's head on the top shelf gave him a start, but he managed to hold his fire.

Emmett hurried to the breakfast counter.

The mail caddy was empty. The bills he had perused that morning were gone. As was the envelope with the University Park return address. But thinking about that could wait. He wanted to talk to Whitesheep before dealing with the crawl space.

The ex-con slouched on the porch with a pack of cigarettes rolled up in the sleeve of his T-shirt and his thumbs hooked in the front of his beltless Levi's.

"What'd you hear?" Emmett asked, keeping his voice low.

"Somethin' crawlin' 'round under there. Something *big*. And it was diggin'—you know, tossin' gravel against the sidin'."

"How long ago?"

"Stopped just as you pulled up." An amused grin. Whitesheep was enjoying the apprehensive reaction of the cops to his call. Emmett would get to the bottom of that later.

"How can we get under?" he asked.

"The porch steps move. That's how Bert got down there to fix things. The pipes was always freezin'. I told him to buy heat-tape, but he didn't want to spend the money."

Emmett was tempted to borrow Whitesheep's dog to make a sweep under the mobile home. But if the animal wound up shot, a reservation mongrel would suddenly have American Kennel Club papers and a stud value of $100,000. BIA's Risk Management would settle out of court for half of that, and everybody would come away satisfied, except Emmett's supervisor in Phoenix, who'd already warned him by phone that his part in this investigation was stressing the division's dwindling third-quarter budget.

He let out an angry breath.

A tribal cruiser pulled in. The bullnecked patrolman who'd chatted briefly with Yabeny last night got out. He slid his nightstick into the ring on his Sam Browne belt as he walked ponderously up to Emmett. Introductions, especially the involved Navajo kind, could wait.

"Where's your nearest canine unit?" Emmett asked.

The officer replied, "Chinle."

An hour away, at least.

Emmett ordered Whitesheep to sit on his steps. The man squatted down with a smirk. Parker asked the patrolman to keep tabs on the man while he and Summerfield searched the crawl space—an ex-con who'd done time for assault against any kind of cop wasn't going to go unsupervised over the coming minutes.

Anna, still poised behind the Suburban, flicked her chin for him to come over.

Emmett went to her. "What?"

"I'm going under with you."

"Listen, no use you messing up your clothes too—"

"Fuck my clothes. I'm taking the point."

The only thing he could think to say was the utter truth: "I don't want you down there." But then he hedged, "Not yet."

"What do you mean—*not yet*?"

"Just that. Do I need to bring up how yours truly got awakened this morning?"

Wrong thing to say. Her eyes turned hot. "When will *yours truly* decide I'm ready?" Cutting his losses, he held his tongue. "And who's calling the shots here, anyway, Parker? I thought you told Esquivel I was leading. Having second thoughts?"

He had an utterly ridiculous impulse to tell her how he felt about her. Then and there. Thankfully, it passed.

But she read something else into his silence. "Then what the hell did you call me down from Vegas for?"

She was right. And for the first time since his telephone conversation with the U.S. Attorney in Phoenix, he regretted having asked for her. But he hustled around the open passenger door to the Suburban's cabin and reached inside the glove compartment—past Summerfield's German edition of *Dine bahane*—for a flashlight. He thrust it into Anna's left hand and relieved her of the shotgun. "Hold the goddamn light out to the side of your body," he snarled. "That way you might avoid taking a bullet to the face."

Furiously, she jacked a round into the chamber of her pistol.

Summerfield had emerged from the mobile home and was keeping a nervous eye on the ventilation holes in the skirting. Emmett gave the Gallup agent the Remington. "Turnipseed and I will crawl toward the back of the trailer. Go around there and get yourself ready for somebody to bust out."

Summerfield moved off at an ungainly trot.

Emmett scanned around again. This call had all the makings of a setup. Ex-con reporting party. Everybody in the tight-knit little community of mobile homes lying low. And this was Anna's and his second trip into the park, so they'd been observed. In Indian Country, the bad-asses watched you the first time. Studied you for weaknesses. The second time, they hit. He gestured for Anna to watch the space behind the stoop as he scooted it away from the gap in the skirting. The heat in her face made her seem exasperatingly pretty to him. He laid his revolver on the top step, keeping it within reach, and dragged the stoop out. The wooden base made a flesh-crawling moan as it skidded over the driveway cement.

Anna breezed past him and squirmed through the opening. Into the darkness. He took his small metallic flashlight from his windbreaker pocket and followed.

*　　*　　*

A KIND OF NETTING had been tacked to the joists to hold the panels of pink fiberglass insulation in place beneath the floor. With time, much of this had rotted, leaving tatters of the gauzelike material to hang like dirty white veils. These created dozens of dark, partitioned spaces. Each capable of concealing a man.

Anna scuttled forward a few yards, then stopped again.

She could hear Emmett moving behind her, but she kept facing forward, trying to penetrate the netting with her beam. All kinds of menacing forms took shape through it, but she struggled to hold her imagination in check. For fear she'd miss the true thing that could cause her harm.

Emmett tapped one of her boots to let her know he was right behind. He wasn't using his little flashlight. So as not to backlight her, she realized.

Drainpipes snaked down into the dusty ground. Bert Knoki had used copious amounts of household rags to wrap his water lines, giving them the appearance of mummified arms and legs. She thumbed off her light. And listened. Overhead in the kitchen, the refrigerator droned. Other than that, and her and Emmett's breathing in the confined space, she heard nothing.

But they were not alone.

The conviction had taken hold of her as soon as she'd passed through the gap in the skirting.

She switched her light on again.

There were impressions in the earth. Broad and scraping, as if someone had wallowed along just as she and Emmett were. Bert perhaps, down here to add more insulation to his pipes? Protected from any moisture, tracks could survive for years in this environment. She shaded the flashlight lens with her fingertips, so as not to illuminate Emmett, and directed the beam backward for a quick inspection of her own trail. Indentations punctuated the drag marks left by her body. Where her boot toes had pushed against the ground. No such divots showed in the impressions before her.

She rested her pistol on the crook of her forearm and wiped her sweaty right hand on the seat of her jeans.

Then she crawled on.

Her left arm trembled from holding the flashlight so far out to the side. But Emmett had been right. Anyone confronting the light would probably assume that the holder was gripping it directly in front of his or her eyes. Each time she came to another veil of netting, she had to brush it aside with her 9mm and peer into the shadowed recess behind it, deciding in a split second whether or not someone was lurking there.

The dirt was littered with mouse droppings. Hopefully, not deer mice droppings, which carried the dreaded hantavirus—first identified in the Navajo Nation, although cases had gone unrecognized all over the West for generations. The illness began like the flu, but swiftly deteriorated into respiratory failure. The victim drowned in his own fluid-filled lungs.

You're drifting. Quit it.

Emmett tapped her bootsole. Urgently.

She stopped, sweeping her muzzle back and forth in front of her. But Emmett swatted her foot again, and she went dead-still. After a moment, she glanced over her shoulder.

He was holding a finger across his lips. He'd heard something. All she could make out was the swish of her own excited blood in her ears. Then Emmett pointed at the trailer's rear axle.

Whatever he'd heard had come from that direction.

He started to crawl up on Anna's left side, but she stiffened her leg against his shoulder. He halted. Setting down the flashlight, she used hand signals to tell him that she would approach the axle. His eyes widened, but the need for silence kept him from arguing.

She ran the beam over the area.

It was partly shrouded by netting, and the large shadow from a forced-air duct pooled over the ground there. As she steeled herself to get moving again, an image filled her mind's eye: Bert and Aurelia, blackened and shrunken, fists upraised at each other. If someone lay between her and the end of the mobile home, that person had had something to do with their murders. Someone capable of setting a cop and his wife on fire. And enjoying it.

She inched forward.

As she drew closer to the shadow, it began to show the depth of a shallow excavation. Like that scratched out of the ground by a jackrabbit. Except that this depression was six feet across. Hard to tell how deep, not without training the flashlight over its lip, which was formed by the axle on her side.

She crawled closer.

Emmett was working around to the side, his face lost in the darkness. She began raising the flashlight, hoping to slant it down into the hole.

Something hissed.

In the first split second, it felt as if a fist had bumped her hand. The flashlight tumbled out of her grasp, casting everything into silhouette. Something cold and wet closed around her wrist with a chilling, fluid grace. Sudden panic made her jerk back her forearm, but the teeth had already sunk into her flesh. Instantaneous searing pain. She doubled her thrashing to free herself.

"Emmett! Something's got me!"

Dropping her pistol, she groped for the point of the mounting pressure—and brushed some kind of scaly head. Her palm slid down over a crescent of writhing muscle to a blunt tail that effortlessly swatted her free hand aside. The squirming thing wrestled her forearm over the axle and down into the depression. She hurled her body over the shaft, trying to take back her arm. The creature's razor-sharp teeth began to masticate her wrist in the relentless vise of its powerful jaws.

"Emmett!"

She'd lost track of him, but now he appeared from the bottom of the depression, blinding her with his small flashlight for a second before lowering the beam onto her arm.

"Go limp, Anna!" he shouted.

"What!"

"Play dead! It'll let go if it thinks you're dead!"

"I can't!" Pitiless reptilian eyes blazed out at her from a black head. Folds of armored skin with striking bands of pink, orange, yellow and white. The beam flitted away from the creature as Emmett clamped his flashlight under his arm. Then he steadied the light on its huge snakelike head. Growling in either rage or terror, he dug his forefingers into both sides of its mouth and began prying.

"Damn!" He gave up, pressed the muzzle of his revolver against the Gila monster's head. "Hold still!" The blue flash blinded her. In the smoky aftermath of the roar, she asked herself if the teeth still gripped her. Yes. Decidedly. The .357 round had decapitated the creature, but still the head remained attached to her wrist. Her vision bleared. Images of the severed head spun in a nauseating circle before her.

"I said don't move!" Emmett fired again. Again. Then dropped his wheelgun and pried at the powerful jaws once more. They gave with a sound like a wishbone snapping. Immediately, he began sucking the bloody puncture wounds. He sucked and spat. He'd done this for less than a minute when he suddenly said, "Won't work . . . too many punctures." He untied a boot lace, ripped it out of the eyelets and made a tourniquet around her upper arm.

"Too tight?" he asked breathlessly.

She didn't know. The pain was still here, lodged like a thorn in her brain, but she felt as if she was losing control of her arms and legs. As if they belonged to somebody else. And she was getting sick to her stomach.

Emmett seized her by the belt and started pulling her toward the gap in the skirting at the front of the mobile home.

An absolutely unequivocal voice bellowed with self-contempt inside her head—*You dumbshit, you left Uncle Boston's hummingbird in your purse!*

chapter 7

EMMETT HUNG UP THE RECEIVER, LEANED ON HIS HANDS against the sides of the telephone carrel and shut his eyes. The mechanical chatter in Navajo at the nurses' station at the far end of the corridor faded as the postmortem findings sank in. He'd just spoken to the FBI agent in Tucson who'd witnessed the Knokis' autopsies at the University of Arizona Medical Center—and learned how the couple had died. Time. Agony could stretch time into unbelievable dimensions, distorting the finite into the eternal. Is this what created that malevolent residue of the human soul the Navajo called a *chindi*?

A voice speaking English brought Emmett back to the hospital. Sage Memorial, thirty miles west of Window Rock in Ganado, where three hours ago Summerfield and he had rushed Anna. "Mr. Parker?"

"Yes." Emmett turned.

A gangly young white man stood before him. His frizzy red hair was tied back in a ponytail, and he was wearing a smock with what appeared to be stethoscope tubes looping from the pocket. "I'm Dr. Hennepin."

It took a moment to penetrate the grisly shock left by the call to Tucson. Hennepin: the reptile-bite specialist on staff who'd been called out of dinner at a restaurant in Gallup. "How's Turnipseed?"

"You mind coming with me?"

Even under ordinary circumstances, Emmett disliked

having a question answered with a question. Now it made his stomach churn. The physician started down the same corridor along which Anna's private room lay. Summerfield was at his post on a straightback chair outside her door. Nobody, except confirmed medical personnel, was going to get near her until Emmett had a bead on the son of a bitch who'd set them up at the Knokis' mobile home. And why.

Dr. Hennepin led him into the X-ray viewing room.

A single chart was clipped to the light panel, which remained darkened while the physician took a stool. Unsmiling, he gestured at a chair across the room for Emmett.

"I'm good." He preferred to stand. *Get on with it: You're scaring the crap out of me.*

"Town of Navajo," Hennepin began, "is almost two thousand feet above the highest range of *Heloderma cinctum suspectum*. Common name is the Utah banded Gila monster, but this subspecies can be found at lower elevations in northern Arizona too. Anyway, this got me thinking—"

"Hold it, Doc," Emmett interrupted. "I'll listen to anything you've got to say, but first I've got to know—how's Turnipseed?"

Hennepin was blank-faced for a moment, then said, "She'll be fine in two or three days."

Emmett thought that he was concealing his explosive relief. Until he felt the moisture burn in his eyes.

But the doctor went on, "Unless infection sets in. Gilas have cesspools for mouths . . ." He paused, catching the impatient twitch in Emmett's eyelid. "Or did you already know this?"

"Yes, that's why I had the patrolman retrieve the carcass for your lab. But I've heard conflicting stories about how bad Gila venom is."

"No hemotoxins or nemotoxins. No anticoagulants either. I realize that's hard to believe, given Agent Turnipseed's outward symptoms . . ." Emmett could now vouch for that, having kept one eye on the highway and one on her violent nausea, cold sweats and paroxysmal loss of coordination on the hundred-mile-an-hour dash to the hospital. "But we got a handle on her hypotensive shock," Hennepin continued, "and her pulse is strong and normal again. Gila bites rarely cause lasting damage or scars, even though they're big and general like a dog bite. I gave her something for sleep, so she should be resting shortly."

Emmett flopped into the chair. After a moment, he sat up, rubbed his face with his hands and tried to look attentive. "Go on with what you were saying, Doc."

"Well, examining the decapitated male specimen the Window Rock cop brought in, I noticed he'd been toe-clipped . . ." Emmett waved a hand in a weary gesture of incomprehension, and Hennepin explained, "Research biologists mark their study animals to tell them apart in the wild."

All at once, Emmett had no trouble paying attention. "How can you be sure the nail or nails didn't just break off?"

"Can't. Not absolutely. But that got me thinking. I took a good look at your specimen's abdomen. And sure enough there was a small, healed-over incision . . ." Hennepin unfolded his long frame up off the stool and flicked on the light panel. Emmett had expected an X-ray of Anna's wrist. Instead, the cigar shape of the headless Gila appeared on the screen. In the vicinity of his gut were two unusual things. The first was a tubular structure—metallic or plastic, judging by its opaque blackness—with a tiny rod projecting from one end. *"That,"* the doctor explained, "is a radio telemetry device. Inserted by a biologist so he can track his critter around its habitat."

"Anything like this going on in the Chuskas?" The mountains rising immediately behind the Knokis' mobile home.

"Too high."

"Are you positive?"

"Absolutely."

Hennepin pointed to two tiny, fetuslike lumps in the stomach. "One reason Ms. Turnipseed is doing well is this—

your specimen had recently eaten. Gilas aren't like rattlers. They can't pick and choose when they want to inject venom. *Helodermas* involuntarily excrete it whenever they eat. So this old boy packed a less potent wallop than he might've otherwise, thanks to a recent meal of two pinkies."

"Pinkies?"

"Hairless baby rats. Gilas are baby-killers in the wild. Bird chicks. Infant rodents. Eggs. But I'd guess these two ratlings came out of a pet supply store."

Tapping the telemetry device with a knuckle, Emmett asked, "Can you remove it for me?"

"No problem."

"And I'd like to see Turnipseed."

"For a couple minutes. No more."

"Summerfield will be standing guard outside her door until two this morning. I'll take over after that."

"Is this really necessary?" Hennepin's smile was skeptical.

"Yes," Emmett replied curtly, turning for Anna's room.

Summerfield came to his feet as Emmett strode up the corridor. "Listen, Parker," the agent began, "I'd just like to say—"

"Spare me." But then the man looked so crestfallen, Emmett added, "Don't go beating on yourself, Reed. If anybody, yours truly should've gone under there first. But she wasn't going to allow that, and she's calling the shots. So all our manly inclinations are sadly out of place."

"Are they now?" But before Emmett could ask Summerfield what he meant by that, the agent switched subjects and inquired, "Any word from Tucson?"

"I'll fill you in as soon as I have a word with Anna." Emmett slipped as quietly as he could through the door. But her eyes opened a crack. Her pupils seemed to brighten as they fixed on him, although her face was deathly pale. All but the scar from the acetylene torch burn. It was the color of wood ashes.

"I'm averaging one-point-five injuries per case so far,

Em," she croaked, limply raising her bandaged left wrist for him to see. "How many cases does an agent handle in a career? That's what I've been lying here trying to figure out. A thousand? Two?"

Emmett sat carefully on the bed beside her. "Bad things come in streaks."

"Sure."

"Seriously, dammit," he said more firmly. "Had a partner in Oklahoma City who got shot twice in six months. And never again. Retired to a condo on a golf course near Orlando. Bitches about the boredom every time he calls me. You'll probably go twenty years now before you so much as stub a toe."

She didn't look convinced. "Mad at me?"

"No," he said.

She raised her head off the pillow and peered into his eyes more carefully. "You got the return from Tucson. Didn't you?"

"It can wait."

"I've got to think about something other than that damned lizard. Especially if Hennepin keeps me in here for twenty-four hours, like he wants."

That made sense. But he already felt as if he scarcely had the energy to do one more task he absolutely must tonight before grabbing a couple hours of sleep at the inn. His ears were ringing, his personal warning he was pushing himself too far—the Navajo believed that tinnitus augured death, the withdrawal of the guardian wind that filled each living being. Yet, he found himself saying, "Aurelia Knoki died at approximately ten P.M. on Saturday . . ." The pathologist had found her trachea to be relatively clear of soot, Emmett explained. A strong indication the woman hadn't been breathing when her husband's police cruiser was doused with gasoline and set ablaze. This assumption was bolstered by the carbon monoxide level in her blood. A negative level meant the victim had expired before exposure to the flames. Aurelia's was in the low to moderate range, which was consistent with a chain-smoker's but not with that of a person gulping down fire and smoke. She'd had a two-pack-a-day habit since her mid-twenties, according to her medical records obtained by subpoena from this hospital and forwarded to Tucson. "That's a bit of a puzzler . . ."

"What?" Anna asked sleepily.

"Why Aurelia routinely used a private facility instead of any of the Indian Health Service clinics at no charge. And there aren't many Navajo chain-smokers. As a people, they don't tend to abuse tobacco . . ." She closed her eyes. "Really, Anna, we can cover this in the morning."

"Go on," she insisted.

He didn't want to: The worst was yet to come.

"*Please,* Emmett."

"Pathologist discovered a subdural, subarachnoid hematoma—that's invariably an antemortem injury—on the left side of Aurelia's head. This kind of bruise forms in a thin membrane over the brain—"

"I know what it is," she murmured. "So she took a hard blow to the head with something."

"And a tight contact bullet wound to the base of the skull. Possibly the same caliber as Bert's missing service weapon."

"Which spared her burning to death."

"Yes," Emmett said. Then he waited, hoping she would drop off.

"What about Bert?" she asked.

Emmett massaged his temples, hoping it might alleviate the ringing in his ears. It didn't. "He also had a hematoma on the left side of the head. But the blow may not have brought on full unconsciousness. And there were no bullet wounds anywhere on his body . . ." Here it was. "He had thick soot in both his trachea and lungs. He was hyperventilating at the time of the fire. Toxicologist came back with a high carbon monoxide blood level, particularly for a non-smoker."

"You mean the bastards *waited* for him to come around

before setting him on fire?" A flash of anger broke through her drowsiness.

"Looks that way."

Her eyelids clenched as it sank in. The only hint she was visualizing Bert Knoki's last seconds. Immobilized by the beating he'd suffered. But conscious. Aware. A prisoner of each horrifying second, with no chance of pardon.

Emmett had nothing more to say.

After a while, he reached over her and turned off the lamp. Her breathing had grown deep and regular. Taking the bedside chair, he watched her in the blue slatted light off the parking lot coming through the venetian blinds. She was part Japanese. He sometimes forgot that until he saw her eyes at rest. One of her Modoc grandmothers had reunited two extremes of that long-ago northern Pacific migration by marrying a young nisei. He'd worked the sugar beet fields with her outside an internment camp during the Second World War. Of course, no North American tribe believed that it had come from Asia. Each originated somewhere within or near its range of the last millennium. Or less. *The hold of myth.* Someday, he'd like to have the time to discover how much stock Anna put in her myths, so perhaps he might understand how much he relied on his. It was not the kind of intimacy he would ever share with a male partner. *What a crock—that a man and woman can work together and keep it all safely tucked within the confines of the job.* Intimacy wore a thousand guises.

She was asleep. He was certain of it.

He rose, leaned over and kissed her lightly on the forehead. She didn't react, which made him feel like a thief as he went out the door to Summerfield.

ANNA WAITED UNTIL she heard his footfalls cross the room and the door shut before opening her eyes. She tried to explore the thing within her that had just made her pretend to be asleep. She could blame the doctor's pill, but that wasn't it. The throbbing of her wrist still made sleep impossible. Caution. That was the culprit, she supposed. Not trusting the natural progression of affection. She'd never known natural affection. Not once.

She could hear Emmett explaining something to Summerfield out in the corridor.

And then, five minutes later, the click of the latch made her think a second chance was coming her way. Facing the door, she forced herself not to feign sleep. But it was Summerfield who crept inside. He peered toward her, then frowned. "Sorry. Did I wake you?"

"No."

"Parker said you were out cold, otherwise I'd never have—"

"It's all right, Reed."

"He wanted me to check on you every fifteen minutes. And I decided now was as good a time as any to start." Summerfield quietly closed the door behind him and leaned his back against it. She realized that she'd given him little thought since the code-three race to the hospital, although he'd looked as stricken as Emmett the entire way. Guilt. Summerfield was almost brimming with that peculiar male guilt which followed the wounding of a female cop. Most of the Las Vegas field office had wallowed in it during her convalescence this winter, and one by one the agents had trooped up to her condo door to say the same awkward things Reed was now poised to say.

But he threw her a curve. "I just wanted you to know I was out of line this afternoon. You know, what I said about Parker . . ." In the Suburban, while Emmett had hiked alone up to old man Tsinnajinnie's rest stop. Summerfield made a play on her FBI loyalties and suggested that, if E.Q. Parker was a typical criminal investigator, BIA law enforcement was better abolished and all Indian jurisdiction turned over to the Justice Department, as some in Congress were recommending. Anna retorted that she wouldn't be alive but for Emmett Parker. Nothing had been said after that. "I'm usually better tuned to this sort of thing, so forgive me."

"What sort of thing?"

"The bond between you two." Summerfield's inflection had made the word sound slightly less than innocent.

"We're not having an affair, Reed."

"I see. Then I must have misunderstood . . ." His voice trailed off. Purposely, it seemed.

She was too tired to play games. "What did you misunderstand?"

"Why a vet like Parker would almost go out of his head with fear for someone. Even if that someone is his partner." Summerfield withdrew.

REACHING WINDOW ROCK, Emmett pulled into the police building parking lot. Knoki's burned-out cruiser was now secured behind the fence of the impound yard at the back. It'd taken a day and a half to drag and winch it out of Crystal Wash. The first tow truck had gotten mired, and a bigger rig had to be summoned from Holbrook. Emmett only hoped that if more evidence was discovered inside the ruin of the Ford, a clever defense attorney wouldn't dissect those thirty-six hours for a breach in the chain of control.

He logged into the jail, turned his revolver over to the booking officer for safekeeping. A trusty drew him a cup of coffee from the kitchen, and Emmett carried it down a long, echoing concrete hallway. Inside the detox tank, two drunks were arguing in a jumble of Navajo and English. They looked sixty but were probably twenty years younger. A transvestite—tricked up with permed hair, tight-fitting girl's jeans and a frilly blouse dented at the front—sobbed uncontrollably in the male gang lockup, to the indifference of the other recent arrestees. No doubt prevented by an outstanding warrant from working the truck stops along Interstate 40 tonight.

Emmett took the cleanest-looking interrogation room.

Slipping a quarter from his trouser pocket, he placed it on one of the two chairs opposing each other across the table. He sat in the other. The cubicle stank of falsehoods. The acrid way human beings smell when, under pressure, they look you squarely in the eye and lie.

Five minutes later, a jailer produced Henry Whitesheep.

The ex-con looked completely at ease in a blaze-orange jumpsuit that had been repeatedly washed down to a pale tangerine.

"Sit," Emmett ordered.

Whitesheep noticed the sparkle of the quarter. With exaggerated meticulousness, he picked the coin up off the chair and set it on the table. Beaming like a Boy Scout who has just passed an honesty test. The test had had nothing to do with honesty. And Whitesheep was still standing. "Bookin' officer says I was busted for investigation of assault on a federal officer with a dangerous weapon. What weapon?"

"Guess." Emmett rose to full height. He was at least six inches taller than Whitesheep. *You're beat . . . watch your temper or his attorney will claim you created a nonverbal atmosphere of psychological coercion.* "Sit down . . . please."

Whitesheep finally did, but sprawled. Emmett decided to remain on his feet as he advised the man of his rights. Whitesheep's eyes glazed over as he pretended not to listen. "Do you understand what I've just told you?" Emmett concluded.

"Not so good, sir. You know that stuff in my language?"

From memory, Emmett repeated the Miranda warning in Navajo.

Whitesheep smirked.

"You understand *that*?" Emmett's hands itched to grab the man, hurl him against the wall. Even if Whitesheep hadn't planted the Gila, Emmett doubted the man knew nothing about it. That was just as galling as direct involvement. To have let Anna and him crawl under that mobile home, knowing full well what awaited them in the darkness.

A creature of penal institutions, Whitesheep must have picked up on Emmett's desire to do him violence. His tone softened to an indignant whine. "Last time, the ADW charge was righteous. I'll admit it. I popped a cap or two at that pottery cop. But this time, it's BS. I couldn't believe it when them *Dine* goons showed up after you left, and said the *federales* want me taken down."

That voluntary statement amounted to a waiver, and the man had expressed no intent to vacate the interrogation setting. "I'll give you the opportunity to convince me." Emmett sat, somewhat surprised that Whitesheep wasn't screaming for a federal public defender to be called in from Albuquerque. "Did Bert Knoki help you get paroled?"

"Nobody can help you with a fed early release these days. You know that. Fifty-four days a year for good behavior is all you can get." Whitesheep's cleft lip crinkled in a grin. "But Aurelia saw to it Bert vouched for me with the mill. Before it closed down."

It must have taken some persuading on her part—for a parolee who'd fired upon a fellow member of Bert's department. But clan obligations were taken seriously. Emmett asked, "When'd you move into the park?"

"Last year. Maybe longer. Been there two winters."

"You lied to Agent Turnipseed and me early this morning . . ."

"About what?"

"Bert not having trouble with anyone."

"Did not, man." Whitesheep had stared off to the right. He'd picked up the coin with his left hand, and lefties invariably glanced to the left while spinning a lie.

"All right," Emmett said agreeably. "Let's try it this way. During that same conversation you said all the dogs in the park have been going nuts for a couple of months. True?"

"I guess."

"Any new tenants in the park?"

"No, it's a pretty regular group."

"Any relatives recently visiting any tenants?"

"An old woman from Kayenta, stayin' with her grandson."

Emmett took a sip of coffee, which had gone cold. He took a gulp purely for the caffeine. "So maybe the cause of the disturbance was you sneaking around after dark. Where'd you do your time, Hank?"

"The Tuna." La Tuna Federal Prison in El Paso, Texas.

"You feel the staff treated you fairly?"

"So-so," he replied. "I've had worse."

"Who investigated the charges against you back in '93?"

"FBI and—"

Emmett finished for him. "BIA's ARPA dick?" The Archaeological Resources Protection Act investigator out of his own Phoenix office. He'd already phoned from the hospital to find out.

"That's right." Whitesheep folded his arms across his chest.

"So an FBI agent and a BIA investigator—just like Turnipseed and me—did you in."

The man wasn't going to argue with that. But his wariness made him hold his tongue.

"Let's be honest, Hank—they were out to make an example of you. A Navajo pot-raider. They can nail a *bilagaana* raider any day of the week. But both of us know it's the insiders who're really plundering the Anasazi sites on this and every other rez in Arizona and New Mexico. You served three years in the federal pen. I know of a white boy who got probation for the same damn thing on the San Carlos rez."

"Hold it, Parker."

"Hold what?"

"I know where this is headed," the man said coldly, for the first time revealing the fulminating temper that had made him shoot at the tribal archaeology cop and possibly, years later, set a trap to maim him.

After a moment, Emmett nodded. "Then tell me this— did you plant that Gila under Bert's trailer?"

"No." Whitesheep glanced to the right.

"Do you know who planted it?"

"Okay, I lied before," he confessed, covering his eyes with a hand. "The Knokis *were* havin' trouble. Aurelia told me Bert thought maybe somebody was witchin' him. A skinwalker comin' 'round the park at night to do stuff to him."

The same old quandary. Whitesheep knew something more concrete than this, but it would be revealed so grudgingly, Emmett's probable cause to hold him would wear thin in the meantime. Especially with the public defender poised to intervene the instant the ex-con decided to invoke his rights. Only one last thing of value might be learned tonight. "Hank, who came to Bert's trailer between the time my partner and I showed up this morning and when we returned this evening?"

Whitesheep lowered his hand from his eyes. "What?"

"You heard me."

"But you already know."

"How would I?"

Whitesheep seemed genuinely confused. "What kind of game you playin'?"

"No game. Who came to the trailer?"

"The big lieutenant from Window Rock."

"Tallsalt?"

"Yeah."

"Did you speak with him?" Emmett asked.

"Sure, that's why I don't get what you're talkin' about. He told me he was pickin' up some things you *federales* asked him to get."

chapter 8

EMMETT LOGGED OUT OF THE JAIL AT 12:19 A.M.

He decided to reclaim his BIA sedan, which Anna and he had left in the police complex lot this afternoon. He parked Summerfield's Suburban in the impound yard and let down the windows to air the vomit smell out of the interior, otherwise Anna would be mortified the next time she rode in it. Later tonight, the Gallup agent would hitch a ride with the Ganado patrolman to pick up his Suburban here.

Unlocking his sedan, Emmett looked up. Moths were swirling so thickly around the light poles he couldn't tell if the low hum was from them or the fixtures themselves.

Two minutes later, he slowed for the intersection with Route 264. Right would lead him back to Sage Memorial Hospital. To Turnipseed. Who might have a second nightmare powerful enough to rip through her sedated sleep. She needed him. But Emmett reluctantly turned left, accelerating past the Navajo Nation Inn and his bed, where he'd hoped to catch a short nap before relieving Summerfield outside Anna's door. Rest wasn't possible now. Not after what Hank Whitesheep had told him about John Tallsalt's unmentioned visit to the Knokis' mobile home today.

The street lights of the capital faded behind Emmett, a boundary sign declared that he'd departed the Big Rez. But, within five miles, he reentered its extension into New Mexico by turning up a wide but badly rutted asphalt road. It struck north toward the Chuskas. He'd last come this way over three years before for an impromptu barbecue on a chilly but cloudless October evening when the grass had been tawny, not green. Hot mutton sandwiches and iced tea. A pretty Hopi woman with a sexy laugh had been living with Tallsalt at the time, a special agent for the Burlington Northern–Santa Fe Railroad police, and there'd even been talk of marriage. Never came to pass. Too bad. It would have been like uniting the Capulets and the Montagues, given the long and bitter enmity between the Navajo and Hopi.

The entrance to Tallsalt's driveway was marked by the glittering red eye of a reflector nailed to a tree stump. A chain was sometimes drawn across the entryway between two metal poles, but tonight it was coiled on the ground. The cinder-block house was set back from the road, screened by the junipers, and Emmett considered honoring the local custom of stop, honk and wait. If the owner appeared, that meant he or she was in the mood for company.

But Emmett decided not to give Tallsalt the opportunity to decline this visit.

He barreled on.

As on that autumn day, there was no sign of any other habitation for miles around. No clusters of houses webbed together by kinship. Living this far removed from relatives was an affront to the twin pillars of Navajo society: *k'e,* cooperation and unselfishness, and its derivative, *k'ei,* solidarity with family and clan. Nor had Tallsalt built a ceremonial hogan anywhere on his allotment, signaling that the old ways meant something to him. On the other hand, he was the rising star of the tribal PD and one of only a few native administrators seriously considered whenever the directorship of the Arizona Department of Public Safety came up for appointment. For this, given the Navajo distrust of ambition, he was probably accused of witchcraft by some.

The house was darkened. Understandable, given the lateness of the hour. But the front door was ajar, and that was not. No Navajo, even a nontraditional one, left his door open to the evils prowling the night.

Emmett cut his engine and headlamps.

Cricket song came muffled through his windows, keeping time with the steady, wary beat of his pulse. He slipped his larger flashlight from the glove box and clambered out. Two vehicles were parked side by side in the dooryard. An unmarked police Chevy Yukon and an AMC Eagle with heavy road-salt damage to the fenders. Emmett fondly remembered tooling around Virginia in the Eagle on weekends eight years ago while Tallsalt and he had attended the FBI's National Academy. Mint juleps and lots of laughs. Yet, even the hilarity had been tempered by a mutual, unspoken knowledge that the drinking had to end.

The Yukon's hood was tepid, the Eagle's cool. Almost dewy.

The darkness beyond the front door was so deep Emmett made up his mind to enter through the back of the house. He followed the path along the side. Around a stack of fresh lumber. Cedar, by the smell of it. Something crunched underfoot. He thumbed on his light, and flashes of glass and gold lit up the sandy surface. A brass-plated statuette of a police officer firing a pistol. Emmett turned it over with the toe of his boot. Tallsalt's shooting trophy from the academy. First in marksmanship. Elevating his beam, he saw where the award had been hurtled through a window. He knelt, examined the brass figure. There was a bloody fingerprint on its torso.

Rising, he quickly extinguished his flashlight and drew his revolver. He jogged the rest of the way to the back of the house. There was no evidence of forced entry through the sliding glass door there. But it was unlocked. He crept into the kitchen by the light of the open refrigerator. Shattered beer and condiment bottles littered the floor in a wash of pungent foam.

Emmett held his breath to listen.

Nothing competed with the crickets except a grind and clatter from the far side of a nearby ridge over which an unnatural light was spilling.

Moving deeper into the kitchen, he noticed a maroon smear on the refrigerator handle and another on the door itself—more blood.

Rushing now, Emmett swept through the bath, the two bedrooms and finally the living room. No one. No sound except a *plop-plop-plop*. The stink of electrical smoke hung in the air, and crystalline drops were still sparkling off the TV stand. The screen had been taken out with a bottle of gin. Tallsalt's trophies for distance running—Window Rock High School, University of Northern Arizona athletics and the Police Olympics—had been batted off a sideboard where they'd once stood. His campaign hat and Ike jacket tossed over a box of cat litter. No other indication of the cat. It'd probably fled like any other reasonable creature, finding living with an alcoholic impossible.

Emmett began to understand.

He went through the front door and raked the ground with his beam. A single set of boot tracks headed eastward across the yard in a wavering line. He called out, *"Johnny!"*

There was no reply.

Emmett scanned the ridge. Finally, he picked out a droop-shouldered silhouette. "Christ almighty." He started up the slope.

Tallsalt was squatting on the precipice of a coal trench that began down along Route 264 and ended at the crumbly lip over which the man was carelessly dangling his boots. A hundred feet below, a gargantuan power shovel was gouging away at the layer of coal. Its operator appeared unaware of Tallsalt's presence, even though six stands of floodlights illuminated the pit as bright as day.

Emmett made no sudden moves.

Tallsalt was still in his uniform, although there was nothing crisp about it now. His green-striped trousers were wrinkled, and his shirt cuffs were rolled to the elbows. He held a pint of Bombay gin in his left hand and a semiautomatic pistol in his right. His eyes were fixed glassily on the huge bucket as it bit into the coal seam and lifted a black mouthful into the bed of a waiting dump truck. Emmett thought Tallsalt hadn't noticed his approach, but then heard him say, "Fucking marvel of reclamation, Emmett . . ." His words were only slightly slurred, but he'd always defied the stereotype by holding his liquor well until he suddenly passed out. Curiously, booze brought a vaguely Spanish lilt to his speech. And profanity, which the *Dine* weren't known for. "They strip away the vegetation and pile up the topsoil off to the side. Remove the overburden rock, pile it up too. Then take the coal. Behind this, they fill the waste rock back into the trench, sprinkle the topsoil over and plant crested wheat grass, clover, sage . . ." He paused to take a hefty slug of gin. The side of his left palm showed a cut, and blood was snaking down his forearm. "Geologists say the seam tends toward my house. Any luck, Dinetah Coal Company'll roll right over me. Backfill and revegetate. Won't be a sign John Tallsalt ever existed. I shall be *reclamated*."

Emmett slowly sat on his heels. "I see you tried to swear off the demon earlier tonight."

Tallsalt chuckled thickly. "You know the drill."

"That I do, Johnny."

"Broke every bottle in the house."

"Easy does it. Can't lick the whole thing in a single night."

"No, no—it felt great. I felt so *free* doing it, Emmett. Then I remembered the pint I been keeping lately in my cruiser. Worst damn feeling in the world. To stand there, drunk on your ass, knowing you can't break the last bottle. The fear of breaking your last damn bottle."

Emmett nodded. But a chill went up his spine each time Tallsalt's forefinger carelessly flickered in and out of the semiauto's trigger guard. "How'd it get this bad again, Johnny?" he asked. Hopefully, with nothing like accusation.

Tallsalt stared back at him.

Emmett thought for a moment that the man was going to cry. He'd welcome that—it'd be a step away from the bottle. But instead, Tallsalt threw back his head and chuckled again. "Must've done something to knock the universe out of whack."

"Who?"

"Me . . ." A surly growl. Then the self-pity rushed back into the void created by his spasm of self-hatred. "Don't know where, Emmett. Don't know how. Maybe I jaywalked in Albuquerque one morning. Or delayed somebody to talk about the weather. I don't know, just don't know. But somehow I put into motion a string of fucking improbable events that ended with poor Bert and Aurelia dead down in Crystal Wash."

Partners did this, Emmett thought. Never mind the psychopaths who'd butchered their closest friends. Partners found a way to blame themselves. "When'll the services be?"

"No idea." Tallsalt took another quaff of gin. The bottle was close to empty. "Nobody tells me shit."

"You mean the department hasn't arranged anything?"

"Give it a rest, Emmett," Tallsalt said brusquely. But then his tone softened. "I'm sorry. I'm insane. We're all going insane. Wind up plunging ourselves into the fire . . ." An extraordinary thing to say, given how the Knokis had gone. Emmett was waiting for Tallsalt to go on with this extreme line of reasoning when the lieutenant asked in a voice that seemed remarkably sober, "What're you doing up here?"

"I saw you from the house."

"No, no—why'd you come calling on me in the middle of the night?"

"I've got a few questions for you." The truth was best.

"What kind of questions?"

"Like what happened between Bert Knoki and Reed Summerfield?"

"Oh Jesus." Tallsalt took another drink, then lowered his head.

"There's bad blood there, and I'd like to know why. Even if it doesn't seem to amount to anything."

"No, you don't."

"Why wouldn't I?"

"Ignorant Indian's a safe Indian."

"Bullshit."

Tallsalt seemed to notice for the first time that he was bleeding. He rubbed his bloody forearm on his trouser leg. "Ignorance is the only way to go when you're dealing with the Office of Professional Responsibility." The FBI's internal affairs division.

"Is OPR working something on Summerfield?"

"Not if my people and I can help it."

"Dammit, Johnny," Emmett said crossly, "tell me what this is about."

"No, I love you too much. You're the last friend I got."

"Is it *that* big?"

"To Summerfield it'd be. And to every FBI agent in Arizona and New Mexico, who'd decide all of a sudden that John Tallsalt is out to bust some *bilagaana* balls. What goes around comes around, and I don't want to be dodging a civil rights beef next time one of my boys slaps around some mope for spitting on us. I like my miserable little hellhole of a world just the way it is. I've made my pact with Coyote, and it works for me. All right?" In Navajo lore, Coyote filled a role akin to the devil in Christianity. Tallsalt polished off the gin and pitched the bottle down into the pit, where it disintegrated with a bright tinkle. "What else?"

"You went to the Knokis' trailer today."

"That a statement or a question?" There was a wry smile below Tallsalt's mustache. "Ignore me . . . go on."

"The neighbor, Hank Whitesheep, says you told him you were there to pick up some things for us. That we feds asked you to do this."

"Wrong."

"Whitesheep lied?"

"No. That's what I told him. I lied . . ." The man shook his head in annoyance. "Fibbed to that damned jailhouse lawyer. He has a hard-on for us tribal cops. Lectured me that this was a federal case. I came that close to losing it with the weasel . . ." Clumsily, Tallsalt brought his thumb and forefinger within an inch of each other. "Thank God, I got ahold of myself and just said something about running an errand for you people."

"Why were you there?"

"I'm executor for Bert and Aurelia's will. I gathered up their mail so I can get going on their accounts and all that."

"Where is it now?"

"Their mail?"

"Yeah."

"In my office. Why?"

"I'd like to have a look at it." A closer look, especially at the letter with the University Park return address.

"Sure, whatever," Tallsalt said listlessly.

His painting Whitesheep as a jailhouse lawyer didn't ring true. The ex-con had been almost naively compliant during the interrogation. And Tallsalt should have checked with Anna or him before removing anything from the mobile home. Emmett was on the verge of pointing this out when Tallsalt touched the muzzle of his pistol to his right temple and said, "Fuck it all." He lowered the weapon and laughed at Emmett's shock. "Just kidding, for chrissake."

But Emmett was already lunging for him. He drove a forearm into Tallsalt's solar plexus and wrenched the semi-auto from the man's grasp. The lieutenant fell backward, away from the pit, and doubled up in pain. He vomited. Seizing Tallsalt by the shirtfront, Emmett ignored the hand the man was weakly lofting in surrender. "Don't ever kid that way again!" he seethed, his face close to Tallsalt's and the smell of puke and gin. "My brother kidded that way, and the next thing my mama knew—his brains were all over her kitchen!"

Tallsalt held Emmett's eyes a moment, then nodded

vapidly. "I'm sorry, Em. I didn't think it meant anything. Fuck me."

GILA MONSTER ROSE from the dirty sleeping bag on which he'd fitfully dreamed of Moth Woman. Without warning, she'd flung him into the fire, overturning the pot of stew that satisfied all hungers. Only anger filled the emptiness after she did these things to him.

Damn her.

Ticking came from the dashboard in the delivery van's cab. The watch the Voice had pressed into his hand at their final parting before that clockwork world blew to pieces. *I must leave it all to you, for my breath is short and my enemies powerful. Wisely used, your time stretches before you like a sun ray across the Galilee. Waste not a minute of it, my son. Soon you may be the last of the Elect to carry forth the javelin. Waste not a minute!*

Yawning, Gila Monster peered out the front at the towering wall of stacked truck tires. The sunrise leaked through the chinks in them, showing him his reflection on the inner surface of the windshield.

He was drawn to his own image. To see the extent of his transformation.

One of his hind paws knocked over his vial of red and white capsules on his way to the cab. He was running low on these but couldn't burglarize the pharmaceutical company's warehouse in Santa Fe again so soon. He was not a thief, even though burglary had become a way of life. Still, no more break-ins when he was so close to fulfilling the Blood Atonement. He had an ample supply of speed. Maybe the methamphetamine might somehow ward off his fits. He recalled nothing of the seizures themselves, just awakening to a splitting headache, the smell of his own feces and the derisive laughter of children. That was the worst part of them: the humiliating incontinence.

He'd fallen asleep with his gloves on, again.

He raised his right forepaw into view. Clicked the windshield with his sharpened claws. The thin daylight brought out the carmine, pink and black in the broken camouflage pattern of his scaly skin. He waved his paw back and forth, struck by the savage beauty of it. Made it tremble as if in the orgasmic act of divination. The trembling paw, when run over the body of a sufferer, unveiled all the sickness in the world. So much sickness. Unnatural lust. Unpunished evil. "I come from a northern land to save you from yourselves!" he hissed. His lips curled back from his teeth. Human teeth. Not little daggers like Gila teeth, wet with venom. And he noticed in his reflection the abrupt edge where his man-skin took over from his reptile-skin.

His red-tinged pupils dimmed with disappointment.

The human dermis was soft-looking, despite the bulging of the underlying muscles. Vulnerable. Prone to pain. His man-body was big and intimidating-looking, but it lacked natural armor. He wished his Gila monster gloves would cleave to his arms so he could never take them off—and the brilliant scale-beads would start spreading over all of him, band after colorful band cloaking his naked flesh until he was Gila Monster from his snout to the claws of his hind paws. That his exposed and dangling human penis would retract into the shell of his living fortress. Then he would be totally invulnerable.

Waste not a minute!

Gila Monster felt the sting of the riding crop on the backs of his hands.

It was time to hunt for Moth Man and Moth Woman again. And kill anyone—especially police—who got in the way. Cops were the gatekeepers of hell, and there was no going forth without slaying them. He saw great mounds of cop carrion mixed with tatters of blue and tan uniform cloth, FBI blazers, nightsticks snapped in two, chrome handcuffs bent out of shape, pistols empty of the bullets that had bounced like rain off Gila Monster's armor. Atop it all was a sign on a stake that had been thrust into the uppermost corpse. It read—*They knew nothing of justice.*

Only the Blood Atonement approached justice.

Stripping off his gloves, he sat behind the wheel and gave the key a twist. The engine rumbled to life. He swiveled around and opened the toolbox bolted to the deck. From it he took the Javelin of Vengeance. So very old. He wonderingly regarded the long iron blade—long enough to pierce two human bodies with one thrust. It was fastened with a rawhide thong to an eighteen-inch length of wooden shaft. The original binding had been so frail with age he'd had to replace it. He turned the crude blade in his hands, fascinated by the bloodlike sheen the dawn light left on the pitted iron. Stamped on one side were the words *Dios no se acobarda*.

God does not flinch.

Gila Monster began to glance up—but stopped himself. He knew that the bearded face of the Voice had appeared behind his own reflection on the windshield. Glaring mercilessly at him. Goading him to get moving. To spill blood again.

Avoiding those withering eyes, the sight of the little whip trembling with indignation in that liver-spotted fist, Gila Monster asked, "What would happen if I sought them out in peace?"

Then you too shall be plunged into the flames!

Gila Monster clenched his eyelids for a moment. Then he put his javelin away, unlatched the driver's-side door and slithered nude down out of the idling van. He sampled the cool morning air with his forked tongue. He could taste the owl that just swooshed overhead on its last sweep of the night. The oil dripping from the tired engine of his van. But mostly, he could taste his little brothers waiting impatiently for him in the springhouse across the garden of ashes. Once the four walls built of tires had enclosed a compound, but all that remained of the buildings were heaps of charcoal. He crawled between these piles and over the spent rifle casings glinting in the sand. Old memories. The haunting wail of an air raid siren to warn of demons screaming out of the desert. Buckets filled with water in which to douse incendiaries that dropped like angels felled by lightning.

He had survived the death of that world, of everyone he knew. Did that make him immortal? Or just the walking dead?

Gila Monster opened the plywood door to the springhouse.

He could hear restless scampering in the cool darkness beyond. Claws flinging gravel. A threatening hiss.

He reached for the matches he kept just inside the door and lit a candle.

Three cages lay side by side on the muddy floor. Three glistening pairs of eyes caught the candlelight. Black snouts pressed ravenously up to the chicken wire, and tongues explored through the mesh. At the back of the dripping cavity, where milk and meats had once been stored from the summer heat, was a tin box. It was perforated with small holes. Removing the lid, he peered down into a nest of wood shavings. In it was a huddle of tiny, pink bodies. Hairless. Puny and wrinkled. As pathetically wrinkled as the man-skin of his own scrotum. He shifted the candle close. The pinkies squirmed from the nearness of the flame. He could taste the hot blood visibly pulsing through the blue veins.

Gila Monster had resolved not to feed his little brothers over the past month. To make them more aggressive. But then he'd broken down and given the one he'd left under the mobile home a final meal.

He picked up a pinkie in his fingertips. Felt the stirring warmth. The flicker of muscles contracting. Heard the almost inaudible squeak of alarm. He cracked the door to the first cage and flung the ratling inside. It was over in a blink. The big male Gila spun around and bit with astonishing speed. He held the pinkie fast in his blunt jaws, pumping his venom into it, clamping firmly until the tiny rear legs stopped twitching.

Then he swallowed.

* * *

ANNA AWOKE TO Emmett sleeping in the chair beside her bed.

He'd slid almost completely out of it, leaving his elbows hooked over the arms, his shoulder blades anchored on the seat and his head scrunched between the backrest and his sternum. She debated waking him. He looked uncomfortable, yet his respiration was measured and peaceful.

She smiled, searching her drugged memory for a recollection of his coming in.

The venetian blinds were still parted, and through the slats she could see the dawn. Only a hint of it. Its full eruption over the Defiance Plateau was being dampened by a dull red cloud bar hugging the horizon.

The door clicked open, and Summerfield's face appeared. He put on an uneasy grin.

The sudden draft from the corridor tweaked Emmett's eyelids. His right hand flew to his holster—before he recognized the intruder. It took him a second to settle down, by which time he'd noticed that Anna was awake. "You okay?" he whispered—for no apparent reason.

She tested her bandaged wrist with her other hand. Only a burning sensation this morning. Plus some nominal puffiness. "Better."

"Talk to you a minute, Parker?" Summerfield also insisted on whispering. Whatever his news, it sounded urgent.

"Go back to sleep," Emmett ordered Anna on his way to the door.

"No," Anna said. "Would you both sit down and bring me up to speed . . . ?" Emmett didn't budge for a moment, but then rubbed his neck and sank back into the chair. Summerfield entered the room and took the stool Dr. Hennepin had used last night. "What's going on?"

There were dark crescents under Summerfield's eyes. "I left word with the Washington lab to call me regardless of the hour as soon as they put Knoki's last citation back together. I just got home an hour ago, and there was a message on my machine. From the lab. They've got a name and address off the cite. A Clydine Jumper of Navajo, New Mexico."

Anna asked, "She live in the same trailer park the Knokis did?"

"Uh, no," Summerfield replied. "All I had was her post office box—"

"Had?" Emmett interrupted.

"Yes, until I dropped by Window Rock on my way here from Gallup. I checked with dispatch, and got Jumper's residential ID number off the computerized housing map. I'm reasonably sure I can get us to her home site."

Emmett asked, "Did you explain *why* you needed her address?"

"No," Summerfield answered. Somewhat defensively. "Nobody from Criminal Investigation Services had come into the office yet, and I figured Patrol didn't need to know at this point."

"Good," Emmett said.

"Because I don't know Jumper's clan affiliations— and who with the police staff might tip her off we feds are coming."

Emmett said nothing for several seconds, then: "Maybe."

"The dispatcher did make a comment regarding Clydine Jumper," Summerfield added. "She asked me if I meant to steal her department's bootlegger business."

"Clydine a confirmed bootlegger?" Emmett asked.

"Notorious, I surmise. Although I wasn't aware of her."

Bert Knoki had been a relentless pursuer of bootleggers. His last ticket had been issued to a made rumrunner, and then his corpse, plus that of his hapless wife, was found less than ten miles northwest of this traffic stop: the intersection of Route 134 and the Asaayi Lake turnoff. Buoyed by this realization, Anna sat up and swung her legs over the side of the bed. Her head throbbed, but she kept the pain off her face—Emmett was watching her every move. "Am I reading you right, Em?"

He glanced away. "About what?"

"That we shouldn't invite the Navajo police along to Clydine Jumper's this morning?"

"*Our* visit?"

"Yes, I'm going," she said firmly. Thankfully, he didn't argue. "Now what do we say to the PD so we're all still talking to each other after this?"

Emmett brushed what looked to be coal dust off his pant legs. "It's your call."

"But I'm asking for your input."

He shrugged. "Well, just before we go off the radio at the scene, we might call for a soft back . . ." A backup that waits on the fringes of the incident until summoned. "Then we interview Clydine. By ourselves."

"This isn't like you."

"Pardon?"

"You *always* involve the tribal police," she said.

"Not always." But Emmett didn't explain. And he was careful not to look in Summerfield's direction, which was almost the same as nodding toward the man. Something had happened involving the Navajo cops, and Emmett didn't want to discuss it in front of the Gallup agent.

"Was Clydine's employment block filled in on the cite, Reed?" she asked.

"No."

"Then chances are we'll find her at home."

chapter 9

THE STEEP SWITCHBACK TOPPED OUT ON THE BLUFF above Navajo Pine High School. Here, enclosed by a fenced pasture, was a shanty with a hogan in the rear. Emmett slowed. The traditional dwelling wasn't entirely so, for the walls were covered with scabrous pink stucco. Parked near the shack was a new Dodge Dakota truck. The Arizona license plate—he reminded himself that they were back over the state line—bore the same number Bert Knoki had entered onto his citation Saturday evening. Unfortunately, the Washington lab had been able to reconstruct the charred ticket only down to that box, leaving other questions about the traffic stop unanswered.

"Time to include the PD," Emmett said to Anna.

She grabbed the microphone. "Window Rock, Frank Thirty-three."

The signal from the tribal capital twenty miles to the south was strong and clear. "Thirty-three, go ahead with your traffic."

"Be advised—myself, Frank Two and BIA Seventeen are out at the Clydine Jumper residence near Navajo. Request a soft back from any patrol unit in the vicinity."

Silence from the Window Rock dispatcher.

Emmett pulled up to the closed gate but remained behind the steering wheel. He tapped his horn twice. The echoes overlapped and rolled across the school grounds. No one appeared from either the shanty or the pink hogan. In

Emmett's rearview mirror, Summerfield's Suburban crested the bluff, coming dustily out of the sun. What could this skittish man have possibly done to warrant an internal affairs investigation by the FBI's Office of Professional Responsibility? Maybe it'd just been the gin in Tallsalt talking. Emmett slipped the mike from Anna's grasp. "Far enough, Reed," he transmitted.

The agent stopped. About thirty yards behind them, as previously arranged—it was less tempting to ambush two widely separated cars. Summerfield would keep an eye on the entire site with his shotgun at the ready. And delay the tribal patrol officer, if he or she showed sooner than expected and insisted on learning what this was all about. *Why the hell did Johnny have to fall off the wagon now? Or is that the reason he wanted me here? A cry for help?*

A frantic bleating came from the vicinity of the shanty.

The radio crackled to life. "Frank Thirty-three, Window Rock."

"Go ahead for Thirty-three," Emmett answered for Anna.

"Units are rolling from this station."

Emmett frowned. Units. Plural. Either someone in the department didn't want the feds to talk to Clydine Jumper, or the potential for trouble was greater than he'd anticipated.

A woman sauntered from behind the shanty, a stout Navajo in middle age. Shading her eyes with a hand, she scrutinized the unmarked sedan and Suburban, then smirked and started for the gate. She wore a Grateful Dead T-shirt with a customary woolen skirt held around her thick waist by a silver concha belt.

Emmett stepped out of the sedan. Anna joined him.

The woman draped her fat forearms over the top of the gate but didn't open it. She had a lantern jaw so severely undershot, her face seemed boarlike. There appeared to be blood in the corners of her mouth.

"Clydine Jumper?"

"Who're you?" she fired back at Emmett, apparently acknowledging that he'd found the right person.

"I'm Investigator Parker, BIA. And this is Special Agent Turnipseed from the FBI."

"Who's the *bilagaana* who looks like he ain't had his bowel movement yet?"

Emmett almost smiled. "Special Agent Summerfield from the Gallup FBI office. We'd like to talk to you."

"Can't," she said.

"Why not?"

"I got a case comin' up, and my *Dinebeiina Nahiilna be Agaditahe* advocate don't want me talkin' to no cops."

"Tribal legal aid," Emmett explained to Anna. Then he asked Clydine, "You referring to the bootlegging charge?"

"Yeah."

"Well, I'm not interested in that. I want to discuss the ticket Officer Knoki wrote to you the other night . . ." Her expression remained placid. Had she expected this intrusion? "I just want to cover the traffic stop. Nothing else. Still, if you want DNA present, I understand." Then he added forcefully, "But we're going to talk, Clydine."

Anna's suddenly worried look drew Emmett's gaze down the slope. Several dark-haired figures were jumping the school fence and heading their way.

"Well, Clydine?" Emmett asked, turning back to her. "Do we talk here or in Window Rock?"

She gave an armpit a long, petulant scratch, then sighed and swung open the gate. "Make it fast, BIA man. I'm nuttin' my lambs this mornin' and got no time for you."

Still tracking the advancing figures, Anna warned, "Emmett."

"I see them," he said under his breath. "Tell Summerfield to watch our backs. Then you rejoin me." He followed the Navajo woman, pausing briefly beside the Dakota pickup to inspect the wheel wells on his side of the truck for evidence of Crystal Wash's silty ooze. They looked as if they'd been washed clean.

*   *   *

BY THE TIME ANNA REACHED the Suburban, the six Navajo youths had spread out into a kind of skirmish line and were coming on with an arm-swinging swagger. She could see no weapons, but the teenagers were all wearing the same baggy clothing in vogue with gangbangers in Las Vegas. Some sported black watch caps, others hair nets.

Summerfield let down his window. "What's happening?"

She drew his attention to the youths. "Them." Summerfield's color dropped a shade. "Emmett wants you to cover our backs, okay?"

The agent took his shotgun down from the roof rack.

Anna set out for the shanty, listening to the oncoming scuffle of athletic shoes. Her legs felt wobbly. As if she'd gotten out of bed too soon with a case of the flu. The pasture had been grazed down to bare dirt, and round stones protruded from it like mushrooms. She was careful not to turn her ankle on one of them. *Not now, not in front of these little bastards.* The breeze was uncomfortably cool on her damp face. *Am I still feverish from the Gila bite?* She reached the cabin's rickety wooden porch. Emmett was peering through the open front door into the darkened interior beyond. His right hand was on his hip, close to the bulge in his windbreaker.

"What's she doing?" Anna inquired.

"I asked to see her copy of the ticket. Just in case the lab can't decipher everything on Knoki's original."

Anna checked on the progress of the youths. Only five were in sight now. "Somebody peeled off."

"The smallest one. He's sneaking up that line of junipers to the west. Clydine's probably got weapons stashed all over this garden spot. Any hint of a gun, you fall back to Summerfield."

"You sure you want just a soft back?"

Emmett didn't answer.

Finally, Clydine emerged from the shanty with the citation. The ticket had been crumpled, possibly in a moment of fury at the traffic stop, but then smoothed out again. "Here, BIA man." She thrust it at Emmett as she ambled by him toward a livestock pen between the shanty and the hogan.

Anna couldn't see the east-facing door to the windowless hut.

"Stay with her," Emmett said to Anna as he perused the cite. The five youths swept past the Suburban and a wide-eyed Summerfield inside, then gathered around Emmett's sedan. The largest leaned against its grille, his gaze riveted on Emmett, who ignored him. "Go ahead, Anna," he said without glancing up.

She neared the brush fence surrounding the pen just as Clydine tied the legs of a protesting lamb together. The woman slit his scrotum with a knife, sucked out his testicles and spat them into a pail of water at her feet, then grinned redly at Anna. "It's the best way to do it," she said, letting the castrated animal wriggle free and rejoin the flock darting around the pin.

"You're supposed to wash your mouth out after with wine," Anna said matter-of-factly. "That's how it's done in my part of the country."

"Where'd a nice girl like me get some wine?" Clydine asked with a husky laugh.

Emmett approached the enclosure but drifted east a few yards so he could keep an eye on his car. Anna scanned the top of the bluff for any sign of the boy who'd split off from the others. Summerfield had stepped out of his four-by-four but was standing behind his half-open door. He looked as if he was having trouble swallowing.

"Clydine," Emmett said sharply to get her attention.

Slowly, the woman stood erect after starting to hunch over to snatch another male out of the cowering flock. "What?"

"Did Officer Knoki follow you before pulling you over?"

"No, he was waitin' for me 'round the big curve below Crystal with his radar."

Emmett stared intently at the Navajo woman. Anna wondered if he was thinking what she was: If Bert Knoki had caught Clydine by chance in his radar trap, it was unlikely that he'd been shadowing her in the hope of catching her bootlegging again. Anna believed that a speeding ticket was less of a reason for homicide than an attempted arrest for a repeat offense. But she had no idea how Clydine Jumper's mind worked. She'd known a few Modoc females like this strange woman, but they too had been a mystery to her. Misfits. Outcasts from two cultures.

The youths passed through the gate and strutted into the yard. There, they clustered around the big one, a hulking boy with a concentration camp buzz showing through his hair net. He shook cigarettes out of a pack for the others. She now saw in their faces what made them dangerous. They had absolutely no fear of death. They were young.

"Says on the ticket here," Emmett went on to the woman, "you were southbound on Route 134. Coming back from someplace?"

"Crystal Chapter House."

"What were you doing there?"

"Visitin' with my brother. He cooks for the old folks who get their meals at the house."

"And after that you were headed home?"

"No, Window Rock."

"Why?" Emmett asked.

"To drop some things off for my older boy. At jail." A triumphant grin spread across her face. Ghastly: The woman's teeth were limned in lamb's blood. And disconcerting. *Why is she so pleased?*

Then it hit Anna.

Clydine could account for her presence at a specified time and place on Saturday evening. Did that mean she knew when the Knokis had died? Their estimated times of death hadn't been revealed until last night—and to Emmett by a Tucson FBI agent, not to the public. Anna made a mental note to check her son's property sheet at the jail. To see if the time of Clydine's drop-off coincided with the final agonies of the Knokis at the hands of their killers.

Emmett confronted the sullen gazes of the youths for a

few seconds, then asked Clydine, "You see which way Officer Knoki drove after he finished with you?"

"No, I left first."

"Was he alone in his cruiser?"

Clydine shook her head. "His woman was with him. Aurora, I think her name was."

"Aurelia?"

"Yeah, that's it. He brought her along to gloat over me. Show her the big bad bootlegger he's takin' to court next month."

Anna looked all around. Still no sign of the sixth youth. Summerfield was watching for him too.

Emmett gestured at the rest. "These your boys, Clydine?"

"No."

In fact, none bore a resemblance to her. And the stamp of her blood was bound to be unhandsomely distinctive. Yet, she'd revealed the existence of a younger son by mentioning the older one in jail.

The largest boy took three strides forward, tilted back his head so there was no mistaking the raw viciousness in his eyes. On the side of his neck was a tattoo, something stylized like a kachina, although Anna didn't recognize the mythic figure. He slowly cricked his fingers into claws. A gang sign, apparently.

"That a state or a BIA school you go to?" Emmett demanded of them. When no one responded, he went on, "If it's an Indian Affairs facility, I'm empowered to enforce the truancy law."

"It's a state school," the big youth finally answered.

"Go on back to class," Clydine told them with an utter lack of conviction. She wanted them here. This was the only hint of uncertainty she'd betrayed so far.

"Where's your buddy?" Emmett asked the boys.

"Who?" the big one said, deadpan.

"The peewee who cut off into the trees."

"Takin' a leak, I guess," the youth quipped, and the others laughed.

"Really? Didn't look old enough to shake the dew off his lily by himself," Emmett said, then caught Anna's eye. "Any more questions?"

"Yes," she said. Then to Clydine: "Did you have anyone in the truck with you when Officer Knoki stopped you?"

"Nobody. Just me."

Emmett rechecked the citation, confirming this with a quick nod.

Anna continued, "The articles you left off for your son . . ."

"Yeah?"

"What were they?"

"Oh, some Marlboros. Gum. Stuff like that."

"You already have these things at home here? Or did you buy them before going to the jail?"

Clydine visibly weighed the direction this was taking. "Before. At Bashas' in Window Rock." Whatever, she must've sensed quicksand, for she changed the subject. "Got any idea who killed Knoki and his woman?" There it was. Why she had consented to the interview: She wanted to learn how much law enforcement knew, and that convinced Anna she and Emmett should talk to her again, this time with a better idea of how much it would have meant to defendant Clydine Jumper to have the chief witness against her in her upcoming trial eliminated. She was evolving into a suspect, and there were admissibility hazards to any future prosecution by plowing full steam ahead here, although Anna guessed that Emmett, true to usual form, would take that risk.

"Drug traffickers," he said to Clydine, waiting a beat for her reaction. There was none. "The authorities think maybe some drug traffickers were behind it. Heard that on the radio on the drive up. Mexican drug lords."

"Bad people," the woman observed evenly.

"Well, thanks for your help, Clydine," Emmett said, sauntering toward Anna. "We'll be in touch."

"Only if my DNA lawyer says it's okay," the woman challenged.

Sidling up to Anna, Emmett said, hushed, "We'll go right

through the middle of these yahoos. Set the tone for our future relations. Walk behind me."

"Sorry."

He started to say between clenched teeth, "Anna, we don't have time—"

"I go first, Emmett."

"And if they don't budge?"

"I kick ass and take names."

He measured her resolve a second more, then said irascibly, "Go on."

She began walking.

The youths flicked away their cigarettes and closed ranks. The big one made a fist, flexing it in tempo with each stride Anna took, sneering with mock encouragement as she came on. "Stand aside," she said with a steady voice.

Nobody budged.

Again, she looked for weapons. None in sight. Beside the Suburban, Summerfield was rocking back and forth on the balls of his feet, unable to keep still.

"Stand aside," she repeated more insistently.

The big one waited squarely on her path. He was powerfully built, almost as tall as Emmett. She was now close enough to smell the stale marijuana smoke on his Oakland Raiders jacket. He glared down at her. She looked back at him without blinking. Then, sidestepping, she slipped her right forearm over the top of his, so gently his only reflex was to smile at her deceptively soft touch. But his lips tightened into a grimace as she abruptly wrenched his arm behind him, bending in his hand so that the fingertips brushed the inner side of his wrist. He cried out defiantly, but the blinding pain drove him to his knees. She went down with him. "I told you to stand aside!" she shouted, using both hands to double the pressure of the wristlock. "When I tell you to move, you do it!"

Shadows danced across the stony ground. A fight was taking place over her, but she dare not let go of the big youth. Her Gila bite ached terribly.

A second gangbanger fell heavily alongside her, his nose bloodied. "Everybody down!" Emmett cried. "Hands behind your goddamn heads!"

The three youths left on their feet went prone, and the sunlight found Anna again. It felt like fire on her face. There seemed to be no air down among all these bodies, and she almost didn't blame the big one when he tried to get up. "Lie still." She overcame his restlessness by increasing the pressure again. But he started to gather spit in his mouth. She cut the attempt short with another twinge to the strained tendons in his forearm. "Don't even think about it!"

Gasping, he dipped his head. The tattoo on his neck was fresh, still red and scabby from the prick of the needle. And the image was finally unmistakably clear to her. A slender tongue forking from a triangular head. Armored scales. Five claws on each of the four paws. A Gila monster. Moth wings sprouted from the lizard's sides. Moth and not butterfly—for long, feathery antennae sprung from the Gila's brows.

The boy smiled at her look of shock, and her grip on him momentarily weakened. He flung aside her hands and reared back a fist to strike her full in the face. It was flying toward her when a boot—Emmett's—caught him in the back of the head. The teenager's brow slammed against the ground, and he lay still, groaning.

Anna was half-rising, fumbling behind her for the set of handcuffs she kept looped over her belt—when Emmett violently pressed her flat. "Stay down!" He flopped prone beside her, revolver drawn. "Summerfield's taking fire!" Unholstering her 9mm, she rolled on her back for a look at the Suburban. The white pucker of a bullet hole showed on the driver's side of the windshield, but the agent had somehow managed to squirm under the vehicle. He peered over the sights of his shotgun first this way and then that, betraying the fact that he had no idea where the shot had come from.

Emmett hollered for Clydine to get down. She was standing in the middle of the pasture, turned toward the hogan.

Anna said hoarsely, "She knew this was going to happen."

"No shit."

Anna hadn't heard the shot. But both she and the big gangbanger had been breathing explosively in each other's faces. She was still fighting for breath. Shifting her muzzle across the screen of junipers, she sought a black watch cap as her target. Car engine. She could hear a vehicle approaching. No, two of them. Speeding up the switchbacks. "That'll be our soft back," she said hollowly to Emmett. She felt as if she were glued to the pasture.

"Stay here," Emmett commanded. "I'll warn them."

"By radio?"

Emmett looked at his sedan, fifty long feet away, then said, "No, the little bastard is zeroed in on the cars. When I take off, fire two shots over the tops of the trees. That should keep his head down." Then he raised his voice. "Anybody moves, Agent Turnipseed—blow his head off."

She delayed him by grabbing his jacket sleeve. Still, the words wouldn't come.

"It can wait," he said, then sprang up.

She had the sinking feeling that it couldn't—as she squeezed her trigger twice.

EMMETT HAD VAULTED the fence and was sprinting head-long for the top of the switchbacks when he caught sudden movement to his right. A darkly clad figure darted from the hogan door and melted into a buckbrush thicket. Digging in his heels, Emmett pivoted to give chase. But the hot whir of a bullet inches from his cheek sent him diving for the roadbed instead. The crack of the rifle report reached him as he lay on the hard-packed dirt. Anna answered the shot with two more of her own.

The fast approach of a vehicle made him roll to the downslope shoulder of the road. He flattened himself behind a slight berm. A white Chevy Yukon stopped between him and where he believed the sniper was hiding. Before the vehicle covered him with dust, he jabbed with his revolver toward the probable source of the gunfire. The passenger door flew open, and John Tallsalt crawled across the front bench seat and out, gripping his pistol. Yabeny was right behind in his own four-by-four, and the sergeant exited his cruiser much as his lieutenant had, although he balanced a carbine across his forearms. Both CIS supervisors, and no patrolmen in sight.

Odd. But no time to think about it.

Tallsalt crept on his hands and knees over to Emmett. The lieutenant's eyes were reddened but seemed alert enough. And furious. "What the hell do you think you're doing, Parker!"

"Getting ready to outflank this little prick who keeps taking potshots at me."

"You have any idea what you're dealing with here?"

"Getting a better one by the minute."

Another bullet whizzed overhead, and Tallsalt wisely decided to put his temper on hold. "How many triggermen?"

"Possibly two by now. A Clydine look-alike just boogied out of the hogan."

"That'd be Ivan, her youngest. Craziest banger on the Big Rez. And the worst gang—the Vipers. Real smart not checking with us first."

Emmett glared at Tallsalt. "Figured you'd be *unavailable* again."

Tallsalt's face went to stone, but then he asked with concern, "Where's your partner?"

"With Summerfield and the rest of the bangers below the shack."

The lieutenant took a lightning-fast peek over the hood of his cruiser, then snapped his fingers at Yabeny. The sergeant was hunkered down behind his own car, resting his cheek against the short barrel of the carbine. "Marcellus," Tallsalt rattled off, "Parker and I'll work our way around the hill. You drive my unit through the gate. Use it to shield Turnipseed and Summerfield. You'll probably take a round or two going up to the house . . ." Yabeny shrugged off such a trifle. ". . . so stay low in the seat. When you get the chance—radio Window Rock Patrol for a perimeter to be thrown up all around the hill. Get help from Chinle and Shiprock, if you have to." Then Tallsalt holstered his pistol and held out his hands for Yabeny to toss him the carbine. The cut he'd sustained on the left palm while trashing his own living room was now neatly bandaged, and he was wearing a fresh uniform. He caught the rifle and turned with an abrasive smile to Emmett. "No cattle to steal on this raid, Comanche. Sure you want to go along?"

"Just keep up with me."

Yabeny crept past them and into Tallsalt's vehicle.

"Do it!" the lieutenant yelled.

The sergeant gunned the engine, then sped for the gate. The spinning tires kicked up a cloud of dust. Tallsalt and Emmett raced through it and across the road. If the pee-wee loosed another shot at them, the sound was lost in the howl of the Yukon careening for the shanty. They pushed through the scattered junipers and didn't stop until they came to the three-strand barbed wire fence on the eastern border of Clydine's home site. Tallsalt pinned the lower two strands to the ground with his boot, and Emmett ducked through, spun around and did the same for the lieutenant.

REDDISH DUST WAS FANNING UP into the sky when Yabeny leaped from the cruiser he'd just parked between Anna and the sniper. He landed beside her, grimaced and plucked a rock out from under his groin—before simultaneously transmitting over his Handie-Talkie in Navajo and signaling for Summerfield to stay put. Clydine was sitting on her porch, calmly waiting for the disturbance to subside.

When the sergeant finally pocketed his HT, Anna asked him, "Where's Emmett?"

"With the lieutenant. Tryin' to get behind this guy."

"Kid. He's just a kid."

Yabeny nodded, almost sadly, then said over the sights of his pistol at the big youth, "Stay right there, Garwin, with your hands in sight." His warning was greeted with a hateful grin.

"What's his full name?" Anna asked.

"Garwin Descheenie," Yabeny replied quietly. "Ivan Jumper's straight-up *loco* number two man."

"What's the tattoo mean?"

"No idea," the sergeant said, studying it. "New. Vipers used to have just a snake logo."

"This one looks like a Gila monster with moth wings to me."

"Me too."

Anna had heard no shots in several minutes now. With Emmett out in the trees, she didn't want to think about what the next one might mean. "Why's this kid with the rifle so eager to die this morning?"

"These are the in-betweeners . . ." Yabeny continued to aim his muzzle over sprawled youths. "They fell through the cracks in the years when nobody wanted to be *Dine*. Lost between the traditional grown-ups and the real young ones learnin' the old ways. These bangers have nothin', except themselves and a Hollywood idea of what a gang is. They're lookin' for a god of their own, I guess, and a reason to sacrifice themselves. We've body-bagged eight of 'em since New Year's." The sergeant paused. "Maybe this is what happens when you've got no real way anymore for boys to become warriors. They do it on their own. And get it all wrong."

AN ATHLETIC SHOE TRACK froze Emmett mid-stride.

He measured it against his own boot. A ten medium. One size smaller than his own. Too big for the peewee sniper's, but right for the six-footer Emmett had just seen bolt from the hogan. The line of prints struck due south. Tallsalt came up from covering the rear and noticed the tracks at once. Emmett pursed his lips at a ravine that wound down the south face of the bluff. Tallsalt shook his head at his clumsy stab at the Navajo gesture, but then concurred with a nod: Ivan Jumper was fleeing as quickly as he could. The real problem was whether or not the sniper had pulled back with him.

With Tallsalt training the carbine on the trees, Emmett cut across the top of the bluff. Searching for the peewee's tracks. Thinking it through. The boy who'd separated from the rest of the pack had gone to their arms stash while the others distracted Anna and him. Then he'd laid down fire so Ivan Jumper could make his escape from the hogan. Even hardened gangbangers didn't wantonly shoot at law enforcement unless they believed a felony arrest was imminent. Had all this been planned days in advance to make sure the gang leader didn't fall into the hands of a federal interrogator?

Was the solution to the Knoki homicides waiting down in the willow-choked ravine?

Emmett motioned for Tallsalt to follow him: He'd found size-seven or eight tracks in a running interval, headed for the gully. He began descending the slope. The breeze was in his face, warm and full of sounds. Dogs barking. The distant laughter of a child. A small valley lay below, cluttered with houses, trailers and hogans, and crisscrossed with unpaved roads. He waved Tallsalt forward, and together they knelt behind a knob of rock. Emmett whispered, "I'd like one of your patrol units to set up on the edge of this settlement before we start pushing anybody before us down the ravine."

"Me too."

"Well, how soon before Patrol can throw a ring around this hill?"

"Not very," Tallsalt admitted. He worked his tongue against the roof of his mouth as if trying to relieve a cotton mouth. His hangover must have been ferocious, but this was the first sign he'd given of it. "There was only one unit on duty to cover both Window Rock and Ganado. That's why Marcellus and I jumped on the call to back you."

So Clydine's son would get away, unless Tallsalt and he managed to hem him in by themselves. But Emmett couldn't blame the Navajo department. With federal cutbacks, it was operating on half the manpower it needed.

Tallsalt asked, trying to sound blasé, "And what led you to Clydine?"

"FBI lab. They got the name of the violator off Bert's last cite. Things came together pretty fast this morning, John."

"Yeah, right. You get a look at our sniper?"

"Black knit cap. Thirteen years old, if that."

"Great," Tallsalt said bitterly, "a wannabe. He'll die trying to prove himself to the ranked-in members of the gang." But strangely, he seemed more like his old self than he had at any time over the past two days. There was some fire in his eyes. "I'll go down and wait for you to herd them to the foot of the slope." He gave Emmett the opportunity to object.

But he too saw no other way. "Just don't shoot me if it turns out they've already given us the slip."

"Insult me, why don't you?" Tallsalt rose. "Eight minutes, then shove off." He trotted up the way they'd just come, light on his feet, scarcely making a sound. He'd venture east before turning south again, skirting the ravine altogether. Exactly what Emmett would do if the roles were reversed. Nothing remained of the sodden ghost beside the coal trench in the vigorous man zigzagging up the brushy hillside. Maybe he would find his sobriety again—as long as he had some help.

Emmett checked his wristwatch—9:11 A.M.—then peered around the knob to watch the willows for movement. They were in bloom, and he could hear bees droning. He felt slightly better about the dilemma he'd faced this morning. Tallsalt needed hospitalization. He was toying with suicide, and nobody got away with that for long. Yet, for Emmett to declare on the protective custody admittance form that the lieutenant was a danger to himself would shatter the man's career just like the gin bottle Tallsalt had chucked into the pit last night. In the end, Emmett hadn't been able to do that. Not to the best cop on the Navajo Nation. So he'd tossed Tallsalt into bed and driven back to Sage Memorial Hospital in Ganado with the fragile hope that the man wouldn't unravel before a way could be found to help him without jeopardizing the only thing holding him together. The job. It hadn't seemed a satisfying choice, leaving him, until now.

Emmett consulted his watch again, then stood. "Close enough for government work."

He sprinted down the slope and over the embankment into the willows. A ribbon of jungle in a dry land. Dappled shade under a canopy of silvery May leaves. The ankle-deep stagnant water was carpeted with cress that gave off a peppery smell as he duckwalked downstream. A cicada skirled angrily at the quiet splashing of Emmett's boots. A goat and sheep trail formed a shadowy tunnel that meandered down through the thicket, a secret highway entirely hidden from view. There were pocks in the cress but no tracks of a size approaching Ivan Jumper's, which meant he'd avoided the ravine and probably beaten Tallsalt to the settlement below— and friends among its inhabitants. Leaving behind a fearless thirteen-year-old rear guard to delay the cops while he made his escape.

Emmett picked up his pace. Nothing indicated that the boy was slowing to set up another ambush. That could mean he was already inside the settlement, and Tallsalt would be facing him alone. No way to tackle a sniper.

Where the ravine drained into an irrigation ditch something glittered under the burble of falling water. Emmett stooped and picked it up: a .223mm rifle cartridge. The pee-wee had dropped it while reloading on the fly.

Swiftly now, he followed the size-seven tracks down the

canal, keeping his head down because the first houses were just above him.

A dog was barking as if something threatening was very close. Emmett didn't believe that he was the cause of the commotion, as the breeze was still in his face, not behind him, and he could see where the shoe prints angled up the sandy bank. He peered over the top, keeping his head parallel to the ground so it was less likely to be recognized for what it was. A juicy target. His right eye had a tilted-on-end view of the scene, but he could make out an old travel trailer set up on blocks as a permanent dwelling, its silver luster turned a flat gray by the relentless sun of the plateau. Across from the trailer was a derelict log-and-mud hogan, its roof partially caved in.

There was movement across the open ground in between.

At first, Emmett thought that it was a small animal. Then he realized that a toddler had scrambled off the trailer porch to chase a big black stink bug across the yard. The child giggled as he pursued the insect, one of his diaper fasteners undone and the dried stream of mucus under his nose red from the dust his bare feet were padding over. The bug was wary and elusive prey. The chase continued to his laughter.

Then Emmett's gaze rushed to the middle distance, where a flash of tan showed against the junipers. Tallsalt was coming cautiously through the trees, a large mongrel snapping and barking at his heels. Suddenly, he cuffed the dog across the muzzle with the back of his free hand. It whimpered off toward a cabin across the road. Tallsalt shifted the carbine back to both hands. Obviously, he had yet to come upon either Ivan Jumper's or the sniper's tracks. Which got Emmett wondering. Had they gone west? The country was more open in that direction, virtually treeless, making escape from the gathering manhunt almost impossible. Jumper, born and raised here, would know that the nearest sanctuary was the Chuskas. The highways would be roadblocked, so borrowing or stealing a car offered less of a chance of successful flight than simply darting across Route 12 into the mountains.

Emmett waved over the top of the irrigation ditch.

Tallsalt flinched the barrel toward him, but then quickly lowered it and relaxed slightly. Emmett brought his hand to his throat—the signal for a hostage, although it stood as well for an innocent in the area. Tallsalt had to work around a John Deere tractor before he could see the child. Then, unable to call out, he looked toward the trailer for an adult. No one was in sight, so he broke into a jog. He was reaching for the startled toddler when a spurt of sand appeared between man and child. As always, the crack of the rifle shot seemed to reverberate through the airwaves an instant later.

Emmett turned on the whitish vapor that was rising from the still unseen door to the hogan. He fired twice, just to try to buy Tallsalt time, then scrambled up the bank and charged the hut. The lieutenant had scooped up the child and was lunging for the trailer—all to the snapping of the .223 rifle. Emmett crashed chest-first into the hogan, staving in the dry-rotted timbers and losing his balance as four of the eight walls collapsed before him. He tumbled into a choking swirl of dust with every expectation of landing on things hard and sharp. But the dried mud coating cushioned his fall.

The shooting had ceased.

Nor was there any sound of the sniper stirring in the debris beneath Emmett. He was spreading his hands, feeling for vibrations in the jackstraw pile of timbers, when there was a groan of wood overhead. He squinted up into the lingering dust as the remaining portion of the roof slabbed off and crashed down around him. Darkness. He thought he'd been spared the worst of the weight until he tried to crawl backward. And found himself pinned.

"Emmett!" came Tallsalt's muffled voice from above.

"How's the baby?"

"Okay. We're both okay. What about you?"

"Pissed. Get the roof off before this little son of a bitch suffocates under me."

Tallsalt went for help. Five minutes later, he returned with a half-dozen men, who grunted and heaved the roof aside.

Emmett immediately started digging through the rubble with his hands. He found the rifle and tossed it to Tallsalt. But no peewee. His apprehension grew. Then he glimpsed dusty, black hair between two logs. He pulled away the closest timber, and a pair of terrified eyes peered back at him.

"You little fucker," Emmett said.

chapter 10

SHUTTING HER MOTEL ROOM DOOR, ANNA SAW THAT Emmett had left his open. She peeked inside. He sat bare-chested at the table, an assortment of greasy chicken, two salads and some dry-looking biscuits spread before him on the paper sack he'd ripped open for a place mat. So far, he appeared to have touched none of it. Glancing up at her, he asked, "Where you headed?"

"Down to the coffee shop for a bite."

"Care to join me instead?"

"Got enough for two?"

"More than," Emmett said. "No appetite. Thought I would when I went down to the drive-through. Must be the heat."

"I know." She sat across the table from him. "Lowering the thermostat does nothing."

"I already complained. Front desk says the Navajo Nation Inn offers either warm or cool air. Not both. The chiller was shut down during last week's rainy spell, and the boiler re-fired. Maybe tomorrow the air-conditioning'll be brought back on line. Maybe not." He winked. "Between us, I admire this native indifference to mechanical efficiency. The resistance of our forefathers lives on."

She examined his tired eyes. Two nights with virtually no sleep, but he only talked this way when his spirits were low. "How're you doing, Em?"

His gaze shifted through the open door to Window Rock

Ridge a half mile beyond. The red and yellow tones of the sandstone were darkening with the going of the sun. "I've just been sitting here, trying to figure out how close we are to a wrap." He didn't go on.

"And . . . ?" she prodded.

"Well, if our *Dine* associates nab Ivan Jumper in the next couple days, as they fully expect to do—I suppose a lot closer than we were yesterday." But he didn't look persuaded.

The tribal department was pulling out all the stops on the manhunt, canceling days off and leaves, enlisting the help of the sheriff's offices with overlapping jurisdiction and the Civil Air Patrol. Tallsalt had been heartened by what Jumper's arrest would mean, ignoring his own ambivalence the previous day over the possibility locals were helping the Sonoran drug lords ship loads through the Big Rez. Ivan Jumper and his gang, the Vipers, fit that profile. Ivan especially. It seemed that the modern offspring of bootleggers seldom followed the family trade. They opted instead to deal drugs—even though, according to Tallsalt, Clydine had been clearing $10,000 or more a month before Bert Knoki shut her down. Greater profits were to be had from manufacturing speed in crude labs. Of which the Vipers were also suspected. But if the gang was doing that, it was competing with its alleged Sonoran partners, who could manufacture better-quality methamphetamine at lower cost in Mexico.

Anna chipped away at the silence that kept building between them. "If we buy Tallsalt's drug-connection theory, we've still got a problem with those months-old airplane tracks. And nothing else to prove some Sonorans swooped down out of the sky last Saturday night and murdered the Knokis."

"How about that?" Emmett offered her some chicken.

She took a leg, contemplated it, then took a bite. Cold. How long had he been at this table, reflecting? At two this afternoon, he'd left her off at her room to change the dressing on her bite wound and rest, while he drove back to the

Navajo police complex, hoping to use Tallsalt's office to tie together some loose ends. "You get a chance to check the property sheet on Clydine's oldest son?" she asked.

"Yeah. Jail clerk logged in her drop-off of sundries at a quarter to eleven on Saturday evening."

Close enough to Aurelia Knoki's approximate time of death. So Clydine had indeed known that she had an alibi. But Tallsalt hadn't wanted her arrested along with her son's fellow gangbangers after this morning's melee. She was either bait, encouraging Ivan's return to the shanty for money, or she'd eventually lead the Navajo cops to his hiding place. Anna had a sudden question. "What's the older Jumper in jail for?"

"His third driving under the influence. Yabeny insists he's not a player. And he started serving his six-month sentence in January, so whatever Ivan did it was without his big brother's help. But he and the Vipers did *something*. Otherwise they never would've gone down so hard this morning."

"So what do we do tomorrow?" she asked.

He stuck a plastic fork into a half-pint of coleslaw and slid it across the table to her. "Not sure."

"What do you mean?"

"Well, the bangers are locked up in Tohatchi, awaiting their detainment hearing . . ." The tribal juvenile detention facility on the east side of the Chuskas. "Their court-appointed attorney isn't going to let us talk to them. Ivan Jumper's hunkered down in the mountains somewhere and won't move till he gets hungry. I'm just not sure."

"You don't have *any* ideas?"

"Didn't say that." He left his chair, went to the sink and splashed his face with cold water. There was a stripe of purple across his upper back. A bruise left by one of the timbers from the hogan roof that had collapsed on top of him. Tallsalt had told her. Emmett had said nothing about his capture of the thirteen-year-old sniper. He dried his face on a hand towel, then returned to the table with a slightly more even-tempered look. "There are two ways to go while we wait to follow up on what went down today . . ." She sensed that he was widening his net. For some reason, the capture of Ivan Jumper wouldn't be the tidy and complete solution he desired. "Dr. Hennepin cut the telemetry gear out of the Gila that bit you." Seeing Anna's puzzled look, he asked, "He tell you about this?"

"No."

"That particular lizard was a research specimen. Outfitted with a radio device for tracking it in the wild. Well, I phoned the doctor this afternoon and he advised me the device was made by Telonics Corporation in Mesa. They traced the serial number to one of three purchased by the Bureau of Land Management. One of their wildlife biologists doing a study on Gilas in southwest Utah."

"That's where mine came from?"

"Probably." It was becoming obvious that Emmett was struggling for a new overview. Otherwise he wouldn't spend time on any of this.

"Okay," she said, "we go to Utah in the morning."

"Not both of us. That'd be a waste of manpower. Besides, planting that Gila under the Knokis' mobile home may wind up being unrelated to the homicides. Not that we shouldn't investigate it as an assault on you—that's the biggest reason I'm willing to give two days to it."

"Hank Whitesheep?"

Emmett gave a vague shake of his head. "I interviewed him last night. Didn't get the feeling he did it. Even a stupid bird won't shit in his own nest, so I had him kicked loose this morning."

Anna idly plucked the fork out of the coleslaw. "You want me to go to Utah?"

"It's hard country."

"I grew up in hard country."

"I know, Anna. Please don't read gender into every goddamn thing I say."

"I didn't *have* to read anything. It was crystal-clear what you meant." The blood had risen in her face, and she took a breath to calm down. "You want me to drag Summerfield along?"

"Worse yet." He heaved himself out of the chair and shut the door, then sank onto a corner of his bed. He looked perplexed. It was disturbing to see him this way. "And don't read anything into what I'm about to say . . ." For a moment, she was afraid he was on the verge of picking up their awkward and humiliating exchange following her nightmare. But then he continued quietly, "I'm giving more credence to what you said out at Sonsela Buttes yesterday."

"What was that?"

"You asked me if I was pissed off at John Tallsalt."

"Are you?"

"Enough to take him on sooner than I wanted."

"What changed your mind?"

"When we went back to the Knokis' trailer last evening, the mail was missing from the kitchen. Turns out John had been there before we arrived. He took it."

"How do you know that?" Anna asked.

"He admitted it. I saw him after I left you at the hospital last night. Claimed he gathered up the Knokis' mail as executor to their will and was safekeeping it in his office."

"So?"

"Remember the letter with the University Park address? The one addressing Bert as *Hosteen* Knoki?"

"Box 444."

He smiled at her having remembered the number. "Right. Well, I didn't get it back with the rest."

Anna had sensed from her first meeting with Tallsalt that the lieutenant was pursuing his own agenda in regards to this case. Now Emmett was suspicious enough of the same thing to either send her or go himself to the Phoenix neighborhood of University Park and find out who had rented that box. If that person were somehow tied to this, however remotely, Emmett and she would have their answer. And grounds for leaning on Tallsalt.

"You go to Utah," she said, "and I'll go to Phoenix. I'll take Summerfield along if it makes you feel any better. That way I'll have an immediate back if I have to do a little light undercover." She finally took a mouthful of slaw. Her three-hour nap had left her with an appetite, and the woolly-headed funk from the venom had finally worn off.

Emmett lay back across the bed and covered his eyes with his hands. "Dang it," he said morosely.

"Dang what?"

"Johnny saved a baby's life out there this morning. Scooped the little guy up with bullets flying all around both of them. I've seen cops given the medal of valor for far less."

"Can you put him in for it?"

"Tried. He trashed the justification I wrote. Took it right out of the chief's in-basket and shredded it."

Anna didn't have to ask what bothered Emmett about this. And it was one more reason to go to Phoenix, she concluded. A man with a wall full of plaques doesn't turn down a commendation for valor—unless he suddenly didn't want to draw attention to himself. "Flip a coin for who goes where?" she asked.

"No," he replied, pulling his hands away from his eyes to look at her. "Truth is—and you always seem to know what the truth is—I'd appreciate it if you'd buzz down to Phoenix tomorrow in my car. If he ever finds out, I'll make sure John knows it was my idea."

"That doesn't matter."

"It does to me." Emmett sat up again. "Take Summerfield. He can use the bright lights and I can use his four-by-four. Is he getting the windshield fixed?"

"Yes—this afternoon in Gallup. And the rear hatch window. The bullet went all the way through."

"Then we'll all regroup here in Window Rock Friday and hopefully have Ivan Jumper to interrogate by then." Emmett dug his keys out of his trouser pocket and detached two from the ring for her. "Your bean counters have been talking to my bean counters."

"Who says?"

"My super. Just got off the phone with him. In light of the anticipated budget crisis in Congress, we're to keep the expenses down for Uncle Sam. Otherwise my position will be the first to go in the next cut. Stay at my apartment. But I expect the toilet seat to be up when I get home." She was starting to protest when he interjected, "Just advise Summerfield."

UPPER LOWE CANYON was thirty miles of jeep trail north of St. George, Utah, not counting the four hundred miles of highway Emmett had put behind him since leaving Window Rock at six o'clock that morning. *All the goddamned driving for this job is giving me saddle sores.* One-hundred-and-eighty-million-year-old red sandstone cliffs were capped by black lava that had gurgled and hissed onto the canyon floor only a few thousand years ago. Periodically, he came upon white sandstone formations that looked as if they'd been wrapped together like turbans. Ancient sand dunes frozen for eternity. Two years ago, he'd monitored a physical geology course at Arizona State University simply because he'd tired of passing through this stark country in ignorance of how it'd formed. Yet, something within him remained at odds with science. He hoped it might one day come full circle and validate the creation stories of the tribes, an earth shaped by the tussling and conniving of primordial beings.

He was beginning to wonder if he had enough daylight left to locate the wildlife biologist's camp. He'd gotten directions at the regional BLM office in St. George, but what had measured out as two inches on the resource area map was turning into an endless, serpentine trek up the sun-baked canyon. He didn't trust the air conditioner not to overheat the Suburban's engine at low speed, so he made do by letting down the windows.

The canyon floor was alive with small lizards. There seemed to be one on every outcrop, doing push-ups to cool down. At least that was the folklore. Was this how it began for someone who ultimately devoted his life to studying a single species? Simple curiosity that somehow got out of hand? Only obsession could induce a human being to spend from April to October alone in this arid wilderness. With only a radio as a link to the outside world. "Stepanek checks in at one each afternoon," the BLM ranger at the office had told him. "I'll advise Nick you're on the way up."

Nick Stepanek had to be a misanthrope.

But then Emmett caught himself in a Comanche prejudice. Only persons who had something to hide failed to live communally.

The track wound through contorted masses of lava and over dunes. After nine hours behind the wheel, Emmett's bruised back was killing him. But he hadn't had to shoot the young sniper. Compensation enough for the pain.

Anna.

He knew that he'd confused her yesterday afternoon by spinning the investigation off into these geographically opposed directions. But now that he'd had most of a day to mull the issue over, he realized what he should have told her—the extreme defensive behavior of Ivan Jumper's gang could be explained by some other crime they'd been involved in, not necessarily the Knokis' murders. If that is all the future interrogations of the Vipers yielded, he and Anna would be back to square one. He didn't want to be caught that flat-footed.

At last, he glimpsed a tiny square of white canvas against the red sandstone.

The biologist's camp was tucked up against the south wall of the canyon for some relief from the midday sun. An even less distinct jeep trail branched off the first and meandered through the lava toward the tent. Emmett would have lost the route several times but for the ruts a wide-tired vehicle had left in the sand. It was not parked anywhere near the tent.

Still, Emmett braked a hundred feet below the camp, shut off the motor and stepped out. "Hello, the tent!"

His shout roused no one. But the echoes off the cliff set some finches to flight. They'd been foraging in the wildrose hedge that bordered the campsite on three sides. This flat spot in the dunes had probably been a corral in Mormon pioneer days. The tent flaps were drawn back, and through the screen he could see that the single cot was unoccupied. The interior of the tent looked breathlessly hot.

Stretching his back, he told himself that he admired Stepanek's fortitude.

A butane cookstove was set up on one end of a collapsible aluminum table, a lantern on the other. The residue of a meal was soaking in a skillet. Under the table were a dozen plastic jerry cans, filled with water. A dry camp. How far did Stepanek have to go to replenish?

Emmett was scanning the bases of the cliffs for willows, the surest sign of water in this country, when he spied a white and brown Ford Bronco wending down the main track from the upper reaches of the canyon. On its door was the triangular emblem of the U.S. Bureau of Land Management. Along with the Forest Service, the BLM was the chief custodian of the federal government's vast public holdings in the West. Nearly all of them pre-treaty Indian lands. This had been Southern Paiute country, a people with a genius for scratching a living out of apparent nothingness.

Five minutes later, a tall and willowy woman in her late twenties stepped from the Bronco. Her sun-bleached hair might once have been auburn, and there was a spray of freckles across her high cheekbones. "I'm Nicole Stepanek." A firm shake, during which she flashed a quick grin, her teeth white against her deeply tanned face. A long moment passed before she let go of his hand, and then her fingers slid ticklishly across his palm.

"Emmett Parker, Bureau of Indian Affairs."

Her hazel eyes registered surprise. "Not the FBI?"

"No, though I'm teamed up with an FBI agent right now for a homicide investigation on the Navajo Nation."

"You mean you're not after whoever's bagging my

research area?" She removed a pair of binoculars from around her neck and set them on the table.

"Who said—?"

"The ranger radioed me that an investigator out of Phoenix was coming up, and that he had some leads on the bagger."

"The bagger," Emmett repeated. His mouth was dry. "May I have a drink of water?"

"Of course." She went to an ice chest in the shade of the tent. There was no ice in it, but she knelt to take out a one-gallon milk jug filled with water. The denim of her hiking shorts spread tightly over her shapely buttocks. He glanced away before she turned back toward him. "Sorry for not meeting you here," she said, offering him the jug with her right hand, "but I've been out reassessing the damage. Just to make sure one of my Gilas didn't voluntarily vacate his burrow."

The water was lukewarm but sweet. "What damage?"

"Three years' work," she explained, her eyes welling up. He realized that she'd been holding back tears of infuriation. "Whoever he is, he damn near depopulated the canyon. I can't find four of my study specimens, though he probably poached more than that out of the whole area. All males."

"Any idea who'd do this?"

She was exceptionally pretty, in a sun- and wind-frazzled sort of way. She smelled of woodsmoke, and he noticed a gray wisp rising from the ashes in a ring of stones. A fire to fend off the loneliness of the dark? "No, I don't know who," she said, glancing downward and to the right. She was right-handed. Emmett frowned—but what reason would she have to be evasive about any of this? "He hit when I was back home in Ogden for the winter." Her voice cracked a little. "It's just that he *taunted* me. That's what really gets my goat." Almost a tone of betrayal.

"How?"

She slipped the jug from his grasp, poured some water into her cupped hand and wetted the back of her neck. "I'd have to show you."

"Within walking distance?"

"Not this late in the day. But I'm low on gas. All the tearing around I've been doing to inventory what's left."

"We'll take mine."

They drove up the canyon for six miles, then she directed Emmett off into a side drainage. A Mars-scape with reddish soil and random boulders sweeping up to eroded palisades. Along the way, he'd told her about the Knokis, but she appeared not to have been listening.

Now, she suddenly asked, "What's that smell?"

Emmett had to think: He'd grown accustomed to it. "Oh, after my partner was bitten, she got sick."

For the first time since leaving camp, Stepanek seemed to put aside her agitation long enough to pay attention. "The poor woman. How'd it happen?"

Emmett told her. Unfortunately, that included confessing that he'd had to shoot the Gila monster.

Stepanek sat in steely-eyed silence for a minute, then said, "She should have played dead. The Gila would've backed off."

Emmett wanted to add he'd told Turnipseed just that, but it would have felt too much like selling out Anna.

Unexpectedly, Stepanek took hold of his arm. "I'm sorry. That was an idiotic thing to say. How was she to know what a Gila will do?" She let go, but Emmett was struck by how unselfconsciously she'd touched him. And he recalled how Anna had shrunk from his kiss.

"So what led you to me?" the young woman asked.

"The radio telemetry gear in your specimen. I traced the purchaser through Telonics Corporation."

"Were any of this male's claws clipped?"

"Yes."

"Do you remember which ones?"

"Second digit, left front paw. Fourth digit, right front."

"Twenty-four . . . specimen twenty-four . . ." Then, with her eyes filling again, she said, *"Buckley."*

"Who?"

"Oh, I called number twenty-four Buckley. You know, the conservative commentator? He flicked his tongue just like William F. Buckley." She squeezed her chapped lips together. "I'm not being much help, am I? I mean, we're talking about the murders of some people here, aren't we?" She searched her T-shirt pocket, presumably for some Kleenex.

"Glove box," Emmett suggested.

She found a packet. Plus Summerfield's German edition of Zolbrod's *Dine bahane*. "Yours?" she asked.

"No, I borrowed this car from an FBI agent out of Gallup. You know the myths?"

"Almost by heart." She snuffled into a fluffy wad. "It's not Navajo, you know."

"What isn't?"

"To abuse a Gila. The *Dine* revere Gila Monster as the original diviner of illnesses. He did it with his trembling forepaw. That's why Hand Tremblers, people with partial epileptic seizures, are believed to have diagnostic gifts. I just can't see one of the People doing this," she said adamantly.

Perhaps, Emmett thought. But the Vipers weren't very Navajo, and thus far the gangbangers were the likeliest candidates for having planted Stepanek's specimen under the trailer. But an enormous gulf lay between his suspicion and proving even the gang's marginal complicity in the murders.

"Any of the other missing Gilas outfitted with transmitters we might be able to track with direction-finding gear?"

"No, the other two units went in females. Besides, the range is no more than a quarter-mile. Park here."

The sun had dipped behind the Bull Valley Mountains, making their trek up an arroyo cooler. Crickets set the cadence, and Stepanek fell into it, her long legs eating up the rising ground with an easy gait. "You're Indian, aren't you?" she inquired.

"So Mama tells me." He liked the way her hair flowed like liquid copper. The skin of her neck was milky white from not being exposed to the sun.

"What tribe?"

"Comanche."

"West Texas?"

"Used to be my band's heartland. Got moved last century onto a reservation in Oklahoma."

"What brought you out to Arizona?"

Bittersweet flight from his second wife. In the midst of their brutal divorce, he'd suddenly started to fall in love with her again. But he told Nicole, "The job."

"Do you like it?"

"Most of the time."

She led him out of the arroyo and across a lava field. Here the wildflowers were already beginning to wilt, and in the windless hollows the valedictory sweetness of spring lingered. He could sense that Stepanek was taking pleasure from his company, although she didn't press the conversation. She knew full well that he was hungrily watching her. Yet, as they clambered up the crevices and around the boulders, his mind wasn't entirely on Nicole Stepanek. This was the kind of volcanic country from which Anna's ancestor, Captain Jack, had frustrated the U.S. Army for five months. *Why the devil do I remember this now?* "Nicole . . . ?"

Slowly, she turned at the top of a low ridge, smiling, her eyes clear.

"Did your law enforcement ranger see anything over the winter that might be related to the baggings?"

"No. He went through all of his patrol logs for me."

"Did he recall any Navajo at all coming up the canyon?"

Her smile vanished. "I didn't ask. But quite a few live in St. George. And there's some intermarriage with the Shivwits Paiute in the area."

Emmett nodded, and she moved on.

The slope turned to ankle-grabbing sand again. Halfway up it to the cliffs, she squatted at the base of a chest-high ledge of rhyolite and peered into the foot-wide opening of a burrow. "Buckley's," she announced. The full impact of the loss returned to her voice.

Standing behind her, Emmett gave her neck a gentle

squeeze. "I'm real sorry, Nicole. Sorry all your hard work's been spoiled. It's not fair."

She turned her head and briefly rested her cheek against the back of his hand. "Thanks, Emmett." Then she rose, and he reluctantly let go of her. "Let me show you what this poor confused soul keeps doing," she said.

Emmett followed her down the length of the ledge. "More than one site?"

"All of them. The same design." She halted and pointed. The daylight was failing, but he could make out the petroglyph that had been meticulously pecked into the desert varnish, a patina of iron and manganese, on the rhyolite. A Gila with moth wings and antennae. Instantly, his mouth went dry again.

"Emmett . . . ?"

"Yes," he said, although his eyes never left the glyph.

"Can you stay for dinner?"

chapter 11

IT WAS A TANTALIZING URGE. TO BE INTIMATE WITH AN-
other human being—but at a safe distance. To get inside
Emmett Parker with none of the risks that had come so close
to the surface two days ago in her motel room. To run the
fingers of her mind over all the things that had made him the
way he was.

But Anna resisted the impulse to pry.

She was sprawling in Emmett's easy chair with one leg
hooked over an armrest. The sunset streamed in through the
sliding glass door to the balcony. She'd opened the windows
to clear the stuffiness out of the apartment. The breeze was
hot, but she preferred it to air-conditioning. The pool in the
courtyard below was ringed with dwarf citrus trees, and the
scent of tangerine blossoms was blending with that of car
fumes off nearby Interstate 10.

Driving into Phoenix two hours ago, she and Summerfield
had agreed that he'd go on alone to the University Park post
office to learn from the postmaster the name of the renter of
Box 444. Anna would hold back, not showing her face anywhere near the postal branch so she could follow up on the
physical address.

A prudent plan, she believed, but it gave her nothing to
do until Summerfield returned.

Emmett's apartment so resembled her own condo in Las
Vegas it seemed as if the same unimaginative interior deco-
rator was to blame. Western-Sterile Design Studio. Bare

walls, nondescript furniture and the sense that the place was not fully lived in. Just a utilitarian flop for when the job finally let go of him for a few hours.

Pushing herself up out of the chair, she strolled into the bathroom. A shower would be nice after the long drive from Window Rock. Her hair and clothes stank of Summerfield's brown-papered cigarettes. She removed the bandage on her wrist, revealing the bracelet of little scabs left by the Gila's teeth. But she was running the taps when she decided not to bathe. Summerfield would be back any second. She smiled to herself as she shut off the water, struck by a thought that almost made her laugh out loud. Emmett had proposed it and she'd gone along without batting an eye: her spending the night alone in this apartment with a man who was almost a complete stranger to her. Obviously, they'd both come to the conclusion sometime over the past week that Summerfield posed no threat.

But by suggesting this arrangement, was Emmett also saying he had no further grounds for jealousy?

She opened the medicine cabinet door, and watched her troubled reflection glide out of view with the mirror.

A reasonable woman, she saw the wisdom in safe sex. Yet, another side of her—the one that had been encapsulated by the sexual terrors of her childhood and was only now trying to break out—distrusted this drugstore premeditation, this latex-armed lying in wait for the sudden moment. Did that mean that, deep down, she still wanted to trust in passion?

She closed her eyes in thanks: no condoms.

But most of the contents of the cabinet were almost equally disturbing to her—for a completely different reason. Tums Extra Strength. Pepcid. Tagamet. Pepto-Bismol. The job was attacking him through his stomach. *The way to a man's heart is through his stomach.*

She shut the cabinet door.

She'd glimpsed something that Emmett no doubt didn't want revealed. The offense had been committed. In slight degree. But committed, nevertheless. And so it seemed slightly less unconscionable to go on to his bedroom closet. She suspected he'd keep his most personal memorabilia here.

Her hunch proved right.

There was a shoe box filled with photographs and keepsakes on the hat shelf. She carried the box to his bed, stretched out on the coverlet and began ransacking his past. A tassel off a mortarboard. Oklahoma State graduation? Her fascination with the minutiae of his life was demeaning. Schoolgirlish. She knew that, but then chuckled over the image of a fat Comanche baby grinning toothlessly at some long-ago camera. Emmett, of course. The same grumpiness around the eyes.

However, the next photo sobered her: Emmett at age nine or ten, standing on the steps of an institution beside a skinnier and younger version of himself, the boys' hair slicked back for that ritual of heartache instantly recognizable to anyone who'd lived in Indian Country anytime over the past century and a quarter. *Not our children. Take all but our children.* Emmett and his brother were being left off at boarding school. The promising brother, the law student, who later shot himself. Only now—as she saw his arm in a stiff but protective clasp around Malcolm Parker's shoulders—did she have a full idea of what the suicide had done to Emmett.

At the very back of the box was a manila envelope.

She opened it. Wedding portraits. They appeared to be in chronological order. His first and longest-lasting marriage was to a Comanche girl who'd attended the female wing of his Catholic boarding school. He'd looked like he was nineteen on this wedding day, despite the somber black tux. The next was to a Plains Apache math professor at OSU. And finally a social worker, tribe unknown. The three women were striking-looking, beautiful even. Anna realized that her own damaged self-image never favored her in comparisons, but she asked herself if she looked anything like the three. *Is he simply drawn to a type? Does he even care who the hell I am?*

A knock at the front door made her jump.

She stuffed the shoe box back onto its shelf, and let Summerfield in. Sweat darkened his white shirt. "Grand weather," he groused, sloughing off his blazer onto the couch. He looked longingly toward the refrigerator. "Think Parker would mind if I raid his fridge for something cool?"

"Let me. How'd it go?"

"All right." He tumbled into the chair. "The box is rented to a Terry W. Rowe."

She brought him a Diet Coke. "Male or female?"

"*Definitely* male." Summerfield popped the lid and drank gratefully. "Sorry it took so long, but I swung by our Phoenix office to run his name through NCIC. Is the cooler on, by chance?"

"No, I'll get the air going." She started shutting windows. "You get a physical address?"

"Yes."

"And any return from NCIC?"

Summerfield, trying to swallow a mouthful of Coke without it effervescing up his nose, jabbed his finger at his blazer on the sofa. Anna slipped the three-page facsimile of a National Crime Information Center rap sheet from the inner pocket. It was damp from Summerfield's perspiration.

Terry Wade Rowe was a thirty-six-year-old white male born in Huntington, West Virginia.

Anna paused.

Bert Knoki had been addressed on the envelope as "*Hosteen* C. Knoki," a Navajo title of respect. Not likely used by a white West Virginian with an extensive criminal record. And the fluid handwriting had struck her as being feminine. Summerfield's comment about Rowe's being "definitely" male was explained on the first page: two forcible rape convictions, one in Kentucky and another in Illinois. His listed occupation was radio and microwave repair—learned while incarcerated? But as Rowe drifted west between prison stints, his focus had shifted from sexual violence to drugs. Not counting a spousal battery arrest in Pueblo, Colorado, which may have been a statutory euphemism for another rape. Possession of controlled substances evolved into sales, and sales into transportation. A shipment out of Hermosillo. *Sonora*. That cost him five years in the Federal Correctional Institution at Phoenix, for which he was still on parole.

She felt Summerfield's eyes on her.

Emmett's parting words over breakfast this morning had been a warning not to tell the Gallup agent too much. Only that Anna and he were to chase down a lead arising from the Knokis' mail. No mention of Tallsalt's involvement in this, although Anna was left wondering if the lieutenant's seemingly spurious drug theory might have some merit. It now appeared Bert Knoki had been corresponding with a known narcotics transshipper. *Why?*

Summerfield gave her a probing glance. "What're you thinking, friend?"

It was obvious: He knew the reason behind this trip went beyond a mildly suspicious letter. On the drive down he'd asked—almost hopefully—if Parker had caught a whiff of corruption in the loose ends of Bert Knoki's life. When Anna muttered she didn't think so, Summerfield's disappointment was visible. And his edginess increased. But now, since discovering the identity of the renter of Box 444, he seemed calmer.

"I'm thinking we should grab a bite now," Anna said. "It could turn into a long night. You like Tex-Mex?" Emmett had told her of a place around the corner.

But Summerfield made a face. "Let's go somewhere nice. My treat."

His tone was unmistakably celebratory.

THE UNIVERSITY PARK DISTRICT in central Phoenix was a tawdry neighborhood of strip malls, flophouse motels and cocktail lounges. Few of the dwellings looked well-maintained enough to be occupied by their owners. The bungalows were fifty years beyond whatever southwestern charm they once may have had, and even the newer apartment complexes were run-down and sprayed with gang graffiti.

For Anna, the ride evoked high school memories of going to Reno on summer nights, a carload of Modoc, Klamath and Paiute kids, hungry for lights and noise after the long winter isolation on the ranchería. For food not made with surplus government cheese.

Summerfield leaned back as he drove stop-and-go with the heavy traffic, his right hand draped over the steering wheel and a cigarette smoldering between his fingers. Dinner had found him in a garrulous mood once again, recalling his eleven years with Foreign Counterintelligence in Washington, D.C. Now he seemed to be basking in the afterglow of those memories, as he took no notice of a chesty young prostitute who rose from a bus stop bench to catch his eye. "Where do you want to be assigned next, Anna?" he asked pleasantly.

"I don't know."

"You've given it no thought?"

Not since she'd been injured in January. Projecting herself into the future seemed absurd, like remodeling the house on the eve of a hurricane. "Vegas is all right." But then she amended, "For the time being."

Apparently fooled by Anna's short hair into believing two men occupied the Dodge, the hooker finally realized her mistake and blew her a sarcastic kiss.

"How about you, Reed?"

"Oh, back to Washington, of course."

"Foreign Counterintelligence again?"

Summerfield nodded. "Screw the dawn of peace," he said, exhaling smoke through his nose. "Can't last for long. Another year or two, the politicos will have a clearer idea who our adversaries are. And then they'll loose the hounds like me on embassy row again."

Anna had wearied of counterintelligence talk over dinner. She wondered where Emmett was tonight. He'd mentioned staying in St. George, Utah, but hadn't named the motel he used there. It would have been reassuring to discuss Bert Knoki's link to Rowe with him—before venturing into central Phoenix with Summerfield. She'd come down here expecting to close out a minor lead. Not to verify what Tallsalt had told them from the beginning: that drug lords were behind the homicides. But how? Had Knoki double-crossed the Sonorans? If that was the case and Tallsalt knew, wouldn't he keep that to himself? His department's reputation was on the line. His too.

Anna glanced up just as the sign to the cross street slipped past. "I'm sorry, Reed—that was Fillmore."

"No problem." He made the next right turn. "First, we'll drive right by the address." He switched off the dashboard lights so both of their faces were in darkness. "I won't slow down, so give it a thorough looking over."

"Okay," she said quietly. He was far more at ease than he'd been tripping through the brush near Sonsela Buttes. "Left here to hit the ninety-two-hundred block."

"Got you."

Few porch lights were on. Which made no sense in a high-crime neighborhood until she realized that one of those frequent crimes might be drive-by shootings. Still, it was hard to pick out house numbers. Fortunately, a street lamp stood in front of the residence Terry Wade Rowe had listed with the post office. Two date palms threw shaggy shadows across the lawn, which seemed long dead except for a few green tufts resurrected by the spring rains. The windows were darkened, and the driveway empty of vehicles.

"Doesn't look promising," Anna said when they reached the end of the street.

"Not to worry." Summerfield made a U-turn and started back for the house. "Gives me a chance to inspect the premises."

She shook her head. *Why does it always get down to this with a male partner?* "That wasn't the deal, Reed."

"Pardon?"

"You covered the post office. I'd do the physical address."

Summerfield parked several houses down the street from Rowe's place. He sat a moment, staring at it, before shutting off the engine. "True. But our boy's apparently out for the evening. I see no reason why we both can't take a gander."

"Because if he's there, I can come up with a story for being in the neighborhood. If he saw you anywhere near the post office—you can't."

Summerfield surrendered to her logic with a sigh. She took Emmett's flashlight from the glove box and crammed it into her purse, which was already bulging from her 9mm pistol. "I'll give you two flashes if I need help."

"Please do," Summerfield said coolly. A different man from the one who'd crouched pasty-faced in front of the Knokis' mobile home. Why was he so eager to find out how Rowe had fit into Bert Knoki's life?

Anna stepped out into the smoggy evening warmth.

"Leave the door open, if you will," Summerfield said as she let the last of the air-conditioned coolness gush away.

She crossed the street and started down the sidewalk. The houses on either side of Rowe's were lit. Over the past few minutes, she'd decided that her conservative pantsuit and the fact that she was braving a neighborhood like this at night could be explained only one way. To establish her cover before she reached Rowe's, she strode up his nearest neighbor's cement path and knocked on the screen door. A breathy grunt came from somewhere inside. It was followed by the appearance of a middle-aged man in a sleeveless T-shirt. He had a paunch so massive it'd begun to split into two distinct halves. Anna faked a charitable smile. "Good evening, sir, I wonder if you've given any thought to letting Jesus into your life?"

He replied with an utter lack of expression, "I wonder if you've given any thought to gettin' the fuck off my front porch?"

Pivoting, Anna started back down the path.

The neighbor's voice chased after her: "You lousy Jehovah Witnesses wanna do some good—get after those broads peddlin' their asses down on Jefferson Street and quit pesterin' decent people!"

Her steps shortened as she neared Rowe's front door. A hefty padlock barred entry. There was a notice beside it. The glow from the street lamp wasn't enough, and she pulled the flashlight from her purse to read: *Closed to Occupancy for One Year by Authority of the Crack House Abatement Ordinance.* A date had been stamped inside the city seal. April 12 of that year. If Rowe had been caught running a crack cocaine house, he was certainly back in federal detention. There was often a lag in state reporting to NCIC, but she couldn't believe that it could exceed six weeks.

She shone the light through the curtainless window beside the door. The living room was barren. The lead was withering before her eyes. Rowe might well have been back in the joint by mid-April. Five weeks before Bert and Aurelia Knoki were murdered.

One constructive thing remained to be done: contact his probation officer tomorrow and arrange an interrogation at the prison.

Yet, she paused as she turned back for the car and Summerfield, glancing at the neighboring house, a pueblo-style box with ersatz roof timbers jutting from the plaster. Anna was tempted not to bother. It was almost 9:30. But, promising herself that this would be the last chore of the day, she cut across the yard to the front door. At first, her knock was answered by a minuscule parting of the velour curtains. Then the porch light came on, followed by the clack of a deadbolt being thrown back. The door opened as far as a security chain allowed, and the wizened face of an old white woman squeezed into the narrow space. Her hair was the color of cotton candy, and her denuded eyebrows had been repainted into rusty-looking arches that went too far up her forehead. "Yes?"

Anna had had enough of being a Witness. "Excuse me, can you tell me where Terry went?"

"You know Terry?"

"Yes."

"One moment, sweetie . . ." The old woman reshut the door to unlatch the chain, then invited Anna inside. Her initial trepidation seemed replaced by a craving for company. "So you know Terry?"

"Not real well."

The old woman's hands flew to her rouged lips. "You're Lolly's sister, I bet."

Anna debated the consequences of lying. If the house had a swamp cooler, it wasn't on, and the sultry atmosphere of tobacco smoke and scotch breath made her want to back out of the living room. The windowsills were lined with strings of multicolored Christmas lights, giving the room a garish carnival atmosphere. At last Anna asked, "How'd you know we're sisters?"

"Saw the resemblance right off. You Indian girls have such nice cheekbones and big dusky eyes. Sit down, sweetie. I'm Gladys Ogilvie. And you're?"

"Annie." As much as she detested this corruption of her name, it seemed to fit the moment.

"Care for a scotch sour?"

"No thanks." Anna had to move some movie magazines off the sofa and onto the floor to find a place other than the rocking chair. So Rowe's wife or girlfriend was Indian. But how to ask which tribe, now that she'd let herself be cast as the woman's sister? "Did you ever live on a reservation?"

"Oh no." Sitting, Gladys gestured with her drink at a huge frame on the wall. Pressed flat behind the dusty pane of glass was a black serving uniform and white apron. "I was a Harvey girl at the Holbrook station. You know, one of the Harvey restaurants for Santa Fe passengers. They were wonderful. Each one had—" She cut herself off and frowned with vague suspicion. "My goodness, Annie—didn't Lolly tell you Terry and her moved this March?"

Anna let some unease creep into her voice. "No. See, we had a falling-out a while back, and I figured as long as I was in town . . ."

"Sisters," Gladys said with a matronly smile.

"Where'd they go?"

"I don't know. It was so sudden."

"Trouble with the rent?"

"No, with the prowler. He really shook up Lolly with his shenanigans." Gladys took a quaff. "How I miss them. Terry had his nasty temper, sure, but I'll take that any day of the week over what the coloreds who moved in after were up to . . ." She lowered her voice. "They were selling dope right out the front door."

"Really. How quickly did my sister and Terry move out?"

"Overnight."

"You didn't hear them load up?"

"Sweetie, they left most everything." The old woman's lips thinned in indignation over her false teeth. "Which the coloreds tore up in no time. They set the couch on fire, and it laid in the front yard for a week."

"Who was this prowler?"

Gladys hiked her shoulders, slopping some of her drink onto her housecoat.

"What kind of shenanigans was the prowler pulling?" Anna persisted.

"You want to see?"

"Please."

"Let me get my gun." Gladys went into the bedroom, returning a minute later with an ancient-looking revolver. It had an eight-inch barrel. She explained, "It's registered, and I don't step outside the door without it no more. Even to the market. Come on." Passing through the kitchen, she told Anna to grab the flashlight off the sink counter. Turnipseed decided not to reveal that she'd come supplied with her own. "Open the back door for me there, sweetie."

Gladys's rear yard was nothing more than an expanse of hard-packed Salt River silt enclosed by a wooden fence. Several sections had been knocked to the ground. "Big windstorm did this," the old woman said as they passed through one of these gaps and approached the back of Rowe's former house. "I don't mind the heat, but the wind gets to me." Then she announced, "Here it is."

"Where?" Anna saw nothing of note.

"Put the light on the back wall, sweetie."

She shone the beam that way, and a spray-painted figure as red as blood leaped out at her. The winged Gila monster she'd seen on Garwin Descheenie's neck. Her heart caught in her throat. "Did Lolly say what this means?"

"No," Gladys replied. "Terry and her just moved."

chapter 12

EMMETT HAD JUST PULLED OUT OF PAGE, ARIZONA, AND reentered the Navajo Nation by its northwestern corner when the distant calls started coming over the tribal police band through a background of static: "Report . . . man with a gun . . . vicinity of Shonto . . . Post . . . any unit in the vicinity . . . respond . . . ?" Waiting for a patrol officer to answer, Emmett took his foot off the accelerator and coasted down U.S. 89, the quickest route back to Window Rock. The transmissions began coming in clearer. "Kayenta, to any unit available to handle a man-with-a-gun call . . ."

The town of Kayenta with its police subagency was about 120 miles east of Page, and Emmett estimated the trading post settlement of Shonto to lie thirty miles this side of it. He snatched the microphone out of its dashboard clip. "Kayenta, this is BIA Unit Seventeen. Where's the Tuba City cruiser?"

"Out of position down in Gray Mountain. And my unit's on a prisoner transfer to Window Rock. Can you handle?"

"I'll roll," he said, making a U-turn, "but be advised it's from Page."

"Copy." Then the Kayenta dispatcher broadcast with a tone of faint hope, "Any unit in position to back BIA Seventeen?"

Silence over the airwaves.

Emmett took the cutoff to State Route 98. Within ninety seconds, he was heading Summerfield's Suburban into the rising sun at 105 miles an hour. He snapped the visor down on the eye-watering blaze and tried to stay focused on the narrow, pothole-studded road. He'd left Page planning to grab his first cup of coffee of the day in Tuba City. Now that was impossible until the Navajo police managed to rouse a graveyard shift officer out of bed.

He kept waiting for the Kayenta dispatcher to announce that at least two tribal cops were on the way and the services of the BIA were no longer required. But he'd sped through the sand dune country before the radio silence was interrupted. The transmitting unit was so far away the voice was unrecognizable. The dispatcher had to relay: "BIA Seventeen, be advised Sergeant Yabeny is rolling from Mexican Hat." In Utah.

"Is he leaving at this time?"

"Negative. He set out about a half-hour ago. Another back is coming from Shiprock."

"Copy." Shonto Trading Post was now only about twenty-five miles away. Emmett would almost certainly beat Yabeny there. Grunting, he slipped the shotgun out of its roof rack and, steadying the steering wheel with his left elbow, opened the chamber to examine it. Clear. He jacked in a shell and laid the Remington across the passenger seat. *What's Yabeny doing in Mexican Hat? Long way from Window Rock.*

Emmett checked the dash clock: 8:03. Forty minutes since the initial call had been put out. "Kayenta, you still have the reporting party on the land-line?"

"Affirmative."

"Then where's the suspect?"

"Oh, he walked off toward the airstrip a while ago."

A dirt landing field, Emmett recalled. "Without shooting anybody, I take it?"

"Affirm."

A new voice inquired, "Who is he, Kayenta?" Sergeant Yabeny, coming in clear.

"Old Regis."

"Somebody give me a description," Emmett demanded.

But Yabeny had a question of his own. "Where are you now, Parker?"

"Just taking the Shonto turnoff." Emmett had to flip on the yelp siren to clear some kids on bicycles and a feral-looking puppy off the side road. "Description," he repeated insistently. He was nearing the airstrip.

"Indian male adult, late fifties, five-ten and one hundred and forty pounds . . ." Then Yabeny paused. "I know him, Parker. Stand by for me to get there before you try to take him down . . . okay?" His hesitation smacked of clan connection.

But then Emmett transmitted, "Too late."

A hundred yards ahead, Old Regis was clasping the airfield wind sock with his left fist, leaning back and swaying on the taut piece of orange cloth. He had crinkled eyelids and long, sparse white whiskers. A picture of senile play but for the pistol dangling from his right hand. The Navajo seemed to take no notice of the Suburban as it slowed to a stop. Emmett stepped out and raised the shotgun. But hastily lowered it. The surest way to tempt a drunk to open fire was to challenge him.

Regis let go of the wind sock and plopped onto his buttocks. Chuckling phlegmatically, he rose with a gap-toothed grin, tottered and almost fell again, then staggered across the runway to the wreck of a Piper Cub. It'd been abandoned in a ditch, its propeller, engine and wings stripped by scavengers. The man crawled inside the doorless cockpit and sat. Serenely. As if he were leaving his earthbound troubles thousands of feet below.

Yabeny drove up, cloaking the scene in dust. He parked parallel to the Suburban and bailed out. Without having drawn. "Reg say anything?"

"Didn't have to," Emmett replied. "He's got what looks to be a forty-five."

The dust scudded away, and Yabeny squinted at the Piper. His Pendleton jacket rippled in a velvety-moist breeze that had risen out of the southwest in the past minute. "Reg pulled my chestnuts out of the fire last year, Parker. Backed me up when I was alone with twenty gangbangers partyin' here. Came out of his trailer with that same forty-five. He knew damn well they'd beat the stuffin' out of him later. And they did. Almost killed him . . ." Yabeny finally looked at Emmett. "I know he gets wasted every chance he gets. But I can't forget that night he stood up for me, you know?"

Emmett nodded. "Just tell me how you want it to go—"

The roar of the pistol sent him to his knees. He hadn't heard the bullet pass close by, but he glanced behind for the kids he'd scattered off the road with the siren. They were nowhere in sight, but the report of the powerful handgun had sent a shiver down the back of his neck. He shifted around the rear of the Suburban to join Yabeny. The sergeant was crouching too but seemed largely unfazed—except for a quick swipe of his palms on the legs of his stone-washed Levi's. He still hadn't taken out his weapon. "Got to watch it," he said with a sheepish smile. "No windshield in that old airplane."

"Want to put out a shots-fired call?"

Yabeny thought about it only a second. "No."

"Somebody in the settlement might've heard, and then we both know all hell will break loose back at dispatch. They'll roll every cop within two hundred miles."

"Only phone is in the tradin' post. And they can't catch the sound from here." Rising slightly, Yabeny called toward the Piper, "Reg . . . !" He went on in Navajo for at least two minutes, but the man seemed to be too far gone to recognize the sergeant's voice. Or care. Yabeny eased down onto his heels again. "Where's your sidekick?" he asked.

Emmett reminded himself that this was Tallsalt's man. "Turnipseed's in Tucson, following up on the autopsies at the university hospital. With Summerfield."

And there it was. A slight grating of Yabeny's teeth at the mention of the Gallup agent.

"Strange duck—Reed," Emmett observed.

"Yeah," the sergeant agreed.

"What the hell happened between Bert Knoki and him?" Emmett believed that he'd asked this casually enough, but then noticed the tension build in Yabeny's jaw muscles.

Ignoring the question, the sergeant said, "If Reg stays put for a while he'll fall asleep."

But a peek told Emmett that the inebriate was wide awake. When Regis moved again, they'd have to intervene. Something Yabeny was no doubt dreading, realizing that then he might have to drop the man.

Another shot rumbled across the stillness.

"Tell him he just killed a Comanche," Emmett said, "and that he's getting dang close to committing homicide."

Yabeny started to smirk but then appeared to suddenly glean an idea from Emmett's words. Again, he shouted to Regis in Navajo. Emmett caught only the *Dine* word for Comanche, *Naalani*. This time, the man seemed to pay attention. He even waved his pistol as if in acknowledgment. The sergeant turned back to Emmett. "Your keys in the ignition?"

"Yes. What do you have in mind?"

"Regis is willin' to trade his gun for a Comanche's car. If you don't mind, I'll use the Suburban. Drive close enough to jump him."

"It may not work out that way," Emmett said soberly. "And you just might have to shoot him."

Yabeny had nothing to say to that. He knew it was true.

"Let me go." Emmett started around the cruiser when it occurred to him that he'd communicated none of yesterday's findings to Anna. She had to know. "Listen, Marcellus—if something unfortunate happens in the next couple minutes, be sure to tell Turnipseed the Gila monster that got her came from Lowe Canyon near St. George. There's a petroglyph up there she should see."

"Of what?"

"A Gila monster with moth wings. Just like Descheenie's tattoo. The BLM wildlife biologist in that resource area can show her." Yabeny's face revealed nothing—while Emmett visualized Turnipseed and Nicole Stepanek comparing notes about him around the biologist's campfire. "Cover me." He continued on to the driver's-side door and got behind the wheel, unholstering his revolver and tucking the barrel under his left thigh. Regis had clambered out of the cockpit and was coming on in a wavering line that tended generally toward the Suburban. Still with pistol.

Emmett shifted into low gear and inched forward at idle speed. He didn't latch the door.

Regis tracked his approach with the air of amusement some Navajo seem to take from the presence of outsiders. In turn, Emmett watched the man's hands. The perverse impulse to fire would be telegraphed to his hands long before it registered in his bloodshot eyes. Emmett could hear his own hard breathing over the barking of the tires on the gravel runway. Most bullets glanced off the curvature of a windshield. But if any could punch through, the .45 round was at the top of the list.

Regis waved him on with his free hand.

Emmett waited until he was twenty feet from the man. Then he hit the siren. Instinctively, the Navajo ducked in the split second before he thought about elevating his pistol and firing. By then, Emmett had simultaneously floored the accelerator and swung open the door. He caught Regis full in the face, and the man went down. His pistol popped out of his grasp and landed with a rattle atop the hood.

Emmett braked and ran back to the man. He was dazed but breathing normally.

Yabeny trotted up. He looked over Regis, then nodded gratefully at Emmett.

"IF SHIT COULD SPROUT LEGS, it'd be Terry Wade Rowe," Travis Fanning drawled. The beefy U.S. probation officer was driving through downtown Phoenix, with Anna beside him in the front and Summerfield in the back. It was a bit disconcerting for her to hear a cracker-sounding southwestern twang issue from the large black man. But his accent and the cowboy touches to his wardrobe had been partly explained by the photographs on his office wall. On weekends, Fanning was a U.S. 10th Cavalry reenactor. The Buffalo Soldiers, former slaves the government dressed in blue wool and set against the Indians. One of whom he claimed to be descended from. "Knew I was in for trouble as soon as I found out Rowe's change of address was bogus," Fanning went on. "He was in his sixth month of supervised release, so we were down to one walk-in and one phone check-in per month. The last time I saw him, he strolled into my office looking like Crazy Horse and gave me a new address in University Park . . ." A cynical chortle. "Turned out to be the Christian Science Reading Room on Jefferson Street. Before you both think I'm a complete idiot—I'm supervising over a hundred and sixty releasees, or I would've caught it sooner. Then Rowe missed his substance abuse counseling session last Friday evening . . ." At the start of the weekend during which Bert and Aurelia Knoki had been murdered, Anna reminded herself as she studied Rowe's mug shot: a typical drug flake with washed-out, scoffing eyes and a so-you-got-me sneer. "At that point I knew I had me a bona fide absconder and started the process." Fanning glanced back at Summerfield. "You asked why Rowe's warrant didn't show up on NCIC till this morning?"

"That's right."

The probation officer gave a disgusted harrumph. "First, I had to write the violation report. Then route it to the sentencing judge, who dillydallied around for two days before issuing the arrest warrant. From there it went to the U.S. Marshal's Office to be entered into NCIC. And their data clerk is as backlogged as everybody else caught up in this paper rodeo."

There hadn't been time to cover all of this in Fanning's office in the U.S. courthouse. Almost as soon as the probation officer had heard the words "Rowe" and "homicide" fall from Anna's lips, he ushered her and Summerfield down to his car. They'd sped off through the late-morning traffic, hopefully to an eleven o'clock rendezvous with Rowe's girlfriend.

"You just said Rowe came into your office looking like Crazy Horse."

"Yes, sir. A real wannabe."

"Gang?" Summerfield sounded confused.

"No, Indian." Braking for a red light, Fanning looked aside at Anna.

She answered the question in his eyes. "Modoc."

"Tenth Cavalry never fought them."

"They were lucky."

Fanning laughed as the light changed. "At FCI Phoenix, Rowe fell in with the Aboriginal Brotherhood, a self-help inmate group that uses native spiritualism to kick drug and alcohol addiction. Kind of like the Red Road, except AB is more willing to let in a polite white boy now and again. And Rowe can be ingratiating when he's not beating on his girlfriend. Anyway, that's what I meant by the Crazy Horse comment. Rowe wears his hair in braids. Has a beaded choker. Also, he was *armed* every time he was taken down. So watch your booties." Fanning eyed his dash clock. "Five minutes from arrival. May I suggest a plan?"

Anna looked to Summerfield, who shrugged. He'd seemed withdrawn all morning. "Go ahead, Travis," she said. "We're the new kids on the block."

"The place is called the Feathered Serpent. Nightclub lounge with an Indian clientele. Lolly Blackhouse comes in every morning at eleven. Has a milk and bourbon at the bar, then phones her escort service for her nooner date."

Anna closed her air-conditioning vent. It was chilling her. "Does she have any solicitation priors?"

"Yes, but all of them are at least ten years old." The eastbound traffic began jamming up, and Fanning's gaze flickered to the dash clock again. Eight to eleven. "Lolly worked the streets in El Paso and Albuquerque under several aliases. After that, she signed on with the escort service. And it's protected her from arrest ever since."

Anna asked, "How?"

"Has more to do with the clientele than anything else. Tribal bigwigs and their corporate suitors in town for business and conferences. All by referral. There are damn few Indian cops, as you well know, and they're pretty well known throughout the West. So it's been almost impossible to set up a decoy john, although Phoenix PD makes a halfhearted try now and again. But for what? A misdemeanor rap that's only going to piss off the tribes for targeting them? It's called racial politics, and nobody wants to get any of that stuck on their boots."

"How old's the woman?" Summerfield inquired.

"Thirty-seven."

"And she's still making a living at it?"

"You should see her." Fanning turned up a side street. "But that presents a problem. One look at you, Reed, and she'll smell posse. She knows me by sight, so she'll bolt the second I come through the door. That leaves—"

"I'll do it," Anna interrupted, although her throat tightened a little. "Should I approach her straight up— credentials and all?"

"No way," Fanning said. "Lolly's a Southern Ute and, according to Rowe, has no love for the FBI. Her brother was shot dead by an agent in Cortez, Colorado. I've been chewing on an idea . . ."

Three minutes later, the probation officer stopped halfway down the block from the nightclub. It was a commercial district, and—except for the garishly painted plumed coils of the Aztec god Quetzalcoatl twined around the walls—the club still looked like the warehouse it had once been. Fanning winked encouragingly at Anna as he pointed at a blue delivery van parked across the street. "Not only will Summerfield and I be lying low in the neighborhood, it seems SWAT is on the scene too."

Anna gave him a thin smile, then got out of the car.

Fanning drove on but turned up an alley instead of cruising past the front of the Feathered Serpent.

She stood alone in the middle of the street for a moment. *SWAT.* She smiled again at Fanning's quip, although the Utah-plated van was too battered and sand-pitted to resemble a police vehicle.

The door to the nightclub was upholstered with dusty red Naugahyde and brass studs. She stepped inside, waited for her eyes to adjust to the gloom. A staleness of cigarette smoke made her want to back out. But she let go of the door, and it shut behind her, increasing the darkness. Out of it a high-pitched male laugh flew at her. At last, she could make out the long bar and the bartender standing behind it. Apache, maybe. An unlit cigarette was tucked in the corner of his seemingly lipless mouth. The laughter had come from one of three young Indian men hunched around a table on the edge of the empty dance floor. She caught their shifting glances and held them, and one by one the men dropped their eyes back to their beers.

The bartender finally lit up and slowly shook out the paper match. "Howdy."

"Hello."

"What'll it be, sister?"

"Shot of Wild Turkey and a Diet Coke in the can." Anna took a stool toward the center of the bar and checked her wristwatch. Eleven o'clock. The bartender brought her setup, then took a carton of milk from the small refrigerator under the counter and mixed it with four fingers of Jack Daniel's and some ice in a tall glass. Anna regarded her own amber-colored dose of alcohol with unease. She didn't drink. And more to the point, this is what her father had drunk when he went off to binge in the nearest town. He'd come home smelling of bourbon and Coca-Cola.

The door let in a burst of sunlight and the yellow of a departing cab.

The shape of a woman stood momentarily in this

luminous square, her short white dress transparent enough to reveal that she had a good body. The same young man laughed inanely.

Anna downed several swallows of Coke, then poured most of the Wild Turkey into the can to make it appear that she'd been sipping from the shot glass.

Lolly Blackhouse sat at the bar three stools to her left. The woman gave her a probing glance, then turned with a radiant smile to accept the bourbon and milk from the bartender. The smile appeared on her face without warning and vanished just as swiftly. "Thanks, Carlos." But Fanning had been right: This thirty-seven-year-old had to be seen to be appreciated. Her eyes seemed extraordinarily large and prescient, and her smooth brown skin was flawless—except for a pale green bruise on her upper right arm.

"Lolly . . . Lolly Blackhouse . . . ?"

The woman's eyes snapped toward her. "Have we met?"

"No."

"Then how'd you get my name?"

Anna grabbed her purse and slid over the stools separating them. "I'm Ginny Grass Rope."

It apparently meant nothing to her, which reassured Anna that her cover would hold up at least in the short term. "So . . . ?" Lolly challenged.

"My brother, Oscar, was in Phoenix FCI with Terry. They belonged to the Aboriginal Brotherhood together." Fanning had hastily supplied her with this tidbit. Grass Rope had been one of his former parolees, a Lakota Sioux who'd died ten days ago in an auto accident on the South Dakota reservation to which he'd returned after meeting his early release obligations.

Lolly bought time to sort through her suspicions by pointing at Anna's setup. "Don't you want your drinks?"

"Naw, I shouldn't be drinking anyway. I'm in a program, you know?"

Lolly nodded apathetically, her long, prune-lacquered nails clicking the lip of her glass. "So how's Oscar?"

"Dead." Anna was surprised when her eyes filled slightly.

Lolly looked up. *"Dead?"* Then her expression went blank. Was she calculating if this posed some veiled danger to Rowe and her? Had she known Oscar Grass Rope?

"Yeah," Anna went on, letting her voice turn husky. "A car wreck on the rez."

"In South Dakota?"

"Yeah."

"Sorry to hear it." She patted the back of Anna's hand. Her palm was cool and dry. While the woman had visibly relaxed at the explanation of how Grass Rope had died, Anna had the sense that she wasn't buying the story, that something in it had raised her guard instead of lowering it. "I don't know where Terry is right now," Lolly volunteered.

"That's a shame."

"Why?"

"Well, Oscar told me that if ever something like this happened, he wanted the AB guys to hold the Wiping Away of Tears for him." A grief-relieving ceremony conducted some time after the funeral.

"Back in Dakota?"

"Yeah, but most everybody with the group's out here."

Lolly stared at her. "Who the hell are you?"

Anna's heart pounded. She picked her purse up off the counter and offered it to Lolly. Even though her credentials and pistol were inside.

The woman slowly reached out and ran a fingernail along the purse's zipper. "You sure, little sister?"

Anna dipped her head once.

But Lolly withdrew her hands and clasped them around her glass again. "I don't care who you are. Don't care who anybody is." She polished off the last of her milk and bourbon, swiveled around and started for the back corridor. The young man laughed as she passed near, but she cut it short with a look that told him she was impossibly beyond his means.

Anna returned to her Wild Turkey and Coke, feeling

weak in the knees. How had she done? Passably well, she hoped, but she had no idea what she'd do if Lolly simply walked out after making the call to her escort service. She resisted stealing a glance at the woman, although she could hear Lolly talking in pithy, obviously coded phrases on the phone. Then she hung up. The sound was followed by the clip of her heels over the hardwood dance floor.

Anna flinched as Lolly touched her shoulder. She faced the woman.

"You're a cop," Lolly said without any apparent special feeling. "Probably a fed, because nobody wants Terry right now except his PO. But that can be helpful if things keep going like they are. Maybe we can use each other. You know what that's like, don't you? To be used . . . ?" Then came the same smile she'd flashed on the bartender. "Give me your number, Ginny Grass Rope. Your *real* number. I'm not promising I'll use it. But we'll see."

After a moment, Anna broke off eye contact and took a pen from her purse. She wrote Emmett's apartment phone number on a cocktail napkin.

EMMETT SAT NUMBLY behind the wheel in Summerfield's Suburban, vaguely thankful for the shade thrown by the Navajo police headquarters in Window Rock. The restless air smelled of rain on the way, although no clouds ruffled the horizons. How did the old saying in the desert Southwest go? *Is it going to rain today? Yes,* came the hedge that was always true to some degree—*somewhere.* But John Tallsalt hadn't even hedged about being executor of the Knokis' will. There was no will. The judge of the Peacemaker Court inside had just told Emmett. This branch of the tribal judiciary handled probate in addition to dispute resolution, and as the attorney for the patrolmen's association fourteen years before, this particular judge had represented Knoki at his disciplinary hearing on the incident in Mexican Hat. The bitch Bert hadn't contested. Recalling that from Knoki's personnel jacket, Emmett had decided to call on him in chambers. And the justice had explained that few *Dine* had wills drawn up, preferring to leave the disposal of their property to the dictates of clan custom.

Emmett started the engine and backed onto the highway.

Returning to the capital from the man-with-a-gun call in Shonto two hours ago, he'd ducked into his room at the Navajo Nation Inn for a quick shower, then gone straightaway to the Peacemaker Court. He'd also dropped by Tallsalt's office. The lieutenant had been absent from the complex again. Unavailable. And nobody had seen him since yesterday afternoon. So there'd been no chance to confront him. Emmett needed to discuss his bald-faced lie with Anna as soon as possible. To tell her that the letter with the University Park return address deserved greater attention than ever.

Had she and Summerfield made any progress?

He pulled into the inn's rear parking lot. Locking up the Suburban, he scanned the vacant fields surrounding the inn for anyone who might have followed him. No one, this time.

The phone message light was blinking. But the room was skin-crawling hot, and first he went to the thermostat. A distant, tiny rumble followed his lowering of the dial, and then—miraculously—cool air gushed from the wall vent. He shut the door and phoned the front desk. "Message for Emmett Parker?"

"Yes, Mr. Parker." A delay in which papers were heard being shuffled. "A Section Chief Vernon called at two o'clock . . ." The clerk then gave him a number with an area code he recognized covering the northern Virginia suburbs of Washington.

"Thanks, honey." Dialing, he glanced at his watch. Six-thirty on the East Coast. Section chiefs were supervisors at the FBI's lab, and Vernon obviously had news worth disturbing the man at home. His wife answered, and Emmett sank onto the bed, waiting for him to be summoned from the backyard. Roses. He didn't know Vernon, but envisioned him to be the sort who spent his twilights tending roses.

"Investigator Parker?"

"Speaking."

"Craig Vernon with the FBI laboratory." A slightly nasal tenor. "Reed Summerfield left instructions that I was to contact you if I couldn't get in touch with him."

"He's in Phoenix with my task force partner."

"I see. Well, interesting latent paw prints you folks shipped us."

"I'd imagine." Emmett rubbed his aching eyes. Too much sun today.

"We're calling him Lizard Man. Although we didn't know what to think until we called in our on-tap herpetologist from Patuxent Wildlife Research Center. Did you know the skin pattern is that of *Heloderma suspectum*, commonly known as Gila monster?"

Emmett decided not to spoil the technician's fun. "No."

"He told us the pattern was left by the skins of at least two lizards. The tubercles, or beads, were of different enough size to indicate age variance. So, hearing that, we took a closer look under the scope and found seams. Even indications of nylon thread used as stitching. This guy made gloves from a protected species . . ."

Once again, Emmett saw the clawed prints on his windshield being highlighted by dawn's light. Now those marks, and the other bizarre particulars of Tuesday morning in the Knokis' mobile home, were his only hope that the letter Tallsalt had palmed had nothing material to do with the murders. That the capture of the being who'd fashioned gloves from the skins of Nicole Stepanek's Gilas and patiently etched petroglyphs on the rocks of Lowe Canyon would ultimately absolve Tallsalt of any responsibility or knowledge.

"Mr. Parker . . . ?"

"Yes, I'm sorry."

"I was just asking if this is useful to you and the task force?"

"Extremely. Thanks for expediting it for us."

"Don't get many like this."

"I'm sure. Goodbye." Emmett replaced the receiver in the cradle and lay back across the bed. What was the meaning of this bit of evidence? He already knew that the individual involved either had a mania for Gilas or wanted to give the appearance of such an obsession—there was still the chance this was all artifice. But if you wrap yourself in the skin of another species does that mean you wish to assume its powers? *Dine* lore abounded with entities capable of physical transformation. Was that the desire here? Or was it merely withdrawal into the animal world? A serial killer in Oklahoma City, a loner like most, was incapable of all but brutal interactions with his fellow human beings, yet had been fastidiously kind to his cats. Loner. That psychological profile was at loggerheads with the two sets of tracks that had led away from Knoki's torched cruiser.

Yet, solo killer or not, the leaving of a signature often revealed an unconscious desire to be caught. To be stopped.

Eat.

He'd had nothing since dinner with Stepanek last night. For a moment, he remembered the firelight on her freckled face. Her lonely voice. Groaning with regret, he heaved himself to his feet and went to the sink vanity. He wanted to pop a couple of Tums, hoping they'd improve his appetite.

But then he noticed that his toilet kit was zippered shut.

He was certain that he'd left it open after showering earlier. Gingerly, he lifted it. To feel if it was heavier than usual. It wasn't. Still, he leaned through the door into the bathroom proper and laid the kit on the floor behind the wall, creating a shield for most of his body to deflect a possible blast. Only then did he undo the zipper. No device. He stood and examined the contents. On top were two three-by-five cards labeled: *Navajo Nation Police Field Interrogation Card*. FIs. He'd last filled out one as a patrolman in Oklahoma City. For bitch insurance, mostly. If your beat got burglarized on your watch, you might luck out and avoid a verbal berating if you'd FIed anybody suspicious in the area.

Then Emmett's pulse quickened again: Both cards

were signed by Officer Carbert Knoki. And the first field-interrogated subject was Reed Avery Summerfield. No occupation had been noted, but the address he'd given was in Gaithersburg, Maryland. Just far enough outside the Beltway to comfortably commute to the Washington Metropolitan Field Office. Summerfield had identified himself with a Maryland driver's license. Apparently not with his FBI creds. Emmett checked the date beside Knoki's signature. October 7 of last year. Before Summerfield reported for duty in Gallup? The location was given as the flat rocks on the south side of Asaayi Dam. Emmett recalled this somewhat remote, forest-ringed lake lying about eight or nine miles east of Navajo, the Knokis' hometown, in the Chuskas. The comments box on the card was reserved for the probable cause behind the temporary detention and questioning. Here, Knoki had been cryptic: *Sunbathing with trunks.* The *Dine* were a notoriously modest people—beholding female genitalia was believed to invite a lightning strike, and looking at a penis caused illness. But Bert's justification escaped Emmett.

The second card was cross-referenced to the first, meaning that Knoki had questioned both subjects at the same place and time.

Dieter (NMN) Preuss. No middle name. Of Dresden, Germany. Occupation: antiques exporter. Identified by passport and work visa. And then Knoki's comment on Summerfield came into sharp focus: *Sunbathing with no trunks. Poss. kids in area any time. Nadleeh.* The mythic creature of this name had both male and female sexual organs, but excelled at women's work and was more empathetic than most men. Emmett had little doubt Bert Knoki had intended the coarser, homophobic application of the term. *Think. What did this mean to Summerfield, other than a momentary embarrassment?* It wasn't a fireable offense with the FBI to be homosexual. But an agent could be canned for *lying* about the fact, if discovered. Had Summerfield been confronted by his Office of Professional Responsibility once before and denied it, making these FI cards the smoking gun that would clinch his termination?

The cards were trying to tell him something else. Emmett couldn't quite put his finger on it.

He went to the window and looked east toward Window Rock Ridge, letting his mind go blank so the answer might creep in. *East.*

Dresden had been in East Germany. And Summerfield had been with Foreign Counterintelligence.

"Shit," Emmett said, turning back for the phone.

chapter 13

"HAS TO BE HIM." SUMMERFIELD TOSSED ANNA THE binoculars and turned the key. A quarter-mile across the Gila River Reservation, a male figure had sauntered from one of the scattered houses and was getting in a 1980ish Chevy Monte Carlo. His name, most likely, was Juan Morada. He was an Akimel O'odham, a people formerly known as the Pima. They'd joined the growing number of nations that refused to perpetuate the indignity of going by names the Spanish or enemy tribes had given them. Akimel O'odham meant *River People,* and River Person Juan Morada drove east toward Interstate 10.

Summerfield followed him.

The face of the dash clock was obscured by a sun glint. Anna shaded it with her hand: 4:32. They'd been waiting since one o'clock for Morada to show himself. After the apparent disaster with Lolly Blackhouse at the Feathered Serpent, Fanning had suggested an alternate plan to find Terry Wade Rowe. The probation officer knew of another member of the Aboriginal Brotherhood, although this brother had served his full sentence at FCI Phoenix and was subject to none of the pressures that could be brought to bear on a parolee. Fanning had supplied Anna and Summerfield with Morada's mug shot and rap sheet, plus directions to his mother's house on the Gila reservation just south of the Phoenix city limits.

Summerfield tailed the Monte Carlo up the freeway on-ramp. Onto the northbound lanes. A massive thundercloud was building over the Mexican horizon, and the wind had risen. It buffeted the car, making it yaw on an overpass.

Letting up on the gas, Summerfield drifted back several hundred yards to blend into the traffic.

Anna had confessed to him and Fanning that Lolly Blackhouse had made her. And made her as a federal cop. Summerfield nearly went ballistic because of this setback, but the probation officer had seen opportunity in it: "If Rowe's still in town, Lolly will tell him about you, Anna. He might start meeting with the AB brothers, if only to make sure they throw us off his track." Then Fanning had come up with the idea of Summerfield and her staking out Morada.

The man had started weaving through cars. "Did he spot us?" she asked.

"Don't think so." Summerfield punched in the cigarette lighter but kept his eyes on the Chevy as it completed the big curve in Tempe and headed west toward the high-rises of downtown. He'd been on edge all afternoon. As if finding Terry Rowe meant everything to him. She herself wanted to talk to the absconder, certainly, but was more inclined to believe that Lolly, not Rowe, had written the letter to Bert Knoki. And strangely, she looked forward to seeing the uncannily self-possessed woman again. Even though those oversized eyes turned even the thickest skin into cellophane.

She frowned as Summerfield's smoke curled around her face. "If tailing Morada doesn't pan out for us in the next few hours, let's quit pressing Rowe."

"Why in the name of God would we want to do that?" he asked.

"If we don't run Lolly's lover to ground, she just might phone me. And I'm sure we can use her help."

The rush hour was at its height, and thousands of brake lamps winked on as the traffic slowed for the interchange with Interstate 17. Morada veered off onto this freeway, which skirted lower downtown. Summerfield followed, swerving in behind a big rig and using the trailer for concealment as all four lanes slowed to a jerky crawl. Periodically, he eased left to keep tabs on the Monte Carlo, which was about ten car-lengths ahead. Anna remembered that it was the start of the Memorial Day Weekend.

"Let me get this right . . ." Summerfield took an abstracted puff off his cigarette. "You want to break off trying to collar Rowe simply because a hooker—who detests the bureau—might give you a jingle?"

"I've got a hunch she can put us on the right path."

"Or the wrong one, if that suits her purposes," Summerfield said. "Don't you—?" Something big thudded against his side of the car, making both Anna and him flinch before it disintegrated into a shower of spiky twigs. A tumbleweed. The wind was picking them up off the freeway embankment and stampeding them among the vehicles. "Don't you see what we have here, dear woman?"

"No."

Summerfield grinned. "We've got Bert Knoki cold!"

"How?"

"How, she asks," he muttered rhetorically, checking on the Monte Carlo once again. Tensing suddenly, he flipped on his right signal and inched the sedan over. Anna saw that Juan Morada was taking the Seventh Street exit. "Ask Parker," Summerfield went on. "Parker knows. Why else would he send us down here . . . *unless* he knew damn well Knoki was dirty? Look at the facts. The Sonorans use the Big Rez for routing shipments to Santa Fe and Albuquerque—"

"Says who?" Anna interrupted.

"Tallsalt, for one."

"Has his department or the DEA made a single arrest to back up that theory?"

"None I'm aware of," Summerfield conceded, following the Monte Carlo north on Seventh. Fortunately, the surface street was just as traffic-bound as the freeway off-ramp—otherwise they would have lost Morada. "But the man heading Window Rock Investigations most assuredly has some idea what's going on—even if Tallsalt insists on covering for a friend. Or a clan relative. Has anybody absolutely ruled out a clan tie between Knoki and him?"

"You ready to take this to the grand jury?" Anna asked.

"Forget Tallsalt," he said irately. "Behold the facts, dear woman. Terry Wade Rowe writes a letter to Knoki. Rowe served time for drug running. Who was his employer? Some cartel in Hermosillo, Sonora. You ask why no arrests were ever made on the rez? Carbert Knoki. He always made sure the coast was clear before a plane out of Mexico ever touched down. God only knows how many loads he greased through before he displeased somebody powerful. In Sonora or Window Rock. Have you or Parker ever considered that someone within his own agency whacked him? These Indians do prefer to take care of their own soiled laundry, you know."

"The ballpark," Anna said shortly.

"What?"

"Morada headed for Bank One Ballpark."

Summerfield acknowledged this with a distracted nod. "Don't you see where it all leads?"

"No."

"Why not?"

"A cop on the take doesn't have to wrap his pipes with old rags to keep them from freezing."

"I don't—"

"The pipes under the Knokis' trailer were insulated that way. I saw when I was down there." Nothing inside the mobile home had hinted at lavish spending, although she understood that even well-to-do Navajo didn't flaunt their riches. To do so invited accusations of witchcraft. But beyond any evidence of unexplained wealth, why would a patrolman who was obsessed with catching bootleggers jump into bed with a drug cartel?

As they bounced over a set of railroad tracks, Summerfield griped, "Oh grand!"—Morada had peeled off into the parking lot directly across Seventh Street from the stadium. There were too few vehicles in it for Summerfield and Anna to follow and go unnoticed.

"Next right," she suggested. Morada had left his Monte Carlo beside the attendants' kiosk. He came out of it wearing an orange safety vest and a Diamondbacks baseball cap. He diddy-bopped toward the entrance on Seventh. "Keep going, Reed. Make a U-turn as soon as he can't see us." Before the Akimel O'odham's face dimmed in her memory, she compared it to the mug shot. Undeniably Juan Morada. The same falcon's beak of a nose.

Obviously, Summerfield had been simmering over her grand jury remark. "I *do* have enough to approach the U.S. Attorney, you know," he said stubbornly as he looked for a place to turn around. "Particularly with Lolly Blackhouse's involvement."

"How's she involved, other than being Rowe's lover?"

"You heard Fanning. Blackhouse works for an escort service that caters to tribal officials. She and Rowe are a potential link to the Sonorans. Now we're talking RICO." The same Racketeer Influenced and Corrupt Organizations Act he'd tried to apply against *Dine* rumrunners.

Anna was skeptical. But she waited until Summerfield had pulled into an alleyway, backed out and started again for the parking lot before asking, "What if the solution to this comes from some dark corner we haven't even looked in yet?"

"How do you know that?"

"I just do." Although she didn't want to be pressed for her reasons. Not yet.

Summerfield faced her. His eyes went cold. "I wouldn't put my faith in intuition, if I were you." He found an open stretch of curb from which they could view Morada collecting money from fans arriving early for batting practice. Summerfield killed the engine, and they sat in silence.

*   *   *

EMMETT SLAMMED DOWN the receiver. For the third time in an hour he'd just been taunted by his own voice asking him to leave a message on the machine in his apartment. He couldn't do that. Not knowing if Summerfield might be listening in when Anna punched the playback button. He'd considered simply asking her to call him at the Navajo Nation Inn, but then wondered if Summerfield might scope on the stress in his voice. And, forewarned by Emmett that the federal government would never reimburse her for massive roam charges, Anna had left her personal cell phone at home.

Time out. Sift through this again to make sure you're not making too much of it.

How precisely did Summerfield and Preuss—whoever Dieter Preuss was—fit together as co-conspirators? Two sets of human tracks had led southeast out of Crystal Wash, away from Knoki's burned-out police cruiser. *Unfortunately, impressions in this soup collapse in on themselves as soon as you take your next step,* Summerfield himself had reported Monday night at the crime scene. With a sense of relief? Emmett couldn't recall. But Crystal Wash lay within ten miles of Asaayi Lake, and two men familiar with the back shore of the reservoir might have scouted the surrounding countryside as well. Summerfield had driven away from the grisly scene an hour before he, Anna and Yabeny had called it a night. Home to Gallup? Or to join Preuss at the Knokis' mobile home to give a false overlay of native belief to the murders? The copy of Zolbrod's *Dine bahane* in Summerfield's glove compartment. The Navajo creation story recounted the exploits of Gila Monster. And Summerfield's had been a German edition of the myth. Had Preuss bagged Nicole Stepanek's specimens and then etched the winged Gila petroglyphs on the walls of Lowe Canyon?

But can this circumstantial soup be boiled down to a credible motive?

Undeniably, Bert Knoki had had a twist on Reed

Summerfield. Yet, had he ever threatened to use it? Or had the two field interrogation cards gone no further up the chain of command than Tallsalt, who secreted them away in his office safe and refused to tangle with the FBI's Office of Professional Responsibility?

How terrifying was this twist to Summerfield?

Lying about homosexuality could result in termination. But not necessarily. Other agents had been caught in a lie and survived the ax. So that might not have been enough to justify murder even to a badly rattled man. But an espionage conviction could lead to life in prison, or even execution.

Emmett reached for the phone again. The Navajo Nation Inn line was by no means secure, but he was running out of time.

The number eluded his normally infallible memory. "You have reached the McLean Library . . ." a Virginia-accented recording cooed.

Depressing the button for another dial tone, he realized that he had transposed the last two digits. He tried again. Twenty seconds later, the raspy, almost burpy voice assured him that he'd connected. "This better be good. I was on my third scotch and second Havana."

Emmett smiled, although Cuban tobacco had probably cost the man his larynx, forcing him to speak—and smoke—through a stoma, a surgical opening left in his throat. He'd always managed to get the contraband cigars, despite the embargo and the vagaries of the Cold War. "Emmett Parker, sir."

"I'll be dipped and plucked. That debt been burning a hole in your pocket?"

"Not till tonight."

"I'm listening."

Emmett simply said, "Dieter Preuss."

"Means nothing to me. What is it, a Kraut dildo?"

"Close."

"Well, give me your shopping list."

"First, I need to know if there's any chance if Preuss was

a member of Stasi . . ." The East Germany Ministry for State Security, which had collapsed along with the Berlin Wall. "I've got his stats."

"Give 'em to me."

Emmett read the information off Knoki's card, then exhaled, knowing full well what headaches his next request entailed. "Second, if Preuss was Stasi, is there any possibility this was a RIP op?"

The voice didn't respond right away. In counterintelligence parlance, a recruitment in place was the turning of a foreign operative, keeping him in his old job, often for years, and mining him at will.

"Shit. What do you savages think a debt is, a grudge?"

"I wouldn't ask unless it really mattered."

"I know that, Parker. Who would've been his control?"

"An FBI agent named Reed Summerfield. Until about eight months ago, assigned to FCI, Washington Metropolitan."

"Okay. The first part's a snap. Thanks to a Hun mob that ransacked Stasi headquarters in '90, you can damn near get their old roster over the Internet. But chasing down an FBI RIP? That's dicey. It'll take a few days, at least—unless I want to set off every whistle and bell inside the Hoover Building. Understood?"

"Understood. But the sooner the better."

"Give me your number."

"I'll phone you from the Gallup airport in about an hour."

"Don't you have a cellular with a scrambler?"

"Not even one without a scrambler."

"Why the fuck did you ever go to work for a two-bit outfit like Interior?"

"They're Equal Opportunity. They hire savages." After a moment, Emmett realized that the phlegmy rumble following his remark was a chuckle. "I won't forget this, sir."

"Yes, you will. You're the first son of a bitch to call in six months." Then he hung up.

Emmett grabbed his lightest jacket and hurried out the door.

Paper trash swirled around the parking lot. Drumming down the stairs, he was thankful that the old man was as good as his word. Many in his place would have pretended not to remember the lowly BIA investigator who'd confirmed for a high official arguing against an air strike on Tripoli that Libyan funds were not bankrolling American Indian Movement activities. The raid had proceeded, of course, but the old man hadn't forgotten Emmett's favor for his unnamed boss.

He was unlocking the Suburban when he noticed Yabeny. The sergeant was leaning against the side of his cruiser at the far edge of the lot. He'd not been at headquarters early this afternoon.

Emmett went to him. "Appreciate it, Marcellus."

"I need 'em back," Yabeny said without smiling, his face sallow in the lot lights. "They've got to be in the lieutenant's safe when he returns."

"Fair enough." Emmett took the FI cards from his shirt pocket and handed them over. "Any idea where Tallsalt is?"

The sergeant just shook his head. Then tried to appear less severe—not by openly thanking Emmett for sparing Regis up at Shonto this morning, but by offering something more of possible use to the investigation. "Vipers—at least those who aren't in Tohatchi—are checkin' a mailbox near Crystal. One nobody uses anymore."

"As a drop?"

"Maybe."

"Can you stake it out?"

Yabeny gave a hardbitten laugh. "Bert's dead, the lieutenant's AWOL, overtime budget's shot to hell . . . and a fed's askin' me if I can put some twenty-four-hour manpower on a mailbox?"

"Do what you can." Over the sergeant's head, Emmett saw the pinpricks of car headlamps flash in the central Chuskas. Despite his urgency to get to the airport, he found himself inquiring, "Why would there be small fires in the Chuskas?" He'd been reminded of what old man Tsinnajinnie had seen.

"Meth labs. Bangers use old hogans for drug labs, then burn 'em when they think we're closin' in. You here tomorrow for Bert and Aurelia's funeral?"

Emmett didn't reply.

ANNA WAS FIGHTING DROWSINESS when a cheer erupted from the stadium. "Home run," Summerfield murmured, sounding as sleepy as she felt. In three hours, they'd observed nothing more than an uncomfortable-looking Juan Morada fighting the wind as he guarded the Seventh Street entrance to the right field parking lot. And a switching locomotive busily assembling freight trains in the yard to the immediate south of the stadium. At sunset, the top of the thunderhead had been whipped into an anvil shape, and with darkness it began to sheet blackly over the city. Still, not a drop of rain. But veils of desert sand had sifted through the light fanning upward through the retractable roof of the stadium—before it was closed ten minutes ago. "My father played baseball at Yale with George Bush," Summerfield went on over the thrumming of the radio aerial in the wind. "Wanted me to play ball."

"Did you?" Anna asked, yawning again.

"No. At least not well. Mother could have cared less about baseball. She was a war bride . . ." He shook his head. "I mean a *post*-war bride. German. Musical family. Dad was a provost major with the occupation forces. She wanted me to play the cello."

"And did you?"

"Dreadfully." He laughed. "At least I managed to disappoint both of them. That's what they get for having an afterthought like me. The woman was forty-six when she had me, for godsake."

She didn't feel like conversation, but it seemed the only way to stay awake. "You didn't really want to be an agent?"

"Oh, I don't know. With an accounting degree, the only other alternative was to become an accountant."

Anna smiled. "Know how that goes."

"You too?"

"Accounting minor. Sociology major." She sat up slightly. A car, briefly delayed at the tracks by the switching engine, was slowing for the parking lot entrance. "Then what'd you want to be when you were a kid?"

"The most impossible thing in the world. Myself. Should've known better."

"Why?"

"You don't want to know."

Anna found herself mildly irked with his self-deprecating evasions. They might wind up working together for years, and she decided that there was only one way to put him at ease. "I don't care, Reed, who was sitting across that table from you in Santa Fe. That's your business. Not the bureau's. Not mine." She expected a moment of discomfort from him. But not a dark, hunted stare. Glancing back toward the lot, she reached for the binoculars. Morada's bored posture of the past three hours had stiffened, and he took his hands from his vest pockets. "Reed . . ."

"I see."

The car—a beat-up-looking Plymouth Gran Fury—crept past the lot entrance and continued north, leaving Morada to stare curiously after it.

"Down," Summerfield ordered as the Fury turned right onto Jefferson and rolled toward them. "He's casing the entire block."

Anna scrunched down in her seat, her knees crammed under the dashboard. Headlights penetrated the interior of the sedan, making her feel ridiculously exposed. She rested the binoculars on the floor mat and nudged her purse, the pistol inside it, closer. The hummingbird within. But the throaty pitch of the Fury's engine didn't change as the vehicle lumbered past.

The shadows returned like a security blanket.

Anna inched up, peeked through the slot between the

back of her seat and the headrest. The Fury took the next right.

"You see his face?" she asked Summerfield.

He was still staring at her. "No."

Two minutes later, the Fury emerged back onto Seventh from Jackson Street. This time the driver showed no hesitation as he braked beside Morada. He rolled down the passenger-side window to talk, and the Akimel O'odham attendant crouched to listen. Again, Anna swept the binoculars up to her eyes. The interior of the Plymouth was dark, but she could tell that the silhouetted figure leaning toward Morada had braids. "It's got to be Rowe," she said.

"Let's catch him in a pincer," Summerfield said rapid-fire. "I'll walk down Jefferson from here, and you drive around the block as he just did. Not both of us in the car. That'd just kick off a high-speed pursuit. Okay?"

"I guess."

"Your signal to pull in behind him is when I stroll past the front of his car. Come out drawn. Cover Morada and the passenger side while I take down Rowe."

"All right," she said, "except you drive and I walk."

"But—"

"No buts. Rowe's less likely to bolt if he sees a woman coming at him."

Summerfield studied the two men through the binoculars. Finally, he said, "Go, then."

She reached up, turned off the dome light, then pushed her door open against the weight of the wind and stepped out. The flying grit stung her cheeks, and she half-closed her lids to keep the blast from peppering her eyes. Her pace down the sidewalk was too fast, too purposeful. She made herself slow down. Morada continued to listen to the driver through the open window. The attendant seemed increasingly somber. No laughter. She unzipped her purse and turned her pistol over so the grips would be more accessible when the moment came.

Behind her, Summerfield made a U-turn, using none of the sedan's running lights, and drove east. What had he meant by having Bert Knoki cold? A *murdered cop* cold?

She turned the corner onto Seventh.

There was now lightning to the southwest, but it seemed to be strobing deep within the muffling cloud, for the only thunder was the crash of the locomotive coupling freight cars together.

Morada stood, and the braided figure sat up out of his conversational lean to watch her approach. A powerful neck. Definitely male. Something unpleasant occurred to her. After Lolly's warning, Rowe would be looking for a female Indian cop. Her argument to Summerfield began to ring hollow.

Where the devil is he?

Emmett's sedan had yet to appear at the intersection of Jackson and Seventh. She halted, began rifling through her purse. "Sir . . . ?" Morada pointed questioningly at himself. "Yes, please . . . can you hail me a cab?" She came out with a five-dollar bill.

Waving the fiver put Morada at ease, but the darkened face inside the Plymouth remained immobile. She could feel the eyes appraising her. "Lady," a smiling Morada cried over a gust of wind that made the pennants lining the top of the stadium flap wildly, "I ain't no valet. Go 'round to the Third Street side!"

At last, Summerfield nosed into the intersection. She started to angle in front of the Fury, but Morada stopped her with a shout. "Hey, you're goin' the wrong way!" He gestured toward the north end of the stadium. His arm was dropping to his side when a dazzle blinded Anna. Pulling in behind the Plymouth, Summerfield had punched up his high beams. All she could see were glittering waves of sand passing between her and the vague outlines of Rowe's car. Still, she drew her 9mm, dropped her purse to the pavement and clicked the muzzle against the window glass of the driver's door. "Terry Rowe, FBI—you're under arrest! Don't move!"

She heard the engine growl to life, but the car remained stationary, straining against an invisible force. Rowe must have realized in the same split second she did: He'd left his parking brake on while clamping down on the gas pedal. His driving skills had apparently eroded in prison. She reached for the door handle with her free hand. The sand cleared enough for her to see him lock down the button with his elbow and begin to grab the brake release. Pivoting toward the rear of the car, she jammed her pistol barrel against the sidewall of the right rear tire and fired twice.

The Fury exploded forward, but then careened on the flat. The metal rims of the wheel left a trail of sparks that curved to the opposite side of Seventh. There, Rowe plowed into a planter outside the right field gate.

He was left slumped over the wheel.

She spun on Morada. But he knew the drill: He spread-eagled on the sidewalk and clasped his hands behind his neck. Summerfield stood behind his open door, face flushed, one hand filled with the radio mike and the other with his pistol. Between barks at Morada for him to remain prone, he was trying to raise Phoenix PD.

"Turn off your lights, Reed!" Anna didn't want to be backlit. The headlamps went out. She scooped up her purse and started cautiously for the Fury, clenching her pistol before her. Smoke or radiator steam was escaping from under the crumpled hood.

Rowe suddenly reared up, and she froze.

Unsteadily, he reached across himself for the lock button and pried it up.

"Don't move, dammit!" Anna hollered, dropping to a knee.

But Rowe staggered out of the car and refused to obey her command to show his palms. Either feigning uncomprehension or genuinely dazed. Blood was flowing from a gash over his left eye. A hard face for thirty-six years. He had a simian build, powerful shoulders and arms triangulating down to a thin waist and short, stubby legs. He started gagging. Taking hold of the beaded choker Fanning had mentioned, he ripped it off, scattering hundreds of beads on the street around him. He continued to gurgle and gasp for air. But he was also backing up.

Then he crowed, "You ain't nothin' to be afraid of, bitch. I'll show you somethin' out there to be afraid of!"

"Stop or I'll shoot!"

But somehow, he caught the movement before she did. Fans giving up early on the game, trickling through the gate directly behind him. Anna sidestepped, trying to find a clear field of fire. But it was impossible, and Rowe skipped playfully through the pedestrians, patting some of them on the tops of their heads as he cavorted by. He vaulted over the turnstile and knocked down the unarmed guard who confronted him.

Already sprinting, Anna hollered over her shoulder, "Reed, advise the PD—I'm in foot pursuit!"

EMMETT'S COMMUTER FLIGHT was delayed at the Gallup airport because of a sandstorm hovering over Phoenix. One of those caused in early spring by a decaying thunderstorm that, instead of expending itself in rain, died in paroxysms of wind and sand. Emmett glanced morosely at his wristwatch. Nine-forty. He swiveled on the plastic seat inside the phone booth and tried his own number in Phoenix again. No answer but his own voice.

He dialed the number in McLean, Virginia, again. "Parker, I presume?"

"Yes, sir."

That was the end of the joshing. "Are you on a reasonably secure line?"

"No, but I'll take the risk."

"Very well, I have the answer to your first query. Yes, positively."

Emmett squeezed his eyes shut against a sudden acid flux in his stomach. Dieter Preuss had been a member of Stasi. Reed Summerfield had been sunbathing with his former enemy. But maybe that hadn't been the case. Maybe the agent had been fondly mulling over old times with a man he had recruited in place as part of an operation that had been duly reported to and approved by the FBI. In that case, the biggest challenge awaiting Emmett in Phoenix would be to explain to Anna why he had flown in without warning. "I don't suppose you've made any progress on my second query."

"You know better than that. And it's going to get territorial real quick if I push hard, according to my little birdie."

"I'd still appreciate it if you do push, sir."

"I will. In due course. Where can I reach you?"

"I'll phone you in the morning."

"Oh, one of those nights."

"Yes, sir, one of those nights. Thanks and goodbye." Hanging up, Emmett gazed through two panes of glass—the booth's and a terminal window—at the turboprop commuter. It was still parked on the tarmac, but a line of exhaust smoke was issuing from the starboard engine. Promising. He folded back the door to hear the announcement that his flight was finally boarding.

AS ANNA DUCKED UNDER the turnstile, the guard started to challenge her, but she explained her drawn pistol with her credentials. "FBI, which way did he go!"

"Come on!" The guard led her at a labored trot toward a tunnel-like passageway. He was soon huffing as he reported the incident over his radio handset. "One subject . . . white male . . . armed with a small chrome-plated semiauto."

Mention of a handgun jarred her—she hadn't seen one. It was soon apparent that the guard was holding her back. She seized the radio from the wheezing man. "I need this. What channel can I raise the PD on?"

"Two," he gasped, giving up and doubling over to brace his forearms on his thighs in a dizzy-looking squat.

Anna burst alone from the tunnel into the artificial daylight pouring down onto the brilliant green ball field. She scanned the aisles for Rowe's white sweatshirt. But the Diamondbacks were losing by six runs in the top of the eighth inning, and thousands of fans were streaming for the exits. An elderly woman almost swooned at the sight of the pistol. Anna dropped it back inside her purse. Then ran again, the spongy feel of spilled popcorn underfoot. She had to jostle her way through the human logjams at the entrances to the tunnels. A boy collided with her just-healed right elbow, making her grimace.

No sign of Rowe.

She pounded up an aisle to the main corridor ringing the next level, hoping to rise above the fugitive and spot him. Trying to blot out the irksome organ music, she stopped and strained for a glimpse of white matching Rowe's frame. Chatter came over the handset, but it sounded like nothing more than stadium dispatch repeating the guard's report of a man with a gun. She switched to channel two and attempted to raise Phoenix PD or Summerfield, who might still be monitoring that frequency. No response. All right. She'd have to do this on her own. *Where is Rowe headed?* Out of the stadium. And the longer he remained inside the greater the chance security would nab him. He would know that. His sole intent was to shake Anna—along the most direct possible line. In on the right field side and out somewhere behind home plate. Onto Third Street, if possible, where Morada had mentioned she should go for a taxicab.

Anna raced toward the seating behind the backstop net.

There, she ducked into a tunnel and let the crush of sweaty bodies carry her along. The dry, itchy atmosphere of the sandstorm had left the people quarrelsome. One man shoved another from behind to hurry him up, and the answer was a cupful of beer in the face before friends of both separated them. Anna realized that all the outer gates of the park would be opened to let the capacity crowd out. She tried to raise security dispatch, but the tunnel held in the transmission. She keyed the mike again on the escalator ride down to the concourse level, but the dispatcher responded suspiciously, "Unit, identify yourself."

"Special Agent Turnipseed," she said. "FBI. The gates—"

But there was a squeal as the woman overrode her: "Be advised this is not a federal-use channel."

Anna raced out the front—and saw something that surprised her: The foot traffic was still relatively light on the broad, plazalike concourse. Rowe would wait for more of the crowd to exit the stadium to screen his crossing to the taxi line. She hurried through the gate to the island between the passenger drop-off lane and Third Street, joining a small group of people waiting for a city bus.

Come out this way, you son of a bitch.

The blood caught her eye before the man himself. Rowe had wiped his bloody forehead on the shoulder of his sweatshirt, adding to the drips there, although the wound itself had stanched. He came across the concourse at a nonchalant lope, the fingers of both hands tucked into the pockets of his Levi's. He looked straight ahead as if his only concern was to hail a taxi. No guards were in sight. Had they all rushed inside the stadium to answer the man-with-a-gun call?

Anna walked out of the bus zone and up to a taxi waiting in the middle of the long line of them. The driver's-side window was down, and when he turned his face toward the sound of her approach she thrust her credentials in his eyes. "FBI, I need your cab for a minute."

"No shit?"

"No shit. Hurry." He got out, and she slid onto the seat just as Rowe stepped off the curb and whistled for a ride. Accelerating, she extinguished the dash lights and shot past the other cabs, cutting off the lead one. The drivers laid on their horns in protest. All her attention was focused on the front pockets to Rowe's Levi's. No bulge of a small semiauto was visible, but he could be carrying it in a back pocket. Her own pistol was already out and lying beside her. Slowing for him, she picked it up.

The first thing he saw when he opened the rear door was the muzzle.

"Freeze, you son of a bitch!"

Before she could react, he had vanished from the opening—and she had a shifting horde of fans in her sights. "Damn!" She flipped the wheel hard to the left and accelerated. One wheel up on the curb. Against the one-way traffic using the loading zone. This time, she had Rowe's white sweatshirt glowing like a beacon as he raced along the sidewalk. The pedestrians were too few for him to melt among them. She pulled alongside and shouted, her finger beginning to depress the trigger, "Go down or I kill you right now!"

Astonishingly, he obeyed.

But she had to brake so sharply to keep from barreling past him, the taxi went into a four-wheel skid. It no sooner stopped spinning than Rowe leaped up and tore for some freight cars.

She abandoned the taxi and ran. Bile scalded the back of her throat, but she refused to let Rowe open the distance between them.

Finally, she saw a glint in his right hand. He was armed, just as the guard had said. And he kept half-turning. As if thinking about cranking off a shot at her.

She was out of warnings for Terry Wade Rowe.

She fired twice. The reports slowed him for three or four seconds. Then he laughed demonically and passed between two boxcars of a stationary train—with Anna right on his heels. He jumped over the couplings but she had to duck under, nearly tripping on the far rail.

Emerging from the space between the cars, she had the sense of something massive and thunderous flying at her. She stopped dead in her tracks and protected her head with her arms.

There was a crash of metal in the darkness. And a blood-curdling scream. Then silence.

Still gripping her pistol before her, Anna dug inside her purse for her penlight. She thumbed on the feeble beam and held it out to the side of her body. The light found Rowe's eyes. They bulged. His face was corpse-pale, and his fists were beating at something clasping him around the waist. The joined claws of the knuckle coupling that had slammed together around his hips when a pair of tanker cars had been connected by the switching engine. The vise was so crushing only a few drops of blood were falling to the gravel between the ties. Close to where a small-caliber semiauto sparkled. "Can you understand me, Terry?"

He gave a remarkably alert nod, although he appeared to be on the verge of convulsing.

"I'm going to stop the engine before it comes back with another car. I'll get medical help."

"Just get Lolly," he begged.

chapter 14

THE ROTATING EMERGENCY LIGHTS GAVE ANNA VERTIGO. The fire department paramedics had wedged their ambulance between the two trains with only inches to spare on either side. One of the medical technicians was fighting hay fever, and he motioned with a damp handkerchief for Anna, Summerfield, a handful of city patrolmen and the railroad investigator to huddle around him. "Listen, folks," the paramedic quietly disclosed, for Rowe was within earshot, "everything this guy's got between his upper thighs and lower abdomen has been crushed. It's all bone splinters and pulp."

"Then why isn't he already dead?" the Southern Pacific dick asked.

"Coupling's acting as a giant tourniquet . . ." The paramedic sneezed, then gestured toward the waiting engine. "Soon as the engineer decouples the car, the bottom's going to drop out of this guy's circulatory system."

Summerfield asked, "Any possibility he'll survive?"

"Jesus," the paramedic replied, "he's been cut in two."

Summerfield took Anna by the elbow and made her go with him over to Rowe. She was sick to her stomach. She wanted to find someplace quiet and lie down. Rowe already looked dead. His skin was translucent, showing a tracery of bulging purple veins in his slack arms. His eyes were barely open, and the slivers of his pupils were opaque.

On the other side of the tracks, a Phoenix motorcycle cop

squatted on the heels of his boots, smoking a cigarette. Summerfield had positioned him there to keep watch on the Raven .25-caliber pistol Rowe had dropped when the cars pinned him.

"Terry Wade Rowe," Summerfield said severely.

After a beat, the man stirred with a shudder. "Who're you?"

"Special Agent Summerfield, FBI. I've just been advised by competent medical authority that you will not survive this injury. Do you understand what I'm saying?"

Rowe chuckled. A corpse mimicking gaiety. "I get the picture, motherfucker. Where's Lolly? I'll talk if you get Lolly for me."

Anna explained, "The police department sent a car to pick her up . . . what, ten minutes ago, Officer?" The motorcycle cop dipped his helmeted head. In the first minutes after the accident, Rowe had given Anna a new address in University Park, but she had doubts the prostitute would be found there on a Friday night. "Are you sure she'll be home, Terry?"

"Yes," he said thickly. "She's waiting for me. We had things to talk about. No chance this afternoon 'cause of you motherfuckers."

Summerfield drew Anna aside. "Help me," he said urgently.

"How?" She wanted to return to the privacy of Emmett's sedan, which Summerfield had parked on the north side of the tracks. But Juan Morada sat handcuffed in the backseat.

"Help me get a dying declaration. A few words from this scumbag and we tie the whole thing together." Summerfield's eyes were feverishly excited. "And you can rely on me, Anna."

"For what?"

"Shooting review."

"What do you mean?"

"The Phoenix SAC and his assistant are on the way here. That's why I wanted no one to touch Rowe's weapon before our people had a chance to see it for themselves at his feet. Did he fire at you?"

"No."

Summerfield winced, then asked, "How many rounds did you wind up expending?"

The SAC, the special agent in charge of the local field office, was coming. For the first time, she realized that her judgment might be questioned. "What'd you say, Reed?"

"How many rounds did you cap?"

"Three. No, four." Two in the tire and two at Rowe as he fled into the railyard.

"Any of them inside the stadium?" Summerfield pressed, raising his voice over an approaching siren.

"No, I wasn't even drawn inside the park."

"Good. That will help."

Then she recalled. She'd had her pistol in hand as she emerged from the tunnel. What was the truth about those minutes? They all seemed unreal now.

A PD cruiser stopped briefly in front of the idling locomotive, and its siren died. The engine's powerful headlamp shone through the grease-smudged windows of the car, illuminating a dark-haired woman in the caged back compartment. She pounded her fists against the Plexiglas partition. The patrolman got out to spring the rear door latch, and Lolly Blackhouse ran headlong for the ambulance lights. Rougeless and unpowdered, she scarcely resembled the slinky creature Anna had met that morning at the Feathered Serpent.

Rowe greeted her with a shrill laugh. "Some fix—huh, babe?"

Anna thought Lolly was going to collapse in horror. But instead she took the man's hands with a tenderness that almost seemed servile and kissed them. "I'll get you to a hospital."

"No, you won't. Not this time." Then Rowe dropped his voice slightly, probably not realizing in his state that he could still be heard by everybody within twenty feet. "I tried, babe. Went every place you asked . . ." He finished by shaking his head.

"It doesn't matter," she said with a loving smile. "Nothing matters except getting you to a hospital."

But Rowe was staring at Summerfield. "Tell her, motherfucker. Nobody's going to say I was a sap."

The agent asked, "Then you understand your death is imminent?" Right out of the textbook.

Rowe gestured at the viselike coupling and his legs bowed limply below it.

"I'll take that as a yes, witnesses," Summerfield said, meaning Anna and the motorcycle cop. "Terry Rowe, did you for a fact write a letter to Officer Carbert Knoki of the Navajo Nation Police?"

Rowe's clouded eyes shifted to Lolly, who looked stricken. Then he said, "Yeah, I guess."

"Yes or no?"

"I did."

"And what was the nature of that communication?"

"Personal business."

"Did you *kill* Carbert and Aurelia Knoki?"

"What?"

"You heard me."

Rowe turned his now tremulous face toward Anna. "Get this sick fuck out of here so I can die in peace. It's a good night to die."

As Anna led Summerfield away, he said hotly, "The scumbag did it!"

She gazed down the line at the Southern Pacific engineer. He'd cocked his head out the cab window, awaiting the signal from the railroad detective. As she watched, two men in suits strode into view off the sidewalk and turned toward her. Both spare, erect and well groomed. White shirts and muted ties. The J. Edgar Hoover ideal surviving more than a quarter-century after the first director's death. "Turnipseed?" the blonder of the two asked.

"Yes, sir."

"I'm Jim Niehaus of the Phoenix office, and this is my ASAC, Fred Waggoner." His assistant special agent in charge. Letting go of Anna's hand, Niehaus reached across her to grasp Summerfield's. "Good to see you again, Reed. Thanks for calling me so promptly."

"My pleasure, sir."

But Niehaus quickly focused back on Anna. He rested his hands atop her shoulders and looked warmly into her eyes. "Are you all right, Turnipseed? That's my first question."

She supposed his concern for her was genuine. She had no reason to think otherwise. But she immediately distrusted him. The knee-jerk paranoia toward white bureaucracy from growing up on a remote Modoc ranchería? "I'm fine," she replied coolly.

"Jim," Summerfield interjected, "I'd like to show you both something, if I may."

Anna remained glued to the spot on which she stood. Rowe was singing what sounded like a death song in Lakota. She couldn't bring herself to look at him again. Emmett. If here, he'd help her navigate through this. Not that she hadn't been catechized by the academy on the reasons for shooting and not shooting. But none of those simulated incidents came close to what had happened tonight.

She startled as a hand clamped onto her shoulder. Niehaus again. Smiling. As was Waggoner, who was now holding Rowe's semiauto inside a plastic bag. "Why don't you tell us what happened?" the SAC asked. Stepping even closer. Was he sniffing for alcohol on her breath?

"Well . . ." She hadn't wanted to start with the word *well*. She attempted to sound more decisive as she explained the reason for the stakeout. But her voice cracked slightly when she related how she'd disabled Rowe's car by flattening the tire with two bullets. Had that been ill-advised? At the time, it'd seemed the only way to prevent a high-speed pursuit through downtown Phoenix. Hadn't a dangerous car chase been Summerfield's chief concern in the first place? Would he say that in her defense? ". . . at which time, the security guard at the right field gate advised me that he'd seen a weapon in Rowe's possession."

"Had you?" Niehaus asked casually.

"No," she admitted. "I wasn't able to verify this until—"

A scream made her jump. Two patrolmen had grabbed Lolly under the arms and were dragging her away from Rowe. "Let me go!"

The paramedics were stepping back from the man, and the Southern Pacific investigator waved a red-lensed flashlight. The engine advanced. The cross gates came down on Third Street to the dinging of the warning bell. The paramedics may have given Rowe something, for his head was now sagging. The engineer brushed up against the leading tanker car as gently as his huge locomotive would allow, but there followed a jerk that made Rowe groan.

Niehaus's voice was in her ear. "You still have your weapon on you, Turnipseed?"

"Yes, sir."

"I've got to take it. Procedure, as you well know. Drop by the office as soon as your administrative leave is over and we'll either return your nine-mil or issue you a temp."

She was suspended with pay awaiting evaluation of her actions. That too was procedure.

"Go back to Emmett's place, Anna," Summerfield said soothingly. "I'll dump Morada in a cruiser, and you take the sedan. I can wrap up. Impound Rowe's wheels and interrogate Morada. Get a ride from the PD back to the apartment later. Go rest, dear woman."

Then there was a shearing clank as the coupling was disengaged. Anna couldn't watch. Neither could Lolly, apparently, for the woman, still being restrained by the patrolmen, was glaring tearlessly at Anna. She grinned viciously and spat, "Got to have that excitement to get him out of your cunt . . . don't you, little sister?"

*   *   *

FOR NEARLY AN HOUR, the commuter had been circling the great sandstorm socking in the Phoenix area. The lights of the city were visible but bleared, partly from the airborne sand and partly by the constant jouncing of the plane in the turbulence around the unraveling anvil cloud. Helplessly strapped into his seat, Emmett picked out his own neighborhood, wondering if he should have the pilot radio the tower and relay a message to Phoenix PD. Or one of his fellow criminal investigators at BIA.

Quit catastrophizing.

Anna would be all right as long as she didn't confront Summerfield over Dieter Preuss. And she knew nothing about the former Stasi agent, so all was well in the near term. Having a PD or BIA cop barge in on the two FBI agents—on the basis of a secondhand briefing rife with potential misunderstandings—might be more dangerous for her than letting sleeping dogs lie until he himself got to Phoenix.

Lightning forked inside the dying thundercloud.

A sudden downdraft whipped his forehead against the window, and he grunted as a woman across the aisle screamed. His upper back, already sore from having a hogan roof collapse on it, was cramping from all the pounding.

How would he confront Summerfield?

That was of secondary importance. He could take his time plotting his next move as soon as he isolated Anna. He didn't know what he'd do if he discovered only Summerfield at his apartment, claiming that he hadn't seen her in hours and was growing worried himself. He didn't trust his temper if he heard something like that from the agent. But reason told him the man had no reason to harm Anna. She was a stranger to the Navajo police, and it would be doubtful to Summerfield that either Tallsalt or Yabeny had confided the existence of the FI cards to her. Emmett was well acquainted with the tribal department, and it'd been like pulling teeth for him to find out about them.

"Folks," the pilot's voice came over the intercom, "we're

starting to run a tad low on fuel, so I've been cleared to land at Tucson International. That's about a hundred miles southeast of us. Sorry for the inconvenience."

SPECIAL AGENT IN CHARGE Niehaus's initial warmth at the scene had only been a marinade. He'd grilled her, and Anna now asked herself if she felt violated. She was unsure how exactly she felt. Her service pistol had been taken from her. Administrative leave until further notice. She had nothing to do until at least early next week, when it'd be determined if she'd shown good judgment. Or not.

Tonight, good judgment seemed like a hopelessly subjective thing. *You had to have been there.*

She parked outside Emmett's building, gathered up her FBI windbreaker and seemingly weightless purse. As light as a dried hummingbird. The storm had stripped the dwarf tangerine trees of their blooms, and they were floating as a white scum on the pool. The only lighting to break up the shadows in the courtyard came from mushroomlike fixtures thrust into the planters.

She trudged up the stairs to Emmett's entryway, fished in her purse for his key. He must have called by now.

But there were no messages on his answering machine.

She realized how much she'd wanted some word from him when she almost started to cry. Then she decided to go ahead. Quietly and efficiently. To purge the night out of her. Its whole new raft of hideous images. She wept soundlessly as she relocked the door behind her, kicked off her shoes and tossed her windbreaker and purse on Emmett's easy chair.

She went to the bathroom, groped blindly for the wall switch.

The fluorescent light hummed to life.

At midday, between meeting with Fanning and grabbing a bite at a coffee shop in South Phoenix, Summerfield and she had swung by the apartment to freshen up. She'd neglected to rehang the hand towel after hurriedly washing. Now she buried her face in it and laughed through her tears. Undeniably, there was a hard kernel of self-satisfaction lodged somewhere in her numbness. She had survived the tumultuous evening. Even taken control of events. While it'd occurred to her on the drive back that Rowe might still be alive had she not pumped two bullets into his tire, she had only to recall her repeated warnings for him to halt to know in her heart that the man had caused his own death.

It was possible to live with everything that had happened.

She wiped her eyes and nose, then dropped the towel. Unzipping her pantsuit, she let it fall to the floor. Her underwear joined the small pile, and she vowed to do a load of wash before rejoining Emmett in Window Rock. She looked at her nude body in the mirror. *Got to have that excitement to get him out of your cunt . . . don't you, little sister?* Lolly Blackhouse knew just where to twist the knife. Her gift was to spot scar tissue, no matter how old. And that made her a less sympathetic figure than she'd seemed earlier in the day. Even when Anna added the loss of the woman's lover into the mix. Had Rowe given her the bruise on the upper arm? Anna examined the backs of her own arms in the mirror. No sign remained of that phantom grip that even to this day tightened around her arms whenever she smelled Wild Turkey whiskey and Coca-Cola.

Too tired. Too spent to wade back into the past.

She shut the bathroom door and turned on the taps. The splash against the bottom of the tub covered all sounds beyond this steamy and protected space—especially the crash of two railroad cars being coupled together. She dipped a toe in the water. Just right. The body could be cleansed of experience. She wasn't convinced the same was true of the mind.

GILA MONSTER AWAKENED.

The sandstorm had died away, but a dusty-smelling stillness continued to pervade the interior of his van. A mercury vapor street lamp shined through the curtains that could be pulled around on a curved track to cover the windshield and front windows. He stretched, his forepaws trembling against an isometric strain that ended as a pleasurable spasm in the small of his back. But the lumpy sleeping bag beneath him was wet from his perspiration, so he rose and lumbered forward to the cab. Parted the curtains with the back of his right forepaw.

It was still there.

The bronze Dodge sedan that had parked in the same spot outside the pool gate during the noon hour today. He'd followed it here from the federal courthouse downtown, and before that tailed an unmarked but obvious police car from the Feathered Serpent—only because *she* had gotten out of the second vehicle and strolled into the club. Not Moth Woman. But the same young native woman he'd spied through one of the ventilation panels in the skirting of the Knokis' mobile home. A cop who at any time might ruin everything. Two plainclothesmen, one black and one white, had dropped her off at the club and then cruised the area, forcing Gila Monster to pull back a few blocks.

His hands shot to his temples as the hot tornado of the Voice filled his head. *Where atonement is not the issue, induce others to do the killing for you. Especially if the target is one in authority!*

"I have," Gila Monster whispered. But the Voice was never satisfied.

Listen, you imbecile—only in this way will you extend your years of service to the Elect, for there are many who will try to ensnare you on your errands!

But was that possible in this case?

No. He was friendless in Phoenix. As in so many other places, other times. Adrift all those years in a sea of children. A row to himself at the rear of the little schoolroom. And alone this evening in the diner until the flirty waitress knelt beside his table and said that *nobody* ever ordered the mutton stew. *What makes you so different, honey?* Laughing at his unease, she touched his arm, making him whip out his wallet, fling a ten spot at her and bolt from the place.

"This too I must do by myself," Gila Monster now said.

Ninety minutes ago, the native woman had stepped out of the bronze Dodge—*alone*. And gone through the apartment door at the top of the stairs. Her name was Turnipseed. He read the papers. She was the head demon charged with running him down.

Gila Monster let the curtains close.

He could hear the pocket watch the Voice had given him ticking on the dashboard. *I must leave it all to you, for my breath is short and my enemies powerful.* And from the cargo area drifted the sounds of his three remaining brothers stirring in their cages. Claws shredding the newspaper linings. The almost inaudible wisp-wisp of tongues slithering in and out, testing the air for pinkies. It was awful to deprive them, but only at the brink of starvation would they clamp voraciously onto anything warm-blooded and hang fast until all resistance went limp. They were proof to the Voice that he had completed his errand. To the world.

He reached down into the toolbox behind the driver's seat and removed a large buckskin pouch. From that, he took out his Gila gloves and slipped them on. He'd filed down the claws until their tips were like needles. Ever so gently, he raked his left paw over the bare human skin of his right shoulder. Despite the scant pressure, five streaks of black appeared on his flesh like an empty bar line of music. Blood was black in low light. Despite all the Atonements he'd visited on the wicked these past five years, this never ceased to amaze him. Tonight, he would see great gouts of the stuff, splashed like tar over a bedroom.

Picking up the pouch again, he removed his javelin and carried it to the cargo area, where he used its point to stab holes in a cardboard box.

*   *   *

ANNA SENSED THAT she wasn't alone in bed. Whose bed? It didn't quite feel like her own in her Las Vegas condominium, but the drone of the air conditioner was familiar. Or was it the rumble of the locomotive, waiting to decouple the tanker cars? She could smell diesel fumes. *You're dreaming, you're dreaming.* But Terry Wade Rowe was in bed with her, his nearly severed halves deathly quiet beside her. *It's a good night to die.* A train horn blatted. Reed Summerfield poked his balding head out of the engine cab, waiting callously for Anna's signal. She dropped her hand like a guillotine blade, and the engine pulled away the leading car. Rowe folded backward, almost in two, as he plunged to the track bed. Into her bed.

Something brushed her cheek. It was cool and scaly.

Her startled eyes opened.

A fetid-smelling glove clamped down on her mouth and nose, muffling her scream. And then she couldn't scream because she was fighting for air. Reaching up, she flailed against the arms pinning her to the mattress. Her blows glanced off thick biceps and slablike pectorals. The pressure increased around her face, and for the first time she felt claws digging into her scalp.

Her hands tore uselessly at the air between their heads.

"Lie still and I won't hurt you." The voice was a soft reptilian hiss that gave her gooseflesh.

She forced herself to stop struggling for a moment, just to see what he would do. The glove remained like a seal around her mouth and nostrils. He was going to suffocate her no matter what she did.

"Stop," he warned with rising fury.

But she drove her fist into his groin. He growled. She struck him again, and the glove lifted from her face just long enough for her to suck in a painful, gasping breath. Her head cleared a little, and she could begin to think beyond the struggle for her next breath.

His face was obscured by shadow, but she could make out the cold, red sparks of his eyes. They glided closer, as if he intended to say something more, but she plunged the heel of her palm into the base of his nose. Felt a mustache.

He tumbled off the bed.

She jerked the drawer out of the nightstand and fumbled inside for her pistol. There was no weapon there, and the reason why sank in, paralyzing her for an instant. Only an instant. He had risen again. As slowly as if he'd materialized out of the floor. He was as tall as Emmett, she judged, who was six-two. And massively built. Bare-chested. She hurled the drawer at him, driving him back a step as he batted it aside, splintering the wood. He was wearing gloves that went all the way up to his elbows. Gauntlets made from Gila monster skin.

And from the left one he now slid a long-handled blade.

She seized both of Emmett's pillows and scurried up onto her knees.

He paused before lunging.

Black spots appeared on the luminous rumples of the sheets. She'd bloodied his nose. Possible only because she'd been close in to him. Precisely how the academy instructors taught how to handle a knife wielder. Stay in close and go for the eyes. Work inside the arc of the blade.

But she couldn't force herself to do that. She'd be within range of those claws again.

She waited for him to come at her.

"What brought you down here?" he demanded. A curiously puzzled tone.

No time to answer. She stood. Slowly. So she wouldn't lose her balance on the wobbly surface of the mattress. Should she scream? Or would that only make him spring his attack sooner rather than later? And all the air conditioners in the complex were running tonight. She might not be heard. But vibration was another matter.

She slammed her heel against the headboard. It sent a tremor through the wall.

"Stop it!" he snarled, although trying to keep his voice

down. Despite his frightening size, he showed a juvenile infuriation that he could be defied. "You stop that right now!"

A chastising knock came from the other side of the wall. And then the doorbell rang. Two chimes before the ringer gave up and began rattling the doorknob. Either the manager or Summerfield. Perhaps even the police, although she refused to let wild hope distract her.

She snatched the reading lamp off the nightstand and hurled it through the window. The crash was followed by the tinkling of shards on the courtyard pavement below. The drapes were gone. They'd wrapped around the plummeting lamp, but no more light than before spilled into the bedroom. She continued to confront a silhouette. Faceless. Towering. Poised to run her through with the blade.

From the living room came the wall-rattling pounding of someone throwing his shoulder against the front door. When her attacker's head snapped toward the sound, she rushed him. By the time he reared back the object to strike, she was inside his reach. She pushed strenuously against the ropy muscles of his chest while laying her hands over the back of his left arm, slipping down the length of the prickly-feeling glove to his wrist. She was bending the joint inward, suppressing a dawning exhilaration that she just might disarm him—when he opened his fist and allowed the blade to fall to the carpet.

There followed a gut-wrenching moment in which nothing happened. They gasped in each other's faces as the pounding at the front door went on.

Then he grabbed Anna by the hair with his free hand and rammed her head into the wall.

A PHOENIX PD CRUISER passed Emmett in the opposite direction as he drove up the street he lived on. He was already coasting into the parking lot; otherwise, even a block earlier, the patrolman would have stopped him for excessive speed. The car he'd rented at the airport in Tucson was close to overheating after covering the hundred miles of interstate in less than an hour. He pulled alongside his own sedan, bailed out—and froze before he took a step.

Every apartment in the building was lit—except his own.

He pressed the glow button on his wristwatch: 12:23 A.M.

Throwing open the pool gate, he again tried to reassure himself that Summerfield had no reason to blow his charade of innocence and go after Anna.

But then he noticed the poolside concrete. It was glittering with shapes too jagged to be water spots. He glanced from the dented reading lamp that ordinarily stood on his nightstand to his reamed-out bedroom window. Then broke into a run. His revolver was drawn by the time he mounted the top of the stairs. It taxed all his self-control to halt at his threshold and listen. The only noise was the tinny rattle of his Sears air conditioner laboring to cool off Phoenix: The front door had been bashed in, kept from entirely collapsing only by the bottom hinge.

His muzzle still trained on the darkness, he reached around the wall and found the switch.

He'd witnessed the brightly lit scene before. A hundred times throughout his career. The only incongruity was that it was now in his own living room. His home had been invaded, and he strained to hold down a burst of rage. A fully clothed white male was lying on his left side, right arm twisted under him and the barrel of a pistol projecting out from under his back. Two pools of blood—one large and one small—had seeped from the body. Both a deep red and wet.

It was Summerfield.

Emmett had to advance three steps into the room to see this, for the agent's features had been contorted into an agonized death mask.

He rushed into the bedroom, flicked on the ceiling light and swept his .357 Magnum from side to side.

Anna was heaped against the wall beneath the broken

window, her head angled back. At that moment, he came as close to passing out as he ever had in his life. His vision started to fade to gray. He had to stand straight to keep from compressing his lungs and letting his light-headedness overwhelm him.

Her neck had been broken.

Slumping to his knees, he went still, scarcely able to hang on to his revolver, his hands felt so weak. He didn't want to confirm the apparent. He wanted to cling to hope for as long as possible. But finally, he holstered and touched two fingers to the left carotid artery in her throat. But he couldn't tell if the jack-hammering pulse he felt was hers or his own. He brought his ear down to her slightly parted lips. Was he just imagining the faint beat? He licked the back of his hand and held it to her mouth. A hint of evaporation made him briefly shut his eyes in thankfulness. Only once before had it been this personal. His mother had called him instead of the sheriff's office to check on his brother. That time there'd been no hope.

Emmett whispered, "Anna."

Her eyes clicked open. The pupils seemed normal. No apparent neurological damage.

"Don't move. It's Emmett."

Her hands twitched to life. He tried to restrain her, but she sat up and rubbed the back of her neck. Then, whatever had happened here, it came back to her in its full horror. She threw her arms around him. "Where's—?" She couldn't finish.

"Summerfield?"

"Who?" She looked so bewildered, Emmett suspected temporary amnesia. Her dumbfounded mind may have found it easier to forget than try to rationalize why Summerfield had attacked her. Emmett swept her up and rested her on his bed. It was splattered with blood. Hers or Summerfield's? There were some scratches near her temple under the hairline. But they hadn't bled much. There was also a shallow bruise on her forehead.

A shaken-sounding but familiar voice wafted from outside to him. "Emmett?"

Leaving Anna, he headed for the front door. Stepping around Summerfield. The meekly alcoholic manager of his apartment complex ventured halfway up the stairs before his nerves got the better of him. "Quent," Emmett said, blocking the man's view inside.

"What the hell's going on?"

"I've got to phone the police. I want you to keep everybody away from here until they arrive."

"Are you all right?"

"Yes."

Quentin was retired Air Force, used to taking orders. "Okay."

Careful not to touch the knob, Emmett jammed the door back into its frame. Then, turning, his stomach roiling, he tried to make sense of Reed Summerfield lying dead on his carpet. Had he actually assaulted Anna? And had she killed him in self-defense? Emmett knew that he should be on the phone to the PD right now, instead of struggling to fit the square pegs of the physical evidence into the round holes of his assumption that Summerfield had done the unexpected. *How far will I go to protect her?*

Swiftly, he had to understand this death.

He parted Summerfield's jacket. A gust of foul-smelling heat was released, and Emmett backed off a few feet. As soon as a gag reflex subsided, he leaned over the man again. The wound track was big. From the navel to the xiphoid process, the bottom segment of the sternum. There was savage trauma to the underlying organs, yet the copious bleeding meant that he'd lived at least some seconds after being stabbed. The instrument had been sharp enough not to fray his white shirt while slicing through it. And the tip had come out his back near the spine.

Anna didn't have the arm strength for that.

Slowly, Emmett came to his feet, stunned by the realization that she hadn't slain Summerfield. And the killer was fleeing at this very minute. So far, he hadn't imagined that she might not be responsible. He'd just spent too many frantic hours visualizing this possible outcome to her being left alone with Summerfield.

"Oh God," she said behind him.

He spun around in time to watch her lean unsteadily against the kitchen counter. He ran to her before she pitched over. "Going to throw up?" he asked, and she nodded. He helped her to the sink, where she relieved herself. Twice. When she stopped at last and ran the cold water, he asked, "Somebody was here . . . other than Summerfield?"

She nodded again.

"Description?"

"Male," she rasped. "Six-two, muscular build. Mustache. Too dark to see much else. Except the Gila monster gloves he was wearing."

The hair on the back of Emmett's neck electrified.

"Want to brush my teeth," she added feebly. "Wash my face."

"Go ahead." But first he kissed her on the cheek. Mindboggling to be so rattled and overjoyed at the same time.

As she trooped into the bathroom, he grabbed his telephone off the counter and returned to the corpse. It was difficult to see Summerfield as a victim and not a threat. But he would try. Bending down from a crouch, he sniffed the muzzle of the agent's pistol. No tang of cordite. It hadn't been fired. Sitting up, he started to dial 911. Had Summerfield sustained any defensive wounds? They would plausibly account for the splatters on the bedsheets.

But the man's hands and shirtsleeves were uncut.

Emmett craned to examine the smaller bloodstain. And promptly replaced the receiver in its cradle. Blood had dripped onto the carpet directly under Summerfield's throat, forming a circle three inches wide. Emmett untangled the man's silk tie, which had flipped around his neck as he fell. Summerfield's Adam's apple. It wasn't so much crushed as pulverized. Masticated. Emmett shifted around so his shadow didn't fall across Summerfield's upper body. As soon as the light improved, he saw the distinctive ring of tooth marks—and jolted to his feet.

To one side of the front door was a medium-sized cardboard box. He nudged it with the toe of his shoe. Nothing in it. He inspected the sides and top: perforated.

The box slipped from his hands.

He rampaged through the living room, overturning the couch and the easy chair, peering through the back of his television console into the cavity under the circuitry. Next, he hurried to the bedroom and upended his bed, checking under the mattress and spring. They slammed back onto the frame as he raced for the bedroom, seizing a straw broom out of the hall closet on the way. The knob was locked.

"Anna!"

At first, she couldn't hear him over the faucet. He pounded on the door with his fist.

"What?" she asked anxiously.

"Unlock the door and stand up on the vanity!"

"What?"

"Let me in, then get above the floor!"

There was a snick on the other side of the door, and he crept into the bathroom. She crouched on the vanity, her bare legs straddling the sink. Hands fisted. Emmett advanced, sweeping the broom back and forth in front of him. He glimpsed the black snout in the same second a blur of vividly colored bands darted out of a small pile of dirty clothes. Hissing, the Gila clamped down on the handle just above the neck where the bristles were joined. The soft wood crunched under the pressure of the jaws. But the handle held. He hoisted the writhing crescent and carried it into the living room. There, the stick gave as Emmett held the Gila over the box. And the big lizard dropped inside.

He closed the flaps and went back to Anna, who'd eased down onto the floor. He held her.

chapter 15

THE INSTANT THE MARICOPA COUNTY JAILER APPEARED AT the top of the basement garage stairs with Juan Morada, Emmett knew the aquiline-nosed Akimel O'odham would talk. He had the dazed look that comes over the chronically guilty when, by chance, they are innocent. "Cuff him to the railing, please," Emmett instructed the deputy, then turned again to Rowe's 1983 Plymouth Gran Fury.

The jailer plodded back up the stairs, and the prisoner, now handcuffed to the railing, sank down onto a cement step. A big, golden shaft slanted down into the basement, illuminating the dust stirred by the comings and goings of sheriff's cruisers.

"I'm Investigator Parker from the BIA." Emmett's voice echoed in the cavernous space.

"I know. Everybody knows you."

"You been told your rights, Juan?"

"Yeah. By the FBI agent. Didn't he tell you?"

"He couldn't."

"Why not?"

"He's dead." Letting that sink in, Emmett took a large screwdriver from his toolbox and pried the trim panel off the inside of the driver's door. Nothing of interest behind it. *Why the hell did Rowe try so desperately to flee from Anna?*

Morada sighed. "What d'you want to know, Parker?"

Everything. And Emmett seemed as far from knowing it as he'd been five days earlier while descending into Crystal

Wash. Summerfield had arrested Morada on the spurious charge of willfully harboring a fugitive. The reason for the hold could now be stretched to include the investigation of the murder of a federal officer. But Emmett realized he wouldn't have long before Morada figured out that his interrogators were on thin ice. "All right," he said evenly, "tell me how a lily-white boy got in the AB?"

Morada's eyes were fixed on the swirling motes in the sun ray. Not on the car. "The truth?"

Emmett took a utility knife to the threadbare upholstery of the driver's seat. "That'd be nice."

"The warden at FCI wouldn't let us have religious privileges on account he said we was just a racial group. All Indians, you know? And back then, the admin tried to discourage separatin' different colors like that. So, one of the guys—"

"Who?" Emmett asked, peering up into the maze of wires beneath the dashboard.

"Oscar Grass Rope. Lakota. So, he says, listen, my cellmate is white, and he might be interested. Thing is, Terry *was* interested. He really got off on native religion. Either that or nobody'd ever asked him to join anythin' before. I mean, here was this squared-away guy, business-wise, but it came out in our talkin' circles during the sweats that he was real tore up inside."

"What do you know about his business?"

"He was a mule for some Mexicans."

"Taking shipments into the Navajo Nation?"

"Never heard that. It all ended here in Phoenix. DEA took him down at a hangar at Sky Harbor."

"Was he a pilot?"

"No. It was his job to stay with the shipment from Mexico to here. He was real good with radios and microwaves. An electronic wizard. So he helped the pilots get under U.S. radar."

"What were most of the hauls?" Emmett asked. "Coke?"

"No, meth."

That blew another hole in John Tallsalt's coffee shop tale that the Colombians were moving their product through Sonoran middlemen. Mexicans made their own methamphetamine.

Emmett sat on the shredded seat. A lingering staleness of perspiration hinted at days of habitation inside the car. Reddish sand and food crumbs all over the rubber floor mats. But no papers or wrappings to reveal where Rowe might have been. Emmett grabbed a hammer from the box, then smashed the center console, narrowing his eyes against the flying plastic chips. But the destruction revealed only the inner workings of the shift lever. He'd already been through the trunk, the backseat and the recesses in the body shell. All this left him mildly confused. The most common reason a parolee with a drug rap suddenly drops out of sight is to haul another shipment. So far, the Plymouth had given up no signs of having been modified for trafficking. And not once had Morada stolen a glance at any particular portion of the car, betraying the location of a stash learned from Rowe.

"How'd Terry approach you last night?" Emmett asked.

"He just drove up."

"You can do better than that, Juan." Anna had told him about Rowe's casing the block before finally pulling up to Morada.

"Okay, okay," the Akimel O'odham quickly said, "he cruised a little before stoppin' by me at the entrance. That's pretty much the same as just drivin' up, ain't it?"

"Rowe tell you he was on the run?"

Morada hesitated. He knew this is where he could get himself in trouble. Now aware of Summerfield's death, he was savvy enough to realize that the issue had gone far beyond aiding a fleeing felon. He didn't want to lie without knowing the risks.

"Didn't Summerfield cover your conversation with Rowe?" Emmett pressed.

"Not really. He was just interested in what you are now—drugs and the Navajo rez. Plus this cop named Knoki. He must've thought Knoki was crooked or somethin' because he kept askin' if him and Terry knew each other."

There it was again. The possibility Summerfield had murdered the Knokis, which was now diminished by the agent's own death. "Tell me what Rowe said to you last night, Juan."

There was a rattle of handcuff chain as Morada shifted his weight on the hard step. "Terry said his PO might be lookin' for him, but he wasn't runnin'. He'd missed a check-in and a counselin' session, but he wasn't no absconder. Somebody was after his old lady—"

"Lolly Blackhouse?"

"Yeah. And Terry had to go on the road to find out who."

"Go where?"

"Sounded like all over upstate. New Mexico too, because he said somethin' about his alternator goin' out in some burg called Canoncito."

It wasn't a burg. Canoncito was the most easterly of the three Navajo island reservations, scattered tribal enclaves outside the contiguous boundaries of the Big Rez. "Why would somebody be after Lolly?"

"Terry figured one of her johns was stalkin' her. That really ticked him off, and he was out to square away this dude."

"Did Rowe have this man's name?"

"No, and I think that's what was drivin' him crazy, you know? I didn't whack no FBI agent, Parker."

Emmett ignored the statement. "Tell me what the female agent did during the takedown last night. You saw it, didn't you?"

"Yeah. She was pretty cool. Told Terry to give it up, but I think he was too wired over his old lady to keep his head, you know? Wasn't goin' to let Fanning violate him till he caught this dude."

"So she clearly warned him to surrender?"

"Oh yeah, sayin' she was FBI and everythin'. But he took off like a bat out of hell."

"Recklessly?" Emmett prodded, walking around to the Plymouth's grille.

"Pretty much."

"Pedestrians?"

"Sure. It was the eighth inning, and the Diamondbacks were gettin' their asses whipped. People comin' out of the right-field gate."

Emmett wrenched open the collision-buckled hood.

The rebuilt alternator looked like it'd been stored on a shelf a long time prior to being installed. No distinguishing marks or labels. Simpler to drive up to Canoncito than begin the process of tracing the serial number. "I don't think you had anything to do with Summerfield's death, Juan . . ." Otherwise, he would've done what the Navajo gangbangers in Tohatchi Juvenile Detention Facility were doing: refuse to be questioned by anyone but a grand jury. Then take the fifth, if their attorney couldn't stonewall the appearance in the coming weeks. Just as Morada began to look relieved, Emmett added, "But I'm not with the FBI, and it's one of their own who bought it. What'd you do your most recent time for?"

"Intent to commit murder," Morada admitted matter-of-factly. "Can't you at least tell the feebs what you think?"

"You ready to deal?"

"Sure," Morada said eagerly.

"Sign a statement to what you just told me about the female agent's conduct last night, and I'll talk to the honcho in charge of the FBI office here."

ANNA BRUSHED HER TEETH at the window of her bedroom in the Embassy Suites at Camelhead Airport. She'd expected to draw back the drapes on a view of the morning desert, but only city spread smoggily out to some scarred hills in the west. Still, underneath her numbness was that day-after-death gratitude she was seeing something Reed Summerfield would never behold again.

Suddenly, she spun away from the window.

West was the direction of the dead, of evil. Facing it in sleep could bring nightmares, or an uncontrollable urge to devour snakes and walk into fires. With so much death around, her repressed Modoc beliefs broke through her doubts. Evil waited everywhere.

Her eyes fell on her purse at the foot of the bed.

Last night, it—and Uncle Boston's hummingbird—had been in Emmett's nightstand drawer when she was attacked. Reason told her that by any reckoning she should be dead. She'd been caught asleep. With her pistol locked up as evidence in the local FBI office.

Yet, she had survived by hovering just outside the sweep of that monster's blade. Like a hummingbird.

At 1:30 this morning, Emmett had checked her into this hotel while a joint team of FBI and Phoenix PD evidence technicians photographed, fingerprint-dusted and vacuumed his apartment. She'd slept for a while, then snapped wide awake at four with the crawling sensation that someone had stolen into the suite. She even groped inside the nightstand drawer for the snub-nosed .38 Special Emmett had left with her. His own spare. But no one had disturbed her.

Until now. A knock at the door.

She slipped the revolver from the nightstand drawer, then spat out a mouthful of toothpaste into the efficiency's sink on her way to the minimal living room. Through the distortion of the peephole, she saw two balloon-sized tie knots and a blond pinhead above each of them. Before unchaining the door, she dropped the .38 Special into her purse and zipped it shut.

"Turnipseed?" Jim Niehaus asked with an embarrassed smile. The Phoenix SAC and ASAC looked surprised to see her.

"Morning," she mumbled.

Niehaus noticed the wet toothbrush she was clutching. "Sorry to disturb you. Is this Parker's room, by chance?"

Then the implication hit her. They thought she'd spent

the night shacked with Emmett. "No, he was kind enough to drop me off here last night before he went out again. Don't know when to expect him."

"Parker asked us to meet him here at nine o'clock," Waggoner said uncomfortably. It was almost that now. "Meeting of the minds."

She knew at once what Emmett had done by inviting them here: He was testing the limits of the administrative leave they'd imposed on her. She decided to do the same. "You sure you want me present?"

"Of course," Niehaus said. Anything else would have been rude, and she could tell from his quick frown that he knew he was being maneuvered.

To hell with him. Someone had tried to murder her last night, and her emotional hangover was slowly giving way to anger. The only real fear she had now was that she'd be sidelined. "Won't you please come in?"

The two men shuffled inside. For the first time, she noted the differences in their Northern European looks: Niehaus had a thin Prussian face and hair like goose down. There was a peasanty robustness to Waggoner's ruddy cheeks and bristly, hay-colored crew cut.

"Can I make some coffee for you?" she offered.

"I'll brew it," Niehaus volunteered. "You finish getting ready."

His comment made her suspect that something was awry with her appearance. There was. A fresh bruise on her forehead—from being slammed against the wall by her attacker—and a foamy smear of Crest fanning out from the right corner of her mouth. Plus the scar from the acetylene torch burn last January. What'd the self-defense instructors used to say at the academy? *They can kill you, but they can't eat you?*

Two minutes later, the sound of Emmett's voice made her hurriedly finish her makeup and return to the living room. Niehaus was saying to Emmett, "Naturally, we're pulling out all the stops on this one. I'm throwing in every agent

I've got. So's the Gallup office. Plus we're ready to tap Washington's offer of whatever else we need to run this bastard to ground."

Emmett's weary eyes were on Anna as he said from the only armchair in the room, "We need an unhobbled coordinating agent."

Waggoner reared up on a sofa cushion as if it suddenly seemed too spongy for him, and gruffly asked, "How the hell are we hobbling you, Parker?"

"Not me," Emmett clarified. "Turnipseed. She's ramrodding this task force. Has been from day one. And if you add more personnel to the mix, that makes her the coordinating agent in my book."

"And how exactly are we hindering Turnipseed?" Niehaus asked carefully.

"Putting her on administrative leave right when I most need direction from her. And leave for what? A shooting incident in which a shot wasn't material to the cause of death? She righteously capped a few rounds Wednesday morning during the sniper attack on the Navajo rez. So'd I. And you let that slide on a short-form report from the Gallup office."

"No one died then," Niehaus noted.

"And nobody got shot last night. A druggie-mope crashed into a train while fleeing. Had he done it with his car instead of his body, Phoenix PD Traffic would be handling this. If he'd died of a heart attack, Animal Control would've been called to pick him up. Christ almighty, Jim—let's expedite. I want closure *today*. We've got things to do, and nobody's better acquainted with this case than Turnipseed."

Niehaus turned nonchalantly toward Anna. "Ready for some coffee?"

"No thanks," she said, sitting in a chair. She was dying for a cup, but wanted nothing to slow Emmett's push toward resolving her duty status. Which was Niehaus's intent.

Waggoner, obviously, wasn't as fast on the uptake. "It's bullshit to rush a shooting review. At any time." The ASAC glared at Emmett.

"It's bullshit to interview an officer at the scene of the incident. It's our practice in the BIA to get them to a quiet environment. Let them settle down and get their wits about them before we hold their feet to the flames. And what about an offer to let her phone her legal rep?" Emmett took a sheaf of papers from the pocket of his dust-streaked windbreaker. "I find a number of omissions, Fred, in your report on Anna's actions—"

"How the fuck did you get that?" Waggoner blurted. "It hasn't even been routed upstairs yet."

Niehaus cautioned him with a light touch on the arm. "I gave it to him last night. Only fair. It impacts the task force."

"And I appreciated it, Jim," Emmett said. A shade less than sincere. "First off, Anna had every reason last evening to believe Rowe might be a murder suspect. A cop killer. She came down here with Summerfield to investigate that possibility, and I'd be glad to supply you with the linkage that spun us off in this direction . . ." He flipped to the next page. "Where's Probation Officer Fanning's admonition that whenever Rowe was collared he was packing heat? Or didn't Anna get a chance to tell you while you were all standing around waiting for Rowe to die . . . ?" Waggoner began fiddling with a loose thread dangling off his trouser cuff. "Anna's able to recount four separate occasions during the foot pursuit when she ordered Rowe at gunpoint to give it up. He disregarded each of those warnings. She didn't actually fire at him until she saw the weapon in his hand, he turned with it toward her and they were in an area clear of bystanders. She also had a freight train to stop any rounds that missed. I see only two of those warnings listed in your report, Fred."

"What're you trying to pull here, Parker?" Waggoner finally plucked off the loose thread. "Since when do we shoot tires in the middle of downtown Phoenix?"

"Don't know how the FBI operates, Fred, but I'd sure as hell plug Mr. Goodyear before I let a possible cop killer waltz."

"No, it's been obvious for years you don't have a clue how legitimate law enforce—"

But Niehaus had rested a heavier hand on the man's arm to silence him.

"Thanks, Jim," Emmett said. "I'm just trying to make sure all the facts get aired. You know, Anna got in this fix only because the senior agent with her came up with a hare-brained scheme to take down Rowe. Is it FBI procedure to split up partners for a felony stop? Seems like a dandy way to get a cop shot, but I'm sure Reed knew what he was doing. Point is—Summerfield impressed upon Anna the need to avoid a high-speed pursuit through the stadium district at that hour."

Waggoner sniped, "Too bad he isn't able to verify that."

"Well, I've got the next best thing, Fred. I believe Juan Morada gives us an objective picture of Anna's conduct during the first minutes of the botched takedown. He's as much in the dark as we are about Rowe's part in all this, so I advise we kick him loose as soon as possible. Otherwise, we risk losing the confidence of the magistrate who short-ordered me a search warrant on Rowe's car in record time this morning." Avoiding Anna's gaze, Emmett sat back as Niehaus read the two pages he'd handed him. She was as much irked with Parker as she was grateful. His tactics bordered on overkill, although last night Niehaus and Waggoner had left her with a feeling that she'd used less than sterling judgment. Maybe Emmett had a keener grasp than she of the bureaucratic morass she was in.

After a minute, Niehaus lowered Morada's statement and peered expressionlessly at Emmett. Parker didn't move a muscle, and at last the SAC broke off eye contact and asked, "Well, Turnipseed, what's your game plan?"

Waggoner's jaw dropped. Anna was off the hook, although she was conscientious not to show any relief. That might be misconstrued as guilt. "Any progress on locating the van?" she asked. The blue van with Utah plates parked down the street from the Feathered Serpent yesterday morning, and then a dark-colored van, that might have been the same one, she dimly recalled driving past in a cul-de-sac near Emmett's apartment complex last night.

"I've got a query in with Motor Vehicles in Salt Lake. But with no make and year, it'll take a while."

She ignored the hint of censure in Emmett's voice. "And the bloodstains the attacker left on the bedsheets?" She didn't say *Emmett's bedsheets,* sensing that Niehaus and Waggoner still didn't buy Summerfield's and her staying in Parker's apartment as an economy move.

Waggoner said glumly, "On the way to the Washington lab, as we speak."

"Make sure the DNA work is started. In addition to the blood-typing. Any idea how he got in the apartment? I threw the deadbolt before going to bed."

"Picked the lock," Niehaus said. "The techs found minute brass scrapings in the mechanism. That means a pick was used."

"Then maybe we should add a possible burglary history to his profile," Anna said. "Anything to broaden the NCIC computer scan. And Fred—please see what we can turn up on Lolly Blackhouse. According to parole, she has a rap sheet for solicitation. So look for all her aliases. I'd like to know who she really is. And then I need the report of a bureau-related shooting that left her brother dead in Cortez, Colorado."

"Never heard of that one," Waggoner muttered.

"Utah plates," Niehaus mused out loud. "Parker, didn't you just return from southern Utah?"

"Right. A BLM wildlife biologist lost several Gila monsters to poaching over the winter. No doubt, the male specimen left in my apartment is one of them. Our boy celebrated these thefts by making petroglyphs. Gila monsters with moth wings. The same design Anna found on the back of Rowe's former house in University Park."

Still jotting, Waggoner asked, "Name of this biologist?"

"Nick Stepanek."

"What office does he work out of?"

"She," Emmett said. "I should have said Nicole. St. George Resource Area."

Niehaus had been visibly weighing all this. "What do moths and Gilas mean in Indian terms, Turnipseed?"

"Emmett's more of an expert than I, but the Gila monster is sacred to the Navajo. Diagnoses illnesses with his paw. Isn't that right, Em?"

"Yeah," he replied. Still evading her eyes after clumsily revealing that the biologist he'd visited was female. "And envied by warriors for his armor. Makes him impervious to all harm."

"And moths mean?" Niehaus asked.

"There's something called the Mothway Myth, but what little I know about it has nothing to do with Gilas." Emmett leaned forward in the armchair. "Listen, Jim and Fred— things got dang hectic last night, as you well know, so I never got the chance to bring this up. But something has come to my attention that goes beyond the expertise of this task force. Plus our resources to thoroughly investigate it." He paused, and Anna couldn't decide if it was for effect or if he earnestly didn't want to go on. "I got an anonymous call in Window Rock. Voice muffled by a washcloth or something. I believe it was somebody on the tribal PD, but I'll never be able to confirm that. Anyway, the voice said Knoki came upon two men sunbathing at a lake in the mountains last autumn. One nude and one in swimming trunks. The one in trunks was Reed Summerfield, between Counterintelligence in your D.C. office and his new posting in Gallup. The nude was a German national by the name of Dieter Preuss. Now, don't get the wrong idea, but I thought it was worth zipping an inquiry through channels to your Washington office to find out if there was any possibility, however remote, that Preuss had belonged to Stasi."

"And what was the result of that inquiry?" Niehaus asked. Until now, Anna hadn't seen either of the supervisors blink since Emmett had dropped Reed's name. She herself felt a buzz in the base of her skull as Emmett's news sank in.

"It appears I've been stonewalled," Emmett said.

Niehaus's slender face hardened. "Give me the name of your contact with us, and I'll make sure it doesn't happen again."

"Oh, that'd be counterproductive, Jim. Let it slide. All that matters is that we get a line on this Preuss fellow as soon as possible."

"Agreed," Niehaus said. "What do you have on him?"

Emmett handed over a piece of paper he'd already prepared. An amazing volume of paper on his person this morning—for an investigator reputed to write crime scene reports on matchbook covers.

Niehaus and Waggoner stood in unison. Doubtlessly anxious to begin damage control. "Where can we reach you?" the SAC asked.

"If you don't mind," Emmett answered, "Anna and I should head back to Navajoland to confirm as much of this as we can."

chapter 16

EMMETT HAD JUST TURNED NORTH OUT OF SOCORRO,
New Mexico, onto Interstate 25, when Anna asked quietly
from the backseat of his sedan, "Where'd you wind up spending Thursday night in Utah?" She sounded wide-awake.

Two miles away, cottonwoods hugged the Rio Grande.
He'd been wondering if his ancestors had camped in that
same belt of lush foliage. Certainly, the Comanche had
raided this far west. And spring had been the season for raiding. *Spring, and a young man's fancy turns to raiding, to
taking female captives.* "What'd you say?"

"Nothing."

"Thought you said something."

Pause. "Where'd you spend Thursday night?"

"Oh, you know me. Any old place I can lay my head
down."

"St. George?"

"Not that I recall." Lunch at a greasy spoon in the mountain town of Magdelena had left him drowsy. And oddly
content. Coming into Socorro a few minutes ago, he'd had
one of those little epiphanies that seem doomed to fade as
soon as he gave it more thought: He did indeed have a kind
of life with Anna Turnipseed. An intimate one in a back-
handed sort of way, for they'd just covered 390 miles together since leaving Phoenix at four this morning without
having shared more than a dozen words. Or feeling the need
to. Until now. Had they seemed like the other southwestern

couples in the café, out for a spin on a warm Sunday in May?

Except that Anna and he were hunting for a murderer who'd now struck twice in the same week. Once with an accomplice. Once without. Even the most violent of human beings were infrequently violent, so this meant he was spinning out of control. Less and less in touch with reality. Her thoughts had gravitated toward the killer too, for she asked somberly, "How'd he find Reed and me?"

"I thought you were going to catch a nap."

"Can't."

He bent the rearview mirror down on her reflection: She was propped up on the two pillows he'd brought along, her arms folded behind her head and her eyes shut. "You and Summerfield somehow got too close," he said.

"To his nest?"

"No, he ranges. Probably doesn't have one permanent place he stays too long. I meant you got too close to his fixation."

"And what's that?"

"I'm not sure. Lolly Blackhouse, maybe." Last night over a room-service dinner in Anna's suite, he'd repeated what Juan Morada had said about Rowe's suspicion his call-girl lover was being stalked. But how could a john's obsession have ensnared Bert and Aurelia Knoki, who'd lived more than three hundred miles away? The dead couple's only established connection, thus far, to either Rowe or Blackhouse was a letter that was still in Tallsalt's possession. Rowe, facing death Friday night, had given Phoenix PD his and Lolly's current address so she could be brought to him. Emmett had gone there yesterday morning after the meeting with Niehaus and Waggoner, only to find the furnished studio apartment in University Park vacated. Obviously, Lolly was a pro at sudden vanishings, although Emmett had found several rusted flakes of metal in her parking space. From her vehicle?

Anna's mouth was slightly agape as if she'd finally drifted

off. She had yet to ask him why he'd taken on the FBI brass yesterday, and he intended never to tell her. They hadn't known what he did: If Anna Turnipseed sat around for a week on administrative leave, she'd talk herself out of ever getting back on the bicycle. He was amazed she was taking the attack on her and Summerfield in apparent stride, but he also understood the limits to her resilience. As well as he understood his own. He'd made himself spend the night in his own apartment last night, and once he'd awakened with the hair-tingling sense he was sharing the disinfectant-scented rooms with Summerfield's bleak presence. Sadly, thanks to his job, he'd already known of a janitorial service that specialized in crime scene cleanup. The two bloodstains in the carpet had been scrubbed out, and he'd stepped on one of these wet spots with his bare foot during a peptic rush to the refrigerator for some milk to wash down a handful of antacid tablets.

Anna climbed between the front seats and belted herself in.

"Give up?" he asked.

"Yeah. Where are we?"

"Valley of the Rio Grande, heading toward Albuquerque."

"This the shortest way to Canoncito reservation?"

"Always two yardsticks in this country—driving time versus distance." But he caught her skepticism about his choice of highways. He hadn't wanted to take the more northerly route, Interstate 40, which brushed the lower edge of the Big Rez. It'd be reported soon enough to Window Rock headquarters by the tribal cops assigned to Canoncito that the task force was nosing around the island reservations. *Do I have a justification I'm willing to share with John Tallsalt?*

Anna looked wrapped in thought, and Emmett asked, "A penny for them?"

She sighed. "I don't know. About Lolly, I guess. Wondering how she's doing today."

The Southern Ute woman had made an undeniable

impression on Anna. "What kind of relationship you figure she had with Rowe?"

"It's called compulsive reenactment," Anna replied.

"Of what?"

"Whatever happened to her as a kid. Lolly uses self-punishment to relieve the stress of the terror she still feels. Others have other ways, but it's all like hitting your hand with a hammer. Feels so good when you stop."

"So Rowe abused her?"

"Yes."

"Then why'd Blackhouse come unglued on you for running him down?"

"That's the sick part, I guess. You wall off your emotions from the abuse. And when the abuser finally dies, those feelings give you grief. Not any sense of being free."

Emmett frowned. "What set Rowe off his nut about this particular stalker, if that's what he is? Christ almighty, Blackhouse had sex with a mess of men all week long, and Rowe managed to swallow that."

"Domination over Lolly."

"You've lost me."

"The others just *rented* the illusion of having that power. The stalker might be after the real thing. That's all Rowe had in this world. A loser like him would never let anybody else have her that way. Even if it meant going back to prison." Then she added with a tenderness that somehow singed him, "Not all men are like you, Em."

He shifted uncomfortably in his seat. Anna's aura of knowledgeableness had put him on edge—it seemed to call up experience. "You cover this at the academy?"

"No."

Emmett was no longer drowsy. Or contented. The stretch of interstate required little attention, for which he was grateful. He was vaguely sickened. *Talk through this with her.* He found himself searching his memory for any hint of sexual desire he might have let slip over these past months—other than the libidinous fiasco in her motel room Tuesday morning. Asking himself if at any time he might have come across as aggressive to her. He was angry too. Angry because he was feeling guilty about something he believed to be normal and healthy. He wanted to make love to this woman, and it shook him to realize that she might find that revolting.

"Why'd you fly home Friday night without calling, Em?"

Was she trying to change the subject?

His relief made him feel cowardly. "I had no idea what Summerfield might do to you. And I did call. Several times. But I didn't want to leave a message he might overhear. Or send somebody by who might screw the pooch and set Reed off."

She was gazing out her window. At the cottonwood forest cloaking the Rio Grande. Into which he wanted to pull off, spread a blanket on a grassy bank along the turbid, green river and make love. Why did that fantasy seem so deviant now? "Then you had reason to believe Reed or Dieter Preuss killed the Knokis?" she asked.

"I did." Falling into his witness-stand monotone.

"And had an out-of-line relationship?"

"Yes."

"I'm not talking about them being gay. I got a feeling Reed had come to terms with his sexuality, and the bureau wasn't going to buffalo him into being less than candid about it."

"You're probably right." Emmett paused. "I found out Preuss was a former member of Stasi."

"But you told Niehaus and Waggoner—"

"I told them just what they need to know to follow this lead, then cross it off the list."

"Why cross it off?" She sounded less shocked than he'd imagined she might be.

"Because I'll bet my bottom dollar it's a dead end. There's a chance Reed enlisted the East German as a double agent. In that case, Summerfield's contact with Preuss even last October at Asaayi Lake was legit, despite the romantic overtones."

"Before I forget—there's a possible photo of Preuss in Reed's book of Navajo myths."

"Okay. The Gallup office can collect it when they pick up the Suburban at the airport."

"So what if Summerfield didn't turn on Preuss?"

"Then I'm wrong," Emmett said. "But I've also alerted the highest levels of the FBI to the problem. So they can take it from here. How can Niehaus bitch about that?"

She cocked a leg up onto the seat and rested her chin on it. The pose was maddeningly appealing.

"Sit like a lady," he snapped. Didn't she have a clue the effect she had on him?

She glowered, but then lowered her leg, too preoccupied to argue. "Was that Dieter Preuss in your apartment?"

"I've wondered. But what reason did Preuss have to kill Summerfield?"

"Jealousy?"

"Possible, especially with folks of that persuasion . . ." Emmett caught her disapproving look at his political incorrectness. "But I'd say you were the target, and Summerfield just stumbled in at the wrong time. You were staked out, and this crazy prick struck only when he thought you'd be alone . . ." He saw that this upset her, but couldn't come up with anything comforting to say. It was his best guess. "Then there's blackmail. But how could Summerfield have dangled that over Preuss's head? Stasi and East Germany are *kaput*. And what interest would Preuss have had in Lolly Blackhouse?"

A mile passed in silence before she asked, "Then what are we doing today, Emmett?"

"Retracing Rowe's search for the stalker who spray-painted that Gila with wings on the back of his rental." Emmett added irascibly, "Had I known about that tag, I doubt I would've bothered coming back to Phoenix at all."

"Why?"

"Hell, that's what gets Summerfield off the hook, as far as I'm concerned. He had a reason to go after Bert Knoki. But not Rowe and Blackhouse."

After a moment, she said, "I'm thankful you came back. And stood up for me to Niehaus and Waggoner."

"No thanks necessary. It was a pleasure. I *hate* the goddamn FBI."

EXCEPT FOR THE HOGANS behind the mobile homes and shingle-sided cabins, Anna could imagine that she was back in her ranchería along the California-Oregon border. The same rolling grasslands and far-flung junipers. Mountains in the distance blue with conifers. The same gnawing sense of isolation, although Canoncito was twenty-six miles from Albuquerque, New Mexico's largest city. Maybe the atmosphere of neglect came from the fact that it was separated by eighty miles from the Big Reservation. Almost beyond the pale of tribal government, but for a trailer in the community school compound marked *Resident Post—Navajo Police*. The cruiser wasn't parked beside it, but Emmett wasted no time driving past.

"Rowe had his alternator swapped out here," he said, apparently looking for anything that resembled an auto repair shop. There seemed to be no commercial district, unless one counted the modular buildings of the various government agencies.

"You sure it wasn't somewhere along the interstate?" she asked.

"No, I'm not. But the alternator in his Plymouth didn't look like one you'd get installed by a big chain. Beat-up and rusted. Something ripped out of a wreck and rebuilt."

Two Navajo youths were swaggering toward them. Baggy shirts and pants. Hair cut to stubble. Headbands so low over their eyes they had to tilt back their heads to peer out on the world. They were on Anna's side of the wide gravel road, and Emmett started to veer that way so he could talk to them.

"Don't," she said, powering down her window and letting in the smell of hot grass. "I'll ask." Emmett braked and the two teenagers shambled to an uneasy halt. They immediately began curling their fingers: letters that stood for their gang. *C . . .* something. "Can you tell me if there's an auto shop around here?"

One of them sneered, *"Me vale madre."*

"Why don't you give a shit?" Anna fired right back at him.

His eyes watered in surprise that she'd understood him, but he signaled his companion to move on with him down the road. *"Justicia,"* he muttered contemptuously. The law.

Anna asked Emmett, "They speak *Spanish* here?"

"Comes from being so close to Albuquerque," he said, moving on. "Even have a Spanish accent to their English and Navajo. Folks on the Big Rez call them the *Enemy Navajo* because they rode scout for the Mexicans and then Kit Carson against the *Dine* farther to the west. They secede from Window Rock every chance they get just to show that they can return a compliment." Again, his restless gaze roved the settlement.

Yet, he was in control.

He'd managed to sidetrack a now massive FBI operation, removing all bureaucratic obstructions in his path so he could pursue what he believed to be the most promising lead. But he'd asked her along for the ride. That alone kept her from being too miffed at him. "Do you sleep well at night?"

"Why wouldn't I?"

"Telling lies like the one you did to Niehaus and Waggoner?"

"A lie is known misinformation. I'm only half sure about Summerfield and Preuss." He turned up a narrower street toward a band of homeboys the first two had apparently peeled off. These were hanging around a cluster of mail-boxes. Emmett pumped the gas pedal three times, turned off the engine, coasted briefly, then restarted.

The backfire startled Anna. "What'd you do that for, dammit?"

But he'd already stopped beside the youths. "Having a bit of car trouble, gents," he said amicably to them. "Hate for my partner and me to have to spend the night here. Don't happen to know if there's a mechanic around, do you?"

The reply was almost instantaneous. A boy with a watch cap said, "Dominguez'll look at it."

"And where's he?"

A half-dozen arms pointed at a group of buildings about a quarter-mile across the steppe—apparently lip-twitching wasn't the custom here. One structure glinted spectacularly in the late afternoon sunlight.

"Much obliged," Emmett said, starting that way.

"How'd you do that?" Anna asked as soon as they were clear.

"The minute we drove onto this rez everybody began holding their breath. Who are the feds after this time? How long will they stay? Hint that we'll be here for more than a few minutes, and everybody will go out of his way to help us get back on the interstate."

"You're a deceitful man, Emmett Parker."

"Not at all. I just value the truth too much to throw it around."

She also sensed that he was taking care not to look at her. *He knows about me. At last he knows.*

Across an arroyo, filled to the tops of its banks with junked cars, was a large tin building and a single-wide mobile home with no skirting. The glint proved to be a hogan covered with hubcaps. A shrine to Detroit. Emmett braked at the open gate and honked his horn twice. A Navajo soon appeared at the trailer door. He was potbellied, with bird legs showing beneath his khaki Bermuda shorts. He scrutinized

Emmett and Anna through binoculars, then gave a reluctant wave for them to approach.

Emmett parked on the near embankment of the arroyo rather than test the sandy-looking track through the smashed and cannibalized vehicles. Anna and he got out, trekked across the wash to the doors of the shop building, where the Navajo now stood beneath a sign declaring his willingness to buy old car batteries for a dollar each. He was just old enough to show gray at the temples. At his side sat a shepherd mix of some sort, watching the partners' approach, his tail dead to the ground.

"Afternoon," Emmett said, producing his credentials and dropping his pretense of looking for a mechanic. "I'm Investigator Parker from the BIA, and this is Special Agent Turnipseed, FBI. You Dominguez?"

"Yep." That was it. No recitation of clans. Dominguez swung open the big doors and flicked his chin for Emmett and Anna to step into the shade of his shop. The heat trapped inside nearly took her breath away.

Turning, Dominguez leaned against the brace of a long shelf crammed with spare parts. None new-looking. "What can I do for you?"

"A *bilagaana* recently had the alternator replaced in his Plymouth Fury somewhere here," Emmett replied. "We need to talk to the mechanic who did that job."

"You feds or Department of Consumer Affairs?" Before Emmett could answer, Dominguez chuckled. "Look, most of my trade is *gringo*. You think these grabass *Dine* got the money to get their wheels fixed?" He pointed languidly at the wrecks in the arroyo. "That's my local business. What'd this guy look like?"

"Blond and blue-eyed," Anna said, "but he dressed Indian. Braids and a beaded choker. His name was Terry Rowe."

Dominguez's eyes turned wary. The implication of the past tense hadn't gotten past him.

"That's right," Emmett said with just the right tone of veiled menace. "Rowe's dead, and it's important we interview all the folks who last saw him."

The mechanic waited for them to go ahead with their questions.

"When'd he show up?" Anna asked.

"Last Tuesday afternoon," Dominguez replied. "Said his warnin' light come on in Grants and he drove all that way without stoppin' . . ." Fifty miles west on Interstate 40, she estimated. Back toward the Big Rez. "He paid cash. My kind of *gringo*, because I don't take American Express. What more can I say?"

"Where was he coming from?" Emmett demanded.

"Utah, I suppose."

"What do you mean *you suppose*?"

"He had a paper sack from a grocery in Mexican Hat. Kept takin' crackers and cheese—stuff like that—from it. Never said where he was from. Arizona plates, but Mexican Hat's not that far from the border."

Anna watched as Emmett digested this. He himself had gone to southern Utah two days later. Had he and Rowe been seeking the same man? Emmett remarked, "Canoncito's a helluva place to come looking for a mechanic."

"Tell me about it. No, he was headed here in the first place. Wanted to make it here after his alternator conked out."

"How do you know that?" Anna asked.

"Rowe asked me if anybody on the rez here owned a blue bakery van."

She hoped that her poker face was as fixed as Emmett's. "And you answered?"

"Nobody I know. And I know everybody."

"Have you seen one around?"

"No."

Emmett strolled out to the doors, knelt and stroked the dog's ears. Anna was powerless to leave the spot on which she stood. Her knees felt weak. Had Lolly Blackhouse spotted the same van she herself had Friday morning down the block from the Feathered Serpent? And had either Lolly or Rowe seen it in their University Park neighborhood prior to the appearance of the winged Gila on the back wall of their house? The image of Summerfield's corpse on Emmett's carpet came back to her, leaving her cold and overheated at the same time. They were close again to the monster's trail. Frighteningly close. What had Rowe shouted outside the ballpark? *I'll show you somethin' out there to be afraid of!*

"What made you so sure Rowe was anxious to reach this reservation?" Emmett asked the mechanic.

Dominguez shrugged. "I don't catch your drift."

"Well, he could've been cruising all the rezes in the area, hunting for the van. Acoma, Laguna, Isleta."

"Oh." The mechanic nodded in comprehension. "He was lookin' for Bernadine Altasal too."

"Who?"

"This old woman."

"Did he find her?"

"Yeah." Dominguez chuckled again. "Ten years in the dirt."

ACCORDING TO THE MECHANIC, Bernadine Altasal had one surviving granddaughter on the Canoncito reservation. The sunset was fading to a bruiselike purple as Emmett sped toward the residence Dominguez had described to him. It was barely visible in the evening shadow of Mount Taylor. The Turquoise Mountain. One of the four sacred and sheltering peaks of the *Dine,* outside which this orphan rez lay. The unpaved road was badly rutted, and Anna's voice vibrated as she asked, "Are the tribal police aware of the blue van?"

"They should've gotten the BOLO," Emmett said, meaning the teletyped be-on-the-lookout. "But I'll phone Yabeny tonight just to make sure."

"Why not Tallsalt?"

Emmett didn't answer.

Darcy Altasal was waiting at her gate as if she'd been expecting them all afternoon. Even though no telephone line drooped down to her plywood hogan. No modern dwelling stood on the allotment in addition to it, an anomaly in Navajoland. In her early thirties, the woman wore a faded cotton dress that hung over her emaciated-looking frame. She seemed small and, despite her youth, wizened. Her inquisitive eyes were abnormally wide-set.

Killing his engine, Emmett asked, "Is she all right?"

"No," Anna said. "Fetal alcohol syndrome. I'll handle her."

So Emmett hung back as Anna walked smiling up to the young woman. "Darcy Altasal?"

"*Sí* . . . ?"

"I'm Anna, and this is Emmett. We're police officers. How are you this evening?"

Darcy gripped the top rail of the gate. "I don't see no bangers no more. Ms. Newton says don't see no bangers no more."

Anna slowed the tempo of her questioning. "Who's Ms. Newton?"

"Services lady."

Anna glanced at the hogan. "Is somebody home with you?"

"*No bangers,*" Darcy said defensively.

"I mean, like your mother or father?"

The woman let go of the gate and stabbed a finger toward the southeast. A dome-shaped glow had developed there over the last few minutes. The lights of Albuquerque. Darcy meant one or both of her parents lived there. Then Emmett noticed white crosses scattered in the brush about a mile off. Also to the southeast. "She means they're deceased," he quietly observed.

Anna smiled at Darcy again. "Do you have any relatives who watch out for you?"

"*Mi tía.*" This time, she both jinked her lips and pointed westward. Did she mean that this aunt lived on the Big Rez? There were no more houses before the massif of Mesa Gigante took over. "And Ms. Newton."

"Is she a relative, Darcy?"

"What?"

"Is Ms. Newton *Dine*?"

The woman giggled at the absurdity. *"No bangers. No touchin'. Or back to the home."* Mimicking the Social Services employee?

Anna's look softened, but Emmett couldn't hide his disappointment. The promise of learning who or what Rowe had been after was starting to fray in retardation.

But Anna persisted. "Did Terry Rowe see you, Darcy?"

The woman's face lit up. "Terry." Then, just as swiftly, confusion clouded it. *"Bernadine. Where's Bernadine?"*

"Did Terry ask to see your grandmother?"

The woman seized the top bar again and began wrenching. "And the baby."

"What baby, Darcy?"

"Ms. Newton gave it to some real nice *Dine* on the Big Rez. Real nice."

"Your baby?" Anna asked.

But Darcy adamantly parroted, *"No bangers. No touchin'."*

"How long ago did Ms. Newton give your baby to these people?"

The woman hesitated, then said, "Ten years."

Anna patted the backs of Darcy's hands. "Boy or girl?"

"Boy."

"And where was he born?"

Darcy pointed at the hogan.

"Not a hospital?" Anna pressed. Emmett saw the direction her questioning was taking: Was it possible that Summerfield's and her attacker had been this son? An age of only ten years discounted that, but he had little doubt the woman had a poor temporal sense. But what if Darcy had gotten pregnant at age twelve or thirteen? Not unheard of. Hospital or Social Services records would verify the date of birth. Why would Rowe have been interested in Darcy's child fathered by a gangbanger, unless that grown offspring posed some threat to him and Lolly

Blackhouse? "Wasn't your baby born in a hospital?" Anna patiently continued.

"Awee," Darcy said argumentatively. *"Awee haliili."*

Anna glanced back at Emmett. "What's she saying?"

"Baby something. You got me."

Turnipseed faced the woman again. "What's *awee haliili*?" But an answer wasn't forthcoming.

Darcy let go of the gate and trudged forlornly toward the hogan. Emmett realized that he'd possibly underestimated her capacity for pain and regret. Anna felt the need to stop her: "Darcy, did Terry say where he'd come from?"

The woman twirled around. "Phoenix."

"You liked him, didn't you?"

A poignant grin barely visible in the gathering darkness. *"Sí."*

"Why did Terry want to see your baby?"

Darcy shook her head.

Stepping up to Anna's back, Emmett whispered a sudden hunch to her, and she asked the woman, "Have you seen Ivan Jumper?" But there was no reaction to the name, and Anna concluded, "Well, Emmett and I are going to the Big Rez. Can we take a message to your aunt?"

"No."

"Are you sure? Maybe she'd like to know how you're doing."

Darcy pointed at the distant graveyard.

"How do you know your *tía* is dead?" Emmett hoped his voice wouldn't spook her.

"The bangers told me . . ." Darcy paused, seeming to dimly realize the admission she'd just made. No doubt, Social Services had put her on some sort of supervised probation to see if she could function on her own. Then she said secretively, *"Tía* Aurelia is gone just like *Abuela* Bernadine."

chapter 17

IMBECILE! BUNGLER!

Gila Monster waited until darkness had fallen over Sitgreaves National Forest before ditching his van. He'd taken a logging road as far as it went into the mountains, then wended even farther up Chevelon Creek through the blackjack pines until there was no more going forward. Didn't matter. He was finished with the van. He believed he'd done well by having made it over 120 miles of back roads and jeep trails since setting out from Phoenix at three, Saturday morning—but the Voice was never satisfied. Never praising. *You were told!* it roared. *Make it impossible for them to follow you, and punish all who try!* At first light, he'd promptly pulled back into the scrub and waited for night before driving on. *None of this should have been necessary!*

He now stood still, listening to the wind in the pine branches. It sounded like flowing water, but wasn't.

The creek below was down to a scummy trickle, but at dawn he'd motored past a young man and woman camped along its bank. White tennis shorts and hiking boots. Tanned and happy. Cooking breakfast over an open fire, they waved cheerfully until they caught sight of his face through the windshield. To their evident relief, he'd driven on. Noticing that they weren't in an established campground. Isolated. With a brand-new Lincoln four-wheel-drive parked beside their tent. "Go away," he'd pled under his breath. "Run while you can."

The day had passed in a fog of faint-headedness and growing clumsiness. A fit was just around the corner. He'd been trying to stretch out his remaining supply of medication, and then this morning, in his mounting agitation, had spilled the capsules while opening the vial. Two were all that remained.

And the Voice had been relentless.

For that failure in Phoenix, you shall be locked in the springhouse for three days . . . so you may learn that darkness is the only companion of sloth! But in the springhouse he'd learned that he liked the darkness, that it was to be preferred over the company of the other children. *You are not of the Elect!* they would singsong during recesses. *Not Elect! Not! Not!*

"I don't want to be," he said to himself. "I want to go home. Eat mutton stew."

But he dutifully took a cardboard box from the back of the van. It wriggled in his forepaws. Life awakening, hungry for blood. Hefting the box on his hip, he started down through the trees.

An hour ago, he'd heard the *thonk-thonk* of an ax biting into wood. The man preparing for nightfall. The woman was attractive, with shiny, platinum hair. Gila Monster believed the sight of his face had sparked as much fascination as fear in her. Already, she was terrified of him. Ordinarily, that'd make him feel powerful. But tonight, with so many Blood Atonements behind him, after five years almost constantly on the road, burglaries and Burger Kings, he felt weary knowing exactly what was about to happen.

A carpet of dead pine needles covered the sounds of his descent.

Distant flames flickered through the pines. The evening was warm, but the couple had rekindled their fire. They didn't want to die. Nothing alive wanted to die, except perhaps himself. If death was immortality. And invulnerability.

"Father—he's beating his head against the wall in the springhouse again."

"Go stop the poor imbecile before he kills himself."

Gila Monster abruptly stopped about a hundred feet from the blaze, set the box down and sat cross-legged beside it in the humus.

Get up, you recalcitrant savage!

Noticing a soft gray light glancing off his bare shoulders, he looked up. The moon, slightly fuller than half, cast long shadows across the forest floor. It was within minutes of dipping behind the rocky rim to the west. He liked the sound of the wind in the trees. But the Voice cut through the peace of the moment: *Slay this pair so you may find that other couple as one in their evil!* Success meant discovering Moth Man and Moth Woman together in the sweaty fullness of their sin. The Blood Atonement wasn't possible otherwise.

Why are you letting everything fall apart?

Two months ago, at last, he'd located Moth Woman in University Park. Not so hard—her letter to Knoki. But while he'd schemed and maneuvered for Moth Man to join her, others had found her as well. Cops. The same cops who'd come to the mobile home. Turnipseed and Parker, according to the papers. And their running down Moth Woman in Phoenix was bad. She disappeared under pressure. It might be months before Gila Monster could find her again. His only option had been to strike at these cops, Turnipseed especially, and make them back off. But that had not gone well. Turnipseed lived. Worse yet, Moth Woman had vanished once more. So Gila Monster was headed north again, praying that she was somewhere in Navajoland, drawn like a moth to flame to the reunion that, if properly closed, would dispatch both of them to Paradise.

Tick, tick, tick—the pocket watch the Voice had given him nagged from his Levi's. *Get up! Move, you heathen imbecile!*

People died, yet he seemed no closer to the final Atonement.

The young woman paused in front of the campfire, a glass in her hand. The man said something, and her giggle trilled up to Gila Monster.

Rise! Get moving!

He felt the sting of the riding crop on the backs of his hands. As always, he refused to show his pain. He suffered in motionless silence, trusting that soon his Gila-skin would spread over his entire body and protect him from that little whip. His man-body would die, and his reptile-body would live forever.

But he rose at last.

The moon was down, and only starlight kept the darkness from being total.

Carefully, so as not to rouse his little brother, he opened the box and slipped out his gloves. He reclosed the flaps, planning to return for his sibling later. Inside one of the gauntlets was his javelin—plus a .40-caliber pistol. *This is pigs gun,* the nearly illegible note accompanying it had read, *and you keep it. My mom says you been witchen us. But I don't think so. You saved our ass from that pig. She knows that now and says thanks too a lot . . .* Gila Monster hadn't used the handgun in Phoenix for fear the thunder of the shots would've prevented his getting away from the female cop's apartment. But he figured this site was at least four miles from Chevelon Canyon Lake campground.

Hurry!

He donned his gloves, grasped the javelin in his right hand and the pistol in his left. Then began crawling toward the flames. This low on the slope there were oaks mixed among the pines, and the dried leaves crackled under Gila Monster's paws and knees. But the man had made an even louder crackling by piling some pitchy wood on the fire. Sparks spiraled up into the sky. Laughing, the couple scooted their lawn chairs back from the eruption of heat. Not unlike the children in the schoolroom laughing at him when he stumbled while reading from the Book of the Golden Plates.

Gila Monster tried mightily to detest this couple. Their tennis shorts and their tans. Contempt was grease to a killing. He imagined Moth Woman flinging him into her fire, rasping *lol-lol-lol* all the while he burned.

He slithered across the creek, sliding over the mossy stones. Tongue testing the air. He climbed the far embankment on his hind legs, his paws twisted around so the couple could see neither the javelin nor the gun.

He sprang over the top, hissing, and they startled.

But their expressions swiftly changed to puzzlement. Both were clearly afraid but seemed to be waiting for some explanation from him that would put them at ease. When none came, the woman said with a flat tone, "We saw you this morning." She seemed to know what was at hand. Had even accepted it, perhaps.

But the man shot vigilantly to his feet, tightening his grip around a green bottle of Heineken beer. "Can we help you with something?" He smiled as if that might help matters.

"Run away and I won't hurt you."

But they didn't budge.

Imbecile, leave no witnesses above the age of comprehension!

Gila Monster aimed the pistol at the man but watched the woman for her reaction. *Shoot now!* He hesitated. *Fire!* Her body jerked at the bark of each of the three shots, but her bulging eyes never strayed from Gila Monster's. There was a clatter of aluminum tubing as the man hurtled backward over his chair, overturning it, and then the *glub-glub-glub* of his beer pulsing out of the bottle.

Still, the woman refused to glance aside at the figure crumpled over the chair. Nor did she scream. After a few seconds, she slowly and carefully set her cocktail glass on a folding table. Relieved of her drink, she glided toward the Lincoln as if her feet were scarcely touching the ground. Arms down at her sides. Head lowered.

No witnesses!

When Gila Monster fell in behind her, she didn't quicken

her pace. She continued to flow toward the four-by-four as if oblivious to the steady tramp of paws behind her.

He let her get in and sit behind the wheel, even though the firelight showed him that the keys were in the ignition. But the side window had been left down. He reached inside with his javelin. She froze, eyes straight ahead as he probed with the tip of the blade for the space between two ribs on the edge of her breastbone. But then a tremor racked his right paw. The breath seized in her throat as his claws jerked across her cheek, drawing blood.

Had he waited too long before taking his medication?

Quickly now, he prepared to thrust.

At last, she began to scream. But it was too late for screaming. He forcefully jammed his left paw against the butt of the javelin's shaft, and the blade angled into her heart.

Impaled, shuddering violently, she still managed to hold her head up. Another tremor made him wrench the javelin, which he hadn't meant to. She turned her face toward Gila Monster as if she wanted to ask him not to do that. But the words wouldn't come.

A strand of her hair had caught in the corner of her mouth, and he removed it with a claw. "I only wanted your car," he said gently. "You should've run when I gave you the chance."

Then she slumped.

He yanked free his javelin, and a plume of blood followed it out. Before ebbing. She sprawled limply over the wheel, a tangle of arms and platinum hair.

Leaning back out of the open window, he headed for the woods. And the box. Staggering at first, but then with eventual steadiness. His head was clearing. There would be no fit tonight; he'd taken his medication in time—thank God. He thought to load the couple in the cargo area of the Lincoln and dump their bodies over a brushy ledge somewhere remote. But returning to the camp, he realized that there were few places as out-of-the-way as this.

Plunge them into the flames! the Voice ordered.

Gila Monster put the box on the backseat, then glanced at the woman. In the few seconds between the slide of the javelin and the end, she'd bled copiously over the dash and steering wheel. He dragged her out of the vehicle and to the fire ring, then unzipped the tent door and grabbed one of two sleeping bags within. This he used to mop up the blood as best he could. The inside of the vehicle stank all coppery like the slaughterhouse at the compound. Lambs bleating in the pen, pigs squealing.

Disappoint me and I will smite you as readily as I do these dumb beasts!

Gila Monster tossed the sopping sleeping bag into the creek, then lifted the man under the arms and pitched him face-first onto the fire. The logs collapsed under his weight, and a cloud of sparks sizzled up. He added dry branches from the kindling pile. The air grew foul with the stink of drizzled nylon and burnt hair. When the flames leaped high again, he picked up the woman and draped her over the man.

Go . . . your work is done here.

"Did I do well?"

Make haste!

Stripping off his gloves, he rushed to the Lincoln.

The steering wheel was sticky with half-congealed blood. Ignoring the sensation on his bare hands, he backed onto the logging road and bounced down it toward Route 260. About ten miles away. It was Sunday night. The couple wouldn't be missed until tomorrow night, the end of the three-day holiday. Before that, he'd leave the Lincoln as far from the beaten track as his van. The cloth seat cover was saturated with blood, and the wetness began to penetrate the crotch of his Levi's.

When would it be like this with Moth Man and Moth Woman? Why did they go on eluding him when he only meant them well? The best possible kind of wellness. Forgiveness for the disharmony they had wrought, for their murderous intentions toward him. That was Gila Monster's mission: to redeem all and restore harmony. Wasn't that why the Voice had sent him out into the world on the eve of the compound's destruction?

Yes, it echoed around inside his skull, *yes!*

Gila Monster suddenly growled. A vehicle was speeding up the road, its lights gyrating whitely through the trees. Should he turn around? No place wide enough for it. And he didn't want to back up toward the camp.

Maybe the driver of the oncoming vehicle would yield.

Gila Monster bore down on the approaching headlamps. But the driver refused to brake. And switched on a spotlight.

Gila Monster stopped, his eyes singed by the glare.

"Turn off your engine," a harsh male voice came over a public address speaker. At the same time, a police-style light bar atop the vehicle scintillated to life.

There was no chance of swerving around the Forest Service–green Bronco. Within two feet, the berm gave way to a plunging cliff. Some rangers carried guns. He knew this. The slam of a door was followed by the suggestion of a uniformed figure flitting in front of all the lights trained on Gila Monster. The ranger rounded the Lincoln's grille. "You camping just up the creek here?" he demanded.

Gila Monster quickly decided that this was the best way to explain his presence in the area. "Yes."

"Well, our lookout all the way over on Promontory Butte spotted your fire . . ." The ranger's flashlight beam skipped around the interior, missing the dash and focusing on the cardboard box in the back-seat. "Don't you know open fires aren't permitted outside—*Jesus*!" At last, his light had found the jellied blood still smearing the instrument panel and steering wheel.

Kill! Kill!

Gila Monster fired twice without aiming.

The ranger flew back as if he'd been struck by a baseball bat. Flopping prone, he began making desperate sucking noises, the wind knocked out of him. He was wearing a bullet-resistant vest: Gila Monster could see the slight bulge of its lower edge across his abdomen. The slam of the two bullets had stunned him, but now he was sitting up and reaching for his own pistol.

Steadying his forearms on the door panel ledge, Gila Monster fired once more.

"YOU WANT TO KNOW ABOUT Darcy Altasal's child," Sylvia Newton said. It was less a question and more an expression of incredulity, as if she found little of genuine interest about her clients. By her own admission, she'd been with the Navajo Nation's Office of Social Services longer than she'd ever intended. Twenty-two years. One of those white functionaries who'd never be entirely accepted by the *Dine* but was too habituated to intricate tribal ways to start over somewhere else. On the wall above her salt-and-pepper hair was a U.C. Berkeley diploma in anthropology, but Anna didn't feel the need to tell Ms. Newton that she too was a Cal Bear. The middle-aged social worker had already driven on a late Sunday night from her home in Grants to her office in Crownpoint, the easternmost Navajo administrative center. An office in a complex that, despite it being the weekend, had the stale smell of a place where people wait long hours for resolution of problems that can never be resolved by government. Any government. "Is Darcy in some sort of trouble?" the woman asked.

"No." Emmett looked worn out from the endless day of desert highways. A hundred miles more of them since leaving Canoncito reservation. But he'd wanted to push on to Window Rock, and it'd taken considerable persuasion for Anna to get him to swing by Crownpoint.

Ms. Newton asked, "Is Darcy's child in trouble?"

When Emmett hesitated, Anna answered, "We're not sure if we understood her correctly. But if we did, there are material implications to the homicide case we're working."

"In what sense material?" Ms. Newton asked.

Anna glanced again at the diploma: *summa cum laude* in

anthropology. "We'd greatly appreciate a look at the file."
Instantly, she could tell the woman had no intention of hand-
ing it over, for she sat back and folded her bony arms over
her chest. "Without having to resort to the inconvenience of
a subpoena," Anna added with a smile to soften the implied
legal threat.

"Window Rock might be more than willing to suffer that
inconvenience," Ms. Newton said tersely. "The adoption
file's sealed for the child's protection. I have no authority to
open it. That rests with the tribal judiciary."

Emmett exhaled loudly. "Look, it may not be necessary
for us to go down that path."

"Are you suggesting I just slip the file under the table to
you, Mr. Parker?"

"No. You mind answering a few questions from personal
knowledge? Neither Agent Turnipseed nor I will put any of
it in our reports—without recontacting you for approval."

"This makes me uneasy."

"Me too," he admitted. "You could know something vital
to the prosecution, and then where would that leave Agent
Turnipseed and me? But this involves the murders of three
people, two law enforcement officers and a cop's spouse.
Otherwise, we wouldn't bother asking, believe me."

"The Knoki thing," Ms. Newton blurted. "But what other
officer . . . ?" Then she answered herself. "The FBI agent in
Phoenix. I saw it on television." The visible result of this
rapid-fire monologue was the uncrossing of her arms.

"Was Aurelia Knoki related to Darcy Altasal?" Anna
asked.

"Distantly," the woman began. "I'm not sure it was blood
or clan, but I do believe Aurelia grew up at Canoncito. But
understand, I worked the first half of my career in Tuba City."

"Where were you when Darcy had her baby?"

"Here in Crownpoint."

"And when was that?"

"About ten years ago. Maybe eleven by now."

From the corner of her eye, Anna saw Emmett sag in his

chair. She was beginning to feel guilty for having made him come on this possible fool's errand when he stirred and testily asked the social worker, "Can this be verified by hospital or BIA tribal enrollment records?"

"Hospital or state documents, no. BIA enrollment, yes."

"Then the baby wasn't born in a hospital?"

"No, Mr. Parker. You see, Darcy's grandmother Bernadine Altasal was a midwife—"

"Awee haliile," Anna interjected, finally understanding Darcy's exclamation.

"Correct, a traditional baby deliverer," Ms. Newton said with a quizzical smile. "You don't look *Dine.*"

"Modoc."

"Ah, Captain Jack and all that."

"My great-great-grandfather."

"Sad." Ms. Newton returned to the issue at hand. "I have reason to believe Bernadine delivered a number of babies who slipped through the administrative cracks. But I made sure the birth of Darcy's baby was duly recorded as soon as I caught wind of it."

"How long after the delivery did Bernadine die?" Emmett asked, interested again.

"A few months. It was her last." Then the woman said with a note of pride, "When I first came out here, the accounting system for births was in a shambles. I had to convince Window Rock that the tribe was losing funding because of the incomplete enrollment lists. And there was another problem draining off the enrolled population. The virtual black market in Indian infants. Not just here, but on all the reservations throughout the country."

"Black market?" Anna asked dubiously.

"How else do you think 30 percent of all native children wound up in foster or adoptive care by the late seventies, Ms. Turnipseed? An adoption rate eight times over the national average, and 90 percent of those Indian kids going to white homes? I call it a black market because most of those transactions were extralegal and coerced. With no consideration given to the sovereign status of the tribes. Or the rights of dysfunctional natural parents who might one day overcome their addictions and want their children back."

Anna was vaguely familiar with the Indian Child Welfare Act of 1978, but hadn't believed its impetus, adoptions by non-Indians, to have been this pervasive. So few Modoc remained, there was always a member of the extended family or the tribe to take in a neglected or unwanted child. "But most of these abuses were before the ICWA in '78, right?"

"Most but not all," Ms. Newton replied. "It took ages to get the bureaucracy moving, and many Indian parents—especially those with criminal or substance abuse histories—still don't realize the rights they have under the provisions of the act." She paused. "I hate to imagine the situations some of these children went into."

"Worse than those they left?" Emmett asked. Anna doubted that he approved of these adoptions. He just disliked Ms. Newton. There was something nunlike about her, and Anna had begun to realize that many of his seemingly flippant biases were rooted in his Catholic boarding school upbringing.

"We'll never know how bad it was for these kids, Mr. Parker," the woman said, rising. "But you can be assured Darcy's baby went to a quality *Dine* couple in Shiprock."

THE DASH CLOCK read midnight.

Emmett barreled west on Interstate 40 toward the lights of Gallup. Still so far off, they twinkled. If too exhausted at that point to push on, he planned to find a motel there. Otherwise, he wanted to make Window Rock tonight and confront John Tallsalt first thing in the morning. At his office or at home, wherever the lieutenant could be found. About the letter that now offered more hope than any other lead of clearing this all up. And Tallsalt's reason for withholding it. *Fuck it . . . I'm putting the screws to him.* But he was asking himself if Tallsalt and he remained friends, if the bonds of loyalty still mattered on any level, when Anna said, musing out loud, "Rowe came to Canoncito looking for a baby."

"I guess."

"Somehow not a ten-year-old living with his adoptive parents in Shiprock?"

"No. I've thought about that from every angle, and it leads me nowhere."

"Something passed between Rowe and Lolly right before he died, Em . . ." She paused to get hold of a sudden catch in her voice. Friday night, she'd been at the center of two grisly deaths within the mind-warping space of three hours. He wanted to pull over to the side of the interstate and comfort her. But that'd be misunderstood. Anything resembling desire, no matter how innocent, was now out of the question. That incensed him more than he'd ever confess to her. It was none of her fault. And all of hers. Incredible, the seesaw this had perched him on. "Rowe said to Lolly that he'd tried," Anna continued. "Gone every place she'd asked him. Then he shook his head as if it'd all been for nothing."

Emmett struggled to kick his mind into gear. "Rowe knew about the Knokis' murders, whatever his or Lolly's prior contact with them. How's the Phoenix media been covering the story?"

"Front page and lead TV spots."

"So that gives us two ways to take it. Rowe already knew that Aurelia was related to the Altasals. Or he didn't, though he certainly would've scoped on her name had Darcy dropped it. But maybe she didn't . . ." Emmett drifted into the right lane to take the upcoming Window Rock exit. They'd reached Gallup, and he supposed he was alert enough to go on another thirty minutes. "Juan Morada says Rowe was searching for a stalker, and Darcy says he was after a baby. Who do we believe . . . an ex-con or a poor retarded soul?"

She was silent for a minute, then: "What's the possibility Rowe had a part in killing the Knokis?"

"Still there. But the only round we have from the autopsies

is the possible forty-caliber taken out of Aurelia. Not even close to the twenty-five-cal bullets fired by Rowe's Raven pistol."

"Frank Thirty-three, Gallup."

Anna unhooked the mike. "Go ahead, Gallup."

"Your location?"

"Just north of town." She looked as surprised as he felt that the dispatch at the Gallup FBI office was up and running in the middle of the night. Usually that after-hours chore was handed over to McKinley County sheriff's office.

"Frank Thirty-three, phone the Phoenix SAC ASAP. Do you have his home number?"

"Affirm. I'll do it from your office."

"Negative. Unless that's your first available opportunity. Per SAC Niehaus's instructions."

Instead of continuing toward the Big Rez, Emmett made a tire-screaking U-turn and darted under the interstate in search of a phone booth. The first one was along U.S. 66 in front of a closed BP service station. Anna rushed out of the sedan and shut the folding glass door against the approaching rumble of an eastbound locomotive. The train was a streamliner. Ten hours to Emmett's home in Oklahoma from here. The only communication he seemed to have with his mother anymore concerned the passing of another relative. Mourning ceremonies he never had the time to attend. The past slipping away a person at a time. A year ago, his uncle Howard had died of a cerebral hemorrhage, the last undeniably fluent speaker of Comanche among the Parkers. Emmett had always planned to spend an entire vacation with Howard on his ranch near Lawton, recording the old man, testing his own command of the language against that impeccable ear. Now the inflections and linguistic nuances of his Quahadi-band ancestors had vanished forever in an internal explosion of blood.

His words turned to blood.

The train was gone, and Emmett brought himself back to the present. Anna slowly replaced the receiver in its cradle, but lingered in the booth after folding back the door. That made him get out of the car and meet her on the pavement. A warm night with a miasma of diesel fumes from the locomotive still hanging in the air. She stepped out, and her eyes glistened in the glow of passing headlights.

"What's wrong?" he asked.

"Summerfield was clean. His relationship with Dieter Preuss was sanctioned by the bureau. A recruitment in place, like you supposed . . ." Burying his hands in his pockets, Emmett stared down the wide boulevard. The news made him feel crushingly tired. And not vindicated in the least. "Preuss now lives in Silver Spring, Maryland. Runs an antiques store in D.C., where he's been every day for the past two weeks. Verified. Washington Metro had him on the hot seat all afternoon. He admitted to a weeklong rendezvous with Reed out here last fall. And the sexual turn their relationship took after East Germany fell. Niehaus said the man was badly shaken by Reed's death. I guess they had plans . . ." She shook her head as if unsure how to go on.

"Let's get some rest, lady," Emmett said. "Find a motel here and call it a day."

"That's not all Niehaus had to report." She stood erect again and looked Emmett squarely in the eye. "You know where Sitgreaves National Forest is?"

"Between here and Phoenix."

"How far?"

"Maybe an hour and a half southwest of us. Why?"

"A Forest Service law enforcement officer was shot to death there earlier tonight," she said mechanically. "He'd been responding to an illegal campfire someplace called Chevelon Canyon. Coconino sheriff's office found him inside his cruiser, which had been shoved partway down a cliff. They found the fire too . . ."

chapter 18

IT WAS A CLOUDLESS MOUNTAIN MORNING WITH ONE corpse already en route to the University of Arizona Medical Center in Tucson and two more waiting under a black plastic tarp for transport. Emmett had helped the FBI evidence technician cover the charred heap of flesh and bones after a Phoenix TV news chopper suddenly buzzed down Chevelon Canyon at treetop level. He'd punched a hole in the top of the tarp with his pocketknife to let out the residual heat when the pyre began to smolder. Now a wisp of smoke escaped from the little volcano.

"Is that plastic getting soft?" Emmett asked. The pathologist in Tucson would be livid if the two subjects came to him coated with melted polyethylene.

The tech felt several places on the plastic, then shook his head.

Emmett turned back to the calligraphy of tracks left by the perpetrator. Decidedly male, unless there was an Amazon out there with size twelves. The comings and goings of the killer were written not so much in the mat of fallen pine needles and oak leaves, which Emmett scraped away at even the vaguest hint of deformation, as the underlying duff, the partly decomposed matter that held an impression better than the top layer. And the story here was just that: comings *and* goings. The killer had hiked down the slope from a point Emmett had yet to find, sat for some time in a level spot, then eventually risen.

But not to his full height.

He'd crawled the rest of the way down to the creek, slinking an alligatorlike track through the leaf debris and then across the moss on the cobbled stones lining the streambed. He reared up on the bank just below the camp. To attack his victims, for there Emmett found three .40-caliber shell casings. The same caliber as Bert Knoki's missing service pistol—that had gotten his heart racing. Then, after tramping all around the fire and dumping a sleeping bag in the creek, the killer had run erratically back to the place where he'd sat down, leaving blood spatters flecked across the humus (his or one of the victim's?), only to return to the camp once more.

Why?

Emmett gazed off toward the pair of lawn chairs, one overturned and one upright. Props indicative of awful surprise.

Beyond them, Anna stood in the middle of the dusty, primitive road, conferring with the case agent for this latest bloodbath, an FBI resident out of Flagstaff. A Phoenix agent had been assigned Summerfield's murder. The task force was collecting agents like barnacles, and Emmett had decided to detach himself as soon as possible from the bureaucratic concretion that was hardening around Coordinating Agent Turnipseed. Still, it would be a good learning experience for her as long as he butted out. So he'd distanced himself from her as soon as they had arrived at three this morning above the Forest Service Bronco that had plunged nose-first into the creek. She was ramrodding what was now the biggest investigation in the country, and looking at every turn to a lowly BIA dick for advice wouldn't help her sell herself to the whirlwind of investigators and technicians surrounding her.

She gestured emphatically to make some point to the Flagstaff agent. She could now be emphatic. Emmett smiled. She'd also refused a dab of benzoin under the nose. The horrors were losing their grip over her. At least at the crime scene. Yet, once her gesture was complete, she unconsciously rubbed her almost healed Gila bite.

The killer sure as hell hadn't walked all the way from Phoenix to these mountains. Where had he parked?

Sunlight streamed down through the pines and oaks, although the broad-leafed canopy grew thinner the farther he trudged up the slope. And finally, with no oak leaves crinkling underfoot, he realized how quietly the killer had come down off the heights. Like a breeze felt before it was heard. Craning his head, he glanced back through the foliage at the camp. In darkness, the fire would have been an irresistible beacon. *A moth to his flame.* The positions of the chairs relative to the fire ring suggested that the victims had built the blaze and the killer had only taken advantage of it as a crematory.

After another hundred yards, Emmett suddenly stopped dead, his mouth going dry. Through the tree trunks, he could see a dark blue delivery van.

Slipping his revolver from his holster, he cautiously advanced. The physical evidence at the scene below told him that the killer was long gone. The mud-and-snow-tire impressions on the road—and above the coffin of the Bronco—convinced him the man had taken the couple's wide-track vehicle, probably a sport utility, and had been fleeing Chevelon Canyon when confronted by the law enforcement ranger. The bloodstains in the road dust explained the outcome of that confrontation.

For some reason, had he returned to his van? That would be suicidal, but in Emmett's experience other suspects had taken this way out.

He halted fifty feet behind the rear doors of the vehicle.

The windless forest was quiet but for the distant tapping of a woodpecker against a hollow snag. Sidestepping, he checked both truck mirrors for movement inside the cab. Nothing hinted at occupation. But this monster could spring astonishing surprises. Emmett had never expected him to track down Anna in Phoenix. The advantage seemed always his. He knew everything, each and every player.

Emmett closed on the rear doors, his muzzle trained on

the crack between them. Watching for the latch to rotate in the slightest degree. It didn't. The thumb and forefinger of his free hand touched no more of the chrome handle than necessary to open it. He threw the right door back and went flat against the cargo bed to sweep the interior with his sights.

Sunlight poured around him into the vacant space.

Raising himself up on his knuckles, he lunged down the length of the van and burst into the cab. Empty.

The entire vehicle had been virtually sanitized. Not a scrap of trash had been left behind in it.

Take everything in sequence. From outside to inside. Or you'll miss something.

Holstering, he walked completely around the van. Both license plates were gone. Facing the grille, he saw that it was a Grumman truck body on a General Motors chassis and cab. He stooped to read the embossing on the lens of the amber parking light: 73. The vehicle was a 1973 model. Stepping up onto the bumper, but careful not to hoist himself by grabbing the side mirror, which the killer had to have adjusted, he peered through the badly pitted windshield at the extreme right-hand corner of the dashboard. The small metal plate bearing the vehicle identification number had been ripped out, leaving only the rivet holes and a rectangle of bright blue paint that hadn't been bleached by years of desert ultraviolet like the rest of the dash.

He would touch neither of the cab door handles. Not before the ID tech dusted them for latent fingerprints. The abandonment had been done with extreme care, and all these square yards of metal and vinyl might yield but one tiny partial print. Particularly if they'd been wiped down, as he suspected. He reentered the van at its rear and strode through the cargo bay to the cab, where he knelt before the removable engine cowling. The last clip was snicking open under the pressure of his ballpoint pen—when he let up. Inwardly seeing the enraged Gila dangling off Anna's wrist in the darkness under the Knokis' mobile home.

Removing the small flashlight from his windbreaker pocket, he doffed the jacket and wrapped it around his left forearm. He reached again for the final cowling latch. It gave with a rattle. Pressing his face flush to the metal floor, he raised the covering an inch, listening for the rustle of claws. Another inch. Shielding his eyes, he squinted for a glimpse of beaded skin but remembered that a Gila's snout was the same shiny black as the grease-covered engine. He leaned the cowling against the dash and examined the block with his flashlight. A patch of silver glistened back at him. The engine number had been scratched out with a sharp tool, baring virgin cast iron.

The number that might have told him who had wantonly killed six people over the last eight days.

There was only one more place the VIN might appear. The factory stamped a hidden copy of the identification number somewhere on the frame, then religiously guarded this secret location from all but the most urgent supplications from law enforcement. He'd probably need an auto theft specialist to find it. So, he wouldn't have his answer for hours, if not days. And if the van had been stolen, he might never know who had left it here and then crawled down toward that fire in search of helpless prey. *Gilas are baby-killers in the wild,* Dr. Hennepin had said.

Then he almost missed it. The grate of hinges opening.

He was already rolling to the far side of the cab when an angry hiss made his scalp prickle. The large Gila scrabbled out of the toolbox bolted to the deck behind the driver's seat. The lizard came at him with surprising speed, mouth gaping, daggerlike teeth glinting under a sheen of venom. Jackknifing up, Emmett unwound his windbreaker and flicked a sleeve at the onrushing jaws. They chomped into the nylon. Before the creature's brain could process the fact that the sleeve was not prey, Emmett hoisted the Gila and dropped it into the open toolbox, slamming shut the lid with his boot and holding it closed with a slightly tremulous leg. "Son of a bitch," he grunted. He jammed his pen into the hasp for a makeshift lock.

Then he sat limply on the floor, inspecting the shredded sleeve of his jacket.

Something red and white drew his eye to the seam between two of the diamond-patterned metal plates forming the floor. Wedged in it was a two-toned capsule. He pried it out with the tip of his pocketknife, then dropped it into a Baggie.

So the monster had left something of himself. He was fallible. But that would be of little consolation to his next victim.

ANNA HAD SURVIVED her childhood by partitioning herself into two conscious halves. The unexpected usefulness of this coping mechanism surprised her. One half of her mind was acutely aware of the stench of charred human flesh. Back just when she'd finally gotten the Knokis out of her nostrils. Aware of the grotesquely stiff and blackened figures, one heaped over the other in the shape of a cross—a male and a female, according to the medical examiner's cursory check. The occasional sound of a drop of fat pelting the still warm ashes beneath the bodies. Yet the other half of her mind thought only of ramifications affecting the case. How to salvage and protect the evidence. The breeze had risen, stirring the hot spots hidden in the pyre. The news chopper had vacated the pale blue skies over the canyon, so she'd ordered the tarp removed. If the plastic melted, the postmortem findings might be contaminated.

Nothing seemed to happen unless she sanctioned it.

She was the coordinating agent. All personnel here and behind the scenes in Phoenix and Gallup were like spokes emanating from her will. "Ms. Turnipseed . . ." The Coconino County medical examiner advised her that the initial inspection and photographing of the bodies was done; could he start bagging them? Automatically, she started to look for Emmett, but he was still somewhere on the wooded slope above the camp. Gone looking for his overview. And purposely leaving her to fend for herself, she'd surmised.

A whine approached. Then something dark and windy soared over her and down the canyon. The chopper again.

"Shit," Anna muttered.

Rather than order the bodies covered once more, she shouted over the fading rotor noise at the Coconino deputy sergeant charged with perimeter security, "Have your dispatch phone that TV station and tell them—one more pass and I go to the U.S. Attorney for a goddamn complaint!" She wasn't quite sure for what, but the sergeant touched two fingers to the bill of his cap and trotted for the radio in his cruiser.

The medical examiner was still waiting for an answer.

"Let's see . . ." She licked the taste of dust off her lips. Jim Niehaus was on the way here from Phoenix. But it seemed ridiculous to hold up everything just so the SAC could stroll around the crime scene and tell everyone they were doing a ducky job. The sooner the bodies got to autopsy the better. "Load 'em up," she said.

All this time, the examiner had been holding a pry bar behind him. He now approached the fused corpses with it.

Anna turned away from the sight.

Altasal. She almost uttered the name out loud. It'd been popping into her head all morning.

The Flagstaff agent, a man with a wiry tuft of black hair showing in the vee of his collar now that he'd removed his tie, thrust a rumpled sweatshirt almost in her nose. He let it fall like a curtain. Arizona State University. She'd forgotten ordering him to search the contents of the tent. "Anything else?" she asked.

"That's it," he replied, exasperated. "What, forty thousand students attend ASU? And whichever of the victims wore it might've been alumni. Or related to alumni. Or he or she just bought the damn thing, right?"

The victims' wallet and purse were presumed to be in their presumably missing vehicle. They'd been camped illegally, so there was no record of their visitation with the Chevelon Ranger District in Winslow. Anna anticipated no missing persons inquiries until late tonight or even Tuesday. And she was undecided about how much she wanted to share with the media at this point. Some key details of this crime had to be withheld, if only to weed out any false confessions. She'd discuss that with Niehaus, as his media representative at the Phoenix office had already issued the adroit press releases on the Knokis and Summerfield.

Altasal.

"Anything else, Turnipseed?" the Flagstaff agent asked.

"Is the Sitgreaves Forest supervisor still around?"

"Somewhere." The man was tired. Strangely, she wasn't. No sleep last night, but she felt as if she could go on forever.

"Mind finding him for me?"

The agent scurried wearily off.

Niehaus would expect a full briefing, including background detail on the ranger victim. So far, although she'd spent two hours examining and photographing his body in the battered Bronco, she only knew that his name was Gary Clement. Two bullets had been embedded in his Kevlar vest like lead-colored gumballs. A third had penetrated his skull just above the right eye. His last transmission had been to Fire Dispatch in Winslow: *"I've got a vehicle coming at me. Will advise . . ."* And when Clement didn't after two status checks, the dispatcher put out a distress call to the Coconino sheriff's office. The deputy, used to looking for plunges off precipitous mountain roads, spotted where the Bronco had been rolled over the side.

A white-haired man in a Forest Service uniform appeared before her. Bags under his eyes. "You wanted to see me, Agent Turnipseed?"

"Yes, sir. I wonder if you can tell me something about Ranger Clement."

"Well, he was a great guy. We're going to miss him."

"How old was he?"

"Thirty-three. Two years with us, several years with LAPD prior. Came here to get his wife and three kids away from city violence . . ." The man smiled uncomfortably at the irony of it. "He got on well with the locals. So this just baffles me."

Again, half of Anna's mind took in the mention of wife and children with a cold, sinking feeling, while the other half blotted the emotion out and sifted for anything material. Such as an unforeseen reason for this homicide. However, she believed the killer and Clement had never met prior to last night. "I saw that he kept patrol logs." She'd found his clipboard in the creek.

"Oh yes, indeed."

"I'd like to have copies of all his paperwork for the last month. Just to check if he came across something related to this before . . ." She didn't feel the need to finish.

"I'll make sure you get it today."

The supervisor was walking away from her when she was struck with an odd sense of well-being. She couldn't make up her mind if it was acceptance of her condition or just a sweltering drowsiness catching up with her. *I belong here.* As ridiculous as that sounded, with two immolated corpses not thirty feet away, and a dozen men waiting with bated breath for her to make a mistake. She felt that she'd slipped into a new realm. One which certainly had its demons. But not her old familiar demons, which were apparently powerless to steal into it behind her. For here, she was in control.

But then Jim Niehaus arrived.

The first thing the Phoenix special agent in charge ordered, upon slamming his car door, was for the bodies to be covered up.

"Sorry, sir," she countermanded him. "But we have nothing but plastic, and the bodies are still hot enough to melt it."

He glared at her a moment, then rolled his eyes skyward.

"What about the news copter that just passed right over me?"

"I've asked the SO to phone the station. If that doesn't work, I'm sure your media rep can find some way to punish them. Besides, are they really going to broadcast these shots?"

Niehaus ambled over to her, his blond head like a flame in the sunlight. She realized that he was striving to look nonchalant, that the gruesome spectacle of death bothered him. He glanced down at her clothes. Dusty and caked below the knees with dried stream silt from the hours working Clement's Bronco. He himself was dressed in a polo shirt and khakis, as if he'd driven here directly from the golf course. "Where's the ranger?" he asked, keeping his voice low.

"Already on the way to Tucson."

"Any leads on the identity of these two?"

"No, sir. But I've had every PD and SO in Arizona, New Mexico and southern Utah alerted to forward us any report of overdue campers. Still, it may wind up going dental."

"Might," he agreed, starting to saunter as if out of sheer discomfort. Emmett was right: Everyone reacted, although each in his own way. Parker couldn't stand still either at a homicide scene.

She fell in beside Niehaus. "I guess we can assume news camera teams are on the way here by vehicle."

"No doubt."

"I'd like to know what's safe to tell them. I don't want to screw it up."

The SAC must have appreciated her candor, for he smiled. "My media rep's about an hour behind me. Fred Waggoner's with him. We'll all put our heads together before the microphones are shoved in our faces. I think it's a no-brainer we've lost the fact the bodies were burned." They wove their way between the pyre and a tech patiently scooping wet plaster of Paris into one of the boot prints the killer had left around the scene. "How's your forehead?"

She realized that he was referring to the bruise. "Fine."

He gave a remote nod. "Well, Turnipseed, is this the same unsub who got the Knokis and Summerfield?" Unknown subject. A curiously detached way to refer to the beast. It was a self-admitted prejudice of hers that blonds didn't feel things as keenly as darker-complected people.

"I think so, sir."

"Why?"

"First, he's not afraid to take on law enforcement. Knoki, Summerfield and now this ranger here."

"Then cops are his targets?"

"If they get in the way of his fixation."

"And what's that?" Niehaus asked, stepping around a tech who was photographing tire impressions beside the tent.

"I don't know yet."

"Go on."

"Second, he burns his victims if given the chance."

"Was the ranger burned?"

"No."

"Neither was Summerfield," the SAC observed.

"But the killer was in a rush to get away from Emmett's apartment. As he was to get out of the canyon here."

"Still, you're convinced he did both the Knokis and Reed?"

Anna paused. Two sets of foot tracks had led away from the tribal cruiser and out of Crystal Wash. That made it unlikely that he had slain the Navajo patrolman and his wife without help, unless the murders and the disposing of the bodies were carried out by separate parties. That possible distinction was blurred by the postmortem finding that Bert hadn't expired until the flames took him. Nevertheless, she hadn't forgotten Garwin Descheenie, the big gangbanger with the winged Gila tattoo arrested with five other Vipers after the sniping attack at Clydine Jumper's. If the killer had had assistance, it was he. Or possibly Ivan Jumper. Descheenie was still in juvenile lockup at Tohatchi. And, according to

Emmett, Ivan was yet at large. She realized that she'd left Niehaus dangling too long.

"You're not holding out on me, are you, Turnipseed?" His smile had returned, but it was less than trusting.

Thankfully, at that moment, Emmett emerged from the pines. "Got a spare tech?"

"Why?" she asked.

"There's a dark blue GM van abandoned in the trees about three hundred yards west of us." Emmett obviously enjoyed it when Niehaus's mouth dropped and the others scattered around the scene started leaving their chores to draw closer to listen.

"Utah plates?"

"No plates, no VIN." Emmett and the SAC exchanged a tepid handshake. "You got a capable auto theft man who can get here lickety-split, Jim?" When Niehaus hesitated only briefly, Emmett turned toward Anna. "I'd be much obliged if you requested the assistance of a fellow I know with Arizona Highway Patrol. He could find the tertiary VIN on an Egyptian chariot . . ." She knew he was pouring on his ordinarily constrained Oklahoma accent just to needle Niehaus. But why now? "Just have him mind the toolbox. There's one pissed-off Gila in it."

"You okay, Em?"

"Dandy." He glanced impatiently at his wristwatch. It made her look at her own: almost noon. "Well, I might as well be shoving off."

He intended to dump his coordinating agent in Chevelon Canyon. Most likely, to go on alone to Window Rock to confront Tallsalt over the missing letter, which he'd been hell-bent to do ever since they'd learned from Darcy Altasal that she was related to Aurelia Knoki. She stood there, quietly fighting the sting of betrayal that Emmett would ditch her.

"Where do you want to set up your command post, Turnipseed?" Niehaus asked.

She stared directly at Emmett as she said, "Window Rock."

But the SAC looked more nonplussed than Parker. "Not Phoenix or Gallup? Think of the resources you'll need."

"I am. All this centers on the Big Rez. It always comes back to the Navajo Nation in one way or another. I want to be there ahead of the bastard this time, waiting for him . . ." She could see Niehaus calculating what she already had: Sitgreaves National Forest was on a back roads beeline to the heart of Navajoland. The killer had used it as a way station to exchange vehicles before continuing north. And she'd almost swear that the van had had Utah plates, a state which included a considerable portion of the Big Reservation. "I'd like to keep Parker on tap for anything that develops up there."

Niehaus said coolly, "Whatever you need to get the job done—ASAP."

chapter 19

AGAINST HIS WILL, EMMETT WAS SWEPT THROUGH THE black and white outskirts of Fort Sill toward his mother's house, knowing that he was dreaming, up her walkway, knowing he was dreaming, past her stricken face, dreaming, and into that horrific, blood- and gore-splattered kitchen. He stopped. Exulted that he'd arrived from Oklahoma City in time. His brother still had all that blood and brain tissue inside his head. Although Malcolm Parker sat at the table contemplating the pistol in his hands. But then, with no clash of dream gears, it was John Tallsalt and not Malcolm, twitching his forefinger in and out of the trigger guard. In the strange, ventriloquistic telepathy of dreams, Tallsalt said, *I shall be reclamated.* But Emmett was inching close enough to wakefulness to recall that, according to his mother, Malcolm's last words had been *I shall be redeemed, my dear Numu Pabi.* Jesus. The muzzle began its fatal rise to his temple. Emmett tried to lunge but couldn't move.

The inevitable blast came, and he jolted awake.

For an instant, he thought that he'd fallen asleep while driving. He was unquestionably inside his sedan, but Anna was alertly at the wheel. He recalled her insistence earlier that afternoon that she drive. Wiping a bit of drool from the corner of his mouth, he glanced back. In reality, the bark of the pistol had been the tires of his Dodge clacking over a cattle guard. Had the entire nightmarish dream been inspired by that sound, compressed into a split second?

"Feeling better?" Anna asked.

No. But he said, "Yeah."

The dash clock read 5:12, and sunlight was fanning over the crest of the Chuskas. The rarefied air showed the scattered hogans and shacks with a raw clarity. The cast-off cars. A defeated people still recovering. He hadn't cried following his brother's suicide, but expected to, eventually, if only in his sleep. He was glad this hadn't been the time. Cumulus scudded along the northern horizon like white sails. Tragedy always looked backward for cause and effect, and he now asked himself if Malcolm would still be alive if Columbus's little fleet had been lost at sea. Was it that simple?

Probably not.

The Comanche, as a people, were not overly given to alcoholism. Introduced to booze by American traders, they were astonished that human beings would want to imbibe something that turned them imbecilic. So Malcolm's and Emmett's mutual failing was probably personal, and if there was a scapegoat, it was genetic inheritance. From whom? The Parkers? Quanah's mother had been a white captive.

"Where are we?" he asked, yawning.

"Almost to Tohatchi," Anna replied. "On Route 666."

"Sign of the Beast."

"What?"

"Nothing." He readjusted his shoulder belt, which had ridden up across his throat. Leaving Sitgreaves National Forest, he'd wanted to go directly to Window Rock. If Tallsalt hadn't returned from his weekend trip by the time Anna and he reached the capital, at least they would be ready to question him first thing in the morning. But then Anna had asked, "What good will that do if John's in deeper than we realize?" He'd had no answer to that. Still didn't. He was run-down. And falling asleep during daylight, even when exhausted, was a new experience for him. But Anna had caught him drifting over the white line. Twice.

At Winslow, about an hour north of Chevelon Canyon, she'd found a phone booth, made two calls, then talked about them only after relieving Emmett and accelerating east onto an Interstate 40 sluggish with Memorial Day traffic. Her first call had been to the on-duty supervisor at the Tohatchi Juvenile Detention Facility—which she was now braking for. A flat-roofed, cinder block jail with garlands of razor wire topping the exercise yard fence. She'd told the supervisor she meant to photograph the winged Gila tattoo on Garwin Descheenie's neck. Her second call had been to the answering service of an attorney in Albuquerque who'd been appointed to defend the Vipers in federal court, sharing with him what she'd told the facility super. Emmett had to admire her cunning: The lawyer, as soon as he found out the same design was etched on the rocks in Lowe Canyon and sprayed on the back of Blackhouse and Rowe's University Park rental, would scream that this demonstrative evidence was inflammatory. And Emmett realized it would be excluded by the judge if he felt its introduction to be grossly prejudicial to the defendants. But he also guessed that Anna's true purpose was to shake up the lawyer just enough to persuade him to let at least one of the bangers talk to her.

Good for her. Deceit in a worthy cause is always admirable. A Comanche axiom.

She parked in the visitors' space, and Emmett stepped out into the dusk shadow of the Chuskas. The coolness revived him a little. The only other car in the lot was a Porsche. If it belonged to the Vipers' attorney, he'd been rattled enough by her message to drive from Albuquerque on the last evening of the holiday weekend.

"Borrow your camera from you?" she asked.

"Open the trunk for me." He took his 35mm outfit with flash attachment from his evidence kit and handed it to her. "Know how to take close-ups?"

"Keep the plane of the film parallel to the plane of the object." She opened the steel door for him.

"Why do I get the feeling I've created a monster?"

"Don't offer something unless you mean it," she said with a slightly wounded tone, following him into the lobby.

Unadorned and furnitureless except for a framed copy of the visitation rules and a bank of chairs screwed to the floor. Normal visiting hours had ended at five, and the room was empty. The supervisor, a portly Navajo with a jingling mass of keys clipped to his belt, led them to the interviewing room and not the booking tank, where all photography was done, which Emmett didn't understand—until the man swept back the door on Garwin Descheenie and his attorney. The muscular gangbanger was wearing a regulation orange jumpsuit. And a hair net. The stocky but not fat lawyer was probably a Pueblo Indian. Late twenties with styled jet-black hair. He wore a fawn-colored suit and cordovan shoes. Rising from the table with a high-strung smile, he asked, "Special Agent Turnipseed . . . ?"

"Hello."

"I'm Rod Guzman."

Anna said, "This is Investigator Parker from the BIA."

"Oh yes."

Emmett was used to those *oh yesses*.

Guzman didn't offer to shake hands. He was on guard. Nothing in his manner betrayed that. It was his dress. He'd taken the time on his day off to create the impression that he was no hick Indian lawyer. "Well, Ms. Turnipseed, I sure appreciate your calling our office, and I've explained to Garwin that while we'll submit to your limited evidentiary request, we have the right to know the context in which your photographs will be used."

Descheenie locked eyes with Emmett, who held them as he said, "They'll be used in the context of a serial murder binge that now has a body count of six." The banger smirked. "Stand up, please," Emmett ordered, although he had already grabbed the youth by the front of his jumpsuit and hauled him to his feet. "How you doing this evening, Gar?" Before Descheenie could snarl anything, Emmett turned to the lawyer: "Oh, I'm sorry—that sounds like the run-up to an interview, doesn't it? And that's the last thing we need at this late date—to hear ol' Gar's line of hooey."

"Mr. Parker—"

"Excuse me, Mr. Guzman." Anna cut off the lawyer's protest by stepping in front of him and training the camera on Descheenie. "Turn his head, Emmett."

He did so, briskly, and in the eyeball-numbing flash that followed he saw the winged Gila hovering in the air. She shot the tattoo from three distances, then said, "That's all." She went out the door and took off down the corridor so quickly Emmett figured she was pissed off at him for having blown her opportunity for an interview. There'd been none from the moment Guzman started talking about *contexts*. He'd come here to prevent any of his clients from talking, obviously out of the belief they were guilty of some part in the Knokis' murders. The young attorney had yet to master the poker face he needed to succeed in this game of appearances.

Catching up with her, Emmett was surprised to see that she was fighting a smile. "Slick, Parker."

"What?" he asked innocently.

"The act in there to stampede Guzman into a plea bargain."

"Actually, I just couldn't stomach that goddamn hair net."

"Special Agent Turnipseed . . . ?" It was the facility supervisor. "Is your call sign Frank Thirty-three?"

"Yes."

"Gallup's trying to raise you. I don't know how long they've been at it. Don't get much of a chance to monitor the radio."

"May I use a phone?"

"Control room." The supervisor crinkled his lips at the doorway.

Emmett waited in the lobby, gazing eastward through a thick glass panel beside the door at Chaco Mesa, a distant elevation of rimrock. Where the Anasazi had lived in accord a thousand years ago without resorting to jails. How much did Descheenie or one of his gang brothers fear incarceration? Enough to tell how they fit into this mess?

Christ almighty.

It continued to escape him: the line that could connect the Knokis, Terry Rowe, Lolly Blackhouse, the Vipers, the brutal creature who'd killed again last night in the forest *and* Johnny Tallsalt. He just couldn't find it. For the first time in his career, the solution seemed beyond his experience.

Anna burst through the security door. "Read this." A fax from the Gallup FBI office. Actually a copy of a teletype from the Utah Department of Motor Vehicles. *Search VIN 3748923S66: expired registration on a 1973 General Motors truck. Last registered owner: Church of Living Prophecy, P.O. Box 19003, Mexican Hat, UT 84531.*

"I'll be damned," he said.

THE UNPAVED ROAD wound through the conifer forest on the north slope of Chuska Peak. Emmett had recommended this cutoff as the quickest way of connecting to Navajo Route 12 and eventually the Utah strip of the Big Rez. The 7,500-foot altitude allowed them to turn off the air-conditioning and power down their windows. Anna stole a glance over at him. Again, he'd taken the passenger seat, not having argued in Tohatchi when she offered to resume driving for them. "I guess I'd like to ask you something . . ." His tone made her sit up. "If you don't mind."

"All right," she said, hands tensing on the wheel.

"Have I ever come across to you in, you know, an unseemly way?"

"Unseemly."

"Forward, I guess I mean."

"You're forward all the time, Emmett. *Direct* is the better word. That's just you." But she knew full well what this was about. At last, he'd solved her pathetic riddle and needed to discuss it with her. She needed to talk about it too, but didn't want to wade into the past now. Not when she felt so good. So useful. "I must be too worn-out to follow you," she fudged, disliking herself for it.

But Emmett proved dogged. "Have I made you uncomfortable at times . . . ?" This really upset him, and that moved her. "Because of my intentions . . . or maybe what you assumed my intentions to be?"

She could only waffle so long without making him feel like a fool. They topped the crest and started down the switchbacks on the west slope of the range. "You've always been a gentleman." But that sounded so ridiculously prudish, she amended, "If that's what you meant to be."

"Be what?"

"Gentlemanly." Below, a bonfire threw an orange ray across a quicksilver-colored surface in the gathering darkness she realized to be a mountain lake. "Is it?"

"Yes," he said sulkily.

"You don't want to be a gentleman?"

"It's exactly what I want to be. My New Year's resolution every year."

He was backing away from the possibility of a relationship. She'd been half-anticipating this ever since the scene in her room last Tuesday morning. But hadn't expected to feel so crushed. What was coming next: quitting the task force?

Letting out a big yawn, he laced his fingers together and stretched his arms in front of him. "Getting too old for this, Turnipseed."

"The job?"

"These special gigs. The day-to-day stuff I can handle."

He was bailing. She downshifted, her eyes misting. "What lake is that?"

"Asaayi."

That meant the cluster of lights on the valley floor below was the town of Navajo, where the Knokis' darkened mobile home was. She found herself resenting the murdered couple. Without that nightmare triggered by their corpses, things might have evolved naturally and slowly between Emmett and her. She believed she needed those two qualities to overcome the past and have a normal relationship with a man.

She felt hopelessly trapped in the shadow of Coyote, author of incest—depending on the myth, he'd seduced his sister or daughter. She racked her brains for something casual to say. "Big bonfire, isn't it?"

He agreed with a grunt.

And there appeared to be scores of people around it. As she drove closer, she saw that they were young people. Some of them gangbangers. Their parked vehicles clogged the access lane that ran from the road down to the picnic ground on the shore. Bottles were clearly visible, despite the reservation prohibition against alcohol. Loud jeers floated up to her: They had made the car.

"Ignore them," Emmett said. "Tohatchi's out of bed space."

She drove on toward Route 12, which could be traced below by the headlights blinking along it.

"THIS WAS THE MAIN COMPOUND and headquarters of the Church of Living Prophecy," Jink Brill explained with a sweep of his arm that encompassed everything inside a ten-foot-high stockade of interlocked truck tires. "These piles of ashes and embers mark where the buildings stood . . ." Ambling along between Emmett and Anna, the FBI resident agent out of Monticello, Utah, hooked his thumb at each in passing: "Communal kitchen and dining hall . . ." Broken crockery sparkled among the cinders. "Wash house. Barracks. Main schoolroom and kindergarten . . ." The head of a charred rocking horse reared its head up out of the debris. "Springhouse over there by the willows. It didn't burn."

The agent had met Emmett and Anna for breakfast before driving them seven miles north of Mexican Hat to this swale with a spring. A raw-boned Mormon in his mid-fifties, Brill wore a dark western-cut suit, despite the morning heat, and a turquoise-studded bolo tie, despite the FBI's dress code.

"Started five years ago in the fall," Brill went on. "That's when an army of state troopers and San Juan County deputies tried to enforce a court order for the church to send its children to public school. Hezekiah Pound, the leader and alleged living prophet of the cult, set off the old air raid siren he'd bought surplus from Civil Defense in Provo. Howling like the end of the world. The kids had put out buckets of water to douse the tear gas grenades in. One of the Pounds fired a burst of submachine gun fire at the sheriff as he read the order right there . . ." The agent pointed at the breach in the tire wall they'd just driven through. "That got ATF, plus me, involved for the illegal firearms possession violation. The siege ended four months later with this . . ." Brill rolled a spent tear gas canister over with the toe of his cowboy boot. "Fire started by all the chemical agent grenades took out the structures. SWAT had to take out Hezekiah, three of his sons and one of his wives. Saddest thing I've ever seen. There were nineteen arrests and fifteen convictions. You in on that with us, Emmett?"

"Nope." Luckily. For the closing stages of the siege, nearly every federal cop in the Four Corners region had been tapped to support ATF and local law enforcement in helping take down Pound.

"What are we talking about here?" Anna asked. She'd seemed unusually subdued ever since they'd come down off the Chuskas last night. "Some kind of Koresh-like cult?"

"Much older than that Branch Davidian nonsense." Brill abruptly spun on Emmett with a southern Utah colloquialism. "Oh my heck, Parker—why didn't you tell me last week that this might involve the Pounds? I've been sitting on my thumb in Monticello, wondering how I might help. I knew Bert Knoki. Liked him fine."

"Settle down, Jink. We didn't get the return on the van's VIN till yesterday evening. I knew you were the expert on the Pounds and phoned you as soon as we got to the motel."

Looking slightly mollified, Brill ran Chap Stick over his lips. Most white skin didn't stand up to Western sun and aridity. "That old bakery van," the agent said, almost fondly. "That's what it was. Hezekiah bought it from the Monticello

Bakery. Should have seen him tooling all his kids around in it. He had twenty-seven of them, as near we could figure. You LDS, Turnipseed?"

Not an unreasonable assumption, as many Indians in the Great Basin belonged to the Church of Jesus Christ of Latter-day Saints. "No."

"Anywho, like any other religion," Brill continued, "we Saints have always had our malcontents. But things came to a boil with the Manifesto of 1890. That ended plural marriage. Some folks held on to polygamy, despite what the Church decreed. Not out of any lascivious bent, I must add. They just went on reckoning God requires it of true believers. Southern Utah's pretty isolated, so these groups tended to concentrate down here along the Arizona border. Hezekiah's daddy was one of these early rebels against the manifesto. From him he inherited the mantle of living prophet. That's a sacred thing to us mainstream Saints, and we don't like it being conferred without a divine nod, if you know what I mean."

Anna smiled. She appeared to like this plainspoken man with the sun-wrinkled neck. Emmett knew that he wouldn't mind belonging to the FBI if men like Brill were the norm.

"You don't hold a splinter group together with ice cream socials," Brill said. "The Pounds got heavy into something called Blood Atonement. Assassinations. Executions. Both inside and outside the cult. To us, it might sound like knocking off rivals, backsliders and apostates. But to Hezekiah's way of thinking, it was shedding the blood of sinners to help them atone for their sins."

"Kind of like enforced redemption?" Anna asked.

The agent glanced to Emmett. "How come she can say in a half-dozen words what takes me a hundred?"

"She's smarter than you, Jink."

Anna tried to meet Emmett's eyes, to let something warm pass between them, but he looked away before she could.

Brill dropped his Chap Stick into his pocket. "Truancy issue was just the straw that broke the camel's back. Intelligence has it Hezekiah had one of his wives blood-atoned . . ." Brill's weathered face hardened. "Saphronia, her name was. I knew her from school, before she got yanked out in the sixth grade. Sweet girl. Hair the color of wheat straw." He exhaled. "Next Hezekiah ordered a son killed. That was down in Sonora, where the cult had another enclave. They used El Refugio whenever things got too sticky for them on this side of the border. Then his eldest grandson vanished, although I believe the San Juan coroner's in possession of some of that poor boy's sun-bleached bones. Never did find the skull. And then the leader of another polygamous outfit was gunned down in Moab. It got where Hezekiah's sons spent much of their time in jail for investigation of homicide, and legal fees put a real crimp in the group's finances."

Emmett asked, "But the Pounds are finished, aren't they?"

"The Pounds are never finished."

"Then who among the survivors could be behind all these homicides?"

The agent peered thoughtfully at Emmett, then turned on his heel and went to his car. "Come here, you two." He took a manila folder from under the front seat and slid some eight-by-ten glossies out of it. "These were taken maybe ten years ago by a Utah state investigator posing as an itinerant photographer." The first group photo had been taken with a wide-angle lens to include the more than fifty people. Their dress reminded Emmett of the Amish. Hezekiah would have been apparent as their leader even had he not been at the center of his wives and progeny: his patriarchal beard and pitiless eyes guaranteed that.

Brill tapped the face of a younger man with eyes the equals of Hezekiah's in unrelenting fierceness. "If I had to pick any of them as your unsub, it'd be Eshcol. Hezekiah's youngest son by Saphronia. He'd kill just for the perverse joy of it. And he may have been the one to blood-atone her. His own mother. Can you believe that?"

"Where is he?" Anna asked.

"That's the rub," Brill replied. "In the joint for the rest of his natural life. So are many of the men and women you see here."

"Who's this?" Anna pointed out a face darker than the others.

"Mexican kid Hezekiah adopted while down in Sonora."

"He looks Navajo or Apache," she said.

"No, he was Mexican Indian, as I recall. Maybe one of those Tamahumara. Peculiar little fella, though he sprouted up big. Epileptic or something like that."

Now Emmett found himself interested. "Name?"

"Don't recall. Not without going back through the records."

"What became of him?"

"Shipped off to a foster home or maybe he was just released. He was close to eighteen at the time of the standoff. Or was it that nobody could determine his age? I just don't remember, Emmett."

"But did he take part in the defense of the compound?"

"Uh, no. Now that I think of it, he was on the outside running errands for Hezekiah. In that van. That's how it escaped being destroyed, by golly." The agent flipped to the next photograph. Nothing but children. White children with no sign of the native boy. "Poor babies." He was starting to move on when Emmett grabbed his hand.

"Who's this girl?" He pointed at the attractive fifteen- or sixteen-year-old whose pigtails contrasted with her already womanly legs.

"Interesting you'd ask. That's Nickie Pound, one of the few grandkids to escape the madness before the siege."

"Nicole *Stepanek* . . . the BLM wildlife biologist?"

"Why, yes," Brill said in surprise. "How'd you learn that, Parker? I ran across her only last year on a federal theft case in St. George. Had the devil of a time getting her to fess up she was a Pound."

Emmett could feel Anna watching him. "The Gilas that keep cropping up in this case were poached from her study area in Lowe Canyon. How'd she get out before all hell broke loose?"

"Well, her daddy was the son Hezekiah had killed down in Mexico. Zelek, his name was. I don't think this insanity ever took with him, though he did serve some time for forgery and Medicare fraud. Anywho, his wife was here with their kids when she got word what Hezekiah had done. They all slipped out. Went underground."

"When?"

"Oh, eight, nine years ago. Next thing I know, a grown-up Nickie is telling me over hot cider she's a scientist. And a widow to boot. Married her adviser at Cornell University couple months before the poor fella had a heart attack . . ." Brill flared his eyes to let Anna and him know what he believed had caused it. "Dr. Stepanek, his name was. Polish fellow, some kind of lizard specialist—"

"Herpetologist," Emmett and Anna said simultaneously.

"That's it. Nickie returned to southern Utah only after the compound was destroyed and the cult scattered. Though she's still skittish."

Then Anna annoyed Emmett by breaking his train of thought—he was dredging up everything the young woman had said to him and weighing it against Brill's information. Nicole had given him a somewhat evasive sign when asked if she'd known who was bagging her specimens. "How much do you know about Zelek Pound's convictions, Jink?" Turnipseed asked.

"Some," Brill replied modestly. "I was the case agent."

"Who'd he defraud?"

"Federal government, of course. But he was working at the time as a finance officer for the pediatric hospital in Salt Lake. Overcharging Medicare and pocketing the difference. To help support Hezekiah's operations."

Sergeant Yabeny had mentioned that Bert and Aurelia Knoki had a little boy who'd developed medical problems and ultimately died at that hospital. Twenty years ago.

Emmett said, "We've got to push on, Jink."

"If you insist. I'll check around Mexican Hat to see if that Rowe fella was here last week. The market, especially, where that paper sack in his car came from."

"We'd appreciate it."

But then, once inside the car, the agent asked hopefully, "Have I been of any help?"

"More than we know quite yet, Jink," Anna said. "And if this amounts to the break, we'll make sure everybody knows where it came from."

ANNA HURRIED OUT OF the Bureau of Land Management office in St. George and across the parking lot to Emmett. He was waiting with steely-eyed impatience in the brown and white Bronco cruiser they'd just borrowed from the regional law enforcement ranger. Emmett's sedan would never make it up Lowe Canyon. She got in, snatches of the two telephone conversations she'd just completed reverberating around inside her head. The first had been to Jim Niehaus. "Still no ID on the Chevelon Canyon victims," she repeated the Phoenix SAC's report to Emmett as he sped out of the lot.

"Not even *one* missing or overdue persons report that might be them?" he asked in disbelief.

"Nothing. Either they're not due back for another couple of days or don't have a nine-to-five lifestyle. Oh, the capsule you found in the van—Dilantin. Used to control seizures."

"There's the boy's epilepsy Brill mentioned. Have Niehaus get somebody working the prescription angle. What'd he say about any abandoned sport utilities?"

"Zilch," she answered. They barreled by the local Mormon temple, its fairy-tale spire shining whitely through the twilight. "Niehaus will get the task force working on any leads developing out of the Church of Living Prophecy. Whereabouts of all known members, in and out of prison. I also asked him to route any requests for background info to Jink Brill." Not having cleared any of this through Emmett, she waited for his reaction.

"You tell him about the Indian kid?" he asked.

"No."

"Good."

"That could backfire on us, you know."

"I'll risk it."

She looked through the windshield at a yawning gap in the sandstone formation dead ahead. Lowe Canyon, she presumed. The BLM ranger's backup cruiser had been thrashed by 96,000 miles of teeth-clattering wilderness roads, and the dash clock no longer worked. Emmett checked his wristwatch. He seemed overly eager to get back up the canyon. She said, "I phoned Jink too."

"And?"

"Terry Rowe was in Mexican Hat a week ago Monday. Slept behind the Chevron station and left Tuesday morning . . ." Later the same day, Rowe pulled into Canoncito with a bad alternator and asked Darcy Altasal about a baby. Not hers, undoubtedly, although her confusion about that was understandable. "Brill hasn't found anybody who talked about anything meaningful with Rowe, but he'll check around town more in the morning."

"And he will too."

"What's that supposed to mean?"

"He's Mormon."

"Isn't that stereotyping?"

"Why, yes," Emmett said testily. "He's a stereotypical Mormon. Conscientious and hardworking. Honest to a fault."

"Aren't there any lazy and dishonest Mormons?"

"Name three, Turnipseed."

She gnashed her teeth. *Fuck him.* "And why is it so damn important that you be gentlemanly around me?" *There. Done.*

"Excuse me if the shift here escapes my measly Oklahoma

state education. What do Mormon stereotypes and my behavior toward you have in common?"

Nothing. She was suddenly furious with his comment yesterday evening. And with the Knokis again. And with Emmett Quanah Parker in general, who was slipping away. Plus herself for letting this play out so badly with him. But how could they ever find a reasonable way to talk about her youth? She'd been on eggshells with him ever since they'd left Mexican Hat three hundred miles and five hours ago. No, longer than that. Since last night in the Chuskas when he'd started this business. She wanted to slap him for making her feel so frigid. But then, despite that violent impulse, her anger dissolved into pleading that was disgustingly reminiscent of her mother's. "I want you to be natural with me, Emmett. I want you to be yourself. *Please.*"

"No, you don't," he said icily.

"Okay, I don't."

"Four-wheel on the right."

"What?"

"There's a four-by parked over next to that dune. Does it have Arizona plates?"

"No, Utah. And a dirt bike trailer behind it."

Neither of them uttered anything more until they were well into some lava flows. Then he chuckled out of the blue. Bitterly. "You know, we are to be commended. We've cut to the chase. Skipped over all that romantic crap and gone right to the core of any enduring relationship—routine hostility. I feel like we've been married ten years. And what a bargain. I won't even have to dole out alimony on this one!"

"Fire on the left," she said sharply. It made her realize that night had fallen.

"What?"

"There's a goddamn fire over there on the left."

He peered toward the base of the south canyon wall. "That'll be hers."

"What's she need one for on a night like this? Must be seventy degrees outside."

"Push back the darkness," Emmett said, his tone turning infuriatingly sympathetic. "That girl probably has a lot of darkness to keep at arm's length."

"Don't we all."

No one was visible around the fire. And the solitary stool was overturned. Frowning, Emmett extinguished the car lights and got out. A bat whished overhead. Anna was joining him in front of the grille when a female voice called shrilly from behind a wildrose hedge, "I've got a gun."

Anna instinctively froze. Emmett had already drawn and was gripping the muzzle against his thigh. "Nicole . . . ?" he asked.

There was no reply.

"Nicole, it's Emmett Parker from the BIA. And my partner, Agent Turnipseed, FBI. You get my message that the Phoenix humane society is taking care of one of your specimens? Well, as of yesterday, Coconino sheriff's office has another. They'd like to keep it as a mascot, but I told them it's yours."

"Emmett?"

"None other, sugar."

Sugar, Anna nearly repeated out loud, nauseated.

There was a rustle of thorned foliage as a tall and slender woman passed through a slit in the wildrose, trailing the butt of a shotgun in the sand behind her. As soon as she stepped into the firelight, it was clear that she was exceptionally pretty. Leggy. And taken with Emmett Parker. With absolutely no hesitation, she wrapped her free arm around his neck and rested her forehead against his shoulder. "Sorry. I didn't know what to think. And yes—thanks, I got your message yesterday."

Surprisingly, Emmett unslung Nicole Stepanek's arm from around him and asked skeptically, "You didn't know what to think about a BLM cruiser coming into camp?"

The delight left the wildlife biologist's freckled face, and she took a step backward. "I thought it might be the bagger coming back. Until I saw the emblems."

"And then what'd you think, Nicole Pound?"

Clamming up, she laid the shotgun—a violation to possess on duty for nonenforcement personnel, unless she had a conditional use permit—across her table before righting the camp stool. She sank down onto it and stared vacantly into the flames. "You have to understand—they're masters of deception. Like the Apache. When they can't come stealthily, they appear to be what they're not. You have any idea what they do to apostates?"

"Some." Emmett knelt across the fire from her. "But if that was always the danger, why'd you come back to southern Utah?"

Nicole thought about that, and in the lull that followed, Anna found herself wondering if they'd slept together last Thursday night. The woman's warm greeting said that they had, but Emmett's coolness toward her didn't. Although he had called her *sugar*. "It's scary to realize you don't belong anywhere else but one part of the country," Nicole said, tossing a fond gaze across the star-choked desert sky. "Besides, Lowe Canyon's three hundred miles from Mexican Hat, and I winter in Ogden."

Emmett caught Anna's eye as he came around the fire to Nicole. "Mind getting the photo for me?"

Returning to the car, Anna could hear an almost inaudible exchange between the two. Nicole plaintively asked Emmett if he was badly disappointed with her, and he answered something unintelligible. Anna's only reassurance was his tone. It was still cool. She brought him the glossy of the Pound clan. He took his small flashlight from his windbreaker pocket and pinpointed the beam on the face of the native boy. "Who is he, Nicole?"

Tears welled in her eyes. "You *are* disappointed in me. You think I held things back from you."

"Did you?"

"I couldn't go into this with a complete stranger. I've spent years running from my maiden name. If you'd come right out and asked about the family, I might have told you.

But I'm not sure. They kill people who can bear witness against them, Emmett . . . don't you see?"

"Is the boy Mexican, like Hezekiah told everybody?"

"No. Navajo."

Anna's pulse quickened.

"What's his name?" Emmett pressed.

"Caleb Pound."

"And his name before Hezekiah got him?"

"I don't know." Nicole snuffled into a Kleenex.

"How old is he now?"

"Twenty-two or -three."

Emmett flicked off his flashlight and looked to Anna for silent confirmation if this age might fit the man who'd attacked her Friday night in his apartment. She nodded, and he turned back to Nicole. "Was Caleb legally adopted?"

"I doubt it. Daddy just brought him back from Salt Lake. He worked up there at a hospital for a couple of years before he went to prison the first time. As a baby, Caleb had been brought to the hospital for treatment."

"And your father was Zelek Pound."

"Yes."

"You know anything about Caleb's natural parents?"

"Yes and no," Nicole replied. Emmett seemed ready to object to her waffling, when she held up her hand for him to wait. She had quit weeping and finally regained control of herself. She'd go through all this—but at her own pace and on her own terms. Emmett stooped again, hands joined between his knees and the photo hanging from his grasp. "Caleb's an epileptic. He had bad seizures, especially when he was younger. You know the *Dine*. They think that comes only from violating a tabu. That's why I think they were so willing to give him up."

"But why'd your father want a Navajo baby?" Emmett asked more gently. He'd gotten her to talk, probably with less persuasion than he'd imagined he'd have to use.

"Daddy didn't. Hezekiah did. He wanted a Navajo or Apache child to bring up in the fullness of the gospels . . ."

She abruptly shook her head. "Listen to me. That picture took me right back to the mind-set. Like recovering from alcohol, I guess. Always catching yourself . . ." Emmett rocked uncomfortably at this mention of his personal addiction, and Nicole stuffed the sodden Kleenex in the back pocket of her hiking shorts. "Grandfather believed Indians are natural-born assassins. In part, his reasons were based on scripture. You're probably familiar with the notion in the Book of Mormon that Native Americans are the descendants of the Lost Tribe of Israel. So Hezekiah figured Indians, especially Navajo and Apache, have an Old Testament zeal for vengeance."

"Why those particular tribes?" Emmett asked.

"Maybe because they resisted Mormon colonization more than the Paiutes and Utes. Maybe he just wanted an assassin at his beck and call. Most of my uncles were in jail at one time or another because of his Blood Atonements. I suppose the old bastard wanted a cold-blooded killer."

"Is that what he got?"

"Almost, Emmett," Nicole replied. "It was sickening how Hezekiah and my uncle Eschol conditioned him. Dehumanized him. Taught him how to spy and sneak. To strike and vanish again. I've often worried about Caleb. Hoped he found help—after Hezekiah unleashed him on the world just before he himself was killed."

"But did Caleb strike before the old man's death?"

"I'm not sure. Probably. My father had started voicing his doubts about the church, and my immediate family was out of the loop. That's when you knew you might get blood-atoned—when you were no longer trusted. When you might become a witness against Hezekiah's crimes. This must sound so bizarre to you two."

Anna scooted an ice chest across the ground and sat on its lid, facing Nicole. "You were friends with Caleb, weren't you?"

"Oh, yes. He was so lonely. So lost. He knew he was different. His color. And there were his fits. They scared the other kids."

"But not you?"

"No. I like creatures others find repulsive. My husband was so homely the students called him Swamp Thing."

Anna resisted casting a triumphant glance at Emmett. "Did Caleb know he was *Dine*?"

"Not until I told him. I wasn't supposed to. I just overheard it one day. Then Hezekiah was worried Caleb would run back to the rez. But he knew no one there. Still, it made him feel better, the things I told him about his people. See, when I showed intellectual promise, Hezekiah had me go through the *Dine* creation story, searching for evidence the Navajo were the Lost Tribe. An exercise in futility. But I found the part in the Flintway Ceremony about Gila Monster, whose trembling paw wasn't an affliction. It was a gift. I read this to Caleb. He really latched onto it. And who knows? Maybe that's what got me interested in Gilas. Anyway, it made Caleb feel better about his illness, I think. His being different in so many ways. But things got jumbled up in his head—I can see where Gila Monster and Blood Atonement can become a pretty wicked combination. But back then, he was just a sad little boy chasing lizards around the compound."

Anna asked, "Did you know Caleb was taking your specimens from the canyon here?"

"Suspected, maybe, but didn't know for sure." Nicole eyed Emmett, warily, before going on to Anna, "When I got interested in reptiles, my father brought Caleb and me here to Lowe Canyon to hunt for Gilas. But we didn't know how to look, so we went away disappointed." She paused reflectively. "My dad was different from the others. More intellectual and less dogmatic, I suppose. Born to another family, he would've been a wildlife illustrator. Not a forger. I regret Daddy and my husband never met." And then to Emmett: "But the last thing I wanted to do when you came here was to go back into this. Does that make sense to you?"

"Yes," Anna answered for Emmett. Then she startled slightly when she felt Nicole's callused touch turn over her wrist.

"You're the one who was bitten."

"That's right."

"I'm sorry."

"Not your fault." Anna disengaged herself. "What do the wings on the Gila mean?"

"I'm not sure. Caleb grew up around no Navajo. Never had a chance to talk to any of their medicine people. They appear to be moth wings. But the Moth People are part of another myth. Entirely divorced from Flintway. An entirely different moral instruction. If Caleb's the artist, he may not know the symbolism himself."

"When's the last time you saw him?"

"The night my mother fled the compound with me. After Eschol murdered my father down in Mexico. Nine years now."

Emmett said rather brusquely, "A minute ago you answered *yes and no* when I asked you about Caleb's natural parents."

"That's right." The fire had burned down to coals, and Nicole stirred them with a wire clothes hanger. "A long time ago—I'm not sure when, maybe when I was twelve or so—a Navajo policeman and his wife came to the compound. I don't remember him so well. But she was crying hard. She said she wanted her baby back. While she and the policeman were talking to Hezekiah, Eschol went out the back of the compound with Caleb. Took him into the canyons in case more police showed up. But none did, and Hezekiah lied to the Navajo couple. He said the child was dead. He had only white children, and she was free to look around. When the policeman started to do just that, plus asking the kids questions about Caleb, the men beat him up pretty bad and drove the couple off the property. The last thing Hezekiah said to them was that if they persisted the two of them would find themselves in serious legal trouble. *You knew what you entered into,* he told them."

Emmett had risen and taken his car keys from his pocket. "A fire can be a false comfort, Nicole. Understand what I mean . . . ?" She nodded nervously. "I'd move your camp every few days. Build no fires at night and set your lantern low. Know how to use that scattergun?"

"Hezekiah showed all us children." But then the woman added, "If it's Caleb, hiding won't do me any good. Uncle Eschol taught him how to steal up on people without their ever knowing—until it's too late. He can watch you from hiding for three days without food or drink. He's inhuman. They made him that way."

chapter 20

EMMETT STAYED IN HIS SEDAN AS ANNA STROLLED OUT onto the Navajo Bridge across the Colorado River. As the rising sun struck the Vermilion Cliffs behind him, the ocher flash in his rearview mirror made him squint. The 1920s steel bridge, once the highest in the world, had been converted into a pedestrian walkway, now that a modern span just downstream bore the traffic of U.S. 89A. Anna had asked for this rest stop, their first since leaving the motel in St. George at 4:30 that morning.

There was still no missing persons report conceivably matching the two burned bodies, determined by autopsy to have been a male and a female in their mid- to late twenties. The man had expired from three bullets; the woman from a wound to the heart nearly as deep and gaping as Summerfield's had been to the abdomen. No word yet of any abandoned four-wheel-drives. Last night over the phone, Jink Brill had reported a number of people in Mexican Hat who recalled a wild-eyed white man dressed Indian asking about Caleb Pound as if he meant Hezekiah's former ward harm. Nobody had seen Caleb since the siege five years ago. Emmett told Brill of the postmortem findings, asked him if the Pounds had ever used a weapon that could slice a human body as if it were putty. The agent would go back through the file.

Yet neither of the Knokis had been stabbed. *Crap.* Emmett tilted the blazing mirror downward to spare his sore eyes.

Rowe had been looking for a baby now grown to terrifying proportions. Almost certainly not Darcy Altasal's child. If not Darcy's, her Aunt Aurelia's. Who with Bert had handed her epileptic son over to Zelek Pound in Salt Lake, who thus filled his father's standing order for a male Navajo or Apache to serve as his assassin.

That was it.

In a sense, Emmett was relieved. He at last knew what John Tallsalt had been trying to cover up. The Knokis' memory would be reviled by the *Dine* for having given up their baby to whites. Fundamentalist Mormons who withheld the child's own culture and traditions from him—the kind of adoption the Indian Child Welfare Act had been enacted to prevent. Brill had revealed one more tidbit: Last Friday morning, while Old Regis had been shooting up Shonto, Marcellus Yabeny had been in Mexican Hat. Asking about Caleb Pound.

Johnny should've told me. He owed me the truth.

Anna ran her hand along the top bar of the railing as she peered gingerly below. No wonder. The sign said it was a 467-foot drop to the river. She halted short of the Navajo Nation boundary marker and turned into a divergence of rays that had just splayed over the Echo Cliffs. In minutes, they'd be back on the Big Rez. In Window Rock in another four hours. Maybe she'd wanted to take a moment before rushing into the maelstrom again. It'd been a peaceful morning, so far, the high plateau rolling past their windows like a tawny and crimson sea.

But speculations kept pricking him: *What interest would Rowe or Lolly Blackhouse have had in Caleb Pound?*

Blackmail? Possibly. If Rowe had still been active in the narcotics trade and had known of the illicit adoption, leverage on a cop would've been useful. Is that why Caleb had gone after the University Park couple? Of course, this theory quickly played out if Hezekiah's loose cannon of an assassin had killed his own mother and father. But if he hadn't? What if he'd been trying to avenge them when Anna and Summerfield got in the way?

Emmett climbed out of the car and started down the bridge toward Anna. The dawn was cool and still, the Colorado a distant, purled green hemmed in by vertical cliffs. She watched his approach with an impish smile. "We could seal it in perfection for all time right now, Em."

"How?"

"Join hands and jump." But her smile sputtered out. At the hopelessness of their ever getting together, he supposed.

Incredibly, he heard himself saying, "I didn't spend the night in Lowe Canyon last Thursday. Drove all the way to Page before bedding down."

"I know."

"Christ almighty, don't tell me you *know*."

"What?"

"You're making it sound like a goddamn given."

"A given for what?"

"That I'll always turn the opportunity down because of you. That was my choice up Lowe Canyon. But I can't say what I'll do some other night. I'm human. I've got human needs. As disgusting as that must sound to you."

"Don't talk that way," she said hotly. "You don't know a thing about what I feel. And you don't seem to want to hear how I feel about you. So quit it with the cheap shots!"

Her shout echoed.

"Okay, okay," he relented. He didn't want to argue. Or discuss how they felt about each other right now.

She broke their silence first. "Heard you talking on the phone late last night."

"Couldn't sleep," he said. "Called somebody I know in Virginia. Thanked him for looking into Dieter Preuss for us. Told him it's now a dead issue. Then I gave Marcellus Yabeny a jingle in Window Rock."

"Why?"

"Had a cultural question. He's the night Investigations watch commander right now. Nothing but time on his hands anyway."

A little flotilla of kayakers floated like sleek birds under the bridge. "What kind of cultural question?" Anna asked.

He realized that he'd blundered into it again. The specter that would never cease haunting them from now on. "I asked him to tell me about the Mothway, if he didn't mind . . ."

"Did he?"

"No. But I had to call back because he wanted to get it right from his maternal uncle. You can always tell a true *Dine*—he damn sure wants to get his origin stories straight."

"What's it about?"

"Sibling incest." Emmett was sick and tired of dancing around this. "The Moth People were a race of mythic beings. All brothers and sisters, it seems, who refused to take unrelated partners. They went insane from these unions. And like moths everywhere, plunged themselves into fires . . ." Tallsalt's words that night beside the coal pit. "Yabeny says the Moth People are the reason incest and not homicide is the worst imaginable offense to the Navajo. That's the moral lesson Nicole was talking about last night—the dangers of disregarding family or clan sexual boundaries. How it can unhinge the whole universe—"

But Anna had already started at a rapid clip back for the car.

Shit. He should've kept the Mothway to himself.

"What's with you?" he demanded, catching up with her.

"How much do you trust me?"

"Oh no," he said stubbornly. "I've learned when anything's prefaced with *how much do*—"

"Then I'm ordering you to give me a little space. Just for a day or two. No more than that. I promise."

"Why? Tell me why, and I'll go along."

"Can't, Emmett."

"Oh, bullshit."

"I need the right to be wrong. And if I am, we'll go on from that point as if this never happened."

He pulled her to a stop. "What warrants an approach like this? I'm trying to understand, Anna."

"You already do," she said morosely. "I've got to be careful, Emmett." Then she added with distaste, "And I know all there is to know about keeping secrets. First rule is—tell no one." She hastened on to the car alone and got in behind the wheel.

When he didn't budge from the spot at which they'd paused, she laid on the horn.

"OH, THIS HAS HEALED BEAUTIFULLY," Dr. Hennepin said, examining Anna's left wrist in the on-duty physician's office at Sage Memorial Hospital. She'd dropped Emmett off at the Navajo Nation Inn in Window Rock at noon, then sped on the thirty additional miles over the Defiance Plateau to Ganado. The reptile-bite specialist's ponytail had spilled over the shoulder of his white coat, and in the glare of his headband-mounted light the frizzy red hairs looked like spun copper. How alien those first Europeans to come to the California-Oregon borderlands, the English of Hudson's Bay Company and the Russians of Fort Ross, must have seemed to her Modoc ancestors. "No sign of infection. That's only because we got the chance to cleanse the wound so promptly."

"Or because my partner sucked on it."

"He must have a very clean mouth."

"You should hear him sometime."

Dr. Hennepin didn't react to the joke. "You're speaking of the agent who was killed in Phoenix?"

"You mean Summerfield. No. I was there when he was . . ." She suddenly saw no reason to go on. The doctor knew. Everyone but Nicole Stepanek had read the papers or heard a newscast. Caleb Pound was now the cause of a near hysteria in much of the Southwest, which made it all the more bizarre that he hadn't been spotted. The photograph off his expired Utah driver's license—a dark and symmetrical face, older than its years, that might have been quirkily handsome but for his hateful stare and cruel mouth—had been disseminated by the media.

"You doing all right?"

She shrugged. "Tired but okay."

"I can prescribe something to get you through the next week or so, if that's what you want."

"I'll make it."

"How're you sleeping?"

"What little I get is like being anesthetized."

"Well, at least our Gila encounter has a happy ending."

Rebuttoning her blouse sleeve, she said, "The weekend before last, our Gallup office served a *duces tecum* warrant on the hospital administration here for Aurelia Knoki's medical records."

"That's out of my department, but was there a problem?"

"A small one's cropped up. No fault of the hospital's. Ours, really. The only copies of those records went on to the pathologist in Tucson. Now I need them. Without asking our Tucson office to chase down the file, if possible. Our manpower's stretched thin at this point. Would you get Ms. Knoki's folder for me?"

Dr. Hennepin rubbed a premoistened towelette over his hands, then tossed it in a waste can. "You sure we didn't challenge the warrant?"

"Positive."

"Okay, hang loose."

"Thanks. Mind if I make a credit card call on your phone?"

"Have at."

The doctor whisked out, and Anna dialed the FBI's Salt Lake City field office. Two minutes later, Special Agent Weyman, whom she'd snagged when she called this morning from the pay phone outside The Gap Trading Post, came on the line.

"Got it," Weyman said right off. *Ask and you shall receive.* Her newfound sense of power as case coordinator gratified her more than she'd ever admit to Emmett. "A death certificate for Alcee Carbert Knoki. Born on February 11, 1977, Canoncito, New Mexico. Died on August 13, 1979."

"Cause?" Anna asked, jotting the dates on a breast cancer information pamphlet.

"Status epilepticus."

"What's that?"

"Something that makes no sense to the doc I consulted. It's a seizure that won't stop. Metabolic acids build, blood glucose gets burned up and cardiovascular arrest results. Unless treated. That's what got the doc—it virtually never occurs in a hospital. And the kid was in an IC unit at the time of death."

"One more favor, if you don't mind . . . ?"

"Glad to. For Summerfield." It had become a battle cry among the agents she enlisted to help the task force. One of their own had been murdered. Maybe they felt that outrage more keenly than she did at present because they weren't in the eye of the storm. She didn't let her mind dwell on Summerfield.

"Investigate that death certificate as a forgery."

"Already started," Weyman said.

"If the lab gives you any crap about their backlog, have their director give me a ring at the Navajo Nation Inn."

"Will do."

Hanging up, she saw that she'd doodled a winged Gila alongside Alcee Knoki's dates of birth and death. A Gila monster borne by the wings of a moth. Canoncito. There'd never been a clinic on that backwater reservation, just a string of Navajo midwives, the last of whom had been named Bernadine Altasal.

Altasal.

Dr. Hennepin swept in. "Don't ask me why," he said as he took his chair, "but the head of our records division insists I hold the file during our interview."

"Fine. Did Aurelia Knoki receive prenatal care for her baby here?"

Hennepin began sifting through the papers. "Yes."

"Starting when?"

"Aurelia saw a Dr. Dooley in her third month. That was May of '76."

Anna did a quick nine-month calculation. "How can that be?"

He glanced up. "What be?"

May would've been the approximate time Alcee had been conceived. Not the third month of the pregnancy. "Alcee wasn't . . ." She stopped as the need for secrecy pressed down on her.

The physician made a face. "They actually gave it a name?"

"*It,* Doctor?"

"On the basis of that first exam, Dooley suspected insufficient fetal growth. He ordered an ultrasound for her at the Indian Health Service hospital in Tuba City. Aurelia got the bad news two weeks later—anencephaly."

"What's that?"

"The worst of the neural tube defects. Faulty development of the embryonic nervous system. Virtual absence of the fetal cranium. It shows up at increased rates in diets deficient in folic acid. The *Dine* didn't used to be big on green veggies. Lots of mutton and fry bread. Also there's a genetic predisposition."

"As ridiculous as this sounds, Doctor—is there any possibility, however remote, Aurelia's child could have survived to eighteen months?" Anna found herself starting to shake her head.

"You've just answered your own question." Dr. Hennepin riffled through the rest of the file, then returned to a page and dog-eared it. "Appears Aurelia didn't see Dooley again. Consulted another physician here when she tried to quit her chain-smoking a few years ago. Unusual for a Navajo . . . an addiction to nicotine that strong. She must've been under considerable stress."

"What's that page in front of you?"

Hennepin vacillated, but then replied, "A records release form signed by Aurelia in late June of that year."

"From what facility?"

"A clinic in El Paso. Performs abortions. Among other procedures. But there's no paperwork to indicate she went through with the termination there. And I'm just surmising she traveled all that way for an abortion. It's odd that there's no follow-up material in this file. But that's not unheard of here, believe me."

"So, a layperson—not familiar with that particular clinic—could go through Aurelia's folder and not realize she considered an abortion in 1979?"

"Most likely. Are you having a problem with any of this?"

None. Other than the fact that the Knokis' baby died twice.

EMMETT STRODE TOWARD the Navajo police complex, hidden at this distance by a low bluff. Only the American and *Dine* flags showed over the brow of it, flapping straight out from their poles. The westerly wasn't really hot, but he was sweating. Something had just snapped inside him. Something that had remained fairly pliable over the past several days. Until ten minutes ago, when he'd been standing in the check-in line at the Navajo Nation Inn. Then, without warning, he felt heat rise up his neck and he was seeing the lobby through a red haze. But after receiving his key and having the clerk hold Anna's for her arrival, he calmly went to his room and changed into his Levi's and boots. He didn't want to be overdressed when he rammed John Tallsalt's head through the wall of his office. Anna had made him promise that he wouldn't confront the lieutenant until she returned from whatever it was she was out doing. But what if that side trip to Phoenix could have been avoided? Summerfield would still be alive. And

Anna wouldn't have had her head driven into a sheet of drywall, just as Emmett now meant to do to Tallsalt.

Hands fisted, he mounted the bluff and jogged across Window Rock Boulevard to the tribal police headquarters.

All the reasons for cutting a man slack ended when it came to closing a homicide investigation. And in doing that for Tallsalt, Emmett had violated one of his own rules, all to spare the man some embarrassment that was what no doubt he richly deserved.

Ignoring the receptionist in the vestibule of the Criminal Investigations Service outbuilding, he plowed down the corridor and threw open the door to Tallsalt's office.

Marcellus Yabeny was sitting behind the lieutenant's desk. His face jerked up. Almost hopefully.

"Where the fuck is he?"

The sergeant's startled look of hope vanished. "Close the door." Only when Emmett had stepped inside and done so, did he go on. "I don't know, Parker."

"Don't give me any of that *unavailable* shit."

"I won't. I'm worried sick." Yabeny looked it. Red-eyed and slightly disheveled. His uniform shirt had second-day wrinkles. Babble was streaming from a police radio monitor on a corner of the desk. "I keep expectin' . . ." His voice trailed off as he listened to the transmission until he apparently learned that it had nothing to do with his worries.

Emmett insisted, "Keep expecting what?"

"I don't know."

"You knew something before you opened your mouth."

Yabeny gusted out a breath. "I keep expectin' a unit to find him. Someplace remote. John left here in bad shape Friday. I've never seen him that down." It was now Thursday. Six days with no word.

"Where was he headed?"

"Wouldn't say."

"And what the hell were you doing in Mexican Hat last Friday, asking for Caleb Pound?"

"John's orders. He said Pound might be dealin' crank to the north end of the rez. Wanted me to get a line on him."

"I hope you know now what a crock of horseshit that was."

"Tell me about it."

Yabeny said this with enough barely controlled anger for Emmett to believe him.

"And what's the truth about those plane tracks on the dry lake bed up at Sonsela Buttes?"

"Who knows," the sergeant answered. "But I'll bet it had nothin' to do with the Knokis gettin' it."

Unfisting his hands, Emmett took the sofa and gazed up at the plaques and VIP photos on the wall. The first Indian to be considered for the directorship of the Arizona Department of Public Safety. Could all that promise be slumped over a blood-splattered steering wheel right now, a pistol and a spent casing on the floor mat between his shoes? Emmett's own brother had been breezing through law school when he closed the books with a shot to the head. *I shall be redeemed* . . .

Yabeny boosted the volume to eavesdrop on another burst of patrol traffic.

"I thought you were working nights," Emmett said, trying to settle down.

"Days, nights—they're all blurrin' together," Yabeny hoarsely responded. "I can't cover for John much longer. He's actin' chief."

"Have you tried his place?"

"Yes. The chain's across his driveway. He only does that when he leaves for more than a couple of days."

"But you didn't go all the way up to the house?"

"No," Yabeny admitted.

A patrolman's voice transmitted, "Window Rock, Sixty-one-five—registration and wants on Arizona plate Paul-Baker-Victor-Two-Niner-Four."

"Do you have this vehicle stopped?" the dispatcher inquired.

"Negative. It's been ditched over the side."

"Location?"

"Just up the Chuska Peak grade from Asaayi Lake."

Emmett waited, jiggling a foot, for the dispatcher to run the Arizona plate. Although he told himself that abandoned vehicles were found by Patrol all the time. Especially in jurisdictions with bored kids given to joyriding. His indignation had been partly dissolved by Yabeny's anxiousness for Tallsalt. Had his own distrust, sprung from John's hokum about Sonorans flying recent loads of dope into the Big Rez, prevented him from helping Tallsalt when the man most needed it? His ears were ringing from fatigue. Death was very near, according to the Navajo belief.

"Sixty-one-five, ready to copy current registration on a 1999 Lincoln Navigator?"

"Go ahead."

Emmett sat up. A sport utility.

"Registered to a Timothy and/or Marlene Olson of Four-oh-two Chaparral Knoll Drive, Scottsdale. No wants on the Lincoln."

"That's it," Emmett said, bolting to his feet.

"The Chevelon Canyon victims' vehicle?"

"Has to be. Let's back your man up there. If Pound's still around the vehicle, he won't hesitate for a second to dust a lone cop."

ANNA KNOCKED ON Emmett's door. Repeatedly, thinking that he'd crashed. No response. Turning, she gave him the benefit of the doubt that he might have gone down to the coffee shop. She opened her own door, left it yawning to clear out the stink of tobacco smoke left by the previous occupant. The desk clerk had handed her a thick sheaf of messages. That's what she got for advising the Gallup FBI office by radio on the drive back from Ganado that she was setting up shop in Window Rock. The most urgent seemed to be from Jim Niehaus: He'd left three numbers at which he could be reached. But rather than contact the Phoenix field office, she tried the one-man federal outpost in Monticello, Utah. Jink Brill's answering machine offered the option of paging him. She punched in that number and her own at the inn, then hung up and shuffled over to the sink to wash her face. The neon over the vanity wasn't very flattering. The bruise on her forehead was almost gone, but the skin graft was still visible just below the hairline. She pressed her fingertips to it. An acetylene torch. The same separation of mind from body that had seen her through her adolescence had enabled her to survive that torture session last January. Adolescence. Lolly Blackhouse's outburst in the railyard replayed in the splash and gurgle of the taps: *"Got to have that excitement to get him out of your cunt, don't you, little sister?"*

The phone rang. Brill. "How you doing, lady?"

"Good."

"Got your beep while I was gassing up my car. You find Nicole Stepanek?"

"Yes," Anna replied. "She was helpful. And scared."

"I'd imagine. Had me a long chat with the BLM ranger and then the Washington County sheriff, just to make sure Nicole gets some extra patrol till we find—"

"Tell me more about Blood Atonement." She regretted sounding so abrupt. But time was breathing down her neck: Emmett was up to something.

"Such as?"

"Where does the belief come from?"

Silence.

"Still there, Jink?"

"Yes . . ." Clearly, he didn't want to cover this.

"I really need to know."

"Well," he began haltingly, "the doctrine's allegedly attributed to Brigham Young. But I'm going to caution you— you got to understand Blood Atonement as a product of the times. Ours was a new faith, pressured from within and without. We Saints were getting the stuffing beat out of us everywhere we went."

"Consider me cautioned." Her face was still wet, and she dried it on a corner of the coverlet. "Many Modoc ways make no sense to the modern world. You had to have been there."

"Exactly. Anywho, somebody supposedly threw one of those huge what-ifs at Brigham: *What if I find my brother in bed with my wife?* He said that he'd drive a javelin through the two of them. Not only would it be justified, it'd atone for their sins and enter them in the kingdom of heaven. He also said he had no wife he loved so much he wouldn't do this to her. With clean hands."

Anna sank onto the bed, twisting the phone cord around a finger. How would Caleb Pound translate this into action? To all appearances, he'd burned four of his victims in imitation of the destruction of the incestuous Moth People. How would he play out a nearly forgotten Mormon doctrine? *Through the two of them.* "Jink, I'm not trying to nitpick your faith . . ."

"I trust that, Anna," he interjected, "or we wouldn't even be talking about it."

"Did the offenders have to be caught in the act?"

"What d'you mean?"

"Did they have to be killed together at that time? You know, for the Atonement to have been okayed by the community?"

"Good question." Brill mulled it over for a moment; motorized traffic whooshed in the background. "I'd say—yes. Like manslaughter as opposed to murder. No premeditation was allowed, per se. No bushwhacking after a cooling-down period. It had to be in the heat of a righteous passion. Dang, that's a mouthful, isn't it?"

"So the couple had to be discovered *together*?"

"For that particular kind of atoning. It's broader than that. Maybe you ought to talk to my bishop. I'm just not up on—"

"No, Jink, you're doing fine."

"Well, I'm just saying that Blood Atonement had more to do with meting out divine justice to incorrigible heathens in a world order to come. It just wasn't a means to eliminate backsliding kinfolk."

"Understood. You've answered my question."

"I have?"

"We'll discuss it all over a pot of decaf as soon as Caleb Pound is in custody."

"One more thing—it's important."

"Shoot."

"Parker asked me about a possible weapon," Brill said. "Something that could've done in Summerfield and that gal in Sitgreaves. I think I found what it might be . . . a *Californio* lance."

"A what?"

"Real quick, Brigham Young sent a battalion of Saints out to California to help the U.S. in the Mexican War. A Pound was among them, and he picked up a broken lance off the battlefield at San Pasqual near San Diego. Kind of a crude blade hammered out of scrap metal and stuck on a pole for one of those *vaquero* lancers who dang near turned General Kearny back. If we're talking Atonement, there's your javelin. It may've been used in a double homicide in Nephi one year after the siege. Still unsolved."

She felt a cold squeeze in her belly, recalling the blade in her attacker's grasp. "Thank you, Jink—that fits the weapon I saw. I'll tell Emmett. I know none of this was easy to talk about with a Gentile."

"Just keep me informed."

"Promise. Bye." She no sooner replaced the receiver in the cradle than the phone rang. "Hello."

"Special Agent Turnipseed?" Female. Navajo accent.

"Speaking," she said, spreading her messages out on the bed to prioritize them. Sixteen in total. One from her special agent in charge in Las Vegas, asking how he might help. Two from the lab in D.C. They could wait, as she sensed she was outdistancing anything physical evidence might reveal to her.

"This is Navajo police dispatch. Investigator Parker asked me to call you."

Her antenna went up. She'd kill Emmett if he'd gone back on the promise he'd made and locked horns with Tallsalt. It could ruin all her efforts. Confrontation only stiffened denial. "Is Parker there?"

"No, ma'am. He's on the way up to Asaayi with Sergeant Yabeny to check out a Lincoln Navigator four-by. He said to tell you—*this has to be it.*"

Again, for just a microsecond, the musty stink of the Gila glove was in her nostrils. "Thanks, I'll get him on the radio."

"Won't work, ma'am. At least not car-to-car. The grade above Asaayi Lake is in a dead spot for that. You're welcome to come by our place to transmit on the big set."

"I'll be right over."

ANYONE BUT A PATROL OFFICER intimately familiar with his beat would have missed the luxury sport utility that lay one hundred yards down another steeply pitching slope. The Lincoln was the same jade-green as the newly sprouted scrub oaks into which it had plunged off the back road to Tohatchi. The unpaved byway Anna and Emmett had used two nights ago. Had the Navigator already been abandoned here then? Unlike Chevelon Canyon, there was no berm for the wheels to have disturbed, but the bulled-neck *Dine* cop on the scene—the patrolman who'd backed Summerfield, Anna and Emmett at the Knokis' mobile home—proudly showed Parker and Yabeny the dangling cedar branch that had keyed him to the vehicle that had gone over the side. "I went down right away to check for folks," he now explained. "Nobody."

"You touch anythin'?" Yabeny asked.

"Nothin', Sarge. Just copied down the license number and humped back up to radio Window Rock."

"Got a long gun in your cruiser?" Emmett somberly asked him.

"Yes, sir."

"Appreciate it if you'd cover Sergeant Yabeny and me while we take a gander."

"Sure."

Then Emmett started down the hillside, keeping to the gash left by the diving vehicle, grabbing stripped branches for balance. He could hear Yabeny descending behind him, walking less quietly than he probably could. Due to sleeplessness. Emmett halted and scanned all around. Two vehicles pushed over the sides of canyons hundreds of miles apart. Beyond coincidence.

The question was no longer if Caleb Pound were here. It was how close.

"You actually think he'd stick around?" Yabeny asked.

"No idea." Just as Emmett had had no idea that Pound would hit Summerfield and Turnipseed in his apartment. "But you warn your people to be doubly careful. On and off the job."

The sergeant nodded, and they continued down the slope.

Reaching the scratched and dented Lincoln, Emmett moistened a finger and touched the tailpipe. His spit sizzled. The hood had buckled and popped open of its own accord. He fully hoisted it and unscrewed the radiator cap a twist. Coolant boiled out.

He stepped back for an overview.

The vehicle had come to rest atop a seep, the mud of the spring having snatched the wheels. Yabeny was examining the lacerations the front bumper had left in some red willow canes.

"What do you think, Marcellus?"

"Sap's still runny."

There were foot-sized holes in the clumps of bitter cress. The cop's tracks, almost certainly. Pound hadn't ridden the out-of-control vehicle down here. If he'd left any boot prints, they'd start above. On the road. The interior of the Lincoln, like that of the van, had been sanitized. No luggage that might contain the missing IDs and other personal effects of the Olsons.

"Driver's-side door looks warped, Marcellus." Emmett slogged around to it. "Might need both of us to open it. But first, how about a dusting . . . ?" At Emmett's urging, the detective sergeant had brought a camel hair brush, some black powder and tape for lifting latent fingerprints.

"You sure? Feebs'll have my ass."

"Not going to be an issue, I promise."

Yabeny powdered the handle and then all the surfaces along the back edge of the door—while Emmett kept an eye on the bushes enveloping them. A cicada skirled somewhere in the shadowy depths of the foliage. Had it picked up approaching movement he himself hadn't? He tucked the right side of his windbreaker behind the grips of his revolver. His spare jacket, after his favorite one had been chewed by the Gila in the van.

"You're right, Parker. Wiped clean."

As meticulous as he was brutal, Caleb Pound had obliterated any obvious evidence of himself before pushing the Lincoln off the road, probably with rags where his hands had touched the rear hatch. He'd learned his lessons well from Hezekiah and Eschol.

Yabeny and Emmett each got a purchase on the driver's door. It gave with a groan and remained open even in an upward angle. Wary of Gilas, Emmett thrust his face down into the space beneath the dashboard, which showed water spotting from a recent washing. But he caught it anyway. The coppery scent of blood. Forensic chemicals would confirm its presence, but Emmett had no doubt that one of the Olsons had been slashed to death inside the Lincoln. Perhaps a frantic attempt at escape he didn't want to picture.

He stood erect. "Let's go back up."

"Don't you want to search the rest of the car?" Yabeny asked.

"Pound doesn't leave much behind. Whatever he did, it'll take the techs to find it."

As soon as Emmett and Yabeny reached the road, the patrolman shifted an automatic assault rifle from one hip to the other and said, "Parker, your partner's tryin' to reach you."

Yabeny unlocked his carryall for Emmett, who sat in the passenger seat and asked before keying the mike, "Your department have a tactical channel on scrambler?"

"Three."

Emmett flipped the selector. "BIA Seventeen to Frank Thirty-three on three."

"I'm goin' to start huntin' for tracks," Yabeny said.

"Watch your ass," Emmett said fervently as the sergeant started down the road. Another cruiser arrived, and Yabeny talked to the cop momentarily before melting into the oaks.

"BIA Seventeen, Window Rock—go ahead with your traffic for Frank Thirty-three."

"Turnipseed?"

"What's your call, Em?" Anna's voice asked.

"Oh no, it's yours."

She paused. "I want to cordon off the area. How big is it?"

"Big. The central part of the Chuskas. From Tohatchi in the east to the town of Navajo in the west. At least ten miles north and south of Chuska Peak. If that's the way you want to go, just remember all the assets at your disposal. Civil Air Patrol. FBI SWAT can back up the Navajo tac team. BIA's Emergency Incident Response Unit can be put on standby with a single call to Lieutenant Jimmy Dann at our academy in Artesia, New Mexico."

"How about I use the BIA team and put the FBI on standby?"

Emmett smiled. "Whoa. You might start a dangerous precedent of cooperation here."

"And what's the case coordinator's biggest asset going to do?" Anna asked.

Yabeny returned, and Emmett lowered the microphone. "Trail heads north," the sergeant reported, his voice pitched a little higher than usual. "Looks real fresh to me."

"You want to go after him tonight, Marcellus?"

"It's our best shot. I don't see what a lot of *bilagaana* cops are goin' to do by surroundin' the mountains."

Emmett transmitted, "With your permission, Sergeant Yabeny and I would like to start tracking right now . . ." Silence but for a crackling over the airwaves. He glanced at his wristwatch: pushing four. "Read me, Frank Thirty-three?"

"One condition. We're going to talk. When this is over, we're going to set aside one whole day and talk like we've never talked before."

"Copy." Emmett flopped the back of his head against the neck-rest. Yabeny was watching him. "I'm not sleeping with her, Marcellus."

"I didn't say a thing." Yabeny didn't have to. Nor would the rest of law enforcement that had been within earshot.

"Moon'll be a sliver off full tonight," Emmett noted. "Good and bad in that. You got a Handie-Talkie?"

Yabeny opened the driver's-side door and took a radio handset from under the front seat. He tested the battery by turning the squelch button—a vibrant hiss followed. "Little good an HT'll do us in these mountains."

"That's okay. I feel better screaming into something other than my empty hand when the shit hits the fan. You grab that assault rifle. I'll borrow your shotgun, if you don't mind. But we'll probably never even see him till he strikes. And that'll be from in close. It's his way."

ANNA BORROWED A PHONE in the computer room immediately off the dispatch center and phoned Jim Niehaus in Phoenix. She brought the SAC up to date, not counting a few intentional omissions. At the conclusion of which, he asked matter-of-factly, "You want me to come to Window Rock?"

She pondered the question as long as she dared. It possibly amounted to a no-vote of confidence in a first-office agent, a rookie. And ordinarily, she would have been offended. But not this afternoon. It'd be a relief to have someone handle the mushrooming logistical details. At last, she saw why Emmett detested massive investigative efforts. They obscured the vision of the crime he'd so painstakingly put together, plus beguiled the lead detective into believing he or she could rely on others. It all got down to one mind. One perception based on experience, both personal and professional. This time it was excruciatingly personal.

But she'd hesitated too long, for Niehaus said, "I didn't mean to suggest you don't know what to do, Turnipseed. I just—"

"No, I can use your help, sir. And your media rep's too. I'd guess *Navajo Times* is a stringer for the national media, and CNN's bound to be here any minute. Please come up."

"Glad to," Niehaus said brightly. "I'll call the Air National Guard and have one of their choppers fly us up."

"You and your media rep?"

"Plus our SWAT team."

"As a backup only. I've decided to use the BIA's team as the primary tactical unit."

Niehaus was quiet for a moment. "If that's what you want."

"It is, sir."

"Very well. See you in a few hours."

As she hung up, her eyes fixed on the computer monitor before her. The tumbling screen-saver logo read: Residential Identification System. She pecked a key, and a map of Ganado came up with each apparent home site denoted by a four-digit number. In a box at the bottom was a Navajo name in white. As was one of the address numbers along a rural road. She typed *John Tallsalt* over the previous name and was ready to press enter—when the door opened and a husky voice asked, "You want a coffee urn in your incident command post upstairs?"

The building maintenance man. She took a moment to regain her breath. "That'd be great."

He passed through the room, and she swiftly entered Tallsalt's name. The entire screen went blank, which unnerved her until a new map slowly materialized. A district to the east of Window Rock and north of the highway to Gallup. She hit the print key.

chapter 21

THE BOOT TRACKS WERE SIZE TWELVES. THEY WERE IN-
distinct and appeared sporadically. But Emmett and Yabeny
soon established that they struck north through the Chuskas
from the Tohatchi road for a mile and a half before veering
up a creek that wound around a humpbacked mountain. Then
the fugitive tended south. As the two men followed this wisp
of a trail through the bonelike trunks of the aspens and the
black-green spruces, Emmett had to admire the Pounds' tute-
lage. Again and again, the line of prints came close to van-
ishing in the thick humus carpeting the forest floor. Yabeny,
who'd taken the lead, was often reduced to crawling, running his palm over the duff to feel for the faint indentation of
a track.

All the while, Emmett, armed with Yabeny's shotgun,
shifted the muzzle back and forth across the twilit trees.
Anna had recalled no sound before Caleb Pound suddenly
appeared over her in bed. It'd be like that here. Somewhere,
in one of these claustrophobic hollows or watercourses,
Pound would be there. Standing at their shoulders.

Yabeny motioned Emmett forward.

He trotted up to the sergeant through a cloud of gnats.
The daylight was swiftly fading, and the moon rising
through the growth. A big jaundiced globe magnified by
desert dust and Albuquerque's smog.

Yabeny said, "Not much light left. How about you signcut
on ahead?"

"Show me your line of bearing."

For once, Yabeny had to violate *Dine* etiquette by pointing.

Emmett nodded but didn't think the tracks were sharp enough in the leaf debris for rushing the process. And Pound might be just minutes ahead. Still, this was the sergeant's turf. Emmett sidestepped several yards to the right so he wouldn't trample any prints, then jogged forward. While Yabeny stuck laboriously to the already found sign, Emmett hurried on, hoping to intersect the fugitive's trail as far ahead as possible.

Below on the eastern plain were widely scattered clusters of lights. Tohatchi, where the jailed gangbangers clung to their secret of the winged Gila. Crownpoint, the outpost of tribal government from which Darcy Altasal's incurable fetal alcohol syndrome was monitored by a white woman who couldn't understand why Indians were indifferent to accounting for their own numbers to a bureaucracy imposed on them. There was only a smattering of twinkles to mark Canoncito, for Mount Taylor towered in between, shutting off the little rez from the traditional homeland. *Enemy Navajo.* All this was cramming Emmett's head with no promise of resolution if only because two unsubs, not one, had walked away from Bert Knoki's burned-out cruiser and a Ute prostitute named Lolly Blackhouse had written a letter to the same murdered cop.

He halted.

Another track. Deep at the toes. Where Pound had leaped from the sandy ground to the top of a lichen-encrusted boulder. From here on, he'd skipped from rock to rock, through a weatherworn confusion of them that straddled along much of the east slope of the range.

Emmett signaled Yabeny to come forward.

Rushing up, the sergeant read the situation at once. "Damn."

"You fluent in bootsole rubber, Marcellus?"

Yabeny inspected the crown of the first boulder. He'd stripped off his brass nameplate and pinned his badge to the underside of a shirt lapel so it wouldn't flash in the moon-light. "He's wearin' boots with nice gummy soles. And knockin' off some of this moss with each step."

"Good." Emmett watched the larger potholes in the sandstone for movement. Scoured out by aeons of wind, some still held water, in which fairy shrimp flitted just un-der the surface. "Let's push him."

They had to slow every twenty or thirty yards so Yabeny could hunker down over a possible sign. As it grew darker, the sergeant was forced to use his flashlight, shading the lens with his free hand to keep down the spillage. It was becoming ap-parent Pound would recross the Tohatchi road. Probably within a few miles of where Yabeny had left his cruiser in the care of two Apache County deputies who were also to guide the FBI technicians down to the ditched Lincoln. But this afternoon, there'd been no way of knowing for certain that the fugitive hadn't trekked north toward Shiprock.

And Pound could be counted on to have left no trace of his passing on the road itself.

That was proved forty-five minutes later when the two men clambered down a steep talus slope to the byway. They broke out their flashlights, stooped and swept their beams over the tire-packed dirt. Pound had brushed out his tracks so meticulously neither Yabeny nor he would have spotted them from the cruiser had they driven here. The sergeant went over the side and located the branches the fugitive had used for a broom.

"We can go on," Emmett said, "but I want to make sure you know something."

"What?"

"We'll have to use our flashlights more and more. Which'll make us easy pickings."

"You suggestin' we fall back to my car?" Yabeny asked.

"Not at all. Just want to be able to tell your next of kin I warned you."

Yabeny looked at him as if he didn't quite know how to

take the Comanche sense of humor, then turned and bounded down the slope on his heels.

Within an hour, Emmett wondered if the sergeant had begun to regret his decision not to call it a day. Pound became more careless with his sign, but the pursuit was taking the two men into a strange country of erosion-scalloped ravines divided by gaunt ridges. The moonlight cast the distorted sandstone into otherworldly forms. Some human. Some too grotesque to be human. Even the pines into which they'd descended out of the conical firs had been twisted by gales and frost into demons. Then these few trees straggled out, and they were thrashing through mazes of snakeweed and big sage. The windless scrub seemed to reach out and claw at them. The Navajo distrust of the night could be seen in Yabeny's crouched advance. The way his head jerked toward the slightest noise as if spirits teemed all around him.

Pound was leaving a conspicuous trail. Snapped twigs, some still dripping sap. A curious piece of torn brown paper no bigger than a thumbnail Yabeny plucked off the spine of a banana yucca stem. Cookie-cutter tracks.

Is he running now? Are we that close to him?

Halting Yabeny, Emmett knelt to measure the distance between two elliptical divots in the soil with the shotgun. Previously, he'd determined Pound's walking stride to be the same length. This was twice that. Instead of urging Yabeny to pick up the pace again, he whispered, "He wants us to rush."

"Slow down?"

"Yes."

A copse of box elder impeded them as they crossed a slough. To keep their noise down, they writhed more than pushed through the rangy branches. Pound could rear up within feet of them and not be seen through the chaos of leafy moon shadows until it was too late. Emmett drew his revolver. Easier than the long-barreled shotgun to swing around in the cagelike interior of the dense stand.

Ahead by ten feet, Yabeny sprawled on his belly to pass under a mesh of low limbs. Emmett covered him until the sergeant emerged from the box elder and went to a knee in the strong moonlight. Then he himself squirmed under the same lattice. Icy water seeped through his jacket and Levi's. He was lifting his back out of the muck—when something large grunted explosively. It crashed through the foliage to his immediate left. His gun hand was pinned to his side by the branches. He tried to raise the shotgun, but it too was caught in the mass of boughs.

He saw Yabeny wheel desperately toward the ongoing thrashing. His heart lodged in his throat, Emmett could only watch. Just when the sergeant's hand visibly flexed to fire, the clamorous shredding of leaves was replaced by a rhythmic thud of hooves on the heights above the slough.

"Elk," Yabeny muttered as if he'd known all along.

Emmett crawled the rest of the way out and sat beside the sergeant. He sneaked a deep breath to quiet his heart. Maybe twenty-five miles to the south lay a glow. Gallup. With tentacles of white and red specks streaming out from it. The highways.

"Ready?" Yabeny asked.

"Let's do it." Emmett heaved himself to his feet.

But then Pound's trail completely vanished. As if he'd suddenly levitated. Emmett covered Yabeny while the man circled around in almost aimless confusion, his light winking dimly on and off among the tussocks of bunch grass that dotted the long rise they'd started up. At last, Yabeny clucked his tongue chukarlike for Emmett to approach, then held his beam close to some blades of grass that had been bent and bruised by the edge of a sole. Pound had vaulted over the crowns of the grass mounds as if they were stepping-stones.

"Thinks he's Baryshnikov," Emmett joked.

"Who's Baryshnikov?"

"Some dancer my second wife made me spend the longest evening of my life watching."

"Indian?"

"No, he dances for money."

They moved on.

The tracks continued over the crest of the rise. Emmett waved for the sergeant to come up. Below was a pasture ringed by fence posts casting long shadows; the wire was probably too rusty to gleam in the moonlight. Pound had gone straight down the hogback ridge with no fear it might peter out at a cliff far above the grassland. Had he ever come this way before? It now seemed likely. And even more likely a few seconds later when Yabeny grabbed Emmett's jacket sleeve and said as softly as his excitement allowed, "I know this place. There's a summer hogan behind the cedars there."

"Is it used anymore?"

"Doubt it. Not many folks take their flocks to higher pasture."

Emmett didn't want to find any more innocents like those in Chevelon Canyon. Few people survived an encounter with Caleb Pound if they had something he needed. "Any other dwellings around?"

"None this far up the mountain."

"Roads?"

"An old dirt one about a mile to the east. Closed by washouts."

Smoke passed invisibly over them on a breeze Emmett realized only from a sudden coolness on his sweaty kin. A juniper fire. The aroma tingled in his nose. Yabeny asked, "Figure he got wet back there too?"

"Maybe." But Emmett saw no reason for Caleb Pound to build a fire—unless it was to draw his pursuers on. "How about a radio check?"

Yabeny unpocketed his Handie-Talkie and tried to raise Window Rock, even though Emmett and he were on the wrong side of the Chuskas for decent reception. On his third unsuccessful attempt, a laconic female voice responded, "CIS Two, this is Gallup PD. Want me to relay your traffic?"

"Affirmative, please," Yabeny transmitted quietly. "Advise

my station that BIA Seventeen and I are code four near the summer hogan on the north end of Manuelito Plateau."

"Stand by."

Code four indicated that all was presently well. No further assistance required. But Emmett didn't know how long that would remain true if the sergeant and he went down into the pasture. A medevac might be needed. "Ask Gallup to give us a welfare check in thirty minutes. If there's no word from us, roll a chopper and a tac team to this location."

"CSI Two," the Gallup dispatcher said, "Window Rock acknowledges your previous message and inquires if you have the suspect in sight."

Yabeny looked questioningly to Emmett, who shook his head. "Uh, negative, Gallup . . ." The sergeant went on to repeat what Emmett had just said about the copter. Then he clicked off his radio handset and rose. The two men stutter-stepped down the tumbling ridge. Emmett concentrated on keeping his boots from skidding on the hard spine of the divide. Their view of the pasture broadened, and as he took a glance across the moonlit flats a huge curl of orange flame roiled up out of the junipers on the far edge of the grass. It lit the surrounding cliffs and ridges like day. And silhouetted them, Emmett realized.

Swiftly, Yabeny and he slid down into the deeper of the two draws flanking the ridge. Emmett had to drag his left hand to keep from tobogganing out of control into the rocks at the bottom. Still, he landed with a painful shock to his ankles and knees.

His and Yabeny's dust folded down over them. Both almost gagged trying to suppress coughing fits.

The brightness went on flaring from across the pasture. Waiting for it to subside, Emmett sucked on the tattered heel of his left hand. It was salty with blood.

The flames didn't die down. They grew.

Yabeny clambered up the embankment for a look. Above him, smoke sheeted across the moon. "Hogan's on fire," the sergeant reported, short of breath. "Orange and white—that's an ether fireball. We just found ourselves a clandestine lab."

"Who still uses ether to cook meth these days?" Emmett asked. White gas was the fuel of choice in Phoenix.

"Our gangbangers. This is the rez, Parker." Yabeny skated back down the bank on the soles of his boots. "Chemicals inside that hogan are goin' off like the Fourth of July."

Emmett considered that for a moment. "Vipers?"

"Could be."

"You get a chance to stake out that mailbox near Crystal?" The night Emmett had flown to Phoenix, Yabeny had mentioned the possibility the gangbangers were using it as a drop.

"No." Yabeny laid his rifle across his legs. "There wasn't the manpower."

"All right." If Pound and the Vipers were linked somehow to this remote methamphetamine lab, the conflagration was still probably Caleb's handiwork. Another fugitive would start one as a distraction to further his escape. But not Pound. Everything he did seemed to be an embodiment of myth, however warped his interpretation of *Dine* belief. A blazing hogan was the most spine-chilling omen of death to the Navajo, like the banshee to the Irish.

Yabeny sat in silence.

"Listen," Emmett said, "no use two of us going down there. How about you covering me?"

"No, we'll both go. That *niziz* is callin' us out . . ." Penis. One of the few *Dine* words that could be bent into a profanity, making Emmett realize that most of these, plus the Miranda warning, comprised his limited Navajo vocabulary. "And we can't take him down from up here, Parker."

And Pound would only melt deeper into the Chuskas with the arrival of the helicopter. The next cop along his bloody path would be caught unawares. That's why it had to end now.

"Any ideas?" Emmett asked. You didn't tell a man in his own country what to do.

Nor did you order a visitor around. "Maybe we can skirt the pasture and hit the hogan out of the south," Yabeny offered. "Cut him off, if he's of a mind to keep headin' toward Gallup."

"You figure he's still somewhere near the fire?"

"Yeah. He'll want to use the light against us." The sergeant paused, then added without much conviction, "We might get lucky. Find him before he finds us."

"Then let's do it." Emmett's wristwatch told him that they had another twenty-five minutes to close this out and raise Gallup PD before Anna in Window Rock assumed the worst and started an FBI SWAT team this way. No doubt, Niehaus had persuaded her by now not to use the BIA's.

The pasture was drained at its lower end by a ten-foot-deep gully with crumbling banks of sand. Evidence that, like much of Navajoland, this high plateau had been overgrazed, the grass cropped down to its roots to die and the earth exposed naked to the hard male rains of summer. Yabeny checked the muddy bottom of the gulch for tracks. None, other than deer and coyote. So at least Pound hadn't fled by using this sunken route through the middle of the open field.

Holding his rifle at port arms, the sergeant broke into a steady trot toward the southwest.

Emmett trailed him through a mixed stand of piñons and junipers. Needles slapped against his face and left resin on his forearms. An incongruous Christmasy smell. He couldn't catch a trace of vinyl chloride gas lingering in the hollow. Hopefully, the raging fire had dissipated it.

The trees began to thin out, and Yabeny dropped to peer beneath their ground-hugging branches. To make certain Pound wasn't waiting behind one of the stunted conifers. "Clear," he whispered.

They hurried on. But only briefly. Soon the firelight was sputtering the forest shadows across the rocky ground, making it impossible to pick out any other kind of motion.

Slowing, the two men spread out from each other.

Emmett looked for tracks. But the surface was too rough

to register an impression that could be seen at a glance. He felt the sunlike heat of the hogan fire on the right side of his face. A loud creak penetrated the popping and crackling. From a failing roof timber. Then the entire hut crashed in on itself. The flames wriggled out of the wreckage and disgorged a whorling updraft of sparks. The smell of chemical residue mixed with that of the smoke.

Fifty feet of open ground lay between them and the circular heap of embers. Emmett saw no reason to approach the ruin of the hogan. Pound was somewhere close by. He could feel eyes boring into the back of his neck. Cold lizard eyes.

Make your move, you son of a bitch . . . you want this finished as much as we do.

A shiver on his nape made Emmett do what Yabeny had already done: press his body into the nettlesome boughs of a piñon. The stiff needles pricked his skin through his jacket. He looked all around for a human form. The slight breeze shifted, and abruptly the air was rife with the odor of scorched green grass.

Show yourself.

What at first had seemed an unbroken sweep of pasture up to the hogan was actually fractured by a tracery of narrow gullies. An attempt to control this spreading erosion had been made: a small check-dam built of stones, which lay ten yards in front of Yabeny.

Emmett held his breath. To listen. To try to tell if the pounding he heard was his own heart or footfalls against the earth. Then it was undeniable. Someone was running toward them.

But from which direction?

The encircling heights made it impossible to tell which sound was genuine and which was echo—until the thumping was joined by the *crack-crack* of a rifle.

Pound was coming at them from behind. Out of the trees. Fast.

Emmett heard none of the bullets whir past, but a clipped sprig of piñon dropped down the back of his shirt collar. He lunged away from the sound of the gunfire, somersaulting through grass that was warm and sticky from the fire.

Coming to rest on his back, he rolled over and brought the shotgun sights up to eye level.

But no target appeared.

Frustrated, he saw a bullet spark against the ground within inches of the top of Yabeny's head. The sergeant had dived behind the cover of the check-dam. He was raising the automatic rifle to his shoulder when his entire body went rigid. From a bullet impact? Emmett believed the man had been struck. Yet, Yabeny loosed a burst as a large figure sprinted headlong from the trees.

Emmett pulled his own trigger, then jacked in another cartridge.

The figure continued to rush toward Yabeny, firing a carbine from the hip. Emmett forced himself to slow down long enough to lead the wildly screaming man before letting go with another shell. He didn't hear the blast but felt the recoil kick his upper arm. The figure staggered. Emmett believed he'd hit him in the chest. But couldn't tell. Yabeny's rifle belched another string of flashes in the same split second. The figure spun out of view.

Dust and smoke hung in the air around Emmett.

It felt like an eternity as he squinted down his barrel at the man sprawled in front of the check-dam. Yabeny still squatted behind it, his head slumped forward against the rocks.

"Marcellus . . . you all right?"

No answer.

Emmett wanted to run over to him. But couldn't. Not yet. He made himself forget Yabeny for the moment and advanced on the figure. His muzzle never strayed from the motionless form as he kicked the carbine out of reach. He ran his small flashlight over the head and chest. The face and one side of the head were gone, pulverized by Yabeny's rounds into a red dew that sparkled in the grass for a radius of ten feet behind. There was also a tight grouping of double-aught buckshot holes in the man's Navajo Pine High School sweatshirt.

Emmett took his handcuffs off the back of his belt and shackled the corpse. To keep the presumed dead from attacking again.

Then he turned for Yabeny.

The sergeant's eyes were wide open, and Emmett feared the worst until he saw them flicker in response to the flashlight.

"Marcellus . . . ?"

The man's gaze darted downward, as if to point out something. Emmett lowered his beam onto a glimpse of vividly colored armored skin. Clamped to Yabeny's right foreleg just above his boot was the biggest Gila monster Emmett had ever seen. The reptile was arched into a crescent but had to be at least two and a half feet long. Doggedly chewing its venom into the man's flesh.

"Get your light off me," Yabeny said, hardly moving his lips. "Walk away and I'll be okay."

Emmett did so, even though the sergeant looked anything but okay. His face was quivering with pain and the stoic resolve not to panic. Eventually, the Gila would decide he posed no further threat and crawl off.

But the seconds dragged on so agonizingly, Emmett focused his attention on the corpse. It was over. Like other seemingly insoluble cases, over in a staccato fit of gunplay. He could hardly believe it. Caleb Pound had seemed so formidable. So cunning. The scrap of brown paper Yabeny had found on the yucca plant now made sense. It was from a pasteboard box in which Pound had carried his last Gila of those poached from Lowe Canyon. Not unlike the box he'd left in Emmett's living room.

Yabeny rose woozily. He began hobbling toward Emmett, who dashed forward to support him under the arms. Blood was flowing from the bite and collecting in the man's boot sock.

"That was no *Dine* Gila," Yabeny said between clenched teeth.

"Matter of fact, it wasn't. From Shivwits country in southern Utah."

"Thought so. No Navajo lizard would turn on his own kind."

"Want to sit down?"

Yabeny gave a terse shake of his head. "Gettin' sick to my gut."

Emmett slipped the handset from the sergeant's jacket pocket and raised Gallup. "Roll that chopper ASAP. One deceased in custody and one officer injured . . ." Yabeny sagged against him. "Advise Sage Memorial to call out Dr. Hennepin."

"Copy, is your location marked?"

"Affirmative. By what's left of a burnt hogan. Does this ship have infrared?"

"Stand by."

Yabeny said, "Think I'll lay down now, Parker."

"How's the pain?" Emmett asked, lowering him to the grass.

"Clears the sinuses." And the stomach: The sergeant vomited. Violently, as Anna had.

"BIA Seventeen," Gallup transmitted, "be advised this is not a Search and Rescue chopper. Negative on infrared scanner."

"Copy." The glow of the embers was throbbing against the undersides of Pound's running shoes. Emmett thought nothing of it for a blink. Then he rocketed to his feet. Running shoes. Not boots. And not the same sole pattern Yabeny and he had tracked from the abandoned Lincoln. But most importantly—not size twelves. Approaching the corpse again, Emmett compared his own elevens to the soles. "Christ almighty."

Yabeny spat, then raised his tremulous head and asked, "What's wrong?"

Emmett circled the ruin of the hogan. The heat was yet so intense he whipped the back of his windbreaker up over his head to ward it off. He didn't need his flashlight to see. The ground was littered with the size-ten prints, some fresh and some seemingly days old. Punctuating these were a few size twelves forming a vee: heading into where the east-facing entrance of the dwelling had probably been and then out again—striking south into the trees.

"What's wrong?" Yabeny asked again.

"Ivan Jumper have any marks or tattoos?"

"Knuckles of his left hand."

Dropping the jacket off his head, Emmett returned to the corpse. He'd already rolled it over, so the manacled hands were exposed. As Yabeny had said, a crude jailhouse tattoo had been pecked into the fingers with a ballpoint pen. One letter on each knuckle: I-V-A-N.

Yabeny sat up in alarm. "Is it Jumper?" The dazed way he asked told Emmett that this had been his first fatal shooting. And someone he'd known. Seen shopping at Bashas' or standing in line at the McDonald's in Window Rock. Perhaps even someone with whom he'd had an understanding.

"Yes."

"Oh Jesus." Yabeny clasped his leg in both hands, eyes shut. Wondering if there'd been a clan connection? Always the potential nightmare in a shooting to a Navajo cop. "Whose round got him, Parker?"

"Mine."

"You sure?"

"Yeah." It was conceivable the bevy of buckshot had punched through Jumper's heart before Yabeny's bullets had carried away his face. But he suspected even the pathologist wouldn't have the definitive answer. Let that doubt be a comfort to the sergeant. He lived here. Emmett didn't.

He reloaded the shotgun while keeping his gaze hard on the trees. Amazing. He recalled firing only twice, but the magazine was empty. So easy to spray under stress.

"There was no choice, Parker." Yabeny was now sweating profusely.

"You bet there was no choice. Jumper had me dead in his sights." It'd been the other way around, with Yabeny bearing the brunt of the fire. But that would never matter.

"Did he?"

The strained hope in Yabeny's face made Emmett glance away. The sergeant was an eleven-year veteran, but a first fatal was like having any other kind of virginity roughly destroyed. "You did what you had to, Marcellus."

"You know, Ivan told me the damnedest thing once," Yabeny rattled on. "Said he wanted to be a cop when he was little. No way a bootlegger's son would make it, he figured. But that's what he wanted to be. Said he liked the uniform. The respect."

"A zig instead of a zag, and that could be you or me lying there in cuffs."

"How'd you know that was goin' through my head just now?" Yabeny was shivering uncontrollably.

"Because twelve years ago I was where you are right now. Except my first was in the parking lot of a convenience store in Oklahoma City, not the backside of the Chuskas."

"Man, that *could* be me there, you know? Except for my uncle. My mom's brother straightened me out when I was thirteen. Made me see why it was important to walk in beauty. To be *Dine,* you know? Ivan didn't have anybody like that. And maybe that's all the difference there is."

"Gallup," Emmett radioed, "get me an ETA on that chopper. I've got a man going into shock."

"Stand by."

"I'm all right," Yabeny protested.

"I know, Marcellus. But anything to goose them. We're dealing with the federal government here. Let's have another look at that bite." Emmett crawled over, and the sergeant pulled his hands away from the ragged laceration left by the Gila's grooved teeth. The wound had stopped bleeding. "Looking good. See which way the critter scampered off? Belongs to a friend."

Yabeny chuckled, but then sobered and said, "Hell. I feel like cryin'."

"Do it."

"Naw."

"That's what I did," Emmett fibbed. "Right in the arms of a field training officer who called me a prairie nigger behind my back." That, perhaps, had been the reason he hadn't—not in front of that ignorant cracker.

The HT squawked, "BIA Seventeen, Gallup."

"Go."

"Chopper should be over you any minute."

"Copy." Emmett scanned the piñons again. Pound was fleeing to the south or he would have already come at them. Ivan Jumper had served as his rear guard, delaying the pursuit, just as the peewee Viper had for Ivan himself nine days ago on Clydine's knoll. Time was wasting. And more of it would soon be wasted explaining the situation to an FBI SWAT team leader.

Yabeny's feverish eyes were fixed on him. "You're goin' after him alone, aren't you?"

"Just as soon as I see you lifted out of here."

"Get movin'. Listen—" The thump of the rotor was reverberating in the canyons above them. "I'll be fine."

"You sure?"

"Hundred percent."

"All right. Tell them to stand off till I call for assistance. They've got no infrared to pick up Pound's body heat, and the chopper's searchlight won't do anything but tell him where I am. If the team has to set up a containment line, I prefer it be several miles south of here."

"I'll tell them."

Emmett patted Yabeny on the shoulder, then ran for the trees. The moon had crossed its zenith and would soon vanish behind the crest of the range.

chapter 22

THE MOON HAD BEEN DOWN AT LEAST AN HOUR, BUT a chalky luminosity still backdropped the Chuskas. Anna stood in the parking lot of the Tohatchi Juvenile Detention Facility, wondering where Emmett was in those darkened folds of sandstone. It was 1:30 in the morning. Two hours since the Air National Guard helicopter had flown back from the Manuelito Plateau to Sage Memorial Hospital with a sickened Marcellus Yabeny. Right off, the sergeant told Jim Niehaus and her that Emmett was pursuing Caleb Pound on foot. Alone. The Phoenix SAC advised Anna to have the tribal SWAT team, which had been left off on the plateau to secure Ivan Jumper's body for the FBI techs, join in the hunt. Yabeny interrupted that Emmett wanted a surveillance perimeter set up several miles south of the pasture where Jumper had been shot to death. And no chopper probing the mountainsides with its searchlight. Anna tried to comfort Yabeny as his bite was swabbed by Dr. Hennepin. She showed him her own healed wound, and the sergeant smiled feebly. She too had thought she was going to die. Asking Niehaus to join her out in the corridor, she told him that Emmett would have his way. No one could run the fugitive to ground faster than Parker. And the lethal force review on Jumper wasn't to be kicked off until Pound was in custody. Yabeny was too ill to be interrogated and Emmett too busy. Niehaus hadn't argued but didn't say more than ten words on their drive back to Window Rock.

A light suddenly gleamed in the Chuskas.

The techs had fired up a portable generator to power their floodlights. Before being wheeled into a private room, a sedated Yabeny had mumbled to her that fortunately, the shooting had occurred out-of-doors, sparing Emmett and him too much exposure to Jumper's *chindi,* that contaminating evil residue of his spirit.

Despite the lateness of the hour, news of the head Viper's death had traveled quickly. Anna no sooner got back to the capital, dropped Niehaus off at the Navajo police complex and turned around in the lot than the SAC radioed her from inside the building to wait. He then hurried out with a message from the U.S. Attorney in Albuquerque: Garwin Descheenie's lawyer, Rod Guzman, was now willing to talk about a deal. Would Anna meet with him and a deputy federal prosecutor at the Tohatchi facility ASAP? She had yet to get to John Tallsalt's residence. The first attempt had been scrubbed when she learned from Gallup PD of the firefight on Manuelito Plateau.

Now this.

Arriving at Tohatchi forty minutes later, she'd been told that Guzman and the deputy U.S. Attorney were sequestered in negotiations. She was asked to wait in the lobby. But the stark lighting there so reminded her of the hospital emergency room, she strolled out into the night.

She'd now been waiting twenty minutes.

The air was finally cooling down. Parked on the dirt flats behind the center was a Navajo police cruiser. The patrolman was leaning across the hood, peering through a night-vision scope at the alluvial fans that spilled out of the canyons of the Chuskas. Many of these officers had now been on duty for more than eighteen hours, counting their regular shifts before the Olsons' Lincoln four-by-four had been discovered—dental records now confirmed that the burned bodies were indeed the Scottsdale couple. The BIA tactical unit was close to deploying along the southern spur of the range. And the FBI SWAT team out of Phoenix was sweeping Window Rock Ridge. She herself was so wired she wondered if she'd ever sleep again.

"Special Agent Turnipseed . . . ?" Shoes scuffed down the concrete steps toward her. Walt Coombs, the deputy U.S. Attorney sent by Albuquerque. Mid-fifties with hollow, acne-scarred cheeks and iron-colored hair. "Sorry to keep you waiting. Had a sticking point in there, but I now believe we're past it . . ." He touched a match to his pipe, the flame accentuating his scars.

"Why's Guzman dealing at this ridiculous hour?" she asked.

"Jumper's dead, and he doesn't want Descheenie left holding the bag. It's plain Jumper and Descheenie had central roles in the Knoki murders—and Guzman wants to put his spin on that before matters get beyond his control . . ." Studying Anna, Coombs let the match burn down almost to his fingers before blowing it out. "I understand the last two weeks have been a meat grinder for you and the BIA dick . . . what's his name?"

"Emmett Parker." She glanced toward the Chuskas again.

"How much do you have on Descheenie and the other Vipers relative to the Knokis?"

So little she'd tried to bluff Guzman into doing just this three evenings ago. Had Emmett learned anything from his encounter with Jumper that would now make a deal counterproductive? "Zip, I'm afraid."

"What about fiber evidence in the police car that was burned?" Coombs asked.

"Fire spoiled that, according to the techs. No latent prints either. On the vehicle or a shovel we recovered."

"Anyone else in the gang ready to talk to you?"

"No." Especially the peewee who'd sniped at them to allow Ivan Jumper to flee. He'd die before talking.

"Anybody on the fringes of the gang?"

"Sorry." Anna paused. "You sure Guzman won't wait till early next week for this?"

"If we don't come to an agreement, his offer goes off the

table tonight. We agree to full immunity and disclosure of the deal in court tomorrow morning and Descheenie, who was Jumper's chief lieutenant, will sing now."

"But why the rush? I still don't get it."

"Maybe Guzman knows about someone who'll eventually cooperate if his client doesn't," Coombs said. "It's a gamble. And here's the possible downside—we let Descheenie skate only to find a more credible witness a week from now. But what if that witness never comes forward? Or doesn't exist?"

She wanted badly to discuss this with Emmett, even if by radio. But he had his hands full. And each time she thought of him in those mountains facing Caleb Pound without backup, she found it hard to stand still. *Wait . . . that's your answer.* Pound was the critical target. She doubted he would ever talk, given his conditioning by Hezekiah, who'd executed all who'd talked. Descheenie might be their only means of proving Pound's involvement in the Knoki murders. "What's the deal?" she asked at last.

"Guzman tried to cajole me into letting Descheenie plea to false imprisonment . . ." Little more than kidnapping, Anna realized, alarmed. But then the attorney said, "After some wrangling, he'll accept conspiracy as long as we don't pursue the death penalty. It's your call, Ms. Turnipseed."

Descheenie might know something that could help Emmett safely bring in Pound. She'd trade anything for that. "Take it."

Coombs snuffed out his pipe bowl with a thumb. "Do you have a tape recorder?"

"I'm sure Parker does. It's his car."

"See you inside."

Her hands shook as she removed the machine from the trunk. She prayed that there were no more surprises in this case, that she had it figured out well enough to justify this roll of the dice.

Five minutes later, the corpulent and sleepy-eyed supervisor of the facility left off Descheenie in the same interview room Emmett and she had last beheld the big gangbanger on Monday evening. The youth took the chair beside Guzman, true to form in a natty business suit. Anna sat on the opposite side of the table with Coombs, who was tieless and in shirt-sleeves. He launched into some legal boilerplate, mostly for the benefit of the tape.

Making a show of not listening, Descheenie idly scratched the winged Gila tattoo on his neck. It looked slightly infected.

Guzman argued a point with a meaning that escaped Anna, and for a few minutes it seemed as if the deal might collapse. But then Coombs nodded at Anna.

"For the benefit of the record, I'm Special Agent Anna Turnipseed of the FBI. I'm heading the task force investigating the murders of Carbert and Aurelia Knoki et al. . . ." She stared at Descheenie. *I'm not scared of you, you miserable little fuck.* The only sound in the room was the squeak of the cassette rolling in Emmett's dusty recorder. "Garwin, where is Caleb Pound headed tonight?"

Descheenie's smooth, brown face scrunched up in confusion, but for the first time he squirmed in his chair. "Who?"

"Him." Pointing, she said, "I'll have the record reflect I'm indicating the tattoo of a Gila monster with moth wings on Garwin's neck."

"Oh," Descheenie said. "You mean Gila Monster."

Anna took a Utah driver's license photo facsimile from her purse and handed it to him. "Is this Gila Monster?" Caleb Pound, glaring coldly at the camera.

"I don't know this dude. Never met him. Gila Monster neither."

She'd hoped to quickly learn something that might help Emmett, but it wasn't going to be that easy. "You're telling me you never met Gila Monster?"

"No."

"How's that possible?"

"He's a god. And you don't see gods like regular dudes. Least, that's what Ivan told me."

"Then why'd you get that tattoo?"

Guzman whispered something to Descheenie, and the youth snapped, "I *am*. I know this ain't like jackin' a car or somethin'." Nostrils flared with indignation, he took took a few seconds to gather himself before facing Anna again. "Right before spring break, there was this letter left under Clydine's windshield wiper."

"Of Ms. Jumper's new Dakota truck?" Anna interjected.

"Yeah. And it said Bert Knoki was goin' to stop her on the way back from Gallup Thursday night."

"With a load of alcohol?"

"I guess."

"Was this her regular day to bring a shipment onto the reservation? Yes or no."

"Yes." Descheenie turned to Guzman but got no more than a nervous frown. "What?"

"Just go on about the letter," the lawyer said glumly. No doubt he had colleagues at DNA, tribal legal aid, and their defense of Clydine Jumper had just been demolished.

"It was signed *Gila Monster* . . ." The youth held two fingers to his neck. "With this alongside the name. That Thursday night, Clydine decides to like see if the letter is BS. She drives all the way to Gallup, but don't bring no liquor back. Just makes the trip. Sure enough, Knoki red-lights her just outside Window Rock . . ." The following week, a second letter appeared during the night under Clydine Jumper's wiper. It foretold of another traffic trap Knoki had planned, which she also averted. Plus suggested the use of a mailbox near Crystal as a future drop. Apparently, Gila Monster didn't want to be observed in the flesh by his new devotees. The third message was far more ominous to the Vipers. It warned that Knoki was close to locating their most recent clandestine methamphetamine lab.

"Where's that?" Anna demanded.

Once again, Descheenie got no help from Guzman. The youth sighed, then said, "Up at this old hogan in the Chuskas. Where Ivan bought it tonight, I guess."

The little room vanished before Anna's eyes, and she saw Caleb Pound crouched in the darkness beneath the Knokis' mobile home, overhearing everything Bert had said over the phone to the department, the things he'd shared about his work with Aurelia. His hatred for bootleggers and drug dealers, the misery they brought to his people. That first morning they'd met in the coffee shop at the inn, Tallsalt had complained to her how Navajo cops consulted with their wives over even the most confidential police matters. The legacy of a matrilineal society. Had Pound also heard the couple discuss the spouse-ride-along program? Had that been his solution to eliminating them both at the same time? The people who had abandoned him to Hezekiah? If so, why hadn't he done it himself?

Anna realized that everyone was waiting for her to continue. "Garwin, did Gila Monster tell you in the letter what night the Knokis could be found out together?"

"Yeah. He said how all the cops was ridin' 'round with their women, and Friday night—"

"Said or wrote?" Coombs asked, perhaps hoping to catch the youth in a lie and further strengthen the link to Pound.

But Descheenie was unfazed, almost chilling in his lack of affect while describing these premeditated murders. "Wrote." His gaze shifted to Anna again. "Gila Monster wrote how Knoki and his old lady would be out patrollin' together on Friday night, so we all went up to Asaayi Lake . . ." Several members of the Vipers and their girls, whom Anna had him name. And this, clearly, is what Guzman had feared would devalue Descheenie's testimony: one of the girls coming forward. "We built us a big fire . . ." Large enough to catch Knoki's attention from the valley below. "Ivan was fucked up pretty bad on whiskey and crank, talkin' 'bout how Gila Monster was our god. How he showed up at this time to save us all from bein' witched by skinwalkers who hate us and bein' harassed by the cops. If it wasn't for GM, we'd all be in the joint or dead. Even Ivan's mom."

Which raised a long-vexing question for Anna. "What was Clydine doing down on the highway that evening?"

"Lookin' out for us, I guess. Speedin' on purpose. To make sure it was Knoki workin' the area. If it wasn't, she'd blink her lights three times for us to see. She's a straight-up lady, you know. Took a ticket just to make sure it was Knoki. Then, after he went up the Asaayi road to check out our fire, she split for Window Rock to leave off some stuff at jail for Ivan's big brother."

"And then what happened up at the lake?" Anna didn't want to hear how Bert and Aurelia had died, but nothing in the world could have made her leave that stuffy room.

"Knoki drove down to us on the shore . . ." The youth shrugged, his first indication that he didn't want to go into the rest of it. "While he walked over to us, I snuck up to the car where his old lady still was sittin'—and broke off the antenna with a pair of pliers Ivan gived me . . ." Bert strolled largely unconcerned up to the fire, assured that the dozen bangers and their girlfriends would do no more than bad-mouth him while he confiscated their beer and poured it out on the ground. But he was encircled by the males. A blow to the backs of the knees with a club made of piñon dropped him, groaning. Anna had to keep unclenching her fists as she listened to Descheenie dispassionately describe how Bert was beaten nearly senseless, his service pistol ripped from his holster. Blood pouring down his face. Beseeching them from the ground with an upraised hand. Aurelia rushed from the cruiser to plead for them to stop, but Ivan clubbed her in the head, leveling her. "Then he said there was no goin' back. So he shot her . . ." At the base of the skull, according to the autopsy report. With her husband's own weapon, although the Vipers had brought plenty of their own to the scene.

Anna had to ask, "Did Bert see Aurelia die?"

"I guess," Descheenie replied, expressionless. "He kind of moaned." Anna closed her eyes for a moment: Her entire family had watched her great-great-grandfather, Captain Jack, fall through the trapdoor of an army gallows. They too had moaned. "But then Ivan hit Bert again and said for everybody to load 'em up fast."

"Did you strike either of the Knokis at any time?"

"What?"

"You heard me." Anna hoped for the sake of his credibility as a witness that he wouldn't lie now.

"I punched Bert some. But there wasn't much point, you know? Ivan got him so bad with the club."

Anna inhaled again. "Who drove the police car away from the lake?"

"Me. Ivan sat up front with a carbine, ready for any cops tryin' to stop us."

"Anybody else go along?"

"No."

"How'd the rear window get smashed in?"

"Oh, one of our homies asked us to do it."

"Name."

"Lokey. His uncle's kind of a singer, though not real john like most."

Anna asked, "What's *john* mean?"

"Traditional Navajo," Guzman, a Pueblo, responded for his client. "I've defended the gentleman in the past."

"Anyways," Descheenie went on, "our homie said the Knokis' spirits would get hung up inside the Ford with us and make us sick. Unless we gived 'em a way out. And swapped their shoes on their feet. Ivan laughed, but he broke the window with his club. Lokey did the shoes. Then everybody put water on the fire and split."

"Where were you and Ivan headed with the bodies?" Coombs's curiosity overcame his previous reluctance to intrude.

"A place down Crystal Wash Ivan been before. Where we could bury the whole car easy after we torched it. But then we got stuck in the mud. So we set fire to the Ford where it was and hoofed it out."

Anna wrested control back from the prosecutor. "Whose idea was it to burn the Knokis?"

"Gila Monster's, I guess. It was in the letter. *Plunge 'em into the flames.* I didn't want to do it there. Somebody might see, even though the place was way down the wash. The first spot Ivan picked out was better. In some narrows. But we couldn't reach it on account of the mud and him actin' crazy that night, so I let him have his way."

Guzman asked, "Do you regret the limited part you played in this tragedy, Garwin?"

"Kind of."

The lawyer furrowed his brow at his client.

"I mean," Descheenie went on, "I got scared when the fire started."

"*Why?*" Anna demanded.

"Knoki sat up and screamed in the back of the Ford. I figured he was already dead . . . you know?"

CALEB POUND'S TRACKS struck at a slapdash angle down the mountainside, deviating only to avoid the buckthorn thickets thriving on this southern exposure.

Emmett slowed.

Ahead lay an angular butte of slopes and ledges. Creased with shadows. Was dawn near? Emmett tapped the glow button on his wristwatch: 4:35. Too early.

Pound was up to something. After only grudgingly revealing his sign for mile upon mile, he was now advertising it.

Emmett sat to think and listen.

He decided the butte looked like a medieval castle. Crenellations and turrets. The sand, loosed over the ages by ice and thaw from the decomposing mother stone, flowed around these spires and down to the edge of each successive cliff.

The lights of the coal pit glimmered below. Still miles off, but close enough to hear the giant shovel, he believed, if it'd been running. It wasn't. Good. Not only had Anna kept the chopper from pestering him all night, she'd evacuated the employees of Dinetah Coal Company. Did that mean she'd checked Tallsalt's house as well? Probably, for it lay inside the perimeter he'd suggested. Another hour or so, and he'd be herding Pound into the crosshaired sights of an FBI SWAT team. The bureau's vaunted ninjas could take him down while Emmett hunted up a drink of water.

Waiting, he'd hoped to catch a sound ahead. A rustle of clothing. The click of a disturbed pebble.

But Pound wasn't going to make it that simple for him.

Did he want to bypass the butte? Rising to his burning feet, he noted the long, exposed climb that would require. And if Pound had slogged directly on, needless time would be wasted. No, Emmett told himself, if he wanted to stay close to him he had to clamber over the slanting bench of sand above the last cliff, one so sheer its bottom was lost in shadow.

He sniffed the air. Both Pound and he had been pushing themselves hard enough to smell each other at a hundred yards. But that advantage was the fugitive's—the whisper of a breeze was to Emmett's back.

Shouldering Yabeny's shotgun, he started toward the butte. Ever since leaving the burning hogan, he'd expected Pound to spin around and strike. Better now than later, somewhere below in the presence of innocents.

He began traversing the slope. The sand was deep and coarse. His calves ached from pushing through it.

A slab of the stuff started to avalanche toward the precipice, forcing him to scurry higher on the bench.

Above and to the right he saw a slit of shadow grow wider as he neared it. The mouth of a cleft that ran up the center of the butte. If Pound had hidden there, he'd chosen unwisely. Emmett would have him boxed in. There was no outlet, for the fracture ended at the base of a towering palisade.

Emmett froze.

He'd heard a scraping noise from above. Like denim rubbing against rock.

He dived headfirst into the waist-deep hollow just below the mouth of the cleft. Flopping over, he listened for another sound. None came. And he began to wonder if the first had been as intentional as the tracks Pound had strewn across the mountainside. The beam from Emmett's small flashlight would never penetrate the darkness above him, but his voice would. "Caleb . . . ?"

Silence, although it seemed to have ears in it.

"Caleb Pound? This is Emmett Parker. I'm a BIA cop. I'd like the chance to talk to you before the FBI gets its hands on you. That was one of their agents you killed in Phoenix, and they're spoiling to get even . . ." He hunkered lower in the hollow. In the last few minutes, the eastern sky had begun to brighten. Daylight would make it virtually impossible for Pound to escape the sandstone cage he'd blundered into. "I saw Nicole recently. She sends her love. Still thinks of you fondly. Remembers that time you, she and Zelek went to Lowe Canyon looking for Gilas . . ." Emmett paused, realizing that if mention of his childhood friend tugged at no sensibilities, nothing would. "I feel bad about Ivan. But he refused to use his head. I don't want it to be that way with you, Caleb. I don't—"

A long, sibilant hiss echoed down out of the cleft. It was both inhuman and obviously human.

Then a lull followed.

It was broken by the sound of something thudding from wall to wall down the defile toward Emmett. Like a plastic jug. It apparently lodged in the rocks several yards above him. He'd instinctively crossed his forearms in front of his face, but now picked up and trained the shotgun on the darkness again. The thing was gurgling. His first thought was that a plastic container of gasoline had been pitched his way, but the fumes that wafted over him were sweet. Vaguely intoxicating. Then, as the vapor gathered coldly around his shins in the confines of the hollow and began to sear his eyes, he identified it. Ether. Which could go off like a bomb. He was already coiling his legs under him to lunge—when he heard the rasp of a match being struck. A transparent whoosh of orange flame snaked down the cleft toward him. With absolutely no hesitation, he pitched himself out of the depression and down the slope. He was digging in the stock of the shotgun to slow his tumble when the pooled ether exploded behind him, flinging him out over the cliff.

He heard his eyebrows crisp, but no other sound.

He tucked his head to start somersaulting. Whatever awaited him in the blackness below, he wanted to hit it rolling.

ANNA COULDN'T REACH John Tallsalt's house before the area was sealed off by the BIA's Emergency Incident Response Unit, assisted by an FBI SWAT team out of Santa Fe. A field command post had been set up in a coal company trailer office, and the sunrise was spanning the east as Anna pulled up to it. The BIA team leader stepped out to greet her, unmistakably a Paiute with an affably round face and a barrel chest. "Jimmy Dann. You must be Turnipseed."

"Yes, Lieutenant. Glad to finally meet you in person." They'd consulted several times over the radio since the team had arrived from the BIA Academy.

Dann shyly examined her features. "Modoc or Klamath?"

"Modoc. Northern Paiute?"

"Right near you. Pyramid Lake."

But she wasn't in the mood for old-home week. "Any traffic from Parker?" He hadn't responded to repeated welfare checks since midnight, but she reminded herself that he invariably turned off his radio when the chatter became distracting.

"No," Dann said, seemingly unconcerned. "One of my scouts thought he might've heard a shot about an hour ago. But he finally made up his mind it was a sonic boom."

She was beginning to wonder if their belief in Emmett's

indestructability might work against him one day. "Has the area north of here been evacuated?"

"Only one house on the map. Tallsalt's. And he came down the driveway at zero-dark-thirty this morning in a loincloth and chased us off. Said he wasn't going nowhere for anybody. I'd heard he'd gone off the deep end lately. But there wasn't much we could do—it's his nation, isn't it? I mean, we can drag him out of there, if that's the way you want it, Turnipseed."

"No, it's his right to stay. But I'm going to have to talk to him. Show me where your people are."

Dann led her into the trailer, where the coal company crew, obviously enjoying the holiday atmosphere of the work stoppage, offered her a cup of coffee. For a boost of energy, she poured in as much sugar as she dared without appearing greedy, then joined Dann at a drafting table. The BIA cop rapped off the spots on a topographical map from which five two-man hunter-killer teams from both bureaus were surveying the south end of the Chuskas. "Can any of your sniper teams keep an eye on me if I'm in the vicinity of Tallsalt's house?"

"You sure you want to go up there?"

"Have to."

"Your call." Dann indicated a team on a slight promontory a quarter-mile to the west of the house. "I'll radio Larry Kills Back and Tom Richards to swing around so they can cover the place. Can't see it from where they are now."

"Thanks." She started for the door through the raptly attentive coal miners.

"Be careful, Turnipseed." Then he could be heard adding to the whites, "Tough folks, those Modocs. Just fifty of 'em whipped the entire U.S. Army."

Smiling, she descended the steps. It would be a hot June day. The night's lingering coolness was too frail to last much longer. Her smile went out as she wondered about the possible gunshot Dann's scout had heard. She'd give Emmett another hour before calling out the chopper and the Civil Air

Patrol. She told herself that he was still in the world, that somehow she would know instantly if he'd gone out of it. Or was that just a kernel of faith she clung to in order to keep functioning?

She drove north through the undulating foothills.

There was nothing to indicate that she was inside a tight police cordon. The teams had melted into the landscape. The sun cleared a ridge, and the grass on the opposing heights went from umber to green. She chewed on a thumbnail. But quickly made herself quit. A habit she'd left in late adolescence. After her father had died with the delirium tremens in a county fire ambulance bound for Reno. As the gurney had been lifted through the doors, he'd tried to say something to Anna. *What?*

She sat up, made herself stop drifting.

Window Rock began broadcasting a litany of welfare checks on the far-flung cops manning the perimeter. The dispatcher ended with: "And BIA Seventeen . . . status?"

I know you were willing to try, Em. Through both our absurd posturings, I trusted you were going to try.

"Gallup," the tribal dispatcher asked, "will you relay this traffic?"

"Affirm, Window Rock . . . BIA Seventeen, do you read this station?" Gallup PD waited ten seconds, during which Anna let up on the accelerator, then the dispatcher signed off.

Anna reached for the microphone. "Window Rock, Frank Thirty-three—put Farmington Civil Air Patrol on alert." She hesitated. "And request your SWAT team start following Seventeen's trail from Manuelito Plateau."

"Copy."

Then Niehaus's tired voice come over the speaker. "What's your present location, Thirty-three?"

"I'll be returning to the capital shortly."

Niehaus tersely acknowledged with two clicks of his mike button.

Anna had reached the only driveway she'd seen so far.

Marked by a red reflector nailed to a tree stump. And with a stout chain drawn across it between two galvanized steel poles. Padlocked. She debated honking.

Instead, she drove past the driveway and up the road another hundred yards before parking partly hidden under the shaggy bulk of·a juniper. A raven flew from the crown of the tree and winged northeast toward the cinder block house she could barely glimpse through the pygmy woodland, as if hastening to tattle on her presence. Its caw carried abrasively through the dawn's stillness. *Kak,* Fate personified in Modoc cosmology, the black Punisher.

She got out, donned her FBI windbreaker to conceal her holstered pistol and cut across the road toward the house. There was a possible reason why Caleb Pound had not slain the Knokis with his own hand. Their deaths had not been the Blood Atonements he sought. The murders had merely been his lure to draw more important victims to the couple's mobile home, a complicated plan which had been thrown out of sync when she and Emmett had shown up—in their midnight blue federal jackets. He had not expected feds. He'd been waiting for a specific *Dine* cop.

Anna saw an older-model AMC Eagle with rusted-through fenders. No one was visible around it or the front of the house, yet juniper smoke hung pungently in the air. Nothing issued from the house's chimney. A nearby buzz of flies stopped her. She turned and shuffled away from the house, trying to trace a stench of rotting meat to its source. As she approached a clump of manzanita, flies boiled up out of the bush, only to possessively return to a pair of small carcasses. Pinching shut her nose, Anna inspected them. Juvenile coyotes. Both dusted with what she believed to be corn pollen. At least a day dead, for when she rolled one of them over with the toe of her shoe the body proved to be slack. Out of the last stages of rigor mortis. The rear legs yawned open and she saw that the male sexual organs had been removed with a knife. And those of the other, a female, had been carved out.

Anna backed away from the grisly find, dropped her hand from her nose and gazed all around. It was all incredibly strange and familiar. She knew from her upbringing that this was not an act of wanton brutality. The presence of pollen attested to a sacred use of the young animals, although the Modoc did nothing quite like this.

Singing drifted to her, so faint she half-believed she might be imagining it. Giving the house a wide berth, she halted at a point on the slope out back where the trees became too few for her to go on without being spotted. A raven, perhaps the same one, had been bending the top of a young piñon but now flew ahead, its wings whiffling through the still air. It landed atop a hogan, the newest and handsomest one Anna had seen since coming to the Big Rez. Built of cedar planks. The shallow bank below it was splashed with sawdust of the same color. A strand of white smoke rose straight up from the fire that had been built before the dwelling, and the flames licked at the bottom of a kettle hanging from a tripod of sticks.

Suddenly, a man ducked through the hogan's opening and into the strengthening daylight, singing the same phrase and over and over in Navajo. For an instant, Anna believed him to be John Tallsalt. But the tall *Dine* was elderly, stooped somewhat but not noticeably gray at this distance. A bearskin was draped over his shoulders. He stirred the contents of the kettle with a gourd ladle.

Then his song caught in this throat, and he gazed down the slope at Anna.

She felt no need to hide. Did he think she was *Dine*?

He went back inside the hogan with the gourd. Before the door shut behind him again, Anna had a glimpse of the interior. A white gossamer curtain covered the far inner walls. The door no sooner was closed than it eased open again. A dark-haired woman emerged, clothed in a wrapping of coyote fur. Anna had the impression that Lolly Blackhouse was regarding her with the same resigned sense of inevitability she herself now felt. Lolly had pointed the way with her words in the railyard last Friday night: *Got to have that excitement to get him out of your cunt . . . don't you, little sister?* Nothing prescient had led up to this moment, Anna realized. She'd simply reached back these past days into her own life to eventually unravel the twisted paths in Lolly's.

And so it was with an equal lack of surprise that she watched John Tallsalt, also swaddled in a coyote skin, come from the hogan and stand defensively beside his sister.

chapter 23

"MY BROTHER DOESN'T WANT YOU HERE," LOLLY
Blackhouse said coldly. As if to add punch to the message
John Tallsalt had sent down the slope with her, he turned
scowling and ducked back inside the hogan through its low
door.

"What about you?" Anna asked Lolly. "You want me
here?"

The woman's eyes still loomed extraordinarily large in
her face, but now they were red-rimmed. Lolly looked exhausted. "Just go away, Turnipseed—all right? We'll talk
some other time."

"There may not be another time. Caleb's coming."

The woman's jaws tightened. "How do you know
that?"

"My partner's been tracking him through the mountains
since yesterday afternoon. The trail leads this way . . ."
Again, Anna glanced to the Chuskas. Emmett should have
reported in by now, regardless of how much police radios
annoyed him. "BIA and FBI SWAT teams are in the area,
but you're out in front of their line."

"We don't care."

"Who's here? Just you, John and the singer?"

"Yes," Lolly replied. Anna noted no marked physical
resemblance between sister and brother, so she didn't feel that
she'd missed something conspicuous at her first meeting with
Lolly in the Feathered Serpent. But both had an un-Navajo

stare that cut to the marrow. "How long have you known Johnny and me are related?" the woman asked.

"A few days."

"What tipped you off?"

"Things you said. And then *Tallsalt* and *Altasal* . . ." Anna did feel a twinge of embarrassment over not having realized sooner that Altasal was Spanish for Tallsalt, although the irregular word order—the adjective *alta* before noun *sal*—had thrown her off. "What's your real first name?"

"Joann." Her hands were still clasping her upper arms. Traces of prune-colored fingernail polish were visible around the cuticles. "You've really got to go. It's already iffy enough."

Anna checked the promontory to the west for the sniper team posted there. Kills Back and Richards would be camouflaged and hunkered down—and hopefully covering her through their rifle sights. "What's iffy?"

"Go, Turnipseed."

"I'm trying to understand."

"The Mothway," the woman said wearily. "Nobody remembers all of the ceremony anymore. This was the only singer we could find willing to try. It's costing us a small fortune, and he's not even sure what goes after what. Plus, Johnny and I have no kin willing to show their faces here."

"What do you need relatives for?"

"To help make sure the cure takes."

"Cure for what?"

"You know, little sister," the woman answered with a groggy, damaged smile. As if she'd been hardened against everything except discussing this without vitriolic sarcasm.

"I guess I do," Anna admitted after a moment. "But is it worth dying for when Caleb shows up this morning?"

"Yes," Joann said vehemently.

"I doubt that."

"The cure's the only way to stop him without killing him. And please," the woman begged, "don't kill my son like—"

"Rowe did himself in," Anna said angrily.

"You chased him—"

"That was my right."

"But for what . . . ?" Joann sneered. "The excitement?"

"No—because he ran. And before you accuse me of doing this job for kicks, you might make up your mind about what you're feeling for Rowe right now—relief or sorrow? We both know the type, don't we . . . ?" Joann's eyes were suddenly brimming. "And I can't promise what we'll have to do to stop Caleb," Anna continued with the same unrelenting tone. "Three cops are dead because of him. And three civilians, including Aurelia. All because of this insane notion of his to murder you and John at the same time."

"What're you talking about?"

"It's something the Pounds drove into his head. Blood Atonement. Killing two sinners with one blow. All the death that's gone before has just been a buildup to this morning." Anna recalled something from the Descheenie interrogation. "What's this singer's name?"

"Lokey . . . why?"

"His nephew's a gangbanger. Vipers. They murdered the Knokis for Caleb, and I'm sure he knows through young Lokey that you and John are here right now. That's why you've got to come down the road to the command post with me. We can wait this out together. And maybe give Caleb a reason to negotiate. But we've got to go *now*."

An impatient-looking Tallsalt appeared in the doorway of the hogan.

"Look," Joann went on, "I doubt the Mothway makes sense to anybody but a *Dine*. Even Johnny and I are scared of it. We've got to repeat . . . you know, the thing that brought on all this sickness."

"You mean the *act*?" Anna asked, unable to keep the shock out of her voice.

The sun topped the ridge to the east, and hot light spilled over them, making Joann's tears glitter. Yet, the woman was also smiling. "Wouldn't you do anything to get him out of you, little sister?" Anna started to protest, but Joann plunged on, "Oh yes, that's the first thing at the bar I saw in your eyes—your *him*. That's where we all show it, even though those who did it to us swore us to secrecy."

The point was made less crudely about her father this time, but the words still made Anna feel naked. Then, despite her growing disgust with what John and Joann meant to do this morning, she asked herself: Would she crawl back into the horror one last time to be rid of it forever? The ultimate reenactment. Not through an adrenaline rush or self-degradation. But was it possible to turn reenactment against itself, like setting a backfire to starve a roaring emotional conflagration of its fuel? Had the Navajo of old seen this as the only means to exorcise the demons of incest? If so, Joann had reason not to walk away from that hogan now. That would be a denial of faith in the cure. Did she also believe the Mothway could restore enough harmony—*hozho*—to her troubled family to somehow turn Caleb Pound around this morning?

"I've got to go," Joann said abruptly.

But Anna took her by the arm. She had to persuade the woman to postpone this ceremonial until another time. Otherwise, nothing would stop the creature who'd attacked her in Emmett's bedroom—except a bullet. "I don't think you're ready for this, Joann."

"How would you know?"

"Doesn't the cure depend on your state of mind?"

"What gives you the right to say that?" Joann jerked free of Anna's grasp. But a chord had been struck.

"The same thing that gave you the right to get in my face in the train yard," Anna said. "We don't pull any punches with each other, you and I." Droplets of sweat had erupted at Joann's temples. *Keep her off-balance and she still might go away with you.* "Who talked you into giving up the baby?"

Joann stared at her as if no answer was forthcoming, but then said, "Aunt Bernadine."

"Aurelia's mother?"

"No, more like cousin. Bernadine wanted her to go ahead and have her baby, but Aurelia got it scraped out of her in El Paso. Good thing she did. It had the head of a lizard, she told me. So she came home to Canoncito to get herself together before going back to Bert on the Big Rez. He was real traditional in his younger days. And making a baby like that messed up his mind. Bad. Figured he'd offended the Holy People. Maybe he had something there," she added sadly.

"Were you living at Canoncito at the time?"

"No, Dad hated the old rez. Most backward place in Indian Country, he said. So he chucked our Spanish name and moved us all to Window Rock when I was in the eighth grade. But when Johnny got me in trouble two years later, Mom shipped me off to Aunt Bernadine to have Alcee. So nobody'd know in Window Rock."

"Is that what you call Caleb?" Anna asked more softly, though she continued to watch the Chuskas. She'd give anything to see Emmett stride down out of the dusty, sunlit pines above.

"Forget what those *loco* Mormons called him," Joann said spitefully. "Alcee Altasal's his name."

"But how'd the Knokis wind up with him first?"

"Bernadine's idea. She saw Aurelia moping around Canoncito because she'd lost a baby and me moping around because I was going to have one. The answer seemed simple to Auntie. But Bert took some convincing. He wasn't sure what he'd done that ruined his baby, but he knew the tabu Johnny and me had broken. Bert didn't want Alcee, even though Aurelia had miscarried a lot. Even though he thought the world of Johnny. Everybody did. Including itty-bitty Joann."

"So Bernadine delivered Alcee at her home?" Anna asked.

"Yeah."

"And Aurelia waited for what would have been her full term before going back to the Big Rez and pretending the baby was her own?"

"You got it," Joann said bitterly. "Except a couple of

years later Alcee started with the epilepsy after a high fever from an ear infection. Bert couldn't wait to unload him on the Pounds. Jumped down Aurelia's throat for taking in a Moth People baby."

Anna recalled the only disciplinary rap in Bert Knoki's otherwise squeaky-clean personnel file. The supposedly Ute prostitute in his company had most certainly been Joann. "Did you go up to Mexican Hat in 1986 with Bert Knoki, trying to get Alcee back?"

"Would've done it too. Gotten me an ICWA lawyer and taken the Pounds down like that . . ." She snapped her fingers, obviously trusting in the power of the Indian Child Welfare Act. "But Bert was scared shitless he'd lose his job. He and Aurelia broke some laws by going along with the Pounds. Lying that Alcee died at that hospital in Salt Lake. So both of them talked me out of doing anything. But I think Bert was mostly scared of Hezekiah." She spat into the sand at her bare feet. "And isn't it crazy how it worked out? The Knokis would be alive today if they'd let me go after my baby, right?"

"Probably."

"That's the last time anybody's talked me out of anything, little sister. So don't waste your breath." Joann was now sweating profusely. Rivulets of it twined out of her hair and down her neck. And her lips had turned a pasty blue.

"What about the letter you sent Bert in early March? Was that the first communication you had with him after that trip to Mexican Hat?"

"Yeah," Joann said. "I needed to know what happened to Alcee after the cops shot up the Pounds." She grinned humorlessly. "For once, you guys did something right." The grin swiftly faded. "But my life was in the toilet back then, and I couldn't take care of myself, let alone Alcee. So I didn't write till this spring, when things were going pretty good, asking Bert if he knew what happened to him."

"Did either of the Knokis write back?"

"No. But Johnny found my letter in their trailer. So

maybe Bert was still thinking about it. I know he always felt guilty about giving up Alcee. That's why he got Johnny the job with the police."

A single-engine airplane was buzzing around the summit of Chuska Peak. Niehaus had finally called out the Civil Air Patrol. "How soon after you wrote did the winged Gila get spray-painted on your place?"

"About a week." Then it hit Joann. "You don't think that's how Alcee found—?"

"The Pounds trained him to hunt down people. Then assassinate them. He knows you and John are here. He isn't the child you gave to the Knokis anymore."

"Oh Jesus," Joann said miserably. "I just want to talk to him. That's why I sent Terry looking. Even though I was scared Ter was so mad about the stalking he might hurt Alcee. It was my only chance. Before now." She leaned over and spat again.

"You getting sick?" Anna asked.

Joann nodded sharply. "The singer gave Johnny and me something to drink. Coyote parts in it. So we'll puke up the moths inside us." After two decades of self-destructive doubt, she was a believer, and Anna would do nothing to take that away from the woman. But, lacking any word from Emmett, she had to assume Caleb was approaching. The Tallsalts had to be removed. Joann, at the very least. Caleb might not attack if he found John alone with the singer. He might wait again—as he had for months, if not years—to fulfill all the bizarre, self-imposed strictures of a Blood Atonement. "What happened to you after Canoncito?" Anna asked, backstepping down the slope.

Joann unwittingly trailed her. "It's still happening, little sister. I ran off with this Mescalero jerk who worked the oil fields in Texas. He dumped me in Galveston. One thing led to the next. All of it hopeless till last Saturday morning. After Terry died, I flipped out. Phoned Johnny after all these years, though I promised myself a million times I'd never do that . . ." She started to retch, but dampened the reflex with a deep breath. "He said what he'd done back then was slowly killing him too, and he wanted to put it behind us. Wanted harmony in our lives again. And he didn't need more Knokis on his conscience."

"So he drove to Phoenix to pick you up?"

Joann nodded. "We talked all the way back here. Even about *the big do*." Again, she almost gagged. "Sunday night we started the Mothway. It's five nights long. This is the end, thank God. Johnny and me are the walking dead." Joann halted, which made Anna briefly search the hills again for movement. The woman was smiling once more, despite her nausea. "You ever get a chance to talk about *the big do* with—who was it, little sister—your old man?"

"Yes, my father. And no. I think he tried when he was dying, but it was too late by then."

"How'd he get you to do it?"

"The usual. Fear. Belittlement."

"Like what?" Joann seemed genuinely curious in spite of her urgency to get back to the hogan.

"Oh, old-time Modoc believed a woman won't get pregnant again if she feeds the afterbirth of her firstborn to the dogs . . ." The years-dead face, his skin mottled by Wild Turkey, ballooned grotesquely in the peephole of her mind's eye. "Drunk, my dad would tell me Mom fed my placenta to our dog. That's how much she wanted another worthless little shit like me. Then he'd yap at me until I cried."

"Ever ask your mother if it was true?" Joann asked.

"No."

"You should've."

True, but Anna had been afraid of what her mother might answer. "You have only one confidant, and that's your abuser. You know that." A pair of mourning doves whistled out of a patch of rabbitbrush as if they'd been flushed by something in the gully that ran through the growth. Anna hoped that the BIA sniper team could see down into this watercourse from the promontory. "How'd John get to you?" she asked, walking again, drawing Joann farther away from the hogan, where the singer now stood beside Tallsalt at the doorway. Looking surly in his shaggy bearskin. He now probably realized Anna was more than a momentary interruption.

"Dad always worked half the year as a section hand for Santa Fe," Joann said. "But when I was fifteen, Mom went away too. Maid for a motel in Flagstaff. Johnny was two years older than me, so they left him in charge. He was always a good student, but he started drinking about that time . . ." She snapped off a stalk of buffalo grass and nervously braided it in and out of the fingers on her left hand. "Even then, everybody knew he'd be a leader. He was so big. And smart. So it wasn't violence. I don't remember him even threatening me with it. But he was so important, and I wasn't. So in a weird kind of way it seemed right for me to do whatever he wanted. Even though it scared me to death. Made me feel even smaller. Am I making sense?"

"Yes, Lol—" Anna caught herself. "I'm sorry."

"Don't be. I'm Lolly too, I guess. A real hooker's name, isn't it?" She briefly gave her dazzling smile, before her growing sickness snuffed it out. "But it wasn't supposed to be when I picked it. Maybe I was looking for a way back home even then. It's from the Mothway, the song the old man's been singing since sunup—*Where sun's headplume is my headplume, there the lol sound is, where the light surrounding the Sun surrounds me, there the lol sound is . . . where to travelers on earth maidens prostitute themselves, the lol sound is . . .*" She shambled to a halt. "*Lol-lol-lol* was the song of the Moth People, and now I've got to shake that song once and for all before I get burned up too." She touched a hand to Anna's cheek. "Thanks for getting me ready, Turnipseed. I guess I needed to talk. But go away before you screw everything up."

GILA MONSTER CAME DOWN off the last slope by keeping to a gully that cut through some thick rabbitbrush.

Everything was accelerating.

He wondered how everything could go so fast and not spin off into eternity. He had expected to be chased relentlessly as he struggled closer to the Moment of Atonement. Eschol had prepared him for this by pursuing him through the parched canyonlands of southern Utah with hounds. But neither the Voice nor his favorite son, Eschol, had readied him for the jarring sense that time was compressing as he neared his freedom.

She and her ungodly husband have no purpose other than to lure you to your destruction and damnation on that heathen nation!

Last night seemed only minutes removed in the past, even though the Voice's pocket watch told him that it'd been seven hours since he put the blazing hogan to his back. Gila Monster had never felt comfortable with other people. But never had he felt *adoration* until he slipped into that hut. The air inside was thick with the smell of chemicals, and he couldn't understand how anyone could sleep in there. Brother Ivan roused with a startled grunt and was groping blindly for the carbine under the cot—when Gila Monster pinned his arms to his sides and whispered, "I've come."

He'd never forget the meth-jacked rapture in Ivan's voice as he asked, "Is it really you?"

"Yes."

"You have trouble findin' it?"

"No, the note left in the mailbox was clear. And thank Brother Lokey for telling me about the Mothway. I'd like to stay and thank all of you for your help. But they're hunting me. Two cops. They can read a trail, and I need you to delay them."

"I'll waste 'em," Ivan said fiercely. "I got Knoki, didn't I?" He had too, sparing Gila Monster the brunt of the storm always brought on by a cop killing. Jumper sat up. "Can I see your face?"

The shadows inside the hogan wouldn't permit it, but Gila Monster had a deeper reason for not letting his followers behold him. He could never be greater than how they imagined him. "I can't let you see my eyes," Gila Monster finally responded. "You'd die. Everybody who sees them dies."

"Are you *Dine*?"

"Yes."

"You don't sound it."

"Been away in the north for a long time."

"Unreal. This is *so* unreal." Ivan popped some pills in his mouth, washed them down with a swallow from a canteen. "The old john folks say us *Dine*'ll be saved by a Holy Person out of the north. Are you that guy?"

"I am."

Ivan noticed the box Gila Monster was clasping under his arm. "What's that?"

"A little brother to leave behind. So disbelievers will know me by my works . . ." Yet, he had no need of this final sibling in the Atonement. At the mingling of the blood of his unholy parents, he'd be covered forever more from snout to hind paws in Gila armor for the whole world to admire. He would be transformed at last, invulnerable for all time. Would he be free of the Voice too? No, it was wrong to want that. The Voice was his shepherd. "We've got to hurry, Brother Ivan . . ."

And so together they went outside. It was Ivan's idea to burn down the hogan, to lure the policemen into the ambush while destroying the evidence of his gang's drug lab. After a few minutes, Gila Monster said farewell and jogged away, trusting in the Voice again after the confusion and doubts of the last three days. If he obeyed the Voice, all would turn out well. He heard the rattle of gunfire in the pasture but, within the hour, realized that Jumper—who'd been recklessly high— had failed. One of the cops was still after Gila Monster. Hard after him—until he pitched the plastic bottle filled with ether down on him and lit the fumes, driving the cop over a cliff. He'd heard no stirring below. And nobody pursued him after that.

He now pushed through the rabbitbrush, tongue flitting in

and out. An opening emerged. From there, he could see the woods below. Stopping, he propped the day pack under his chest. Inside were his Gila gloves and javelin, its tip protruding from under the flap. The view was scarred by the coal trench he'd sneaked up weeks ago to see where Moth Man dwelt. And more recently, from a far ridge, he'd watched two old grayheads building the hogan. There had never been a hogan at this place before, so he'd guessed something was afoot. But confirmation had come only yesterday with the note from the singer's nephew.

A Mothway was planned. The supreme cure for Coyote sicknesses, the misfortunes brought on by lust.

Smoke rose from a cookfire near the hut. Good. He wouldn't have to build one. Was that mutton stew boiling in the pot? The mental picture of Moth Woman stirring the pot tugged at his sympathy. Did he really want to kill her?

Yes, yes, yes! the Voice howled. *Do not weaken now!*

Gila Monster stopped thinking about her and made himself run his eyes over the country.

There would be police. Where?

The high ground. They always went to the high places. He located these and shifted his attention from one to another. Finally, he was rewarded by a momentary flash. The sun reflecting off a binocular lens. This was on the slight rise to the west of the hogan. He couldn't make out the men at this distance. But they were there. Set up to protect Moth Man.

Motion drew his eye to the trees near the main house. His heart leaped as he realized that it was Moth Woman, clad in a skin. She cleared the last junipers and continued toward the hogan. Moth Man emerged from its doorway and walked down the slope to meet her. They talked briefly, then turned awkwardly—hand in hand—back for the hut.

So close.

Without warning, Gila Monster's right arm jerked.

He struggled to remain alertly in the present, but the numbing onset of another fit was sucking him into the timeless boom of the Voice. He was back in the sun-baked compound, kneeling penitently before Hezekiah. *It was wrong for Nicole to tell you of your Navajo blood. Because you are no longer Indian, Caleb Pound. You are one of my own. The Elect. And because I believe you saw the man and woman who came here last week asking for you, I'll tell you this. She, who calls herself Joann Altasal, was your birth mother, but the policeman Knoki was not your father. They confessed that much to me. Knoki was simply a demon helping her. You see, the woman mated with her own brother—who is your father. And now they want you back on the reservation so they can slay you. She and her ungodly husband have no purpose other than to lure you to your destruction and damnation on that heathen nation, for they know you must one day kill them to free yourself from their evil, which is the source of your shaking disease!*

Hezekiah vanished under a veil of dizziness, and Gila Monster could see the slope of the southern Chuskas falling away from him again.

So close.

He was so entrancingly close to Moth Man and Moth Woman. But first there were the cops keeping watch from the rise. Always there were cops.

THE INSECT LIFE CHIRRED RAUCOUSLY to life under the morning sun.

After giving Joann Tallsalt the impression she was headed back to the road, Anna had veered west and headed for the promontory. The antenna of the Handie-Talkie Jimmy Dann had given her at the command post tangled in her jacket pocket as she tried to take out the radio. Sweat had soaked through the armpits and back of her windbreaker, adding to her irritation.

"Nest, this is Frank Thirty-three," she transmitted. A new resolve had taken hold of her since parting from Joann: to let the Tallsalts complete the ceremony. They deserved release from their torment. And if Caleb was at hand, as Anna believed, it meant only that closure was but minutes away. An end with well-armed help all around.

"Go ahead."

"Advise Kills Back and Richards I'll be approaching their position on foot from the southeast."

"Ten-four," Dann's voice said. "Eagle Three from Nest . . ."

She hiked over a rocky ledge, wary of rattlers, and through a waist-high colony of ephedra, the broomlike branches whisking against her legs. The sunlight made her sleepless eyes water.

"Eagle Three from Nest," Dann repeated less casually.

Still, there was no response from the sniper team.

Anna picked up her pace as she depressed the mike button. "I should be coming up on them in a minute here, Nest."

"Okay. We've had spotty reception ever since we arrived. Tell them to change locations, if possible, so we can communicate again."

"Copy." Anna clambered over another ledge, reaching the dip in the lower end of the promontory in which she believed Kills Back and Richards were concealed. But the saddle was covered with scrub oak. The leaves fluttered in the light breeze, making the detection of any movement through them almost impossible. Perspiration had gathered on the tip of her nose and chin. She wiped them against her jacket sleeve. Trying to get her bearings, she turned and peered back toward the hogan. The door was now shut. She shoved a lurid and unsettling mental picture out of her mind and concentrated on discovering Kills Back and Richards without spooking them into swinging their muzzles on her.

That meant slowing down.

She was cutting her anxious stride in half when she saw boots under a low-hanging oak branch about ten feet away. "Hold it right there," a male voice said from the depths of the foliage.

Her instinct was to draw her pistol. But she resisted it as

she stopped dead and splayed her arms slightly out from her hips to show that she had no intention of unholstering. "Kills Back . . . ?" she inquired. And when that was greeted with silence: "Richards?"

"Who're you?" he replied with an almost imperceptible relaxation in pitch. It made her want to trust that he was indeed BIA Officer Richards.

"Turnipseed, FBI."

"Nobody told me about any split-tails on the line," the voice said petulantly. "Toss your weapon to the side till I check your creds."

Creds. Federal law enforcement jargon. But Anna examined the large boots again. They were roughly scuffed; not much of the black dye remained on the rawhide. SWAT cops tended to be anal-retentive about their uniforms, and the short hike from the road would never have punished a pair of boots that badly. How well could he see her from behind his screen of oaks?

"What'd you say?" she stalled.

"I said lay down your nine-mil."

Another hint it was Richards. He knew the FBI's service weapon. Had called it by its most common nickname. Nor did the voice coming from the trees resemble the lizard sigh she'd heard during those petrifying minutes in Emmett's apartment with a Gila-skin glove clamped over her mouth and nose.

But, despite all this, it was Dann's radio she chucked to the ground, not her pistol. Its metal and plastic components clattered convincingly enough for the boots to suddenly shuffle toward her. The leaves shivered as a human shape slipped through them, and she found herself looking into the red-tinted pupils of Caleb Pound. Her gaze never left his as she reached for her handgun. He'd inherited his parents' stare, but the Pounds had warped it into a stark, soulless gape. Her hand closed around her pistol grips. The moment was unfolding with a nightmarish slowness. Drawing, she took in more about him. Tall. Massively built and bare-chested except for the straps of a small backpack looped over his shoulders. Hair shorn down to the scalp like a gangbanger's. And he was wearing his clawed, elbow-high Gila gloves once again. Her semiautomatic rose into her tunnel-like field of vision. "Freeze, Pound!"

But in the same decelerated split second she saw him flick something from a metal canteen cup he'd been holding down at his thigh. A big dollop of crystalline liquid broke apart into a thousand drops. She smelled them before they splashed icily around the forearm she'd raised to protect her face. Her eyes smarted as if salt had been tossed into them, and the pungent vapor burned in the back of her throat. But more frightening than that, the last neural command issued by her brain—to squeeze her trigger—got lost in the madcap urge to escape the clinging splatter of cold fire.

Shoot . . . shoot!

But she heard no report. Felt no recoil buck the muscles of her right arm.

She was down. Flat on her back. Trying to suck air into a chest that had been hammered by his flying boot.

A crunch told her the Handie-Talkie had been shattered.

Then the same boot lay painfully across her wrist, and she felt the pistol being pried from her fingers. "Lie still and I won't hurt you . . ." The same soft hiss he'd used while hovering over her in Emmett's bed. Her lungs finally filled with a bright agony that helped bring her around. "I can't have any shooting," he explained. "So lie still."

But both her head and vision were clearing after the dousing of ether. Straddling her, he'd leaned over to retrieve her pistol. He was pausing to inspect it when she scraped up a handful of sand and flung it into his eyes.

He growled insanely—but stumbled back far enough for her to hitch her legs out from under him and roll to the side.

"Heathen!" he shrieked under his breath. "Dirty heathen!"

Rising, she watched him wrestle blindly with the impulse to shoot her. But she'd counted on him not to open fire. The last thing he wanted was to alert the Tallsalts in the hogan, and she'd use that against him. Turning, she crashed through the scrub oaks. Light-headed. Wheezing. Involuntarily arching her back in anticipation of the bullet that still might come.

She could hear him pursuing her.

She stripped off her dark blue windbreaker in favor of her lighter-colored blouse beneath. *Don't cry out. He'll shoot if you cry out.* In passing, she tossed the jacket over a small juniper.

She saw the glint of the long blade in his fist. The broken *Californio* lance.

In his other hand was her pistol.

GILA MONSTER COULD SEE NOTHING but a stinging, liquid mosaic of light and shadow. Trying to blink the grit out of his eyes was of no help. But the woman's nearly black jacket beckoned him on through the pastel greens, tans and yellows of the woodland. An exposed root grabbed at his ankles. He stumbled and recovered his balance by slashing at the trees around him. Palpitations were droning like bees inside his chest. They swarmed into his throat and became a choking sensation. A fit was very near.

Then, thankfully, the woman stopped. Cowered in a dark heap on the earth.

A collapse of nerve had taken her legs out from under her. Like others he had hunted down before. He tucked the pistol in the waistband of his Levi's. She was hugging herself, offering her rounded back to him. He didn't break stride until he brought the blade down with all the strength in both arms. He so expected to feel the resistance of bone and gristle, he nearly cried out when the javelin plunged completely through the windbreaker. As if it held a ghost. He fell forward, stripping most of the branches off the puny tree over which she'd draped her jacket.

Gila Monster lay still, straining to fend off the coming convulsion. His lips and tongue had gone numb.

He raised his head and looked around.

No doubt, the entire area was crawling with cops, but Turnipseed no longer had a radio to summon them. Sooner or later, she would find help. But the minutes before that eventuality were enough for him to complete the Blood Atonement. And escape once more. He'd go back up into the Chuskas, doubling back on his old trail again and again to confuse his pursuers.

Rising, he staggered off for the hogan.

ANNA RAN TOWARD EMMETT'S SEDAN. Making quick estimates. The time it would take her to reach the car, radio Dann at the field CP and grab Emmett's shotgun from the trunk. Then the precious minutes it'd take to return to the hogan to warn the Tallsalts. Driving up to the main house was out of the question. There was a locked chain across the driveway at its entry, and the BIA Dodge was no four-by-four.

Pound would reach the hogan long before she could.

And she was now convinced that he'd given up chasing her.

She slowed, gasping, her chest throbbing from where he'd kicked her. Had to alert the Tallsalts. But shouting would bring certain death. Pound would zero in on the sound of her voice if he believed there was the slightest chance John and Joann might hear.

Anna began jogging again. Toward the sedan. Then halted within a few yards and slapped her empty holster in useless anger. *What has happened to Kills Back and Richards?* They were her closest help. If they were still alive.

Spinning around, she set off toward the promontory once more. The hogan was blocked from view by the junipers, but the smoke from its fire curdled up into the sky, which was now milk-white with heat. Her saliva tasted of old pennies, and her knees felt weak. Did Pound expect her to come back this way? No, she decided. It was the last thing he'd anticipate. Yet, she leaned over without breaking stride and picked up a stone she believed heavy enough to cause damage.

Rocks. I'm thinking of putting up a fight with rocks.

She ran past her jacket. A chill roughened her sweaty skin as she saw the gash Pound's lance had left in the nylon. But the impressions in the dirt among the rocks told her that he'd struck off toward the hogan.

Did John Tallsalt have a handgun with him?

She sprinted full-out toward the crest of the promontory, batting oak branches out of her way with her arms. Again, visibility through the leaves was down to a few feet. This time, Pound would have her if he'd returned.

A sudden roar made her dive for the ground. Heaving onto her back, she looked up. Wings and a fuselage crossed the sky. The Civil Air Patrol plane at treetop level. Skimming so closely overhead the prop wash and exhaust fumes settled over her. Then it was gone.

She lay limp a moment.

Something had brought the aircraft down out of the mountains. *What?* She wanted to think this through—but nothing mattered except finding Kills Back and Richards.

She rushed on through the bruising scrub at a crouch. Welts now crisscrossed her forearms, and she was huffing thunderously despite an effort to keep the sound down. She dabbed at her nose with the back of her hand, expecting the wetness to be sweat and coming away instead with red. No idea where she'd gotten a bloody nose.

The plane would have driven Pound under cover. But only temporarily. The fixed-wing craft couldn't hover. It wasn't a chopper.

Is help on the way? Should I hold up . . . and save myself? Had Dann, having received acknowledgments from neither the sniper team nor herself in the last several minutes, started dispatching every available asset this way?

She came to a stone corral. It was largely tumbled down, but clearly a pair of human beings had waited behind one of its low walls for a considerable period of time. The dirt was pressed smooth as if by buttocks, plus churned up where heels might have chipped away at the ground in boredom. A balled-up gum wrapper glinted in the sunshine.

Her spirits sank. Kills Back and Richards had abandoned their lookout. She turned. The hogan was in plain view below. She scanned the brush for Pound but sensed he wouldn't reveal himself until he was ready to close on the Tallsalts. Her shout of warning would never be heard from inside the hut at this distance.

She set out again—and knew within a hundred feet of the corral what had happened. Two sets of tracks led off abreast toward a bluff to the northwest. And after another fifty feet, sole impressions larger than either BIA man's appeared between the two. Pound had lured Kills Back and Richards out into the rocky breaks, probably with some noise they'd felt obligated to investigate. Then, after leading them on a wild-goose chase—or killing them—he'd circled back, only to stumble upon Anna in the scrub. Had the two cops moved far enough out of the dead spot atop the promontory to transmit to Dann that they were onto something? *Where the hell are they?* They had guns.

But she had no time left to rely on anybody but herself. The sun was full in her face as she raced down off the rise toward the hogan.

GILA MONSTER CRAWLED through the sage and ephedra until it grew so thin there was no further point in trying to hide himself. He rose and walked purposely toward the hogan. He could hear faint singing from within. The singer, Lokey, whom Gila Monster had promised Ivan Jumper not to harm. Even though leaving witnesses behind was against everything he'd learned from the Pounds. *No witnesses above the age of comprehension!* The words of the song meant nothing to him. They were in Navajo, and he knew only the English text to the Mothway. But there was a tone of finality in the old man's voice. The singer was nearing the climax of the arduous ceremony, and within minutes Moth Man and Moth Woman could experience the wonder of Atonement, the joy of soaring into heaven from the depths of a sin that would have damned them forever. Not a minute too soon, for the fit was almost upon him.

The pot did not contain mutton stew. Something vile-smelling, instead.

"Far enough," a voice called from the brush.

Starting, Gila Monster turned toward the man who had just risen from the sage on the flats to the east. He'd seen him before. But where? One side of his head and face was painted a reddish brown from dried blood, and an eye was swollen shut. Indian but not *Dine*. He was holding a revolver, but that didn't alarm Gila Monster. The man was at least two hundred feet away. A tough shot for even an unharmed marksman, and this one seemed scarcely able to stand. He wavered as if in a gale.

"Throw down your weapons!" The command was a gravelly croak.

Then Gila Monster remembered. Parker, the BIA cop. His voice had been strong and clear in this morning's darkness when he'd introduced himself. Before the flaming ether made him leap over the cliff. Gila Monster had feared that the sandy slope continued below the precipice, and now it was proven.

"I'll shoot!" Parker bellowed. Then he fired.

But Gila Monster remained standing as the first bullet whirred a few feet to the right of him. Shucking off his day pack, he returned his javelin to it and took out Knoki's pistol. That gave him two, counting Agent Turnipseed's 9mm. His legs felt leaden and clumsy beneath him. But he charged, firing repeatedly, smirking as he realized that he'd guessed right—Parker had just five rounds remaining. He couldn't squander them at long range. So he was forced to turn and run. Gila Monster laughed as the BIA cop limped furiously through the trees and up the ridge that overlooked the coal pit. He could tell that everything within the man was against turning tail and running. But there was no choice.

A clamor swelled over Gila Monster.

He halted and watched the airplane pass over again, even waved at the pilot and spotter, for they could do him no harm. Then he wedged Turnipseed's weapon in his waistband. The gunmetal was hot against his moist skin. Knoki's pistol, a slightly bigger caliber, would do better for what he had in mind. He lined up the phosphorescent-accented sights on Parker's retreating figure, hissed in a patient breath and—

"Here!"

He wheeled in puzzlement. Turnipseed had materialized out of the brush. Endless demons being pitted against him by his malevolent parents—no longer would he have merciful thoughts toward them. He was squeezing back the trigger on her—when something flickered in the corner of his right eye. Moth Man. He burst from the hogan and positioned himself between Gila Monster and Turnipseed. "Son," Moth Man said with a gentle tone but mocking eyes, "don't do this. Please, let me talk to you. I've avoided you far too long. I want to know you. Will you give me that chance, *she'ye*?"

Gila Monster knew that *Dine* word. It was *son*.

But Parker was coming back at a labored run, shifting across the face of the slope so he wouldn't hit anyone but Gila Monster. He saw a faint spurt of smoke. The bullet came so close he felt it like a searing breath on his neck. The report followed a second later before echoing away into the hills.

"Emmett, don't!" Moth Man yelled, but it was obvious Parker wasn't going to back off. "Don't hurt him! Please don't hurt my son!"

Pivoting, Gila Monster widened his legs for a steadier

aim and prepared to pick off the BIA cop again. He could hear Moth Man lovingly beg for his attention, but he refused to be distracted by this trickery.

Kill him! Kill! Before the fit has you!

JOHN TALLSALT WAS BLOCKING Anna's view. Sidestepping, she pitched the rock as hard and accurately as she could. But it plopped harmlessly in the dirt yards from Pound, who went ahead and fired twice on Emmett. Heartsick, she saw him go down. Roll dustily down the slope. Her cry of horror mingled with Joann's.

But Emmett sprang right back up and answered with a shot of his own. It missed. Still, Pound went to one knee, on which he braced an elbow before firing back.

Anna was going to tell Joann to flee—when she felt herself being driven to the ground. Tallsalt held her flat with a hand to the throat. "Stay down!"

"Do you have a weapon?" she whispered frantically.

"You don't bring a gun to something like this." He scrambled up and faced his sister. "Back inside with the singer. Right now!"

She hesitated, then obeyed.

Meanwhile, Pound had decided that Emmett was his greatest threat, for he ignored the Tallsalts and Anna and rushed at Parker, who was also advancing. But not shooting. He looked so beaten up. Pound filled his hands with both pistols again, and each blast made Anna flinch. She prayed Emmett would withdraw—but knew that none of them would survive if he did.

"Stop!" Tallsalt bellowed, hurrying after his son. "It's me you want! Shoot me! I'm the cause of all this!"

For a moment, Anna didn't think Pound had heard, but then he stopped and lowered the handguns to stare at Tallsalt's fast approach.

"I'd undo everything but you, Alcee," Tallsalt said pathetically, slowing. "You're part of me, and I won't deny that anymore. I'm ready to tell all the people that you're mine. I'll announce it from the roof of the council chambers, if that's what you want."

Pound spoke at last. "I want you to start walking to the hogan."

"Why, *she'ye*?"

"Embrace my mother in lust."

Tallsalt shook his head. "Never again. Not like that ever again."

Pound mulled this answer over. He appeared to be vacillating when he cocked his head as if listening to something in the air beside him. "All right, all right," he muttered wearily. "I will . . . I'll do it." Then he gave a brief cry as if his chest muscles had contracted around his lungs. His eyes fluttered, and blood dribbled from the corner of his mouth. He'd bitten his tongue. A seizure. He was having a seizure, and Anna waited breathlessly for him to collapse. But, staggering, he fired once from the hip.

Tallsalt folded backward from the force of the impact. Blood showed on the coyote skin. Emmett continued to come on at a ragged gallop. Tallsalt lifted his head and muttered something to Pound. Who now stood over him. His face spasming, he listened to his father briefly before baring his teeth and aiming squarely at the prostrated man's head.

"Alcee . . . !" Joann screamed from the doorway.

Shutting her eyes, Anna believed she heard the shot in echo, for the concussion seemed to rumble behind her. Steeling herself for a look, she was astonished to see that Tallsalt's head was intact.

Pound's was not.

Two gouges bled where the high-velocity bullet had ripped from temple to temple. He tottered on his feet for a second, then dropped heavily, burying his quizzical expression in the sand.

To the northwest, two men in dark cammies—Kills Back and Richards—had emerged from the scrub oak. One of them shouldered a scoped rifle.

* * *

EMMETT'S SPRAINED RIGHT LEG would no longer bend at the knee, and his lungs felt scorched. His sight was almost a total wash, although he believed he could still pick out the spot where John had fallen. At dawn this morning, he'd landed on Yabeny's shotgun at the sandy base of the cliff, bending the barrel with his skull and giving himself a deep bone bruise. The rampant swelling was agonizing, nearly blinding him, but he hobbled forward. Past Anna, who reached out and tried to hug him as he lumbered on toward John.

"Emmett . . . ?"

Dropping his revolver, he knelt and ripped back the coyote skin from Tallsalt's chest. The wound gurgled as the man struggled to breathe. Anna had to restrain Lolly Blackhouse, whose presence only confused Emmett. That explanation could wait. He had to get John somewhere he might die in comfort. Tallsalt knew he was finished too, for he gave a convulsed smile. "Want to know something, Em?"

"Anything, brother."

"You can't just neck with the devil."

chapter 24

IN THE DEEPENING TWILIGHT, ANNA SAT ON A FOLDING chair. Emmett was on her right and Joann Tallsalt on her left. A thunderhead had mushroomed up just across the border in West Texas and seemed to be drafting all the air out of Artesia, New Mexico. The turbulent wind fluttered and flapped the clothes of the audience seated outdoors before the granite stela of the Indian Law Enforcement Officers' Memorial. It blew out the candles they'd been clutching and twirled paper programs across the surrounding farmland like untethered kites. Joann clung tenaciously to hers, buried her eyes in it as the names were read by the young cadets attending the BIA Law Enforcement Academy here. The names of all the Indian cops who'd given their lives since a January night in 1852 when Officer Chin-Chi-Kee of the Chickasaw Nation was killed in the line of duty. Where possible, a cadet from the tribe of the deceased read the name, and so it was that far down the line a female *Dine* in academy blues waited to recite the names of Lieutenant John Tallsalt and Officer Carbert Knoki.

With the pronouncement of each name, a Lakota drum group hit their big circle of stretched rawhide as if to mark the silence into which that name should be recommitted. Never a casual thing to summon the dead.

"Officer John Green, Cherokee Nation." *Thump*.

"I don't know if I can stand in front of all those people, Anna," Joann had whispered over lunch in Roswell. Anna reminded her that she looked eminently respectable, matronly even, in her Navajo blouse and skirt, her hair flecked with gray and tied back in a bun.

Emmett seemed even more remote than he'd been on the drive down. His concussion had hospitalized him for one week of the past three since BIA officers Kills Back and Richards had responded to the CAP pilot's sighting of Caleb Pound near the hogan. His eyebrows, scorched off by the ether fireball, were growing back. So enough healing had occurred for Anna to have the unpleasant suspicion Emmett was taking Joann's and her friendship as some kind of alliance against him. He'd said nothing to her suggestion they see her therapist together next week in Las Vegas. A specialist who treated adult survivors of sexual abuse—and their partners. Helped them explore the unexplorable.

"Thomas Cloud, Seminole Nation." *Thump*.

Anna felt Joann take her hand. The woman's palm was sweaty. Three of the four sage bushes encompassing the monument and marking the cardinal directions were visible. They were quaking as if being shaken by a spirit fist. Ten days ago, Joann and her Altasal kin, including Darcy, had buried Alcee in Canoncito. Emmett and Anna hadn't been invited. But Joann had phoned Anna at home that night, talking away much of it, taking solace from a sign that some measure of *hozho* had been restored to her world. Within days of John and Alcee dying, the coal seam had petered out and the trench abandoned before swallowing her brother's home site, the hogan in which he'd striven to redeem himself.

Reed Summerfield had been privately interred in Maryland.

"Joe Big Knife, Union Agency Muskogee." *Thump*.

Bert Knoki was represented by an aged maternal uncle, who was so frail he looked like a baby eagle as he waited beside newly promoted Lieutenant Yabeny at the far end of an entire row of *Dine* cops.

"Officer Cub Burney, Choctaw Nation." *Thump*.

There was lightning in the east now. And a dull hint of thunder barely audible above the wind.

"Officer George Comes at Night, Blackfeet Agency." *Thump.*

Emmett was staring down between his shoes. Anna ran a finger over his clasped hands. He looked up at her, smiling dimly. Last night from the Navajo Nation Inn, he'd called his mother in Oklahoma, allowing Anna to remain in his room while he talked to her in a hushed mix of English and Comanche. Emmett had mentioned his brother, Malcolm, and a lull came and went in which tears had seemed close.

"Officer Carbert Knoki, Navajo Nation." *Thump.*

Joann tensed at the strike of the drums, and Anna tried to reassure her with a squeeze.

"Lieutenant John Alcee Tallsalt, Navajo Nation." *Thump.*

Joann lowered her head.

John's was the last name, and the Lakota head singer stood and prayed that it would truly be the last. Then he called for the kinfolk of the most recent casualties of policing Indian Country to come forward. Joann almost balked, then tried to pull Anna along, who said, "The old man needs your help to get up there." At last, given something selfless to do, Joann approached the monument with Bert's uncle hanging on her arm. The Lakota singer enfolded each of them in a quilt made by women on the Pine Ridge Reservation for this occasion. Joann trembled beneath hers.

The drum group began singing.

"Damn Sioux," Emmett grumbled. "Give them half a chance and they'll sing all night. Wait and see."

"Quiet," Anna shushed.

The audience formed a line and started filing past Joann and the old man. Cops of nearly every tribal department in the country. Anna read the shoulder patches as she and Emmett joined in: Creek, Ute, Mohawk, Blackfeet, San Carlos Apache, Ouray, Crow, Ak-Chin, Jicarilla Apache, Tohono O'odham, Washoe . . . on and on. Sprinkled among them were a handful of white federal agents, including Niehaus and Waggoner, but it gave Anna an unexpected surge of pride to see how differently the Indians honored the two survivors. Unlike the whites, who reservedly shook hands with Joann and the old man and muttered a few words of condolence, the Indians embraced them. Some openly wept. Seeing this, the singer encouraged, "That's it, people. Cry if you must. We Lakota have a sayin'—*We are our most powerful when we cry.*"

The partners had just reached Joann when the singer said this. Emmett's face seemed to tighten around his eyes, and he made a sound as if his breath had snagged in his throat. He began to say something to her, something about John, but nothing broke through his self-conscious fight to hold back his tears.

"Go see that shrink with Anna, Parker," Joann said adamantly.

"What?" Emmett looked completely taken aback.

"You heard me. Johnny had the guts to face the past. How about you?"

"You suggesting I had something to do with what happened to Turnipseed when she was a kid?"

"Not at all."

His eyes clearing, Emmett asked, "Then what the hell am I supposed to feel—some kind of guilt just for being male?"

Joann gave Emmett a cool smile. "When you get serious about a woman, you buy into her past. Whether you like it or not."

Emmett turned to Anna. "That true, Turnipseed?"

"Yes, I'm afraid so." Anna meant not to say anything more, but then couldn't help herself as he continued to stare at her. "What're you thinking, Em?"

After a moment, Emmett took her hand. "Let's move on before these damn Sioux sing all night."

Turn the page for an exciting preview of

KIRK MITCHELL'S

next thrilling novel of suspense:

ANCIENT ONES

due in hardcover from

Bantam Books in May 2001

chapter 1

FOR YEARS, GORKA BILBAO DROVE SHEEP BACK AND forth across the hills of north central Oregon. Each day began anew the search for fresh grass and tender green herbs. He baked his bread in a Dutch oven over a sagebrush fire. He slept alone in a coffinlike travel trailer. That is how his father and his grandfather had earned their living, and Bilbao never dreamed of doing anything else. But when he was forty-two, the federal government cut back the number of sheep it allowed to graze on public lands. The conservationists said sheep were overgrazing the range. Most of the herds went to the slaughterhouses, and Bilbao's old way of life passed away.

What to do?

For a while, he washed dishes at his cousin's restaurant in Portland. But cities were his downfall. They tempted him to do bad things. A woman would get inside his head and not let go of him until he had her. He was completely helpless against this desire. And it eventually cost him his freedom. Released from prison, he returned to the badlands east of the Cascade Mountains. He could find no way to earn his bread there, so he drank up his welfare money and waited to get sick and die. All things without purpose on the desert get sick and die.

Yet the badlands wouldn't let him slide off into oblivion.

Each winter, the rains washed a new crop of fossils and old bones out of the volcanic ash that jacketed the barren hills. For as long as he could remember, Bilbao had stumbled across weathered bones and flat rocks with the imprints of leaves and strange creatures in them. He never gave these oddities much of a thought. But then, while waiting for his next welfare check, he came upon a man in a floppy straw hat and short pants who was scratching at the banks of the John Day River with a pick. A college man, it turned out. On that day, Bilbao heard the word *fossil* for the first time. The college man showed him a fossilized three-toe hoof, explaining that it came from a dog-sized horse that had once roamed this country. Bilbao asked if it had been an Indian pony. Smirking, the college man said no, this was long before there were any men in Oregon, long before there was such a place called Oregon. All this was of mild interest to Bilbao.

But what the college man said next made the unemployed shepherd's ears perk up.

The professor would pay good money for fossils. Others, although not he, would pay even more for human bones that weren't quite fossils. As much as their weight in gold. That astonished Bilbao. It also made him grimace as he recalled all the skeletal remains he'd passed by through the years. The college man said that fossils and bones, once exposed to the elements, quickly crumbled and lost their value.

No more would Gorka Bilbao pass them by, and on that afternoon he became a fossil hunter.

Ten years later now, he was back along the John Day River. His shoulders were hunched and burly from a decade of hacking at the ground with a pick, and his tangled beard was flecked with seeds from the thickets that lined the river. It was the last week of September. Mist hid the canyon walls, although a pale sun kept trying to break through. The unseasonable chill had made Bilbao take out his moth-eaten army overcoat and mittens with the fingertips cut off so he could still pick up fine bones. Soon it would be winter. This was a cold desert. Blizzards howled down the canyons. Ice fogs stole in during the night and left diamonds on the brush when the heatless sun came out at dawn. It'd be nice to hole up in his cabin in the Ochoco Mountains during the bad months, to do nothing but drink, but he always seemed to need the cash from more fossils and bones.

Bilbao suddenly halted. "Here we go," he whispered to himself. "Here we go now . . ."

At the foot of the bank lay a fossil fragment shaped like an oyster cracker. He recognized it right off: a scale from the shell of a giant turtle that had swum the vast, inland lake that had once covered this now parched country.

Bilbao looked over his shoulder for the U.S. Bureau of Land Management ranger who patrolled the area. The cop knew him, knew what he did for a living, and tried to keep an eye on Bilbao. But the desert was a big place.

Seeing no one, Bilbao pocketed the piece of turtle shell. The turtle was an animal with a backbone, and the fossils of animals with backbones were off-limits. Much of what Bilbao collected was against the law to possess, and nothing more so than the remains of human beings. But oh so valuable. Yet, they had to be ancient. Very, very ancient. Once, on a moonless night, Bilbao had dug up a skeleton from the graveyard outside the old Bureau of Indian Affairs hospital in Warm Springs, then soaked the bones in potassium bichromate, hoping to pass them off as being thirteen thousand years old. That was the magic number to the college men; they didn't figure Indians had been in this country much longer than that. He tried to sell the remains to a professor, but the man knew at once they were fakes and refused to do further business with Bilbao. After that, the fossil hunter became more careful.

College men knew bones like shepherds knew sheep.

Still, there were ways to find the genuine article.

Last autumn, the Army Corps of Engineers had finished the Clarno Reservoir—Bilbao could see the sweeping concrete face of the dam from where he stood. And three weeks ago, the spillway gates had been opened, disgorging a manmade flood. This was to help the Chinook salmon make their way up the canyon and over the dam's fish ladder to their spawning places. The torrent had chewed at the banks of the John Day, hopefully scouring out old bones like nuggets of gold. Last night, the gates had been shut, and the river had dropped again. These fluctuations were posted by the Army Corps of Engineers in the local newspaper, and Bilbao was usually first to search any canyon after a water release.

A loud splash turned him around—a slab of bank had just peeled off into a muddy pool.

Bilbao scurried over to this hump of dissolving earth and ran his practiced eye over the debris of centuries. There were flakes of stone left by Indian arrowhead makers. Charcoal from a brush fire that may have swept this way a thousand years ago. Black pellets of sheep dung from a herd he himself might have run when he was younger.

By noon, Bilbao had found the vertebra of an oreodont, a stubby-legged, plant-eating creature.

But nothing else.

He waded across the shallow river. The water slopped into his boots and soaked his socks. He must get used to the cold again. He couldn't let the weather stop his searching, just as he'd never let it make him neglect his herd.

At dusk, a chip of darkly soiled bone caught Bilbao's attention along the east side of the John Day. It was resting on top of another slab of earth that had sloughed off the bank. Anyone but Bilbao, who saw bone fragments in his dreams, would have missed it.

"Slow down, slow down," Bilbao reminded himself. Haste had no purpose here.

Just to the left of the chip was a knee joint. Carefully, he pried the thigh bone out of the silt and examined it. Human. It was definitely human. But how old? Bilbao sucked on his lower lip, studying the bone. By nature, he was suspicious of good fortune, for he'd had almost none in his life, but his heart was beating fast. This was good, so very good.

He peered down.

Strewn around his boots were a jumble of rib, finger and toe bones.

"Jesus!" he cried out loud.

Most of a skeleton, maybe. Rare, so very rare, for with time the Earth scattered her dead children far and wide. But this specimen still might be in one place.

All of a sudden, the hair on the back of his neck prickled. As if he'd blundered into a rattlesnake den. Something rattled angrily all around him, but when he held his breath to listen over his pounding heart, he heard only the murmur of the river. Something was rising from the mud. He could feel it swirling in the air, almost see it spinning into shape. The fog blew back from the mound, and the brush topping the bank shivered as if trying to yank free of its roots and bolt away.

Bilbao shut his eyes.

The nearby Warm Springs Indians claimed that there was bad power in old bones. This power was easy to awaken but almost impossible to put to rest again. He didn't want to see anymore. He was chilled by his find. Evil surrounded it, just as evil surrounded him when the city got hold of his soul and made him do things against his nature.

But there was also pleasure in evil—and profit. As if on that thought, the air went still. Dead still.

Slowly, Bilbao opened his eyes.

There was no sign of the strange restlessness that had just sprung from the ground. Calming down, he began searching for the other bones of the skeleton.

He located the sternum several yards upstream. Grinning, he was reaching for it when the same blustery evil seemed to explode out of the silt. It gave the breastbone life, made it appear to be a gigantic centipede scuttling through the ooze.

Bilbao staggered back on his heels.

This had happened before. In the detoxification tank of the Portland city jail. Things had wriggled out of the lime green walls to molest him, a gushing mass of cockroaches, worms and spiders that vanished only when the jailer answered Bilbao's hysterical screams.

He forced himself to approach the breastbone again. It lay completely still now. Just a sternum. But one stained dark with age. He made up his mind that nothing was going to spoil his good fortune.

Then his breath seized in his throat—jutting from a sand bar was the domed curvature of a human skull.

Splashing over to the bar, he lifted the cranium free. Only the upper portion of the skull. The lower jaw was probably buried nearby. Bilbao studied the specimen. A narrow face and a slightly projecting upper jaw. Not the round face and flat upper jaw of other skulls he'd found. He'd found no Indian skulls like this, but he'd been told to keep an eye out for this very thing—a different-looking skull of great age.

"My God, this is one of them! *This is one!*"

Through the gaping eye sockets, he saw himself sitting in

front of his cabin in the shade of his pine tree, sipping Thunderbird wine, planning his next trip to the listless but complying women who walked Portland's streets.

Bundling the bones up in his coat, Bilbao laughed giddily to himself. "Son of a bitch, yes—I'm on a roll! Nothin' can stop me now!"

OUT OF AN AWKWARD SILENCE—and there'd been several awkward silences so far—Anna Turnipseed's gently smiling, white-haired therapist said, "Well, you're both Native American. That should make communication a snap. And you both have the same job, FBI agents . . ." Anna expected Emmett Parker, her yet unconsummated lover of three months, to correct Dr. Tischler. Anna was the FBI agent; Emmett was a criminal investigator for the Bureau of Indian Affairs.

But he didn't.

He looked like a POW under interrogation. One who'd resolved to give nothing more than name, rank and serial number.

"How's communication been flowing lately, Emmett?" Dr. Tischler asked.

Parker shifted his tall, muscular frame on the sofa as if the simple act of sitting had begun to torture him. "Okay," he finally replied.

Less than a ringing endorsement for Anna's and his progress since their last session three weeks ago in this office.

Dr. Tischler pressed, "Has Anna continued to share things about her childhood with you?"

"This and that," Emmett said indifferently, avoiding Anna's eyes. That stung. She'd told him more than "this and that." Dredging up those malignant memories had nearly killed her. It had amounted to an extraordinary act of trust, running her soul over the cutting edge of the past. For an adult survivor of child abuse, the past was not a stroll down memory lane. She wanted to smack Emmett, but relaxed her fists for fear Dr. Tischler would scope on this hint of aggression.

"Do you appreciate how hard it is for Anna to discuss these memories, Emmett?"

"Of course I do." He slowly ran his hand over his close-cropped black hair. Hair with the lustrous sheen of raven feathers, but for the recently sprouted touches of gray. "I've investigated dozens of cases just like hers, and I can't imagine a worse nightmare for a child than being molested by a parent. But what's past is past. Why can't Anna accept that?"

"Good question," Dr. Tischler said. "People who were sexually traumatized by their caregivers have recurring experiences long after the abuse. Such as flashbacks. The past is very much part of their daily lives." The psychiatrist folded her hands in her lap. Her one concession to Emmett's presence was not to break out the knitting she worked at when alone with Anna. "Last time, Emmett, you promised to be patient with Anna while she develops a perspective toward her late father."

Anna blurted, "Emmett's been more than patient, Myra." Then, too late, she realized that she was rushing to defend Emmett just as her mother had her father. All at once, she wanted nothing more than to get out of this office, even if it was out into the glaring, wide-eyed Las Vegas evening.

"I'm pleased, Anna," Dr. Tischler said. "So you two continue to lay the groundwork for healthy sexual expression..." She took a sip of mineral water, the loose skin of her underarm jiggling as she set the glass back on the coffee table. The psychiatrist was pushing seventy, and Anna dreaded the day the woman would retire. She didn't want to go through all this with somebody new. "And I sense a strong desire for commitment here. Anna, didn't you just turn down a promotion so you could remain relatively close to Emmett?"

"The assistant directorship of the Indian Desk at FBI headquarters in Washington."

"What's that, dear?"

"A special department that oversees cases in Indian Country."

"So at this time in your life you consider your relationship with Emmett to be more important than career advancement?"

"Yes." But Anna's quick reply made her feel nauseatingly compliant, so she echoed, "At this point."

Dr. Tischler brightly shifted gears. "Okay, let's try to figure out what went wrong this time and adjust our tactics. Any ideas, Emmett?"

"None."

Anna had to unclench her hands again. In private to her, Emmett had accused the psychiatrist of showing "survivor bias," aligning with Anna. Now he was apparently out to prove it.

Dr. Tischler said, "Our goal is to create a good sexual experience for the two of you. Right?" Anna nodded, but Emmett's face remained deadpan. "Of all the techniques I suggested, which has come closest to achieving that?"

Silence.

"What about hand-holding?" Dr. Tischler checked the mantel clock over her gas-fed fireplace. Blue teardrops of flame flickered up from the grill. It was the middle of October, and the north winds were just starting to abate southern Nevada's furnacelike heat, enough so for the Boston-bred doctor to celebrate the seasonal change by lighting the burners. Yet she seemed to be one of those easterners who'd been captivated against her will by the desert. The stark and haunting quality of its sunlight, she'd once explained. "Did you enjoy the hand-holding, Anna?"

"Very much so."

"Emmett?"

He sighed.

Dr. Tischler smiled coolly. "Meaning you didn't enjoy it?"

"No, I did," he answered. "It just felt a little funny to me."

"How?"

"Well, sitting in Anna's living room in the dark, holding hands half the night like a couple of teenagers."

"How old are you, Emmett?"

"Forty," he replied as Dr. Tischler scribbled a note on her pad. "Thirteen years older than Anna," he added pointedly.

The psychiatrist asked, "Is hand-holding a traditional

way of expressing affection in Comanche and Modoc cultures?"

Anna shrugged, then saw Emmett do the same. Her mother and father had never held hands in her presence. Nor shown any tenderness to each other, which told Anna that deep down her mother had known what was going on.

"All right," Dr. Tischler said, "how else did you two try to build a foundation of comfort? Any imagery rehearsal?"

Anna replied, "I think we're a little too old-fashioned to talk . . . you know, Myra . . . so explicitly about the act."

"Are the Comanche a prudish people, Emmett?"

He sat up, obviously provoked. "Not at all."

Anna swiftly inserted, "Emmett also shampooed my hair."

"And how'd you find that, dear?"

"It was sweet. He kept asking if he was hurting me."

"Was he?"

"No, he was very gentle. And we laughed a lot."

"Excellent, Emmett," Dr. Tischler said. "So I take it you enjoyed the experience as well?"

"Kind of."

"Kind of . . . *what*?"

"Well, I got this crazy urge to do her nails too." Emmett laid his Oklahoma drawl on thick. "And I dang near asked Anna if I was too old for beauty school."

Dr. Tischler chuckled after a moment. "All right, you character—so you both worked up to taking a shower together. Tell me how you prepared yourselves."

Emmett clammed up again, so Anna volunteered, "The week before, we talked about it over the phone."

"And how'd that make you feel?"

"I don't know," Anna said. "Silly. But safe."

"That's right. Things don't strike us as being silly unless we feel safe," the psychiatrist observed. "In this case, Anna, your sense of safety came from distance. You live here and Emmett lives in Santa Fe."

"Phoenix," he corrected.

Anna could tell that he was smarting from her "safe" remark. She now regretted having uttered it. Regretted everything she'd ever contaminated with her sordid problem. In every other regard of her life, she was strong and in control. But as soon as she stepped inside this office . . .

"Go on, Anna," Dr. Tischler coached. "You're doing fine."

Anna suddenly choked up.

Emmett took over. "She flew down to Phoenix last Friday night. Dinner was great. The drive to my apartment was great. She thought my idea of putting candles in the bathroom was great. Everything was great till I turned on the taps and dropped my Levi's. Then she freaked on me."

"I did *not* freak." Anna raised her voice enough for Dr. Tischler to jump a little.

"Could've fooled me," Emmett went on. "When a woman buries her face in her hands, I call that freaking."

Dr. Tischler turned to Anna. "Flashback?"

Anna nodded vehemently.

"Just because I took off my goddamn trousers?" Emmett said. "I don't know how you Modoc are raised, but everybody in my family showers in the nude. Now, I don't want to be culturally insensitive, but there are a helluva lot more Comanche than Modoc, and I'm beginning to see a pattern that might explain—"

"Thank you, Emmett," the psychiatrist cut him off. "Anna, did your father wear Levi's back in those . . . ?" The woman didn't have to finish.

Her stomach churning, Anna confessed, "Old faded pairs. Like Emmett was wearing Friday night."

"How was I supposed to know that?" he complained. "I always put on my old Levi's as soon as I can get out of that monkey suit and tie the BIA makes me wear."

"Anna tells me you have a scientific degree."

"Criminology major, anthropology minor," he said sullenly.

"Then you'll understand—we're dealing with conditioned stimuli that inhibit Anna's arousal. It isn't you. And this is a trial-and-error process. Now you both know the effect a pair of old jeans can have on your attempts at intimacy." Dr. Tischler checked the clock again. "What's really important—how'd Emmett's disrobing make you feel, Anna?"

"Small," she said quietly.

"Made *you* feel small!"

Anna gave his hand a squeeze. "Don't be mad, Em. It's just that some things you do take me back to how I used to feel. Not all the time. I like the way you make me feel when we're detailed together on a case."

"Good point," Dr. Tischler interjected. "You learned to bond as professional partners over these past months. Now you must learn to do the same as lovers. In either case, it's seldom easy."

Emmett's look softened, and Anna let go of his hand. No one said anything, and the ticking of the clock became audible.

Dr. Tischler was first to break another extended silence. "Anna, did you look forward to the shower or dread it? Be honest with us."

Anna felt the heat of a blush on her cheeks. "Looked forward. There were moments when the thought of it really seemed sexy. That's what so disappointed me Friday night, Myra. I'd really looked forward to being with Emmett like that."

"All right, dear. We have to design a different kind of situation. Another stepping-stone on the path to full intimacy. One that assures you that you're not expected to go all the way, but gives you a taste of sensual pleasure under controlled conditions. Emmett, take Anna somewhere public and show her how much fun heavy petting can be. The only condition—it has to be a place where intercourse is completely out of the question."

Emmett's jaw had dropped. "We're federal law enforcement officers."

"So?"

"We've got conduct codes hanging over our heads."

Dr. Tischler smiled impishly. "Then you'll have to be sneaky, won't you?"

ON THE DRIVE ACROSS LAS VEGAS, Emmett came within a breath of asking Anna how long this delay would go on. Previously, he'd been married and divorced in less time than the nine months he'd known Turnipseed. But as he cooled down after another profitless and embarrassing session with her shrink, he realized that any sign of his growing exasperation would devastate her. He was tired, yet suggesting that they just go back to her condo and relax—before she retired to her bed upstairs and he to her couch downstairs—would be taken as his throwing in the towel.

"You hungry?" she asked. Strange how swiftly after the turmoil of these sessions her self-confidence returned. As if there were two halves of her self that never intersected.

He shook his head at her offer to eat.

She was so damned pretty. Petite, pert bobbed brown hair, big and expressive eyes, a light cinnamon complexion, great legs. But how much more simple and less convulsive his life would be today if that prettiness had left him cold last December when they were teamed up in Las Vegas to investigate the homicide of a U.S. Bureau of Land Management bureaucrat. Long hours together in the field had led to his infatuation with her, and that infatuation had deepened into love over the months of her convalescence. She, an innocent and a rookie at the time, had been tortured and nearly beaten to death by a sociopath who'd been after Emmett, and that made him wonder if his inexplicable patience with her had as much to do with guilt as passion. Endless patience from an impatient man who was used to sensual gratification. For Anna Turnipseed was apparently untouchable. As much as she obviously cared for him, she would not be touched.

Maybe this troubled relationship was Emmett's personal purgatory. The dead were the last to realize that they were dead. He'd been shot on duty out on some lonely reservation and had yet to comprehend this otherworldly reality. Anna was a tantalizing object lesson, and now he had to confront the rampant desires of his youth before moving on to a higher spiritual plane. Or maybe he was doomed forever to try to draw the waters of lust with a sieve. *But what have I done wrong?* Sex was like food to a Comanche, essential for healthy life.

"Any ideas where we can go?" Anna asked.

"Not without getting both of us dragged before a review board," he replied. He'd considered the airport, but just the notion of necking in a phone booth among hordes of pot-bellied, camera-toting tourists was enough to turn his stomach. "You mind just driving out into the desert?"

"Myra said someplace *public*," Anna sharply reminded him.

"How about the nuclear test site? It's monitored around the clock by Department of Defense police. That safe enough?" Emmett turned right on Tropicana Avenue around the New York, New York casino. Manhattan, Venice, Paris, imperial Rome—not one of the megaresorts had a motif to remind the tourist that he was in Great Basin Nevada. Maybe it was a blessing. Emmett couldn't imagine all this chintz invested in a desert-Indian ambiance. The Southern Paiutes who'd lost these lands preferred their landscape unadorned.

Emmett had powered down his car window, and a mix of squeals and screams drifted from the top of the false New York skyline that overspread the hotel.

On an impulse, he veered into the valet parking entrance.

Within minutes, Anna and he were gliding up an escalator out of the casino hubbub to the arcade level. Without looking at him, she touched the back of her hand against his. Again. Then she took his hand. It was done with such silken grace, Emmett felt his pulse quicken. Was she trying to drive him out of his mind? If so, she was close to succeeding. "When I want you . . ." he started, then stopped.

"Go on."

"When I want you, I'm not trying to *punish* you."

"I know, Em." She looked hurt. And extraordinarily attractive. But then, glancing around, she laughed when she saw what he had in mind. "You're kidding."

"Nope. If this ain't imagery rehearsal, I don't know what is." Standing back, he waited until a throng of Japanese tourists had filled the first seats in the Manhattan Express. The roller coaster train resembled four New York taxis jammed bumper-to-bumper in traffic. The taxicab seats were high backed, creating enough privacy from the other riders for Anna to eye Emmett apprehensively as he helped her into the last car. The restraining bar lowered across their laps, locking them in.

The train rolled outside and started ratcheting up a towering incline with no guardrails. The weight of the climb pressed them back into their seats, but Anna looked over at him. "You getting tired of me, Em?"

Of this endless wait for something he'd wanted to do since the first time he'd seen her? Yes. *God, yes.* With his right hand, he reached a few inches under her skirt and brushed the backs of his knuckles against the smooth skin of her thigh.

She braced slightly at his touch, but whispered, "Go on."

Before he could continue his exploration, they crested the top of the steep incline and began hurtling down toward Tropicana Avenue. He let go of Anna as they plummeted, and gripped the handles to the sides of his head. Now he knew what it was like to auger into the ground in a jet fighter. Las Vegas Boulevard, twinkling with white headlights and red brakelights, flashed past in a dizzying corkscrew. He wanted off this mechanical aberration. He had no faith in something that didn't share his instinct for self-preservation. But his only escape was to close his eyes.

The Japanese screamed gleefully.

Anna shouted something he couldn't make out over the rush of the wind. Opening one eye, he glanced at her—she looked exhilarated. And, like some of the tourists, she was actually waving her arms over her head as the car completely inverted again.

An object slid across Emmett's chest. His BIA-issued encrypted cellular phone creeping out of his jacket pocket. It took all his willpower to let go of the handle with his right hand and grab the phone before it fell out. As the train slowed for its reentry inside the casino, he realized that the cellular was ringing.

"Let's go again," Anna said with a huskiness in her voice he'd never heard before. She further encouraged him with a fast, hard kiss.

But Emmett, rubber kneed, pulled her out of the car and answered his phone. It was from his supervisor in Phoenix, a Mescalero Apache of few words.

Twenty seconds later, Emmett disconnected and led Anna toward the escalator.

"What is it?" she asked.

"We've got an unwitnessed death in Oregon."

"Who?"

"Nobody can tell."

She grimaced, no doubt thinking of maggots and decomposition. She wore a certain perfume for homicide calls. Strong. "How recent was it?"

"Several thousand years ago—at least."

ABOUT THE AUTHOR

KIRK MITCHELL is a veteran of law enforcement in Indian country. An Edgar Award nominee for a previous novel, he lives in the Sierra Nevada of California.